Rowan Coleman

The Accidental Mother

New York   London   Toronto   Sydney

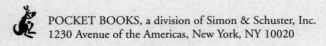 POCKET BOOKS, a division of Simon & Schuster, Inc.
1230 Avenue of the Americas, New York, NY 10020

Library of Congress Cataloging-in-Publication Data

Coleman, Rowan.
  The Accidental Mother / Rowan Coleman.—Pocket Books trade pbk. ed.
    p. cm.
  1. Motherhood—Fiction. 2. Guardian and ward—Fiction. I. Title.
PR6103.O4426A64 2007
823'.92—dc22

                                                            2007010242

ISBN-13: 978-1-4165-3270-5
ISBN-10:   1-4165-3270-6

This Pocket Books trade paperback edition September 2007

10 9 8 7 6 5 4 3 2 1

POCKET and colophon are registered trademarks of
Simon & Schuster, Inc.

Manufactured in the United States of America

For information regarding special discounts for bulk purchases,
please contact Simon & Schuster Special Sales at 1-800-456-6798
or business@simonandschuster.com.

For Mike
1971–2005

The
Accidental
Mother

One

Sophie considered the question Jake Flynn had just asked her.

It wasn't a difficult question. It didn't require a degree in anything to understand it, or any special knowledge of semantics. No, it was much more tricky than that. Jake Flynn had just asked her out to lunch, but that wasn't really the question. The question was—what kind of lunch had he asked her out to?

As Jake waited on the other end of the line for her reply, Sophie sat back in her desk chair and swiveled it so that she could see out of her office window and down onto the plaza below where the wind swept an errant piece of brightly colored litter in whirls and swoops across the near-empty expanse. One of Sophie's main difficulties in life (not a problem, she refused to admit that she had a problem despite her personal assistant, Cal, constantly assuring her that she did), was knowing when men were attracted to her. Other people, other women and most of her friends—okay, all of her friends—seemed to have an innate intuition that kicked in at least a month before Sophie's did. While her friends had frequently planned short engagements and long marriages based solely on thirty seconds' worth of eye contact in a nightclub, Sophie was far too afraid of getting it wrong to wait for anything less than large bouquets of flowers delivered to her desk and an invitation for a romantic break in Venice as signs that a man was interested in her. And because only one man (Sophie's ex-boyfriend, Alex) had offered these in the last decade, her relationship experience was somewhat limited to him and a handful of hopefuls that friends and colleagues had lined up for her. All of whom admitted defeat at the first obstacle.

The first obstacle having been Sophie herself.

In this instance the confusion arose from the fact that Jake Flynn was a client. Sophie's newest and most important client in some weeks and the one she hoped was going to help give her the edge she needed to secure a hotly contested promotion when she wowed her boss, Gillian, with the lucrative long-term contract she was planning to negotiate with the Madison Corporation, Jake's company.

Cal had declared after the very first meeting they'd had together almost three months ago that Jake fancied her.

"He does not," Sophie had told him. "He's just being friendly and, you know—American. Americans are very friendly."

"Not that friendly," Cal had retorted. "Not unless they want a lawsuit slapped on them." Sophie had shot him one of her best silencing glances and told him that the most important thing was persuading Jake Flynn that McCarthy Hughes was the best corporate events company to organize his organization's first U.K. event. And showing him that Sophie's ideas, plans, and budgets knocked all the competition into a cocked hoop, as her mother would say.

And she had.

"I've never met a party planner quite as serious as you," Jake had told her after he left their first meeting. "You could be a general in the army!" Sophie had laughed politely and shaken his hand (and wondered if his comment had anything to do with her forgetting to wax her top lip the previous evening) and walked him to the lift.

"*That* was called flirting," Cal had informed her as she got back to her desk.

"Cal," Sophie had warned him. "He wasn't flirting, and even if he was—which he wasn't—I wouldn't date him because he is my client."

"You're a party planner, not a lawyer," Cal had said. "I don't think it's against the rules."

"It's against *my* rules," Sophie had retorted.

"Everything's against your rules," Cal had told her.

The trouble was that Sophie was not good at working out if a man was attracted to her. In fact, she was terrible at it, so mostly she didn't bother trying to think about it. But as soon as Cal had told her so bluntly that even she could understand it that he thought Jake liked her, she couldn't stop speculating about whether he was right. It was like part of a crossword puzzle that she could not solve.

Since that moment, Sophie had tried to push any thought of whether or not Jake Flynn had been flirting with her to the back of her mind, except occasionally while dozing off in the bath or lying in bed on a Sunday morning. Then she couldn't help but dwell on the fact that Jake Flynn was very handsome in a proper, square-jawed sort of way. And he was dreadfully polite and, Sophie noticed, had very fresh breath. But it would be disastrous to mistake good manners and good dental hygiene for attraction—she would never live it down. Also, Sophie thought it would be a really terrible idea to go out with Jake, her most important client. He really was out of bounds, which made him all the more intriguing. Not because Sophie was the kind of woman to throw caution to the wind and embark on an ill-advised affair with reckless abandon. But because she preferred her love interests to be off-limits. It was much safer and far less time-consuming.

A good five seconds had passed between since Jake had asked her out to lunch later that morning. Sophie did a split-second review of the available facts.

The party was planned, the date was set, and all the arrangements were made. There was more or less no reason for Jake Flynn to be in touch with Sophie now until just before the party itself, and that wasn't for nearly a month. Still, Sophie could not decide what kind of lunch Jake was asking her out on. But either way, she realized in a moment of clarity, she was going to have to say yes.

"Sorry, Jake," she said, efficiently covering the pause. "I was just looking at my diary, and there's nothing in at twelve, so . . . Oh, hang on, what's this?" The initials "T.A." had been penned into the twelve o'clock slot in purple ink. That wasn't Cal, he was far too organized to deface her diary in such a slapdash way. That was her executive trainee, Lisa. Sophie sighed. There were no other details, just the letters "T.A.," written in round, girlish letters. How many times did Sophie have to remind Lisa to ask Cal to put any new entries in her diary? The trouble was that Lisa was scared of Cal, and even though technically he was her PA too, she would rather tear out her eyes with rusty nails than ask him to do anything for her.

"Well, whatever it is, it can be moved," Sophie said, feeling uncharacteristically capricious for a second before feeling her stomach muscles clench and hoping that it wasn't something desperately important that might secure her the promotion she was working toward. It couldn't be that important, she told herself. If it was that important, even Lisa would have brought it to her attention.

"Great!" Jake said the word on an outward breath. "Okay if I swing by and pick you up at twelve?"

"Oh, well, you don't have to do that, Jake . . ." Sophie began before pausing to consider the ambiguity of the meeting. "But you can if you want," she finished a little awkwardly.

"I want," Jake said, with a laugh. "I'll see you at twelve."

"Super," Sophie said.

Jake hung up the phone.

Sophie looked at the receiver and decided that now was not the time to think about the fact she hadn't had sex for over a year, even if Jake innocently saying "I want" had brought the thought forward. Sophie hadn't really had time to miss sex, and besides, although she'd never admit it to her sex-obsessed friends, she'd never been that impressed by it. Even more, she worried if she ever ended up in bed with someone again, she would be really terrible at it.

Sophie tucked the worry neatly back in the darker corners of her mind and looked at her watch. Seeing she had five minutes until her next meeting, with Deutsche Bank, she glanced at the pointed toes of her new pink suede boots and smiled. It had taken a good ten minutes longer to get into work this morning simply because she had to take extra care as she picked her way through the puddles and remnants of last night's dirty, half-hearted snow in a bid to keep the suede pristine. And then, of course, there were the heels. It had to be said that it was tricky and probably even risky to run down a wet and crowded escalator in high heels, but still, as Sophie lifted her right foot and then her left, she felt it had been worth the risk. Of course she could have put her new boots in a bag and worn her sneakers to work, changing them under the desk the moment she got in. She could have, but she didn't. Sneaker changing was for wimps, and besides, Sophie felt the best thing about her new boots was actually wearing them, come hell or high puddles. Sophie may not have been the world's most adventurous or spontaneous person, but she was very hardcore about her footwear—all forty-eight pairs.

Cal had said once that her flamboyant love of shoes showed the inner diva in her struggling to break free from her puritanical, sexually repressed exterior.

Sophie had pointed out that she frequently wore skirts above the knee and so was neither puritanical nor sexually repressed, thank you very much. Cal had snorted in derision and said that, if there was a closet for straight people, she would be in it. He said she wore sexy shoes to cover up her total lack of sexuality. Sophie had told him that actually it was no such thing. It was just shoes. Shoes and boots and mules and pumps. Sophie loved shoes in all colors, shapes, and sizes; her reaction to seeing a new pair in *Vogue* or *Glamour* was almost visceral. It was a gut-wrenching longing that didn't abate until those particular shoes were safely nestled in their box and swinging from her wrist in an expensive shopping bag. And then there was a moment of perfect bliss and satisfaction followed by the anticipation of winning that day's shoe-off with her office rival and general all-around nemesis, Eve McQueen.

Cal often said that there were websites and magazines for people like her, but Sophie shrugged off his comments and told him that actually it was because her mum had made her wear clunky Clarks shoes to school until she was fourteen, even though her friends were wearing gray patent leathers with ankle straps and maroon bows on the sides.

She told him her shoe collection was the little part of her

that could be free and creative. Her shoes were what made her stand out from all the other women in gray or black business suits.

Cal said it wasn't her shoes that did that. Sophie decided not to ask him what he meant.

It might even be, Sophie thought, biting her lip as she straightened her calf and stretched her toes to a point, that her shoes were what had made Jake Flynn ask her out to lunch, if indeed it turned out that he was asking her out to a *lunch* lunch and not a lunch *lunch*.

Sophie frowned. She had succeeded in confusing herself. Luckily, Cal snapped her out of the moment.

"The Germans are coming," he said, opening her door without knocking. Sophie surreptitiously tucked the booted leg she had been admiring behind her desk and sat up. "They're in the lobby on the way up. Do you want to meet them at the lift?"

"I want," Sophie said, allowing herself a tiny smile as she pushed her chair back and gathered up the notes she needed for the meeting. "Let's practice German on the way."

"Guten Tag, Herr Manners." Cal said it first, slowly and carefully. The fact that he was multilingual made him a real asset, as he never tired of reminding her.

"Guten Tag, Herr Manners." When Sophie said it, she sounded like her cat, Artemis, when she was coughing up a hair ball.

"Mmmm," Cal said. "Once more with feeling."

"Guten Tag— Oh, bollocks." Sophie hated it when she could not get a thing absolutely right, and she especially hated the fact that she was no good at languages. It wasn't the actual words so much (although she didn't really know any besides the ones Cal told her), it was the accent. She just couldn't let go of herself enough to really get the accent right.

"I don't think our German cousins use that phrase," Cal told her flatly. "Maybe just stick to English. Germans speak very good English. Most nations speak very good English, and while I approve of your attempts to be transglobal, I think in this case you should take advantage of that."

"I think you're right," Sophie said. "I know," she said, "I just like to pay—"

"Attention to detail." Cal mimicked her mantra with eerie accuracy.

Sophie laughed. She was really very fond of Cal, despite his insistence that his innate bitchiness was really more of a lifestyle-guru, tell-it-like-it-is attitude. They had been together for almost five years; it was Sophie's longest relationship with a man, and she knew she could rely on him absolutely. He was the best PA on the floor. In the early part of their relationship, she had once spent nearly three months being in love with him and wishing that he was straight. But then she'd realized that, if he was straight, she probably would not like him at all, because who likes a straight man who spends that much time reading girls' magazines? Since then, they had become closer and closer friends, and Sophie had fallen in love with an anonymous risk assessor in the building across the street instead.

"Anyway, where *is* Lisa? She knows we've got a meeting at eleven." Sophie scanned the open-plan area of the office for her trainee, the third and supposedly vital member of her team, although Cal cheerfully refereed to her as the "The Dead Weight." "She's got all the costings for this meeting, and they'll be here any minute— If she's crying in the ladies' room again, I swear to God I'm going to—"

"Be nice to her and tell it her doesn't matter?" Cal said. He had his own opinions on how useful Lisa was, and he wasn't afraid of sharing them. "You should just toss her, she's rubbish."

"It's her first job," Sophie said. "Everyone's crap at their first job. I was, and I bet you were. She just needs a bit of time to get into it."

"She's had eight months," Cal said.

"Just get her, okay?" Sophie asked him in her boss voice. Cal saluted her in the way he had a habit of doing whenever she resorted to using it and headed purposefully toward the ladies'.

Sophie watched the numbers on the lift creep up and sighed. She had been training Lisa for close to a year now. Sophie really liked Lisa; she could see she had potential, but Lisa just couldn't seem to separate her head from her heart; it was as if the two organs had been fused into one tumultuous mass. Lisa had such a dramatic love life that the average romance writer would have turned it down as too unbelievable. Sophie had tried to give her pep talks. She had tried to be firm but understanding.

The last time Lisa had had a crisis during office hours Sophie had even wiped Lisa's eyes and gently suggested that she might want to try to cut down on the number of men she dated or even stop seeing men for a while—since it didn't seem to be working out for her.

"Give them up completely like you, you mean?" Lisa had asked her with the typical wide-eyed tact of a twenty-one-year-old. "But what about sex? Don't you miss shagging?" Sophie remembered feeling her cheeks begin to color, and she'd decided against confiding in Lisa that in the eighteen months since her boyfriend, Alex, had left her via email she hadn't had sex once. It wasn't that she didn't miss it, she did in a sort of abstract, romanticized way. But she didn't miss it with anybody in particular. Not even with Alex, with whom she had nearly been in love, did the earth move for her. She suspected that the earth didn't move for any woman at all and that the whole thing was a massive conspiracy made up by women's magazines to make all women feel insecure. But then people like Lisa did sort of throw that theory out the window. Lisa, it was clear, really enjoyed having sex, even if it inevitably ended in emotional disappointment.

"I haven't given men up," Sophie had told her. "I'm just choosing to put my job first at the moment. I think you should do the same. Now is an important time for us. If Gillian decides to give up work, then someone will need to take over her job. Opportunities are opening up. I want the best out of my career, and so should you. I'm giving you a big chance here, Lisa, it's time for you to grasp it with both hands. Don't let me down."

"I won't, I won't," Lisa had promised her. But she had fallen in love with the watercooler deliveryman on the way back to her desk instead, and when he dumped her two weeks later, she was back to square one.

The lift had paused on the floor below Sophie's.

"She's here." Cal almost shoved Lisa at Sophie, who looked at her trainee with a critical eye. She had reapplied her makeup, but her eyes were red and puffy, and her nose swollen. She'd been crying again.

"Dave chucked you?" Sophie asked her in the final few moments as the lift reached their floor.

Lisa's tender eyes widened with distress. "All I did was ask him to meet my mum. Is that too clingy?"

Sophie sighed. "We'll talk about this later," she said. "Just stay focused and remember what you're here for."

And the lift doors slid open.

When Sophie and Lisa returned from the meeting, Sophie was feeling very pleased with herself. It had gone exceptionally well, she was going to look really good at the next new business meeting, and Lisa had made it from the meeting room back to her desk without becoming engaged. Things were looking up. Sophie even had time before lunch with Jake to catch up on her paperwork. Or maybe she should swing by Eve's office and tell her about her new contract, show off her new boots, and generally try to piss Eve off, which was difficult with the undead, because they tended not to be that emotional.

"You don't have to tell me it went well," Cal said, peering at her over the top of a copy of *OK!* "I can tell it went well just by looking at you; you've got that triumphant Boudicca look again. Sophie Mills, Warrior Queen Party Planner."

Sophie stopped dead in front of his desk and took the magazine from his hands. "Do some work," she said. "I've got some free time now, so I'm going to catch up on some—"

"Celebrity gossip?" Cal said, looking miserably at his magazine.

"Filing," Sophie lied.

She had barely made it to the exclusive celebrity wedding pics when Cal interrupted her. "Slight problem with you catching up on your filing," he said, glancing over his shoulder with a fastidious look. He lowered his voice. "Of the unscheduled variety. Elasticized waistband. Head scarf." Sophie blinked at him. "There's a 'lady' here to see you!" he exclaimed, as if his previous description had been more than sufficient. "Your twelve o'clock—the T.A.? Or Tess Andrew, I should say."

Sophie blinked at him. "But I told you t——"

"I know!" Cal said," but I couldn't find anything anywhere and Lisa was in with you so I was waiting for Lisa to come out but she's in the loo again and anyway the woman's here now. She's eight minutes early. So it's not my fault."

Sophie thought about Jake, who might even at that very moment be about to "swing by" and "want," and a part of her was relieved by this obstacle that had presented itself even if she didn't want to let down her most important client.

"Can you cancel her? Tell her my diary's double-booked or

something?" Sophie asked with the justifiable conviction that Cal could get most people to do most things.

Her PA stepped into her office and closed the door behind him, standing close enough for Sophie to smell Chanel Allure mixed with the slightly salty scent of his own skin. She wasn't sure if it was *pour homme* or *pour femme.*

He held out a graying and dog-eared business card. "She gave me this. She said could she have it back please as she's only got one. Budget cuts or something."

Sophie took the card and read it, "Tess Andrew, Highbury and Islington Social Services."

"But we deal only with private companies," Sophie said, looking confused.

Cal shrugged. "Obviously I already did tell her that. But she says it's personal business. She says she's got to see you—now." He paused for a beat. "Look, Sophie, I'm sorry, but she means it, and she *is* in the diary, after all. She says she phoned this morning and a nice young lady fitted her in and said it would be no trouble at all. She says it is really urgent." Any trace of Cal's habitual humor or sarcasm was gone.

"Urgent?" Sophie said uncertainly. What could a social worker want with her? Oh, God, she groaned inwardly. She hoped it wasn't the neighbors complaining about her mother's dogs again, not that she could blame them. It didn't do much for house prices, living next door to a kennel. However, Sophie was not her mother's keeper. She couldn't stop her breeding dogs if she wanted to—they were all looked after. Sophie could vouch for that. She had grown up in the dog-related chaos, and she'd frequently felt the dogs had taken precedent over her. She told as much to the community liaison officer from the council who'd been sent around to vet her mum. But after her dad had died, sixteen years ago, Mum had begun not only to breed dogs but to take in waifs and strays. She needed a farm in Surrey really, not a Victorian terrace in Highbury. Sophie couldn't think of another reason for a social worker to be here, and she could do without all that again, but Cal said she had to see her. If he couldn't persuade this Tess Andrew to leave, then nobody could. She must be one of the few rare humans who were immune to his charm.

"Okay, if I must," Sophie said, briskly managing the moment with her usual aplomb. "Maybe I can get her in and out before Jake gets here."

"Jake's coming here to pick up you up?" Cal asked, raising an interested eyebrow. "He so loves you."

Sophie found Tess Andrew sitting in Cal's chair anxiously clutching a large sequined bag.

"Miss Andrew." Sophie smiled at the pleasant-looking woman, who was probably in her fifties, amply proportioned, and with a kind of innate air of disarray, set off nicely by her hippie gypsy look. "How can I help you? Because I have to say, when it comes to my mum and her dogs—there's no logic there. She sees their 'little faces,' and all sense goes out the window. I don't get it myself. I'm a cat person."

"I'm sorry, Miss Mills? It's not about dogs. Or . . . er . . . cats." The woman followed Sophie into her office.

"Sophie, call me Sophie. If it's not dogs, what is it? Drains?" Sophie speculated out of left field. She wasn't exactly sure what it was social workers did, and the downstairs drains were a bit iffy.

"Thank you so much for seeing me at such short notice," Tess Andrew said. "It must be odd, me, just turning up out of the blue, but it's all been a bit of a rush. I thought we had time—but then there was Christmas and New Year, and, well, it—just ran out, and suddenly, out of the blue—we found you." She beamed at Sophie and then switched off her smile abruptly. "I'm afraid I've got some bad news."

Sophie felt her stomach swell and buckle. Those were the words her headmistress had used on the day her dad died of a heart attack. She had called Sophie out of class and sat her down in her office and said, "I'm afraid I've got some bad news . . ." Sophie felt a cold fear drench her. Was it Mum after all? Was Mum ill or . . . ? "Okay," she said, steeling herself. "Go on."

Tess Andrew composed herself. "I'm very sorry to tell you that your friend Caroline Gregory is dead," she said.

Sophie stared at her. She felt a bubble of relief burst in her chest, and she laughed.

Tess Andrew looked startled, and Sophie realized what it must look like. "Oh, I'm sorry, Ms. Andrew. But there's been some kind of a mix-up. I don't know anyone called Caroline Gregory. I thought you'd come to tell me my mum was ill." She took a breath and composed herself. "I'm sorry, but I think you've wasted your time. I think you've got the wrong Sophie Mills."

Tess Andrew looked puzzled and closed her eyes for a moment as she furrowed her brow. "Oh no," she said, looking awkward and uncomfortable. "Oh, look—I'm so sorry. I forgot. I have made a mistake, but not about you. Of course she didn't use her married name, did she?" Sophie gave her blank look and watched as the social worker composed her face again into its bad news mode. "I'm sorry, Sophie. I meant to say Carrie, Carrie Stiles of St. Ives in Cornwall. She was killed in a car accident, outright. Carrie Stiles is dead."

For a second Sophie remembered laughing with Carrie in the girls' room of Our Lady Catholic High School for Girls, folding the waistbands of their gray pleated skirts over and over as the hems gradually rose above their knees, and standing on the toilets smoking cigarettes out of the open windows.

Carrie Stiles was dead. Carrie, who had been her best friend once. Her sister and ally for a long time, until the friendship had eventually ebbed as old friendships do and dwindled to a phone call once a year or so, with Christmas cards and presents for Carrie's kids, Sophie's godchildren. But if someone had asked her, just out of interest, who her best friend was, Sophie would instantly have answered "Carrie Stiles." She struggled to remember how old the children were. Young, possibly even less than six, she thought. Cal always organized the birthday presents—he would know. She looked at Tess Andrew, who was watching her closely, holding a packet of tissues at the ready.

"I'm sorry—it *is* a shock," Sophie said, still not able to register the information that this Tess Andrew had given her. "We were close once. But thank you. Thank you for letting me know. I didn't realize Social Services did this sort of thing. I thought you were too understaffed and overworked for that. So— When's the funeral, do you know?" Sophie was aware that her voice sounded all wrong. As if she were making an appointment for a routine meeting. Not a funeral. Not Carrie Stiles's funeral. But Carrie had been alive somewhere else for so long, it seemed impossible that she was not still there, leading her life as usual, just out of view.

Tess squeezed the packet of tissues and twisted them. She looked more upset and uncomfortable than Sophie did. It was the shock, Sophie supposed. It didn't seem real yet. Not like the day Dad died. That had been real from the moment she had known. The truth was that, while Sophie still thought about her dad every single day, she hadn't thought of Carrie in ages. She tried to remember signing the last Christmas card she'd sent her, just a couple of weeks ago, but couldn't. Cal wrote out all her cards, including the few personal ones. Sophie just signed them one after another—her name and then three kisses, XXX.

"I'm afraid," Tess said uneasily, "that the funeral was some time ago. A little over six months ago, actually. From what I understand, it was quite an affair. Carrie had a lot of friends in the area. They organized it down there for her. Her mum went down; she was in better health then. She said it was exactly how Carrie would have wanted it, *pagan* I think was the word she used. They scattered her ashes in the sea, at a favorite spot of hers and the children's."

Sophie tried to picture a group of people she didn't know scattering Carrie Stiles's ashes in the sea. It didn't make sense to her. It was like a dream. "Oh," she said. It was strange to know that Carrie had not been in the world for six whole months now, that the Christmas card would have gone unopened. She was unjustly hurt that she had missed Carrie's funeral but not surprised. She did not know any of Carrie's St. Ives friends, and she'd hardly known Carrie's husband. Sophie took a deep breath and tried to bring the real world back into focus.

She had to get on, go to lunch with Jake, she decided. She had to do something now that was normal and that she could control and understand. She just couldn't understand Carrie being dead. She just couldn't think about it.

"Well." She glanced at the business card she was still holding before handing it back as requested. "Tess. Thank you for letting me know. You're right, it was a shock, but I think the best thing is to get on with life as normal, so if that's all?"

Tess looked taken aback and shook her head. "Oh dear," she said, apologetically. "That's not the only reason why I'm here, Miss Mills. Sophie. I didn't come just to tell you Carrie was dead. Oh dear." She took a deep breath. "It's the children. Carrie's children. Bella is six, and Izzy is just three."

"Of course," Sophie said, shaking her head grimly. "It's terrible for them. Just terrible." She didn't quite understand what Tess wanted from her.

"Good, I'm glad you understand how difficult it's been for the poor little mites. That'll make everything so much easier for them."

Sophie was confused. "Make what so much easier?" she asked politely.

"For the girls to come and live with you." Tess studied Sophie's blank page of a face. "You've forgotten, haven't you? I was afraid that you might have—people never take these things seriously." She could see that Sophie wanted her to get to the point. "Carrie named you in her will, but we only just found it, you see, a couple of days ago. Her neighbor had volunteered to sort through her things before they got cleared out—to save anything special and important for the girls. They found it in the bottom of a box of paints, can you believe—" Tess switched her smile back on. "She named you as the girls' legal guardian, Miss Mills. You must remember you signed the agreement. She wanted you to look after them."

Two

Sophie *had* forgotten until that moment. Of course she had—why would she remember a half-drunk agreement she had made nearly three years ago? Carrie was never supposed to actually die.

It had been after the girl's christenings. Carrie's mum had arranged the whole thing in the same Highbury church that Carrie had been christened and confirmed in. It was just after her first stroke, a mild one that she recovered from quickly, but she'd suddenly got a sense of her mortality and a renewed religious fervor that meant she had to see her grandchildren christened before she died, she simply had to, or so she'd told Carrie.

"Of course it's emotional blackmail," Carrie had told Sophie on the phone, sounding strung out and stressed, two conditions her mother invariably inspired in her. "I don't want them christened. But Mum's really turned the screws, so I'm bringing them both up. It's either that or living purgatory for the foreseeable future."

Sophie had felt a lot of sympathy for Carrie. She knew what it was like to have a twilight-zone mother; in fact, a lot of women her age had similar experiences with their mothers. For some reason, it seemed to Sophie that, immediately after becoming mothers, women began a degenerative process that slowly transformed them from bright and interesting people to dotty and eccentric and, especially in Mrs. Stiles's case, unhinged harridans hell-bent on dragging their daughters to the same ruinous fate. It was the main reason among many that Sophie had decided she never wanted to have children: she never wanted to become *her* mother, let alone anyone else's.

And Sophie's mum was crazy only about dogs. Carrie's mum, on the other hand, was a leader in the field when it came to bitter recrimination and emotional blackmail.

"What about Louis," Sophie remembered having asked Carrie. "I bet he doesn't want it. You could say he's put his foot down and blame him, couldn't you?" Carrie hadn't answered for a moment, and Sophie had been able to hear the new baby gurgle and cough down the line.

"Oh well, no . . . I just. Well, no, it doesn't matter. I've said yes now." Carrie's laugh had seemed a little thin. "Poor Bella, God knows what she'll make of it, getting water chucked over her head by a bloke in a dress at nearly three years old! Mum's even sorted out godparents, dreadfully pious cousins from Tottenham. But I put my foot down. I said I'd have at least one friend that I chose. You will do it, won't you, Soph? I don't think I can face the whole eternal guilt trip thing all on my own. You are a product of Our Lady's too—at least you understand. And anyway, you'd make a good godmother, set the girls a good example and all that."

Sophie had laughed at Carrie's description of her relationship with her mother and the church. Carrie had declared herself an atheist and a vegetarian at fourteen. She and Mrs. Stiles had been engaging in a gargantuan battle of good and evil ever since, each thinking that the other was on the wrong side.

"Of course I will," she'd said, looking forward to mulling over old times with Carrie. "But you won't be alone, will you? Louis will be there, won't he? He'll stop your mum checking you into a nunnery!"

Sophie tried to remember if Carrie had laughed at the rather feeble joke, but she couldn't.

"Louis can't come," Carrie had told her, her voice wobbling as Sophie imagined her jiggling the baby in her arms. "It's work. I told him not to worry about it. This whole thing is for Mum anyway. It's her show."

Sophie thought of the one time she had met Louis, at Carrie's sacrilegious registry office wedding. Carrie had been eight months pregnant, in a white crocheted smock with wildflowers entwined in her brown curls making her look like an earth goddess. Mrs. Stiles had managed to overshadow the whole event by not being present. Sophie had barely spoken to Louis. He'd seemed slightly drunk, even during the ceremony, and she'd thought the very least he could have done was combed his hair and shaved off his near-full beard of dark stubble. He was personable enough and friendly, but secretly Sophie had disapproved of the whole relationship; it was too impulsive and somehow hurried.

Carrie had met Louis while she was on a long-planned painting holiday in St. Ives. He was into surfing and photography. They shared a love of art and of the sea. "Met most marvelous hunk," Carrie had written on the postcard she sent to Sophie. "Am going to keep him." She was pregnant three months later. They were married five months after that. Sophie had privately given it six months, as she made her excuses and slipped out of the pub wedding reception. She had felt out of place in her lilac suit and matching shoes, her long blond hair ironed straight over her shoulders. Everyone else had been tie-dyed and sort of a hippie. Carrie asked her to stay longer, but Sophie had explained she had to drive back up to London that night. She'd been working toward a promotion even then. The marriage *had* lasted longer than six months, and Sophie had been proved wrong, a new baby proved her wrong conclusively, she'd supposed. She had agreed to be the girls' godmother.

The christening had gone exactly as Sophie had expected. It was long, the church was cold, and no one understood what the charming but heavily accented Dominican priest was saying. The baby had screamed relentlessly for the duration of the service, and the toddler—Bella—had had the sort of thick cold that made Sophie feel like she had a temperature and sore throat just by looking at her. Sophie had had to hold the baby at one point, and it had looked up at her. Two huge black, blank eyes peering out from a wrinkled, pinkish lump devoid of any recognizable emotion, and Sophie hadn't got it. She didn't understand why Carrie was so crazy about the baby. About both her children, actually. It had to be more complicated than just hormones duping all new mothers into eternal slavery. Kids had to have something going for them, but how could anybody be so in love with a leaden lump of alien life-form that looked like it had no humanity in it whatsoever, just an unremitting, single-minded will to suck mankind dry of everything that it had to offer? No, Sophie hadn't taken to the baby at all, but at least Bella could talk and seemed quite sensible.

"I like your shoes," the three-year-old had told her as they stood by the font. "And your pretty, beautiful clothes. Like Barbie." She had reached for Sophie's hand, and Sophie had held hands with her for twenty minutes, even though she'd feared the slight stickiness of Bella's palm was not caused by chocolate alone.

Later that night, at Mrs. Stiles's house, Sophie had sat up with Carrie long after everyone else had gone home or to bed. They had stockpiled three bottles of wine that Mrs. Stiles had bought for the occasion and were two-thirds of the way through the second bottle.

"Oh, my God," Carrie had said with the practiced, hushed giggle of a mother. "What about that time we got caught in the boys' changing room of St. Peter's! My God. I thought Mum would literally kill me. She didn't, though—she just looked at me and told me she was disappointed in me and so was Jesus." Sophie had remembered the occasion—they had only narrowly avoided suspension. Her own mother had been too busy worrying about a new litter of puppies to be that cross. "Silly girl," she had told Sophie when she heard. "If that Carrie told you to jump off a cliff, you would. Just don't do it again love, okay?" she'd said.

"It was a fifth-grade dare, wasn't it? Who could get Toby Barnes's boxers out of St. Peter's. What were we thinking? It just goes to show what clueless virgins we were. If we had any sense at all, we would have stayed well clear of Toby Barnes's boxers."

"Yes," Carrie had said. "Unlike Ursula Goodman. She got far too close to them. Pregnant at fifteen. Exiled to Welwyn Garden City. Nightmare."

Sophie had poured out the last of the wine. "Well, you're a young mother. You seem to love it," she'd said. "But then again, I suppose it's different when you've got someone to share it with."

Carrie had nodded and drained her glass in one gulp. "God, this stuff is rough," she'd said, laughing. She'd paused then, and Sophie had waited, sensing that she wanted to say something.

"You know we bought the house after the wedding?"

Sophie had nodded.

"Well, mortgages and kids make you think about stuff. We made wills and even got life insurance!"

Sophie had nodded approvingly. She'd made a will soon after she'd bought her flat and arranged a policy to cover her mortgage in case she got knocked down by a bus. It was just sensible. Tidy. She was impressed that Carrie and Louis were even thinking that far ahead. Perhaps Louis was good for Carrie after all.

Carrie went on. "Recently I've been thinking that my will doesn't do enough. I have to make provision for the girls in case anything happens to me, to both of us I mean. Name a guardian, you know." Carrie had smiled at Sophie. "Someone who's not my mother. So I was wondering, Soph—would you do it? Would you be the girls' guardian? You're the only person I know with a proper job."

Sophie had laughed. "Oh, I'm flattered!" she'd said.

"Yes, well, you know what I mean. You're the only person I think I'd trust with them."

"Really?" Sophie had said. "You must have some very irresponsible friends."

"Well, yes, I have," Carrie had replied, only half-joking.

The two women had laughed, and Sophie felt a rush of their old friendship flood back. She had been touched and warmed by the request. It showed that they were still close, even all those miles apart. She had been flattered. Sophie didn't know if it was the wine, the nostalgia, or echoes of a hundred promises that they had made unthinkingly to each other over the years, but in that moment she'd been uncharacteristically impulsive and accepted what she assumed was a kind of token gesture of commitment from Carrie.

"Of course!" she'd said without hesitation. "Of course I will.

If anything ever happens to you and Louis, which it won't, I'm your girl."

Sophie shook her head. Her patience with Tess Andrew was draining rapidly away. It was bad enough to find out that Carrie was gone, but worse still for the news to be mangled by so much ill planning and incompetence.

"Miss Andrew," she said scathingly. "Obviously I do remember that agreement. But that was in the event of *both* parents dying. You didn't mention Louis. He wasn't in the crash, I presume? He is the children's guardian. He's their father. I would have thought that was obvious."

Tess puffed out her chest at Sophie's tone and suddenly looked a lot more formidable. "Yes, technically that is correct, and we're doing our best to track him down, but—"

Sophie cut her off. "Track him down? What do you mean, track him down?" She asked incredulously.

Tess pushed the chair she was sitting in a couple of inches away from Sophie's desk and took a breath. "Louis Gregory left the family home some time ago. We can't trace him. We think he's overseas."

Sophie rubbed her temples with her thumb and forefinger. "Carrie was on her own?" she asked, trying to force her mind to absorb all the information that was being thrown at her.

"Yes, since the little once was a baby apparently," Tess said, looking slightly thrown. "I thought you would have known."

Sophie thought of all the Christmas cards with Louis's name that she had sent, and the cards she had received. To be honest, she'd probably never read them that closely, but now that she thought about it, she was fairly sure Carrie always signed any cards or letters either just from herself or, sometimes, "From us all." Sophie had spoken to Carrie a few weeks after the christening and then a few months after that. Neither time did Carrie mention that Louis had left her, and it wasn't exactly the sort of thing one asked in a casual conversation. After that, they hadn't spoken. Sophie had just always assumed, like she supposed Carrie had, that they would speak at some point. But neither one of them had got around to making that call, and Carrie, her life, and her family had slipped further away from Sophie's life until they were almost entirely separated. Until now.

Louis must have left Carrie alone with a new baby. Sophie had known from the moment she set eyes on him that he wasn't the kind of guy to settle into marriage and fatherhood. She'd thought she had been proved wrong—but she hadn't.

Even so, it didn't make her the children's guardian.

"Their grandmother surely—" Sophie began, watching the second hand of her watch. She wondered if Jake was outside now, talking to Cal and Lisa.

"Oh yes." Tess nodded. "Mrs. Stiles brought them home with her right after the funeral. They're here in London now. But two small children are a lot for an old lady to cope with; they can't seem to settle. Bella has missed a lot of school. And Mrs. Stiles is very frail, you know. High blood pressure, angina. She tried her best, but there came a point when she had to call us in to help her just before everything stopped for the holidays. We've only been onboard for the last few weeks. Anyway, she's moving into assisted living. There's a place that came up just before Christmas, and she has to take it now or she'll lose it. And even if she *could* cope with the girls, you can't take children there. She feels awful about it, as you can imagine—but to be honest, I think the girls would be better off somewhere that wasn't so . . . gloomy." Sophie tried to take in everything that Tess was telling her.

"Carrie had a lot of family," Sophie said. "No brothers or sister admittedly, but tons of cousins—she was Catholic!"

"Yes, well. Most of them have moved away or have families of their own. There's no one willing to take the kids on. And besides"—Tess looked at Sophie with renewed determination—"Carrie named you. You agreed to it. Surely you must have thought about what it would mean when you agreed to be guardian?"

Suddenly Sophie felt the walls of her office close in on her, and the air seemed to leak out of the room. She stood up abruptly. "I have to go, Miss Andrew," she said. "I have a lunch."

Tess stood up too. "Lunch?" she said, looking bewildered. "Lunch can wait, can't it? Look, I know it's a lot to take in, a lot to ask— But Carrie must have thought she could ask it of you or she wouldn't have put you in her will. And we're thinking of what's best for the girls in the short term. There aren't very many options, Sophie. Until Carrie's will was found, there was only one—foster care or a home until we could find their dad. We're not asking you to keep them forever; we're asking you to have them until then. On a short-term basis."

Sophie stopped by the door. "Short-term basis?" she repeated the three words as a question.

"As you pointed out, the girls *do* have a father. We're looking for him, and I'm sure that when he knows what has happened, he'll want to come back and look after them. It would just be until we find Louis Gregory and let him know what's happened." Tess coughed into her hand as she finished the sentence.

Sophie thought for a moment about two bereaved children she hardly knew living in her flat. There were a lot of things that Sophie was very good at. Pushing the envelope, thinking outside the box, making lists about lists, and devising pie charts. She was extremely good at pie charts. But she'd always said that when she discovered her limitations, she'd be happy to admit them. That time had come.

"I'm sorry, Tess," she said. "I really am. But I don't know anything about children. I hardly even know Bella and Isobel. It would be wrong of me to say yes. Wrong for them. They need someone who knows how to help them."

Tess's face remained impassive. "Perhaps you're right, Sophie, in an ideal world that would be best. But do you know how many children need foster care in London tonight? Hundreds. Do you know how many foster parents we have? Nowhere *near* enough. Look, if they don't go to you, I have no choice but to place them under a care order. They'll be going to a home, if not tonight then tomorrow at the latest. They will stay in a local authority home until a foster place comes up or their dad comes back. They try their best at the homes, but trust me, they are always a last, last resort. It could be weeks, months until we find a foster home. I might even have to put them in separate homes." Tess looked intently at Sophie. "If you agreed to take them, you wouldn't be on your own. I'd be able to apply for a supervision order, and I'd be assigned to you as your support worker, with you all the way. They are missing their mum, Sophie. If they could be with someone familiar, it would really help them. Please, please, at least take a moment to think about it. You are their only hope right now."

Sophie hesitated for a moment. She thought of the day her dad had died. After her headmistress had sent her home, Carrie must have seen her out the classroom window, stumbling across the playing field in tears. She'd put her hand up, told the teacher she needed to go to the girls' room, and walked right out of school and run after Sophie.

"Don't tell me you've finally got yourself expelled," she'd said to Sophie when she caught up with her. Sophie had dissolved into tears and told her what happened. She remembered the feeling of Carrie's arm around her shoulders for the rest of the walk home until she'd stopped at last outside the front door. The dogs had started barking.

"I could come in," Carrie had offered.

Sophie had shaken her head. "No, I think I have to go in on my own," she'd said, wishing she didn't have to. "But thanks."

"Look," Carrie had said. "I know it's not the same, I know you love your dad and I hate mine, and that your dad is dead and mine ran off with the neighbor and made my mum go mental, but . . . well, I do sort of understand a bit. I know what it feels like losing your dad. Even though mine's a bastard and yours was great." She'd paused for a moment. "You realize that now there are two fatherless only children at a Catholic school. I'm not the weirdest one anymore!" Incredibly, Carrie's stumbled attempt at words of comfort had made Sophie almost smile. Whereas other people would stifle her with sympathy and sensitivity, Carrie had done the one thing that had made life bearable. She had made Sophie laugh and let her forget for a few minutes every now and then that her dad had dropped dead of a heart attack at a gas station without any warning at all. Carrie had let Sophie be angry, let her cry, let her talk about boys, clothes, and cry again if she wanted to.

"I'm glad I've got you, Carrie," Sophie had said as her mum opened the front door, and the girls had hugged each other for a long time, until eventually Sophie knew she had to go in.

"I'm here for you," Carrie said. "Always, forever, whatever."

"I know," Sophie said. "Me too. Always, forever, whatever."

Sophie hadn't thought of that moment for years, but now that she did, she could remember exactly how it had felt and exactly how much strength the unwavering friendship of a thirteen-year-old girl had given her. "Always, forever, whatever." It was something the girls had said to each other daily, until they'd almost stopped thinking about what it really meant. But when it had mattered, Carrie had been there for Sophie, supporting her through the very worst time of her life. Sophie had been waiting a long time to return the favor. Self-assured, stubborn Carrie, tired and embarrassed by all the handouts she and her mother had received from well-meaning church members after her dad left, had prided herself on never asking anyone for help. She'd never needed help—until now.

"How long?" Sophie said, not quite believing what she was thinking of agreeing to.

"Pardon?" Tess said, clearly expecting a flat refusal.

"How long until you get hold of the father?" Sophie asked her.

Sensing fragile progress, Tess pursed her lips and made a professional judgment. It was important she didn't lose her now. "Well, like I say, Social Services has only been involved for a few weeks. Mrs. Stiles tried to get by on her own for as long as she could— But now we have the case, I don't think it will be long. A week maybe—two at the most?"

Sophie considered the information. "Two weeks—okay then. For Carrie. She would have done it for me. I wouldn't let the girls get split up, I couldn't. So I'll take them for two weeks, as long you promise to move heaven and earth to make more suitable arrangements at the end of that time."

"I will," Tess said, lifting her chin a little.

Absently, Sophie touched the cool back of her hand to her blazing face. It was always the first part, actually the only part of her to show visible signs of stress. She could tame it and hide it with concealer, but she always resented the fact that she couldn't control it. She took a deep breath. "Right, well, let me know dates and times and things. Get back to me later in the week."

"Pardon?" Tess said again.

"I have a lunch," Sophie repeated with some frustration.

Tess looked at her. "Actually, Sophie, I was rather hoping

you could come with me now to pick the girls up. I brought all the paperwork for you to sign." She reached into her glittering bag and produced several forms, which she waved at Sophie as proof.

"You mean now, right now? You want me to have them right now?" Sophie repeated herself, incredulous.

"That is the idea," Tess said with a tight smile. "After all, the girls need your help *now*. Not when you have a window in your diary."

Sophie wondered how all of these events had managed to erupt and tumble down on her head at this precise moment without her even noticing they were coming. She looked at the pink toes of her new boots and knew she just had to accept that her day wasn't going to go the way she had planned, because nobody knew better than she did that sometimes your life turns itself on its head without asking you for permission.

She looked up at Tess and gestured to the visitor's chair. "Okay," Sophie said simply. "If you'll excuse me for a few minutes, I just have to rearrange some appointments."

At last Sophie opened the door and stepped back into the normal world, where things were happening just as they had before she got dragged into the alternate reality that was seething in her office. For a split second, she considered making a run for it, and then she knew she couldn't. She just wasn't the sort of person to walk away from a problem without solving it. Even if she wanted to, and her pride wouldn't let her.

Jake Flynn was sitting on the edge of Cal's desk. He turned and smiled at her as she emerged, and behind his back, Cal swooned in his chair.

"Are you ready?" Jake asked her, smiling warmly.

Sophie looked at him. "No, I'm not ready," she said, feeling every word.

Jake's face fell.

"Look, Jake, I'm really sorry, but I . . . I just found out that a close friend of mine died, and I . . ." Sophie could not put the last part of the sentence together, but it seemed like she didn't have to.

"Oh, Sophie," he said gently. "I'm sorry. Well, of course, you aren't ready. Don't worry about lunch." Jake paused for a moment, as if assessing what he should say next. "Work can wait. I only wanted to go over a few last-minute details you've probably already taken care of. Don't worry about it at all. And I'm really sorry for your loss."

Sophie nodded, not knowing whether to feel relieved or disappointed that Jake had been taking her out for a business lunch after all. She looked at Cal. "I'm going to be out of the office for the rest of today," she said. "Cancel everything, and ask Gillian if she's got five minutes, okay?"

Cal nodded and looked from Jake to Sophie and back again.

"Will you be okay?" Jake said, reaching out and holding her elbow.

It was such a strange, mannered gesture that Sophie found it rather touching. "I will," she said. "It's . . . complicated, Jake."

Jake nodded, and his hand dropped back to his side. "I'll call you," he said.

"I'm not sure when I'll be back in the office, but Cal and Lisa have everything under control, so you don't have to worry . . ."

Jake nodded. "I'm not worried, and I'll call *you*," he said.

Cal watched him heading for the lift. "Mmm," he mused more or less to himself. "Now even I'm confused." He looked up at Sophie. "What else can I do?" he said.

She smiled at him. "Right now? Nothing. In the next couple of weeks—probably everything actually." And she told him as quickly as she could everything that Tess had told her.

"Bloody hell," Cal said, wide-eyed by the time she had finished.

"I know," Sophie said.

She turned around and looked at her office door. She took a deep breath and went back in to see Tess Andrew.

Three

For twenty minutes Sophie sat and listened to Tess talking about words and procedures she had never thought would be part of her life, let alone her day-to-day vocabulary. Tess explained that she would be granted an interim residency order immediately and with it full parental responsibility.

"Technically," she told Sophie, "you have it anyway as legal guardian, but because of the unusual circumstances of this case, I think it's important to keep you and the girls under supervision. You'll have me for guidance and support until thing are 'firmed up.'"

Sophie narrowed her eyes imperceptibly. "Yes, but it is only a temporary arrangement, isn't it?" she reminded Tess. "This all seems a bit over the top for a couple of weeks."

"Not at all," Tess said. "It's standard procedure with a supervision order—a one-size-fits-all policy, I'm afraid, but generally it works very well." She beamed at Sophie. "Now, we have got the girls down for counseling, but—"

"Counseling?" Sophie picked up on one of the stream of words. "Are they— I mean, are the girls traumatized in a—you know—bad way?"

"As opposed to a good way?" Tess asked, looking slightly perplexed.

"There's no need to look at me like that!" Sophie retorted, fully aware that, to be fair, Tess had at that very moment been looking at her notebook. "Look, I don't have much—any—experience with children, except for my own childhood, and that was . . . unusual. My mother didn't raise me, a chocolate Labrador called Muffin did." Tess raised an eyebrow. "Okay, so that's a bit of an exaggeration, but in any case I don't have much to go on. I don't know any children. I have no idea what to say to happy, normal children, let alone ones whose mum had died and whose dad has deserted them!" Sophie caught her rising tone and forcibly lowered her voice. "What I'm saying is, if they need *expert* help, I'm not the one to give it."

Tess paused for a moment just to check that Sophie had nothing further to add. "Counseling is a standard procedure that is available to the children if need be," she said. She thought for a moment. "I have only known them for a little while, but I can tell you that Bella is a very self-contained and mature little girl. She never talks about Carrie at all. I think it's a coping strategy. I think she feels she has to hold it together for Izzy's sake. And Izzy? Well, Izzy is a typical three-year-old, although obviously the crash has left her rather unsure of cars. She prefers not to travel in one. And as in any event as you are only having them temporarily, I don't think you have to worry about their deeper issues. Just a familiar face, someone who knew their mother, will help them. Someone to take their minds off things—that would mean a lot right now."

"But I'm not a familiar face," Sophie said. "I haven't seen them in years."

Tess smiled. "But they've seen you. Carrie kept a photo of you and her together—at your high school graduation party, Bella told me. You've got different hair, different clothes—but apart from that, you look the same." Tess slotted in the compliment with professional discreetness. "The girls brought it with them from the house. They know who you are. They talk about you. Apparently you always get them the best presents."

Sophie looked out her window over Finsbury Circus and watched a woman more or less her age, with more or less her build and probably more or less her life, walk across the concourse wrapped up against the cold in a swath of cashmere. Suddenly she wished she could swap lives with the wonderfully free woman and in the same moment remembered with pressing urgency that she had being trying to find time to make a trip to the ladies' room all morning. Now she *really* needed to go.

"Okay," Sophie said briskly as she stood up. "Well, I have to sort things out with my boss. The rest of the day off, you know . . ."

"Two weeks off, you mean," Tess said.

"If need be," Sophie mumbled, hurrying to the door.

"Well, you can't leave them home alone . . ."

"I realize that, but—" Sophie opened the door and found herself jiggling on her toes. She felt like a naughty child trying to escape class.

"So you'll need to take time off," Tess reaffirmed.

"Fine. I'll take the week off," Sophie snapped at her. "I can always work from home. Now, if you'll excuse me, please, I need to sort things out." She closed the door on Tess with a good deal more firmness than was strictly required.

"I'll make her another tea, shall I?" Cal said as Sophie marched past.

"Don't bother," Sophie said shortly.

"Sanctimonious self-righteous morally pompous . . ." Sophie grumbled under her breath as she headed purposefully for the ladies' room. As she passed Eve's office, Eve fell in line with her, and four metal-tipped heels clicked purposefully along the tile floor.

"In-ter-est-ing," Eve said, carefully pronouncing each syllable as she observed Sophie. "What do we have here? Sour looks and bitterness." She cocked her head sweetly at Sophie. "You didn't nail the Germans did you?"

Sophie lifted her chin. "Signed, sealed, and delivered. Three conferences, summer party, Christmas party, staff. All corporate entertaining. For two years."

If Eve was impressed, she hid it well. "Yeah, well, I think they were ripe for a change. I reckon even Lisa could have landed them." Sophie ignored the gibe and stopped outside the ladies' room door.

"Are you smoking this morning?" Eve asked her, slipping the top of her packet of Marlboros out of her trouser pocket as if they were illegal contraband, which in a smoke-free office they more or less were. It wasn't even that smoking was banned entirely; it was allowed outside, but hardly anyone actually smoked anymore, except for Eve, that is, and Sophie sort of, and their involvement with nicotine was possibly the only thing they had in common. It also provided an opportunity for them to size each other up and see how the competition was doing.

Tess Andrew could wait ten more minutes. "Yes, I am smoking," Sophie said with conviction. Eve pushed open the ladies' room door.

"I'll wait for you," she said.

Five minutes later, feeling considerably refreshed as she stood outside the office building, Sophie found herself lighting a second cigarette from the butt of the one she had just smoked. She was glad that the chill of the morning was providing a cooling anti-dote to the heat of her cheeks.

"So, considering you've done so well," Eve said, looking Sophie up and down as she channeled a plume of smoke though her pursed lips, "why are you so stressed? And don't deny it, your face looks like it's in the early stages of leprosy. You haven't even flouted your new boots—are you ill?"

Like Sophie, Eve wasn't wearing a coat; the cold didn't seem to affect her, probably because she was already cold-blooded. Sophie wound her arms around herself, glanced at Eve, and appraised the situation. Eve couldn't in any way be described as a friend, because it was hard to be pals with your mortal enemy even if she did throw you the occasional Marlboro Light. But Sophie and Eve inevitably spent a lot of time together during office hours and had developed a sort of mutual resentful respect that had evolved into a relationship of a kind. After all, they were the only two of their breed. Gillian was at the top of the tree, and Eve and Sophie were two of three managers beneath her. The other one was Graham Hughes, of course, but he was so incompetent that no-body really counted him; he only had the job because of his fam-ily name. Eve was Sophie's only real equal at McCarthy Hughes, the only other person who knew exactly what it was like to be her and exactly how much she wanted to move into Gillian's job if and when Gillian stepped down from the office in order to spend more time with her family. Sophie had been working for ten years toward this moment, and she wouldn't let her chance to sit in Gillian's chair go without fighting for it tooth and nail.

Outside the office, Sophie wouldn't have gone near Eve with a six-foot pole. In fact, if she'd seen Eve walking down a darkened street toward her, she would have run the other way. But sensing that this was one of those times it paid to keep your enemy clos-est, Sophie decided to tell her everything.

"I just found out an old friend of mine died," she said flatly.

There was no other way to say it. So far, her feelings about the news seemed to entirely two-dimensional, as if she had read the words off a page but hadn't really felt what they meant yet. Maybe if Carrie had still been a regular part of her life, the news would have seemed real, but for now at least Carrie's death didn't seem real. Sophie supposed that would change when she met the children, and that thought terrified her. Not feeling anything would be much easier, she decided, and also much worse.

"Really," Eve said, keeping her voice even as she stubbed out the butt of her cigarette with the black, pointed toe of her Prada shoe. "So, were you close to this friend?" she asked.

Sophie considered the question. "We were once, you know at school," she said. "And for a while after she went to university and I started working here. We kept in touch—met up in the holidays, but you know, we both changed. She got married pretty soon after she graduated and moved away." Sophie considered the length of time and distance that had grown between her and Carrie. "So we weren't so close anymore, no— But, well . . . you know."

Eve tipped her face back to a glimpse of the sun that a passing cloud had temporarily revealed, and Sophie guessed probably she didn't know.

"So it's not all doom and gloom then," Eve said lightly. "You won't be having weeks and weeks off for compassionate leave?" She couldn't help but sound hopeful.

Sophie squinted at her and thought anxiously about the time she would inevitably be out of the office in the next few days. "Not at all," she said. A significant part of her didn't want to tell Eve the rest of the story. The part of her that knew Eve was a natural predator. Show her any kind of weakness, and she would exploit it—especially professionally. But Sophie also knew if she didn't tell her, it would also look like a weakness.

"There is another slight complication that has arisen, though," she said, carefully considering the best way the play out the situation. Let Eve think that her position was being compromised and then, when she showed Gillian she could cope so well with a crisis and still be on top of her job, Sophie would be a stronger contender than ever.

"Did she leave you loads of money?" Eve asked.

Sophie shook her head and paused for effect. "No—she left me her kids."

For the first time ever Sophie witnessed Eve at a loss for words, if only for a second. Then she found two that Sophie considered extremely apt. "Good God," Eve said.

Gillian had two children of her own, eight-year-old Jack and four-year-old Matilda. Sophie knew their names and ages because of the many photos and drawings that adorned Gillian's office walls and because of their occasional visits to the office.

They were the reason, Sophie supposed, that as she relayed the events of the morning, tears welled up in Gillian's eyes. A vital and extremely attractive woman in her early forties, Gillian Hughes was Sophie's inspiration and role model. She had cut a swathe to the very top when other women were still complaining about glass ceilings, and had become a partner in the firm by the time she was thirty-five. She openly encouraged her younger staff to try for promotion and to achieve the dizzying heights she had. With her as your boss, you felt that anything was possible, everything was achievable. Sophie had learned everything from Gillian, and she didn't mind admitting to herself that she wanted to be Gillian when she grew up. She wanted Gillian's job, her sense of presence, her innate authority, and also her really great, wrinkle-free skin. Gillian was so tightly in control of every strand of the business that Sophie had been taken aback by her display of emotion. The plight of the children touched her instantly.

"Oh, my God," Gillian said softly, shaking her head and staring out her window. "It's your worst nightmare, your worst ever nightmare. The thought of leaving your children alone in the world. Every mother's deepest fear." She looked at Sophie. "Your friend must have trusted you very much, Sophie. You should be proud."

Sophie felt a little guilty. Proud was the very last thing she had been feeling. Beholden, embattled, terrified, and shocked—all of those things had registered, but pride had yet to make an entry in her top five chart of whirlwind emotions.

"Of course I do," she lied so as not to disappoint Gillian. "And, well, I'm afraid I will need some time out of the office while the children are staying with me. The social worker says—"

"Of course," Gillian said generously before leaning forward a little in her seat. "How long exactly?"

"Not long at all," Sophie said hurriedly, sensing that already Gillian was trying to find how much exactly all this would affect her business. "I won't need long. . . . It's just for a week or two, just until they find their dad, you see."

"So you'll want two weeks off right away then?" Gillian asked her, sounding suddenly less generous. "To spend time with your godchildren."

"No, I won't—" Sophie began reflexively, not wanting to irritate her boss. "What I mean is that of course I *do* want to spend time with them, the poor darlings, but I won't just walk out on my responsibilities to McCarthy Hughes, Gillian. I know that you are being extremely kind, but I am not the sort of person to take advantage of that kindness. I'll have to be at home mainly, but I'm sure I can supervise Lisa and Cal from home, and I'll be in at least twice a week. Three times maybe. Maybe I'll pop in every day. I'll get a nanny or something."

"For two weeks?" Gillian asked, with amusement.

Obviously Sophie had said something funny, but she wasn't exactly sure what it was. "Yeah, you know, from an agency or something," She said uncertainly.

"It seems a little extreme, Sophie, for a few days. If that's all it is really going to be, the company won't grind to a halt without you, you know."

The comment could not have stung Sophie more if Gillian had leaped over her solid oak desk and slapped her across the face.

"I know!" Sophie said with a little brittle laugh. "But I'm just in the middle of some important projects right now, especially the Madison Corporation ship party. That's coming up really soon, and there is heaps left to do, even though we are completely on top of it, of course . . ."

"Of course," Gillian said, smiling wryly.

"So, I mean, I will take it as vacation, but I'll just keep working too, if that's okay."

Gillian seemed to mull the proposition over, and Sophie wondered, not for the first time, how it was that Gillian managed to wear chic little chiffon neck scarves loosely tied at her shoulder without them constantly coming undone like Sophie's did whenever she had tried it. Perhaps she glues them on, Sophie thought.

"Look," Gillian said at last. "I appreciate your dedication, Sophie. It doesn't go unnoticed. But I wonder if you realize what you are taking on. Let's play it by ear. If things change or you find it too much to do both, then Eve can always step in—"

"No!" Sophie interrupted her and instantly regretted it. It was like interrupting the queen. "Sorry, Gillian, I just meant that I can handle it. No one needs to step in. It's only fourteen days, and that includes two weekends!"

"You normally work weekends, don't you?" Gillian said.

"Well, sometimes . . . ," Sophie said, wondering why she was being made to feel guilty just for being dedicated. "My point is, it's not for very long. How hard can it be?"

Four

For the first ten minutes of the taxi ride to Mrs. Stiles's house, Sophie and Tess did not speak to each other.

Sophie was too busy fretting about the looks on Lisa's and Cal's faces when she had told them what was happening and wondering what the implications of those looks were. They were like theatrical masks. Lisa's face had been the tragic one, and Cal's had been pure comedy. He'd neatly glossed over the whole dead-mother-of-two element to see the funny side and to give Sophie a rundown of all the hilariously calamitous events that were bound to befall them.

"Look," Tess said, breaking the silence as the cab turned onto Upper Street. "I think you are doing an incredible thing here, I really do, and I want you to know I'll be there to help you. It's not as if you're on your own."

Sophie half-smiled at her. "Thanks," she said, tucking a strand of hair behind her ear and looking out the window. The record shop where she and Carrie had spent so much time peeping at boys over the tops of Stone Roses LPs had long since been replaced by a cell phone shop. "I want to help, I really do. I might not have come across like I did, but I do. It was just the surprise of it all. You know, it all happened so quickly, for me anyway."

"I know," Tess said, studying her profile. "That was my fault. I did bungle it a bit. It's not like me at all. I've never worked on a case like this before." She held out a hand to Sophie, who turned and looked at it. "Let's try to work together, try to do something good for these children—okay?"

Sophie nodded and shook her hand. "Okay," she said. "Okay, I'll give it my best shot."

Mrs. Stiles's house, her life, and a large part of Sophie's past had already been packed away. There were several crates in the hallway marked "Storage," and a host of cardboard boxes stacked against any available wall space. The house where Sophie had spent so many hours, laughing and plotting and dreaming with Carrie had been swept away, leaving only faint shadows and outlines to prove that it had ever been there. Even Mrs. Stiles herself had faded to the point where she was almost translucent.

When Sophie had seen her at the christening, she had been looking older and tired, but the last three years seemed to have shrunk her away almost to nothing. She was inches shorter, and her skin was papery thin and gray.

"Mrs. Stiles," Sophie said. "I just couldn't believe it when I heard. I'm so sorry."

Mrs. Stiles nodded and gestured for Sophie to sit down on the same beige velour sofa that she and Carrie had giggled on the night of the christening and countless times before that as girls. "We tried so long for Caroline, her dad and I," she said. "Everyone else was having baby after baby except me. Five years went by, then it was fifteen, and I thought it just wasn't meant to be. It wasn't in Jesus' plan, you see. When she came, I was so unprepared that I thought it was the change! She was my miracle. My gift." Mrs. Stiles's smile faded. "I don't why loving her so much wasn't enough. I don't know why she went away, why she let that . . . *man*"—she spit out the word—"ruin her life just like her father ruined mine." She coughed and gagged as if she might choke on her bitterness. "And now the lives of those poor children too. Everything that has happened to them has happened because of *him*. If he'd been at home like he should have been, supporting his family, Carrie wouldn't have been driving that death trap." She stopped talking abruptly and caught her breath. "I just feel so angry, all of this, *all* of this is his fault."

Sophie did not know quite what to say, so she said nothing and listened to the house, perfectly quiet except for the ticking of a clock.

"Where *are* the children?" she asked eventually.

"Upstairs," Mrs. Stiles said. "I told them to wait there and not make a peep until we were ready for them. They're no trouble, you know, as long as they know who's boss. They packed all their bits. They don't have too much with them, just a big suitcase between them—almost everything is still in Carrie's house—there's been no one really to sort it out. The neighbor's been good, keeping an eye on it—but there's so much that needs doing. I didn't think I would have to do it—" She reached out and took Sophie's hand in hers. Her skin felt dry and rough.

"I just can't do it," she said, and Sophie knew she was talking about the children.

"I know," she said.

"Well," Mrs. Stiles said with a sharp edge to her voice. "I always said to Carrie that you were the sensible one. And now look."

Sophie sat back in her chair and withdrew her fingers from Mrs. Stiles's hand. She had expected her to be upset but not angry.

"Ms. Andrew, call the girls down, will you?" Mrs. Stiles said.

Sophie swallowed hard and counted the last seconds of her foreseeable freedom as footsteps thundered down the stairs, the living room door flew open, and a small child flung herself into Sophie's lap with some considerable impetus, winding her momentarily.

"Goodness, child, slow down," Mrs. Stiles said, but the child in question ignored her and flung her arms around Sophie's neck. At first Sophie thought it was Bella, but then she saw Bella standing in the doorway and realized that this must be Izzy in her lap, resplendent in a lilac fairy costume complete with wings and a glittery net skirt.

The child kissed Sophie wetly on the cheek and patted her head fondly. "My mommy's car is broken," she said. "There was a *bang* and a man in a van, and it's broken now, it's in the garage. I don't like cars, do I? Have you got any chocolate birthday cake? Are you three or seven today?"

Sophie looked at her. "Um," she said.

Bella crossed the room and gave Izzy a sisterly look of disapproval. Sophie thought she saw a trace of Carrie in the expression, just a trace among the dark good looks Bella must have inherited from their father. Izzy clearly resembled her mother, who was fair-skinned and whose light brown hair was almost a honey blond.

"Shut up, Izzy," Bella said. "She's much older than seven, idiot." Bella held out her hand, and Sophie took it and shook it, still struggling to find something appropriate to say.

"I like your boots," Bella said. "I like pink, it's my favorite color."

Sophie smiled at the girls. "Me too," she said.

"Me too!" shouted Izzy, causing Mrs. Stiles to wince. A passion for chocolate and an eye for shoes. Maybe she did have something in common with the girls after all. A shame then, Sophie thought as she smiled fixedly at the girls, that she felt as if she were having her very life pulled inside out by an overwhelming vacuum of fear.

"Right then," Tess said, gathering up the reams of papers she had laid out across Sophie's blond ash coffee table. "I'll be off. See you tomorrow, girls."

"Bye, Tess," both girls sang absently, mesmerized by something Tess had found for them to watch on TV involving huge multicolored puppets and a lot of shouting.

"Off?" Sophie said anxiously. "Off where?" They had been back at her place for less than two hours, in which Sophie had seen a small, quite neat flat transformed into a jumble sale of dirty, multicolored clothes. Tess had suggested that, when she had time, Sophie might clear the girls a drawer, but in the meantime, she helped them sort out what was clean and what wasn't, refolded what she could neatly into the suitcase, and loaded the rest into Sophie's washing machine. Sophie, who was more of a dry-clean-only sort of girl, rarely used her washing machine. When it had juddered and shaken its way into a final spin, Sophie had jumped out of her skin.

"Where do you have to go *now*?" Sophie repeated her anxious question.

"Oh, you know, work," Tess said. "It's almost four, Sophie. I have to get all this signed, sealed, and, er, delivered tonight."

"But so soon? I mean, do you think I'm ready?"

Tess smiled at her and dumped the sheaf of papers into her sequined patchwork tote bag seemingly without the vaguest concern over tears or dog-ears.

"You said before in the cab that you'd help me, that I wasn't alone!" Sophie said tremulously.

"I know," Tess said. "And I meant it, but I can't move in. If I could, we wouldn't have this problem. There are other people out there who need me, plus a load of paperwork that needs doing. The law makes a special provision for cases like yours. I'll be at a night court until late arranging your residency order." Tess looked around the flat, the second floor of a converted Georgian town house, and tucked one chin into another as she smiled at Sophie. "Look, you have nice flat. Obviously a little too small for an adult and two children, what with only one bedroom and no garden, but on the whole I'm satisfied. It will do for now. And the girls seem to have settled in okay. I think they're getting used to moving around, poor mites. You'll be fine."

Sophie looked at the girls. What Tess said was right—she had expected them to be Dickensian waifs, thin and pale and red-eyed. But they seemed to be handling this with much more presence of mind that she was, and they *had* been very manageable since they left Mrs. Stiles's. It must be, Sophie thought, because they don't really understand what's happening. Perhaps they are too young to really feel the loss and upheaval.

Sophie had thought there would be tears when they said good-bye to their grandmother, but the girls hadn't seemed too sorry to leave her. Mrs. Stiles had told them she would see them soon and to keep their chins up, and both of them did, literally in Izzy's case, causing her to walk into the gatepost at the bottom of the garden path. If there had been any hint of tears, it might have been from Mrs. Stiles, who had pressed her lips so firmly together as she watched the girls leave that her mouth had turned pale and bloodless. She'd shut the door before they had closed the garden gate behind them.

Miraculously, Sophie had seen a black cab turn in to the street and had stepped out to the curb to hail it, but just as the cabbie caught her eye, Tess had pulled her back onto the pavement and waved the driver on; he'd sworn through the glass at the pair of them and shaken his head with irritation.

"What's the problem?" Sophie had asked Tess. "Was it money? Because I was going to pay—my place is a long walk from here, you know. I didn't think these two could walk that far. Short legs and all that." Sophie had looked at the battered and brimming suitcase at her feet. "And this is heavy."

Tess had shaken her head.

"Oh look, girls!" she'd exclaimed. "Ants!" Astonishingly, the discovery had seemed to delight both girls, who'd crouched over the crack in the pavement and watched the busy insects track and bustle across the stone slab. After a moment Bella had started to give the ants tiny tinny voices, commenting on their every movement, making Izzy chuckle, her small shoulders shaking.

Sophie had raised a questioning eyebrow at Tess. "I didn't think we'd be stopping for a natural history lesson," she'd said.

Tess had taken a step closer to Sophie and lowered her voice. "I told you Izzy is still a bit iffy about cars," she'd said. "After the crash."

"Oh." Sophie had forgotten that piece of information. "When you say *iffy*, what do you mean exactly—she can't go in cabs at all? Because I didn't think she'd know, you know, that her mum had been killed in a car crash. I didn't think she really got that her mum was killed. I mean, she seems pretty happy."

Tess had chewed her lip. "I obviously didn't make myself clear," she'd begun ominously. "Izzy was in the car when Carrie was killed. A van going fifty hit them on the driver's side at an intersection. Izzy was in a car seat. She was protected. Frightened and alone for almost ten minutes until help came, but physically unhurt. Carrie's seat belt was faulty. Apparently she knew it was, she just hadn't got around to getting it fixed. She was killed out-right. Thrown from the car. So Izzy's a bit iffy about getting in cars, including cabs, I'm afraid."

Sophie had looked down the length of the tree-lined road that she and Carrie had walked along so many times together talking incessantly—making plans, creating dreams for themselves. Carrie was going to be a painter, of course, and a fashion designer. She was going to live right by the sea in a tower and marry a fish-erman. Sophie was going to become a vet and run a cat sanctu-ary. She was going to marry Jason Donovan. It was funny how Carrie's dream never changed and how she had made it more or less come true. Sophie's plans changed from year to year: differ-ent occupation, different celebrity husband, until her dreams and fantasies had faded away into real solid ambition, into her life as it stood now. Even now, even knowing exactly what she wanted and exactly where she was going, Sophie assumed she had enough time left on the earth to make it happen. But Carrie had never planned to be thrown from a car and killed taking her daughter to nursery school. Neither one of them had ever dreamed she'd die. Not now, not ever.

"Does she understand what happened then?" Sophie had asked. To be perfectly honest, Sophie had no idea what three-year-olds could or could not understand. If she'd ever thought about it before that day, and she never had, she would have guessed they had about the same amount of reasoning power as the average dog—maybe a collie or a German shepherd—and much less than a cat.

Tess had shrugged. "She understands that it was very frighten-ing and that she hasn't seen her mummy since. I'm not sure what else she understands. I haven't really had time to talk to either of them properly. I don't think anyone has. Like I mentioned before, I've got both girls down for counseling, but, well, there's a waiting list." For a second Sophie had not known what to say, and she'd felt the weight of the children's terrible loss nudging at her edges. She'd blinked hard and chased the feeling away. There was no time for that now, she'd told herself. Right now she needed to stay focused on the project at hand.

"There's a bus stop at the end of the road," Sophie had said at last, hefting the suitcase off the ground. "We'll get the bus."

"Anyway," Tess said as she checked her cell phone. "I'll pop back in the morning, see how you're getting on, okay?" Sophie nodded and fingered the twenty-two-karat white gold chain around her neck until she caught the half-carat diamond pendant it held between her fingers. It had been her present to herself after her last promotion, material proof that she was making it. Sophie liked to be able to measure her progress through life with things she could see and feel. Hence her shoes and her precious jewelry collection, which was small but expensive. They were more than just objects—they were markers of specific times or achievements. They were three-dimensional memories.

"Right, okay," she said to Tess, desperately trying to fight down the wave of panic that was surging in her chest. "What do I do with them?" she hissed. "They're okay now, but what if they start crying or something?"

"Then give them a hug," Tess told her.

"A hug." Sophie looked dubious.

"But in the meantime, just give them some tea," Tess added, looking at her watch.

"Tea? Really?" Sophie said. "Okay. If you say so."

Tess gave her a slightly quizzical look as Sophie walked her downstairs and opened the main entrance door. As Tess walked out, Sophie's cat, Artemis, walked in, shouldering her way past Sophie's legs without the faintest of greetings. Sophie wasn't of-

fended, that was just Artemis. It took her a long time to estab-
lish complete trust with a human. Sophie wasn't sure exactly how
long, but it was definitely longer than the three years since
Sophie had rescued Artemis from the cat home where she had
been the least popular and most solitary inmate. For some reason, though, Sophie had been drawn to her and had slavishly
adored her from the moment she brought her home. An emotion that was definitely not reciprocated by the cat. Artemis
merely tolerated her.

Normally when she came in this way, she'd shoot straight up
the stairs and into the kitchen, looking for her dinner. But today
she stopped at the foot of the stairs and stared up them.

"Ah yes," Sophie said to the cat. "There's something I've got
to tell you." She scooped Artemis up in her arms. The cat went
rigid in her embrace and tightened her claws on Sophie's sleeves
just enough to make holding her uncomfortable. Sophie took
this as a good sign. If Artemis had been really pissed off, she
would have drawn blood and twisted her way to an escape by
now, just as she used to when Sophie first brought her home
from the shelter. "The thing is, Artemis, we've got guests.
Children. Now, I know you hate noise and mess and people invading your space and touching all your things, but it's only for
a week, okay? So try to be nice. At least try not to be violent. I
mean, you never know, you might really like them, couple of
kids to play with."

Artemis did not look convinced, and neither was Sophie.
After all, the only other creatures that Artemis had ever happily
played with to date were a disemboweled mouse and a not quite
dead starling chick. Still, no need to tell the girls *that*.

Sophie carried a horrified Artemis into the living room and
presented her to the children. "Bella, Izzy," she said. "This is my
cat, Artemis—"

"Catty!" Izzy shrieked with delight and bounded over the arm of the cream leather sofa in one fluid moment. Artemis shot out of Sophie's arms with a yowl and disappeared into the bedroom.

"Um, that *was* my cat, Artemis," Sophie said. "She's a bit . . ." Sophie was going to say "antisocial" but thought better of it. "She's a bit shy. I got her from a cat shelter. Her last owners weren't very kind to her, so people aren't her favorite thing. She'd been at the shelter for nearly a year when I got her. No one else wanted her because she was so . . . shy. We get along okay, though. I love her, and she ignores me. It works pretty well."

Izzy had dropped to the floor and was peering under the sofa. "Catty? Catty where are you?" she inquired. "Come back, Catty. *Izzy's going to cuddle you up!*"

"The thing is, Izzy," Sophie said to the child's bottom, "It's probably best that while you're staying here you leave her alone. Okay?"

"Okay," Izzy said cheerfully. "Catteeeeeeeeeeeeeeeeeeee? Whereareyoooooooooo?" She peeped around the living room door and looked each way down the short hallway before advancing toward the bedroom. Evidently, Izzy's definition of *okay* was different from Sophie's. Well, looking for Artemis would keep her occupied for a few minutes, Sophie reasoned. There was no way Izzy would find Artemis on top of the wardrobe, her favorite hiding place anyway, so they would both probably be quite safe for the time being.

"So," Sophie said to Bella, who remained sitting, her hands primly on her knees. "Tess said to give you tea. How do you like it? Milk, sugar? Earl Grey? I think I've got Darjeeling somewhere . . ." Bella blinked her brown eyes at her from under her thick black and slightly too long bangs.

"I think she meant *food* tea, Aunty Sophie," she said slowly, as if English wasn't Sophie's first language. "Like *dinner?*"

Sophie sat down on the sofa next to her. "Obviously I knew that!" she lied. "I was joking! Ha-ha. Get it?"

Bella shook her head. "No," she said deadpan. "It wasn't funny."

For a moment Sophie was reminded of a film she'd once seen where the world was taken over by evil aliens disguised at kids. She forced the thought to the back of her mind. She was the adult, they were the children. She was in charge. It wasn't like, for example, *The Omen,* at all, nope, not in any way. These were Carrie's children. Not the Antichrist's—although Sophie really hardly knew Louis, so she couldn't rule that out entirely.

"So tea!" She said with renewed vigor. "Let's go and see what's in the fridge, shall we, Bella?"

There was nothing in the fridge except for half a pint of skim milk, three shriveled spring onions, low-fat margarine, and two Marks & Spencer low-fat ready meals, Thai green chicken curry and seafood pasta. They would have to do.

Sophie took the two meals out of the fridge, forked their film coverings with enthusiastic aggression, and shoved them in the microwave. Bella watched Sophie display the extent of her culinary skills, her brown eyes just about reaching over the rim of the counter.

"What *is* that?" she asked Sophie.

"It's seafood pasta and chicken curry," Sophie said. "Yum yum."

Bella said nothing but eyed the microwave warily for a moment. She looked around the narrow galley kitchen. "Your kitchen is very small," she said. "Where do you eat?" It was a valid question.

"On the sofa usually," Sophie said. "Is that okay?"

Bella looked skeptical. "Well, it's okay for me, but . . ."

"Excellent, that's settled then," Sophie said. Just at the moment that the microwave beeped there was a crash from the bedroom and the screech of a furious cat, followed closely by the cries of a distraught child.

Sophie and Bella ran into the bedroom. Izzy was lying sprawled on Sophie's bed, with Sophie's old-style umbrella in one hand and half of one leg trapped underneath Sophie's empty and fortunately lightweight suitcase.

"Catty!" Izzy sobbed, waving the umbrella wildly at the open window. "Catty, come back!"

Sophie looked out the small window that she always left open for Artemis to come and go as she pleased. She was sure that leaving the window open pretty much negated her insurance policy, but she couldn't bear the thought of cooping Artemis up in the flat when she'd been imprisoned in the shelter for so long. Artemis had certainly been glad of the escape route on this occasion. She must have scooted across the little balcony onto the downstairs extension roof, and off into the evening in double-quick time. Sophie didn't think she'd be coming back anytime soon, and she felt a pang of helpless anxiety. She didn't know why she worried about Artemis. Artemis was a pretty tough cat.

Bella climbed onto the bed and pushed the suitcase onto the floor with a thud. She put her arm around Izzy and pulled her into a sitting position. Kissing the younger girl's light brown hair, Bella patted her firmly on the back three times. "There. There. There," she said with each pat. Sophie wasn't sure what she was supposed to do. Perhaps she was supposed to hug Izzy and do a bit of patting too, but she didn't quite know how to go about the whole hugging and patting thing, so she left it to Bella and sat on the edge of the bed instead.

"What happened, Izzy?" Sophie asked her.

"Catty was stuck, I was helping Catty, like when Bob the

Builder helped Pilchard," Izzy sobbed. "But she ran away! I wanted to cuddle her up!"

Sophie guessed that Izzy had spotted Artemis on top of the wardrobe and, unable to reach her, had climbed onto the bed with Sophie's hook-handled umbrella, which had been propped in the corner of the bedroom, and tried to hook the cat down. An event that would have horrified poor old Artemis. Still, it proved that Izzy had at least as much reasoning power as a border collie after all.

Sophie ventured out a hand to pat Izzy's knee, then quickly withdrew it. "Don't worry," she said. "Artemis will be back when she wants to be. Probably best not to cuddle her up next time she comes home. She's not a big fan of the cuddle as a concept."

"Okay." Izzy sniffed. Sophie wasn't sure whether or not to take that as agreement.

The microwave beeped again. "Tea's ready!" Sophie said brightly, and both girls did look more cheerful. They must really be hungry, poor kids, Sophie thought.

In preparation, Sophie positioned them both on the sofa and gave each of them a paper towel to prevent spillage. She gave them each a fork and a knife, and looked through her practically medieval five television channels for something they could watch, settling in the end for a talk show, *Richard & Judy.*

"Oooh, a knife," Izzy said, inspecting the implement she had been handed as if it were a lethal weapon.

In the kitchen, Sophie tipped out each ready meal onto a separate plate. She thought for a moment and then tipped the seafood pasta onto the Thai green curry plate and mixed it around until it was slightly lighter shade of green. Then she split the mixture in two and slid one half back onto the second plate. That way there'd be no arguments about who was having what, she thought, feeling pleased with herself. Foresight, that was what she had displayed there. Foresight. A key problem-solving skill was to solve the problem before it even occurred.

She took the plates to the living room, where Izzy was endeavoring to cut open the sofa with the blunt serrated edge of her knife.

"Um." Sophie made especially sure that she did not raise her voice. "Izzy, don't do that darling, okay?" she asked her, wondering if the exorbitant cost of the sofa would mean anything to Izzy. Probably not.

"Okay!" Izzy said, sawing away regardless.

"Here's tea now anyway," Sophie said. She handed the girls a plate each. "Okay, enjoy, I've just got to make a couple of quick calls, so I'll be back in a minute, okay?"

"Okay!" Izzy said, transferring her sawing attentions to the food.

Bella looked at her food suspiciously and poked it with her fork. "Okay," she said with much less enthusiasm.

Sophie picked up the phone in her bedroom and called Cal first.

"How's it going?" he asked her, unable to keep the amusement out of his voice.

"Fine, it's fine actually," Sophie said, wondering if her voice sounded as high on the other end of the phone line as it did in her head. She made a conscious effort to lower it a half octave. "I've given them their tea, then I expect they'll go to bed after," she said confidently.

"What, at five o'clock?" Cal did not sound so confident.

"Never mind that," Sophie said, brushing his doubt aside. "Did the contracts from the bank come through okay?" Cal confirmed that they had. He gave her a rundown of the day's events and the inside scoop on how Lisa had handled all of her new duties. "Pretty well, actually," Cal said. "She hasn't cried for the whole afternoon. Barely even a sniffle. Well, maybe the occasional sob—but mainly I think you being out of the office is good for her. She's too scared of me to mess *me* around."

Sophie ignored the last comment. "Good. Listen, I want you to come round in the morning, okay? Bring my laptop. I didn't have time to pick it up when we went. Bring all the stuff we talked about today and our schedule for the week. I want to sort out exactly who's doing what when."

"Okay, sir," Cal said. "Should we synchronize our watches, sir?"

Sophie did not laugh. She did not like it when Cal called her "sir." "Any other calls?" she said.

"Jake called to see if we'd heard from you. He asked me for your home number, and I said it was against company policy and all that, but he said what about your cell phone number, and I said I supposed that would be okay if it was really important, and he said he needed to talk to you about the party. So I offered to see if I could help him, but he said he'd just give you a ring and see how you were doing, so he clearly fancies you even though you've just become a single mother. I think you should marry him. He's a keeper."

Sophie gave a short, hysterical laugh. "Look, Cal, I need to get my head round this. Carrie's gone, and her children are in my living room. I can't think about any of that stuff—so please, for my sake, just give it a rest, will you?"

There was short pause.

"I'm sorry, Soph," Cal said, his voice softened. "You know me, the more complicated and emotional things get, the bigger and more stupid my mouth gets. Look, if I can help you with anything, you know I will, don't you?"

Sophie smiled. "I know," she said. "You're a mate. Just come over tomorrow—at lunchtime, okay?"

"Yes, sir," Cal said resuming normal service. "Over and out, sir!" And for once Sophie didn't mind.

She listened for any sound of disturbance from the living room. All was quiet on the Western Front except for the faint jangle of the *Richard & Judy* theme song. She dialed her mother's number. As usual, it rang only twice before she heard the receiver clatter to the floor and the sound of dogs baying and yapping. Her slightly hard of hearing mother had trained her Great Dane cross, Scooby, to answer the phone when it rang. She had not, unfortunately, trained Scooby to take messages or, perhaps more vitally, to let her know that someone was waiting on the other end of the line. Sophie had always thought that was an essential bit to leave out.

"Mum!" she yelled into the phone. "Mum! Mum! Mum!" It was a bit of a lottery as to whether her mum would work out that she was on the phone at all. But the more Sophie yelled, the more the dogs barked, which meant the more likely her mum was to come and see what they were barking at, which usually resulted in a conversation. Usually it did, but one evening when Sophie had called her, she had not answered at all, and after listening to dogs for twenty minutes, Sophie had been forced to go around to her mum's house and let herself in just to double-check that her mother wasn't lying dead in the hallway having her toes nibbled by her pets.

Finally there was a clank and the sound of her mother's voice conversing with the dogs. "Get down, poochies—get *down*! Hello?" Her mother spoke into the receiver at last. She always sounded surprised when she answered the phone as if she'd forgotten that it had been invented until each time it rang again.

"Mum, it's me," Sophie said.

"Hello, dear." Her mother's voice warmed. "Oh, I am glad I

called you. I've got a lot to tell you. Felicity's got to go back to the vet's again—same upset tummy—"

"Mum! Look, I'm sorry, but I've got something to tell you." Sophie told her about Carrie and the children.

"Oh dear," her mother said after a long pause. "How terrible. How terrible."

Sophie agreed once again that it was, she knew it was terrible, but she worried that she was secretly thinking it was terrible for all the wrong, selfish reasons.

"The thing is, Mum, I don't really know what I'm doing, you know. I thought maybe you could come over? Give me some tips? Please, Mum?"

Her mother hesitated, as Sophie had known she would. "Tonight, dear, do you mean?" she said uncertainly.

"Well, it *is* sort of an emergency," Sophie said. She was disappointed at her mum's reluctance, even though she knew that prying her away from her dogs was near impossible, especially in recent years.

"Please, Mum," Sophie said, resenting that she had to ask for help twice. "I need you."

"All right," her mother said, with slow reluctance. "But I won't be able to stay for long, okay? Mitzy's expecting, you know—it could be any minute."

Sophie said good-bye and looked at her reflection in her dressing table mirror. She looked exactly the same as she always did. Neat and efficient. Calm and in control—so why did she feel as if she'd suddenly been sent into a war zone, thrown in among the bloody chaos without the faintest clue what to do, not even any basic training? She made herself take a deep breath. Managing children was no different than managing any other project. It simply required a broad depth of knowledge, a cool head, and brilliant negotiating skills. That and twenty-four tranquilizers and a large bottle of whiskey. Sophie smiled at herself in the mirror. Things were not quite *that* bad. Yet.

"It's just two weeks," she told herself. "You'll be fine."

The bedroom door opened a crack, and Bella's bangs peered around the corner, followed a fraction of a second later by her eyes.

"Um, Aunty Sophie," she said ominously. "I think you'd better come and see this."

Sophie instinctively steeled herself as she followed Bella back down the hallway to the living room, imagining the very worst that could have happened. She did not imagine hard enough.

"My sofa!" Sophie cried, ignoring the child who was covered from head to foot in Thai-curry-seafood-pasta. "Oh, my God! My sofa! My . . . sofa."

Half of her cream leather sofa was now a greenish color, and so were her two faux fur cushions, their once strokable softness now converted into punklike sticky spikes.

Izzy grinned at her. "Tea was all bleugh and yuck," she said reasonably, by way of explanation. "So look, I made a painting with it on the sofa!" Izzy clearly thought that the artwork was something that should impress and not depress Sophie. "Is there any ice cream please?" she asked.

Sophie resisted the urge to weep. She ran through all the legal and moral reasons she knew of why it was not a good idea to throw a child out the window until she was sure she had stopped herself from screaming. She took a deep breath and counted backward from ten just to be on the safe side.

"What have you done to my sofa?" she said, after the countdown with much more control than she felt. "Why have you . . . *ruined* my sofa?" She turned to Bella. "Couldn't you have stopped her? Couldn't you have come and got me? I mean, you're the responsible one."

"I'm only six and a half," Bella said, looking irritated. "And anyway, you were on the phone and you said it was okay for us to eat on the sofa and I thought you realized that she might be a bit messy and I didn't know that she was going to do that, did I? I just went in the kitchen to get some more water and when I came back she'd tipped it everywhere and—" Bella stopped talking, and Sophie was worried that she had made her cry. But when Bella looked up at Sophie, her eyes were dry.

"Really," she said, giving Sophie a look of pure recrimination. "Izzy needs *adult* supervision."

"All right, I appreciate that it's not your fault," Sophie said. She looked at Izzy, narrowed her eyes, and tried a phrase her mum had used on her frequently as a child. "What have you got to say for yourself, young lady?"

Izzy giggled and clapped her hand over her mouth. "Ooops," she said. "I done a wee-wee in my pants!" The child giggled and pointed at a trickle of warm liquid running over the edge of Sophie's sofa and dripping onto her sheepskin rug. Sophie wanted to break down and cry over her sofa, she wanted to weep for her rug, she wanted desperately to mourn her faux fur cushions, but she could not, she told herself. She could not be crying over rugs or cushions or sofa when so far she had witnessed neither one of these children cry over the loss of their mother. Whatever way you looked at it, they had the moral high ground. And children are more important than sofas or cushions. Apparently.

Gingerly, Sophie picked Izzy up and held her at arm's length. This was harder than she'd imagined; Izzy was pretty heavy and, what's more, very ticklish. She giggled and kicked, sending a fine spray of goo all over Sophie's dry-clean-only skirt. Sophie gritted her teeth and thanked God that she had removed her new boots and locked them safely away in her wardrobe.

"I'm just putting you in the kitchen for a minute, Izzy," Sophie told her. "Just while I clear up the mess, okay?"

"Okay!" Izzy said.

Sophie was not reassured. She set Izzy down on the floor by the window and cast an eye about for any more potential disasters. There were no sharp objects in view, no toxic substances, and no box of matches. Everything should be fine, she thought.

"Okay, let's play statues, okay? You stand very, *very* still for as long as you can and don't move. Okay?"

Izzy nodded. "Okay," she said.

Twenty minutes, two rolls of Bounty, and three bowls of warm, soapy water later, Sophie and Bella had made quite a good job of cleaning the sofa, although Sophie suspected there was no hope for the cushions, which she consigned regretfully to a garbage bag that she put outside the flat's front door in the communal hallway.

"Thank God," Sophie told Bella sincerely. "That Marks and Spencer doesn't use artificial coloring."

"Thank God," Bella agreed. Sophie noticed her food also uneaten but mercifully still congealing on the plate.

"You didn't like it either, did you?" Sophie asked.

"It *was* rather disgusting," Bella said, wrinkling her nose.

Sophie suppressed a smile. For a small child, Bella had a remarkably large vocabulary.

"I'm sorry Bella," she said. "This is all new to me. I'm not very good at it, am I?"

"No," Bella said. "But you're trying."

Sophie somehow found the energy to get off her knees and stand up again and held out a hand to help Bella up.

"Aunty Sophie?" Bella said, still holding on to Sophie's fingers. "I love Grandma and everything, but I'm glad we came to stay with you."

Sophie felt herself smile and her resolve strengthened. "Really?" she said, warmly deciding to fish a bit further. "Why's that?"

Bella shrugged. "Grandma doesn't have a telly," she said.

Sophie nodded and glanced at the TV, where the end credits for *Richard & Judy* were rolling.

"Fair enough," she said. "Well, I suppose we'd better go and clean up your sister."

"Yes, before she starts eating the cat food," Bella said.

Sophie laughed. "You're joking, right?" she said.

Bella wasn't joking.

Sophie gave her mum a cup of tea and her very best resentful look. Iris looked offended. "I got here as soon as I could, dear," she said.

"Mum, it's twenty to ten! I was hoping you'd be round before they went to sleep. That's when I needed help the most."

It was shortly after Sophie had discovered Izzy snacking on the dry cat food that she had made what would later prove to be a critical discovery. When a three-year-old girl is determined to do something, she really, *really* means it.

In this case, Izzy had refused point-blank to remove her fancy dress, even for a much-needed bath. At first Sophie had tried reason and logic to persuade the child out of the dress. But then, as Izzy's screams had grown to eardrum-perforating levels and Sophie had clutched at all the available straws, she had turned in desperation to Bella.

"What do I do?" she had asked the older girl, who was watching with detached interest, her hands clapped over her ears.

"Let her keep the dress on?" Bella had suggested casually. Simple, brilliant, and entirely effective.

A few minutes later, Sophie had washed child and dress in her bath, tipping in large amounts of Chanel bubble bath in an attempt to mask the smell, too fraught to resent the sacrifice.

"She's always happy if you let her get her own way," Bella had observed, sitting on the toilet.

"I'm not letting her get her own way," Sophie had said with determination. "I'm multitasking."

Iris was unrepentant. "I would have been here earlier, Sophie, but Oedipus Rex started having one of his turns, and I had to stay with him until he settled down. I don't want the neighbors complaining again, do I?"

Sophie shook her head. "You should move, Mum. You should sell that house and move to the country. You'd get somewhere much bigger for your money, and it wouldn't matter so much that you have the canine version of the von Trapp family."

Iris sniffed. "I don't know anyone in the country," she said, looking a little hurt.

"You don't know anyone here anymore," Sophie reminded her. "No one wants to come round in case they catch rabies."

Iris sighed. "I want to live near you, anyway," she said wistfully.

Sophie covered her surprise. Her mother loved her dogs so much that sometimes Sophie forgot she was probably fairly fond of her daughter too.

"So what do you think about the cat food thing, then?" Sophie said, deciding to change the subject before they somehow got embroiled in one of their long, consistently unsatisfactory, and ultimately life-draining conversations about what it meant to be a good daughter.

Her mother considered the question for a moment. "I think it will be fine," she said. "There was an article about an old lady who couldn't pay her gas bill in the *Express* last week. She'd been living off cat food, the poor old dear, even though when the neighbors broke in they found thousands of pounds in cash under her bed."

"Why did the neighbors break in?" Sophie asked her.

"Because she was dead, dear," her mum said, as if it were a stupid question.

"Dead!" Sophie panicked momentarily as she wondered what the maximum sentence was for involuntary manslaughter.

"Oh, no, no," Iris said quickly. "She didn't die of cat food. No, she died of hypothermia. All alone in the world, you see—her children had abandoned her."

"Oh, thank God," Sophie said with relief. Her mother raised an eyebrow at her. "Well, you know what I mean." Sophie sighed and drew her legs up under her on the sofa. She wrinkled her nose. It still smelled decidedly spicy. "The thing is, Mum, I have no idea what I'm doing. I know I'm only having them for a week or so, but right now that feels like a week or so too long. I'm useless."

Her mother reached into her bag and pulled out a book. She tossed it to Sophie, who was expecting something useful on child care. She should have known better.

"*Dr. Robert's Complete Dog Training and Care Manual?*" Sophie read out the title in disbelief. "Mum! They're children, they're humans—or at least that's what I've been told! How's this"—she wagged the book at her mum—"going to help?"

Her mother pursed her lips. "You'd be surprised, actually. The principles are more or less the same. Sit, stay, come, et cetera. House training. A spot of doggy psychology. It could work wonders, I expect. I wish I'd known all that when I had you. That's the trouble with you cat people. No imagination."

Sophie tossed the book to the floor in disgust. "You must know something about looking after children, Mum, you brought me up after all—more or less."

Iris nodded and looked slightly abashed. "I know, darling, I know, but I've— Well, I've forgotten how I did it. It sounds silly, doesn't it, but it was rather a long time ago, and I don't know— it's just gone out of my head. The only thing I do remember is feeling like I was always getting it wrong. I can't have done too much of a bad job, though—look at you. Successful, independent. Can't get a husband, but that will come . . ."

Sophie sipped her tea and felt it warm the back of her throat. "Don't want a husband, Mum. Don't *want* one," She said irritably. "There *is* a difference." Sophie's mother looked skeptical. Sophie thought about Jake. "And even if I did, I never exactly know when one wants me."

"That's the easy bit, dear." Iris chuckled, thinking that her daughter must be joking. "It's what to do with them after you're married that's the hard part."

"You and Dad never had any trouble," Sophie said.

"Yes, well." Iris smiled fondly. "You father and I always had incredible sexual chemistry. I can't tell you how I've miss—"

"Mum!" Sophie did not want to think about her mother as a sexual being. Especially when she did not think of herself that way.

"All I'm saying is that a woman has needs. I know since your father passed—"

"Mum!" Sophie hissed, afraid to raise her voice. "I don't want to talk to *you* of all people about 'needs'—mine, yours, or anyone's—okay? I need your help with these children!"

Iris shrugged. "Alex was a nice young man," she said, willfully ignoring her daughter's attempt to change the subject. "He seemed to really care about you, and he bought me some lovely flowers."

Sophie felt the muscles tighten in her chest with anxiety and frustration. She had told her mother time and time again why things didn't work out with Alex.

In the end, Alex had told her he was tired of going out with her. Tired of the amount of effort it took to get her to leave her job alone for even a few minutes and spend some time with him. He said he'd jumped through hoop after hoop to get her attention, but nothing seemed to work. So he'd tried a last-ditch attention grabber.

He'd asked her to marry him.

Crucially, Sophie had hesitated. Not for a few minutes or days but for nearly three weeks. When he'd left her that evening with a ring in a box on her coffee table it was the last time she talked to him face-to-face. She just didn't know what to say, so she didn't say anything.

Eventually, Alex had sent her an email telling her he assumed her silence was a no—unless she wanted to let him know otherwise. Sophie had never replied to that either. She'd let the biggest and potentially most important relationship in her adult life slip out of her hands simply because she didn't know who to be in it. No, it was worse than mere negligence. She had deleted it.

And although her friends, especially Cal, had told her she was crazy to let him go, she'd told them she couldn't keep him, because she wasn't absolutely certain she *wanted* to.

Sometimes, though, she did miss Alex. Well, not him exactly, more the warmth he left in bed in the morning. Sophie shook her head. Her mother was managing to railroad again. "Can we just for one moment try to think about the most immediate problem?" Sophie asked.

Iris looked rather vague.

"The kids!" Sophie had to remind her mum.

"I'm sorry I'm not more of an expert of motherhood," Iris said, the slight sharpness in her tone going over Sophie's head.

"But, well, I think you just have to trust your instincts. Listen to your intuition and you won't go wrong."

"I think that's the problem," Sophie said glumly, wishing she hadn't smoked all five of her remaining cigarettes shortly after the girls had gone to bed.

"What is, dear?" her mum said.

Sophie looked up at her blankly.

"What's the problem?" Iris pressed her.

"Well, most women have intuition built in, don't they?" Sophie asked, remembering her point. "Give 'em a kid and they know what to do with it instantly—at least that's what we're all led to believe. But obviously I have that particular gene missing. . . . I never get any intuition about anything, Mum. I mean, how do I know what's for the best, unless I have all the available facts in front of me—unless it's there in black and white? This intuition business sounds like total nonsense to me—like reflexology or astrology."

Her mother smiled. "Your stars did say you were facing great upheaval."

"Really?" Sophie looked interested for a moment until she realized her mum was teasing her. "Anyway. I don't think intuition really exists. I think it's a myth."

"It isn't," her mother said.

"You would say that. And anyway, how do you know?" Sophie challenged her.

"I just know, the same way I know that you have it, Sophie," Iris said, pausing to find a way to talk to her prickly daughter without offending her. "Sometimes I think, with all this work and career and promotions, that you've forgotten yourself. You're always working toward something, but sometimes I wonder if you even know why."

Sophie rolled her eyes. "Mum, things are different now. I know what I want from my life. I want to get to the top. I don't need a man or children to be happy or successful or fulfilled. I want to be successful."

"But *why*?" her mother asked her.

Sophie looked at her mother and wondered how it was they shared the same language, because she never seemed to understand what Iris was going on about.

"I want to be the best I can," Sophie said, frustrated that the conversation had somehow drifted onto her mother's favorite subject—Things That Are Wrong with Sophie. "And anyway, this isn't about me," Sophie reminded her irritably. "It's about now and the next couple of weeks. I've got to come up with a coping strategy, and I thought you could help me. I should have known better."

Iris dipped her face and looked at her tea, and immediately Sophie felt sorry. "I'm not saying you're not a great mum. I mean, you are great and you are my mum and I love you. But you were never exactly conventional, were you?"

Her mother shrugged. "Possibly not," she said. "It was the seventies, dear. Nothing was."

"I know. All I'm saying is that I don't have it. I don't have that way you're supposed to have with kids. I understand Artemis better than I understand children, and Artemis is not an easy cat to understand. She's got issues."

Her mother finished her tea and set the mug down on the coffee table. "I don't think anybody would expect you to instantly turn into an expert under these circumstances, Sophie. I'm sure Carrie wouldn't. In fact, if I remember Carrie correctly, I'm sure she'd think the whole thing was pretty funny."

Sophie felt the corners of her mouth creep into a smile. Carrie *would* be seriously tickled by everything that had happened this evening.

"I'm sure you'll pick it up eventually, a capable girl like you," her mother reassured her.

"Eventually, maybe," Sophie conceded. "But not in two weeks."

Five

Aunty Sophie!" Sophie opened one reluctant eye and looked at Izzy. She felt like she had been asleep for a total of forty-seven minutes. "Pssssssst, Aunty Sophie," Izzy whispered at the top of her voice. "Wake up, wake up. I want breakfast. I want Cheerios *and* Shreddies *and* Crispies *and* Coco Pops *and* milk!" Izzy's eyes widened as she spoke in clear anticipation of the delights that her cereal feast would bring. She would be unlucky, though. Sophie did not eat breakfast and so did not have any of the cereals on Izzy's optimistic list. She didn't even have any bread anymore—they'd eaten it all last night.

Sitting up, Sophie rubbed her eyes and looked at her watch. It was just before 6:00 A.M. It turned out that she *had* been asleep for a total of forty-seven minutes.

Her mother had left just after eleven, and Sophie had been sitting on the edge of the sofa wondering exactly how she had come to this point in her life when she had heard a loud buzzing. For a few moments she'd thought the day was being topped off nicely with an invasion of giant killer wasps. Then she'd realized it was her cell phone vibrating on the coffee table. Nobody ever called on it outside office hours. Its loud thrum against the blond ash had been rather disconcerting. Sophie had picked it up and looked at the display; it had said "Number withheld." Compulsively unable to leave a phone unanswered, Sophie had pressed the Call button.

"Hello?" she'd said uncertainly.

"Sophie?" It was Jake Flynn's voice. Sophie had looked at her watch. Jake at this hour?

"Look, I know it's late, and I've been wondering about calling you all night," he'd said quickly. "I wanted to see how you were. I nearly didn't call you, but then I thought if I were you, I'd be sitting up all night worrying. Tell me to go away if you like, but I thought you might like someone to talk to."

Sophie had chewed her lip. "Um, no—thanks for calling. It's very . . . nice of you," she'd said. She would have to ring Cal in the morning and ask him to verify, but she was fairly sure that phone calls at this hour of the night were quite a good indicator of Jake being interested in her on more than just a business level.

But what if he *did* like her? She had had a secret and happily unattainable crush on him for sometime now. But that was when he was just her most important client. Not a man who phoned her late at night to ask her how she was. If he did like her like that, what did it mean? How would she feel abut him then? A real, three-dimensional, fleshy version of him that would want her in the real world instead of when she was daydreaming in the bath?

Sophie's labored thought processes had crashed, and she'd shut her eyes for a moment to reboot. He still might not fancy her. He could just be being American again. Americans were famous for not being very good at observing boundaries. That was always a possibility.

"So how are you coping?" Jake had asked her, and Sophie had realized that he was the first person to ask her that.

"I don't really know, Jake, there's so much to take in. I mean, Carrie's gone . . ." Sophie had paused to listen to those words out loud again. She still could not make sense of them. "It's a bit surreal," she'd finished after a moment. The mistress of understatement, Cal called her.

"You know you're not alone, don't you?" Jake had asked her.

"I know," Sophie had said. "I've got this Tess woman, the social worker, and Cal and Lisa will handle everything in the office until I can get back in. You don't have to worry, Jake, I won't let anything get in the way of—"

"That's not what I meant," he'd said. Sophie had heard him breathe out. "Look, Sophie, I really like you, and just in case you were in any doubt about what I mean by 'like you,' I mean I like you in a nonbusiness, personal kind of way. I'm very attracted to you."

"Oh," Sophie had said. That cleared that up then.

"I know you have a lot going on now, and maybe I should be stepping back and letting you get on with things, but like I said, I really like you, Sophie. I don't want to let this go before it's had a chance to become something else. Something that might be really great. I understand that right now you just can't think about anything like that, so in the meantime I want to be your friend. I guess that's why I'm calling you at this hour of the night, to put my cards on the table. To let you know I like you and that if you need me I'm here for you." Jake had laughed. "I'm hoping you'll be so impressed by my chivalry you'll fall for me and let me take you out on a date once all the dust has settled."

There had been a short pause in which Sophie had realized

that Jake had been asking her a question. "Of course," she'd said automatically.

"And I was thinking I could come by and take you all out one day. To the zoo or something? I have all this vacation time coming to me, and after all, I'm the boss. I'm sure I can give myself a day off on short notice."

"That would be lovely," Sophie had said, her mind still on the fact that Jake Flynn definitely "liked" her, which left just one question—did she definitely like him?

"So—it's okay if I call you on a nonbusiness footing?" Jake had asked her again, just to be totally clear.

"It is," Sophie had said, painfully aware of her stilted responses.

"Then good night, Sophie," Jake had said, and that time he'd said her name it had sounded different.

"Night," Sophie had said, and he'd hung up the phone.

Sophie had then sat on the edge of the sofa with her phone in her hand and wondered about how different her day might have been if Tess Andrew hadn't turned up. She wondered if Jake would have been so open and up front at their lunch date. She wondered if he had, if they might have met that evening for dinner and he might have escorted her home. She closed her eyes and tried to imagine him kissing her and then opened them quickly again. It wasn't that she wasn't attracted to Jake, but she was glad in a way that this obstacle had thrown itself up between them. Speculating on what might or might not happen with Jake was far too complicated to fit into her present worrying schedule. She had so many other things to worry about. Abandoned children, absent fathers, dead best friends. Sophie's stomach clenched as she ran down the list.

She decided to worry about her cat instead. It was far less worrying.

And so she had lain awake on the slightly too short and rather smelly sofa for most of the night, worrying about Artemis. Artemis liked her routine, she did not like disruption of any kind, it seriously freaked her out. For all the tough and together front she put on, all the girl-about-town swaggering she did, she was a bit of scaredy-cat when it came down to it. She was not keen to be nudged out of her comfort zone. Sophie was worried that she wouldn't come back, that she would take the children's invasion as a breach of trust between woman and cat and leg it forever to live life on the road, murdering small mammals along the way. She didn't want Artemis to leave her. Despite her being the world's most unfriendly pet, Sophie would miss Artemis sitting on what had become her very own armchair, casting Sophie the occasional imperious glance.

Even Sophie, who was not someone who needed a comfort zone, was feeling the pressure. Ordinarily she embraced change and welcomed a challenge. She just wasn't keen on ones that came out of the blue in nothing more than slight frothy fairy dresses.

Fortunately, Artemis did come back, just before 5:00 A.M., which Sophie considered something of a step forward in their relationship, because it meant that the cat must have wanted to come home enough to come through the bedroom window, even though she would have known the girls were sleeping in there. Getting her priorities right, the cat had gone into the kitchen, and Sophie had listened to her eat what was left of her food and have a drink of water. A few moments later, Artemis had stalked into the living room and regarded Sophie with a look of pure recrimination before leaping on to the armchair and curling up on its cushion with her back turned on Sophie, who was somehow comforted by the snub.

Sophie had looked at the ceiling and, for the first time in the last nearly twenty-four hours, allowed herself to think about Carrie. Closing her eyes, she'd pictured her friend the last time she had seen her, three years ago. Small but curvy, with dark honey curls and hazel eyes that glittered when she laughed, and she was always laughing. She'd tied her hair up in a bandanna and worn a pair of paint-splattered dungarees over a T-shirt top. She'd teased Sophie for fretting about the upholstery in her beloved car as Sophie drove Carrie and her sticky children to the station to catch the train back to Cornwall.

"Call me if you need me," Sophie had told Carrie as she helped her with her luggage onto the platform. "Call me anyway, but call if me you need me too—any time, okay?"

Carrie had laughed as she threw her bag onto the train with no regard for who or what it might hit. "Always, forever, whatever—right?" she'd said, hugging Sophie as she reminded her of their ancient pact.

"Exactly," Sophie had replied, not quite able to say it back to her for fear of sounding a bit cheesy.

"Let's see each other really soon, okay? I mean, I know your life is one constant social whirl, but I'm sure you can find time to see us somewhere," Carrie had said.

Sophie had known that Carrie was being gently sarcastic, because although her job did guarantee at least three parties a month, her life outside the office had dwindled to almost nothing.

And Carrie had been right. It wasn't that she didn't have friends out there who wanted to see her and whom she wanted to see. It was just that something always came up at work to prevent it happening, and nine times out of ten she would have to cancel at the last minute. Carrie had lived a couple of hundred miles away, but Sophie had other friends she was just as bad at keeping up with. Christina and Sue from the gym, who both lived in

Islington, for example. She hadn't seen either of them in months, and they were practically neighbors. And she'd been supposed to meet the McCarthy Hughes olds girls for a drink on every fourth Thursday, but the last time she had made it, it was just after last call and all she could do was kiss her friends on the cheek as she exchanged hurried news in the line for a taxi.

"You have to let you hair down more," her recently engaged friend and former colleague Angie had told her. "Don't let McCarthy Hughes run your life. You don't want to turn into Gillian!"

Sophie had laughed but secretly thought that, actually, she did.

Still, Sophie remembered thinking as she had said good-bye, Carrie was different. Carrie was her best friend and as much a part of her life as her mum was—if not more. No one knew her like Carrie did. She had to make more of an effort.

"Let's not let another two or three years go by again," she had said sincerely. "Let's not. I never remember how much I miss you until I see you."

"I'm going to take that as a compliment," Carrie said with a grin. When the train pulled out of the station, Bella and Carrie had pressed their noses against the window and crossed their eyes as Sophie waved good-bye. Sophie had never seen Carrie again. It was possible, probable even, that if Carrie hadn't died, she would never have seen any of her friend's family again, because as soon as she had remembered how important Carrie was to her, she had forgotten it too.

"I'm sorry, mate," Sophie had whispered, "I really am remembering how much I miss you now, believe me." And then seventeen hours of drama had overcome her at last and she'd finally fallen asleep.

That had been forty-eight minutes ago. Right now Izzy was

repeating her breakfast order with increasing urgency. Sophie looked over at the armchair. Artemis was no longer in it, lucky cat.

"Okay, okay," she said, holding the palm of her hand in front of Izzy's face. "Shush." Izzy did shush. Her eye filled with tears, and her lips quivered perilously.

"No!" Sophie said quickly in a conciliatory tone, instantly fearing the wailing and screaming and holding of breath again. "No, no, no, no. Don't cry, Izzy! Aunty Sophie wasn't telling you off, no! Because you are a lovely good girl, aren't you?" Izzy nodded and sniffed in a deep, damp breath. "Yes, yes you are—super-duper good excellent good grown-up girl who isn't going to cry, are you?" Sophie nodded at the child encouragingly, and returning her nod, Izzy climbed without invitation onto Sophie's lap and wound her arms around Sophie's neck until her runny nose teeming with a billion odd germs was only millimeters from Sophie's wrinkled one. That was Sophie's main objection to the whole physical-displays-of-affection thing—it was just so unhygienic.

"I'll be a good girl for you, Aunty Sophie," Izzy said, picking up a thick strand of Sophie's hair and winding it around her fist. "I'll be your friend and we will all be happy and you don't be cross, okay?"

Sophie nodded. She knew that any normal woman would be charmed and delighted by the comment—so why did she feel like it was a Mafioso-style threat?

"It's a deal," she said uncertainly.

"I'll kiss you now, okay?" Izzy said, and without waiting for consent, she pressed her slimy face against Sophie's tensed cheek, leaving her damp noseprint just under one of Sophie's twitching eyes. "Breakfast now. I want Cheerios and . . ."

Sophie wiped the sleeve of her pajama top across her cheek

and was contemplating how to break the no breakfast news to Izzy when she saw the walking pile of laundry that was approaching though the living room door. Bella dropped the sheets onto the rug.

"Izzy wet the bed," she said a little anxiously. "It wasn't me."

Sophie felt the damp of the fairy dress skirt begin to seep through her pajama bottoms. She didn't doubt Bella, all the evidence supported her case. Sophie took a deep breath. She wasn't going to get stressed about it. It was just wee on her leg. It wouldn't kill her. It probably wouldn't kill her, although she might have to look that up on the Internet just to make sure. She'd just have to get changed, put these pajamas in the laundry hamper, and buy a new bed after they'd gone, that's all. And new bedclothes and a new sofa and new cushions and new rugs. She wondered if the presence of a dead friend's children was an acceptable risk on her homeowners insurance. If it wasn't, it should have been.

Sophie lifted Izzy off her lap and sat her on the fragrant pile of sheets, where she could do the least damage.

"Okay," she said to both girls. "Only thirteen days to go." Both children stared blankly at her. "What I mean is, I have no food in the house. We'll have to go out for breakfast. Luckily, there's a twenty-four-hour Sainsbury's at Manor House. We'll get dressed. We'll go there, okay?"

"Okay!" both girls said.

"I'm hungry," Izzy said, glumly. "I'm *starving*."

"I know," Sophie said. "Which is why we have to get ready extra quickly, okay? And why we have to do *everything* that Aunty Sophie says, okay?" Sophie stared at both the girls as if she could hypnotically implant obedience into them. They stared back at her. She formulated a plan.

*   *   *

Of course Sophie's plan, which was to empty Izzy's treacherous bladder completely and get everyone out of the flat before malnutrition set in, did not work.

This is what happened instead.

Sophie sat Izzy on the toilet and told her not to move until she came back. She returned to her bedroom to dress and found Bella holding one of her Manolos in one hand and balancing precariously on the other with one foot. Sophie regarded the scene as if she had just come across Bella with her finger in the pin of a live grenade.

"Nooooo!" Sophie shouted commando style and, in her head at least, in slow motion.

Bella's face fell, and she slumped on the bed facefirst, letting the shoe drop to the floor, from where Sophie scooped it up and cradled it momentarily before realizing that she had things a *little* out of perspective. She had been about to offer Bella a go at her low-heeled pumps when a clatter and a scream sounded from the bathroom. The Manolo was abandoned once again as Sophie realized her rookie error of leaving Izzy alone in the bathroom for longer than a nanosecond. She found Izzy jammed securely in the toilet, her calf sticking out at a right angle from the seat and wriggling furiously, her face and upper torso caked in Sophie's expensive makeup collection.

Which meant another bath. And which Sophie was sure would mean another tantrum.

In any event, though, Izzy was amazingly contrite and even allowed Sophie to remove the offending fairy dress, which was now beyond all help, as long as Sophie promised to replace it with an identical one. Sophie chose not to worry about the logistics of that promise, concentrating only on the results it got.

Eventually she dressed in the bedroom, alongside both girls. Bella selected from the girls' single suitcase a pair of red leggings with yellow dots, an electric blue T-shirt, a lime green cardigan, and a pink cotton ruffled mini-skirt to finish the outfit off. And, robbed of her fairy dress, Izzy carefully picked out items of clothing that were entirely yellow.

In the meantime, Sophie struggled to find clothes that were suitable for taking two small children to the supermarket. Sensible clothes were not Sophie's strong point. Almost everything she bought was chosen to go to the office or a function in. And everything she bought was chosen with a particular pair of shoes in mind. Sophie put shoes first. If she saw a wonderful pair that she had absolutely nothing to wear with, she would buy them anyway. In her experience, shoes were like fashion magnets. The right clothes would simply be drawn to them. Sophie was especially proud of this philosophy she had invented all on her own, although she did have to admit that it sometimes took a lot of hard shopping to reach outfit Nirvana. Consequently, Sophie was limited on casual wear, principally because she didn't do much casual wearing.

Eventually she found a pair of jeans that she had forgotten she had and possessed only because she had felt compelled to help her mum redecorate the house last year with washable stainproof paint. After some rooting about in the backs of her drawers, she found an old pink Calvin Klein T-shirt that had the logo spelled out in diamantés, which she pulled reluctantly over her head.

Sophie looked at her shoe rack, which was neatly attached to the inside of her wardrobe door, and scanned her shoes. The most sensible and expendable pair of shoes she had were from River Island, low kitten heels in magenta pink with pointed toes and a thin strap that crossed each toe horizontally, ending in a tiny bow.

Once, only yesterday in fact—although it seemed like a dim memory now—it had amused her no end that such a pair of shoes were her most sensible ones. Now it dismayed her. Not because she wished she were better prepared for all scenarios but because she wished that her life was back to normal.

When the threesome finally emerged from the flat, Sophie felt curiously triumphant, as if she had survived an apocalypse.

The thing is, she decided, squinting slightly in the glare of the bright winter sun, to keep your nerve. If I can just do that, it'll be a breeze.

Six

Cal was not nearly as enthusiastic about Sophie's plans to turn bounty hunter as she was. Especially when she asked him to look up Louis Gregory on the Internet—as if the man and his whereabouts would be handily listed by Google in an A–Z directory of missing feckless fathers.

"This is not the telly, Sophie," he told her impatiently over the phone the morning after she decided to find Louis Gregory herself, mainly by getting Cal to do it. "You don't type a name into the Internet and then suddenly, *schum-schum-schum,* there's the current location, address, and a satellite image of the person's every movement. Do you know what I got when I typed Louis Gregory into the Search engine? Three hundred and eight-two thousand matches. And is your Louis Gregory *the* Louis Gregory? New Zealand's greatest living sheep shearer Louis Gregory? Not unless he's sixty-two and a Maori he's not. I do have a job to do, you know. Just exactly when do you expect me to go through all of these entries that probably have nothing whatsoever to do with your Louis Gregory?" Sophie had tapped her chipped nails on the edge of her bed. She was nervous about being in the bedroom when the girls were not, but she didn't want them to know she was looking for their dad too. She wasn't even sure they knew they had a dad. They hadn't mentioned him since they'd arrived. She wasn't sure what sort of an effect that kind of news might have on them, but if it was anything on a par with their reaction to the news that she did not have Cbeebies on her TV, she didn't want to risk it.

"Oh, come on, Cal. I need you here. It's an emergency."

"Why don't you do it?" Cal snapped. "You're the one on holiday after all."

Sophie paused. She thought about telling him in detail about the inevitable demise of her laptop, involving a tube of John Frieda Sheer Blonde hair serum, the residue from an empty box of Coco Pops, and a pair of nail scissors, but she decided against it. She couldn't stand the ridicule again; she could still hear the hysterical laughter of the IT support man ringing in her ears.

"My laptop's broken," she said. "I'm not getting a replacement until next week. And anyway, if this was a holiday, it'd be an all-expenses-paid trip to the Siberian salt mines of the former Soviet Union. Cal, you're my personal assistant—assist!"

Cal tutted. "I think you're taking the personal bit a bit too literally," he muttered.

Sophie paused. She never stopped to think about the nature of their relationship too closely, but she had made the assumption that the occasional weekend shopping trip, the odd after-work cocktails in the city meant that it was more than just a professional one, that it was a friendship of sorts. She hoped so, because Cal was the only friend she managed to see regularly, even if the fact that he worked for her did help the friendship along. Perhaps she *was* asking too much of him. Perhaps she was straying into

things-you-can-ask-your-boyfriend-to-do-on-the-grounds-that-
you-let-him-have-sex-with-you territory.

"I'm sorry," she said stiffly. "I didn't mean to impose on you."

Cal huffed again. "Oh, for Christ's sake, don't pull the martyr
act on me, love, I'm immune. Besides—I've got the answer to all
of our problems." He lowered his voice. "I know someone who
can help."

"Who?" Sophie asked, touched and reassured by Cal's reclas-
sification of her problems as "ours."

"Maria Costello," Cal said proudly. "Private detective. She's
not cheap, but she's good—she *always* gets her man. We've got a
lot in common in that respect."

For a moment Sophie didn't know what to say. She'd associ-
ated Cal's friends and acquaintances with a number of profes-
sions, from drag queen to car mechanic, but she would never
have guessed he'd know a private detective.

"A private detective?" she asked. "How do you know a private
detective?"

Cal's voice was rich with drama. "Oh, you know. I've done a
little . . . let's call it 'freelance' work for her."

"Freelance work?" Sophie questioned him anxiously. "What
sort of freelance work?"

"Well," Cal whispered. "Have you ever heard of 'the honey
trap'?"

"Yes?" Sophie said uneasily.

"Well, honey, I was the honey in the trap!" Cal giggled.

"You're lying!" Sophie cried, utterly scandalized. "Please tell
me you're lying. If this ever got out . . . you have to be lying," she
repeated.

Cal sighed. "Yes, all right, I am lying—spoilsport. Her offices
are in the shop below my flat, but that's just boring. Anyway, she
is very good, and I've told her all about you, and she says she can

find him, no problem. She says it will be, quote unquote, a piece of cake. Do you want to see her?"

"How much would it cost?" Sophie began uncertainly before she and Cal reached the same conclusion at exactly the same moment.

"Actually, I don't care how much it costs," she said.

"Trust me. You don't care how much it costs," Cal said simultaneously. "And besides," he continued, "you have nothing better to spend all your money on."

Sophie had to agree that, right at the moment, she did not. "All right, ask her to come to the flat today," she said. "We'll be here. I've worked out that, if we don't actually leave the flat, we've got an eighty percent better chance of survival."

"Righty-ho," Cal said jauntily. "Now if you don't mind, I think I'd better get back to my real job."

"Is everything okay there?" Sophie asked anxiously, thinking about *her* real job. After all, she'd been out of the office for nearly forty-eight hours.

"Everything is fine. Nobody misses you at all," Cal said, specifically to irritate her. "Except possibly your new boyfriend, Jakey."

"He's not my boyfriend," Sophie said wearily.

"Of course he's not, because you only like men when you're not sure if they like you. Now Jake's actually come out and said he wants to be in your life, you'll get cold feet and run away and do spreadsheets or something—"

"Cal!" Sophie interrupted impatiently. "Why are we talking about this now?"

"Because Jake is too good to run away from." Cal pressed on regardless. "If you want to keep him, you have to get over your fear of intimacy and stop acting like you're a closet lesbian. Or a frigid closet lesbian."

"Now I think you're taking the 'personal' part of PA too literally," Sophie said.

"I'm just saying, don't make the mistake you made with Mr. Luscious Loss Adjuster."

"What mistake?" Sophie asked him. "I only ever saw him from a distance. I never even spoke to him."

"And that," Cal finished matter-of-factly, "was the mistake!"

Maria Costello arrived at ten minutes past ten that night. It was a night that had followed a day that was, Sophie's exhausted brain reasoned, as stress-free as a day was ever likely to get as long as the children were invading her flat. This was largely because she had worked out a fairly efficient containment system, involving food and television. She drew the curtains to exclude any unwanted foray of daylight onto the TV screen, and she watched daytime television all day, with the girls sitting on either side of her, occasionally rising from the sofa to bring them another snack. Fortunately they had been so starved of TV at Mrs. Stiles's house that they were prepared to watched anything with awe, like a couple of cave girls who had just been brought forward in time fifty thousand years or so to marvel at the modern world inventions. As for Sophie, well, she didn't care what she watched as long as it wasn't another one of her precious possessions being executed.

"You are very old to have blond hair," Bella had told Maria Costello as Sophie showed her into the blanket and clothes-strewn living room.

The detective had wrinkled up her slightly hooked nose as she looked around the room and then down at Bella. "And you are very young to be up this late," she said, with a slightly stern upper-class Liverpudlian accent.

Sophie put her hand on Bella's shoulder and drew the child a step closer to her, suddenly sensing how very small the little girl was in comparison to the rather large and rather solidly bosomed Ms. Costello. Sophie didn't know exactly what she expected from a private dick, as Cal had begun to refer to her with a little giggle after every reference, but it hadn't been a Day-Glo orange tan and jewelry almost as brassy as her hair.

Maria Costello must have guessed exactly what she was thinking. "You don't need to blend in these days, love," she said. "I can do almost all of my work from the office." She winked at Bella. "Mind you, I'm a master of disguise when I need to be."

"Who are you and what do you want from us?" Bella asked her, quoting verbatim a line she'd heard on *Neighbours* twice earlier in the day, once at lunchtime and once in the teatime repeat. At this point Sophie decided it was a good plan to get her back into bed. Nobody had to know anything until there was something to know.

"Maria is here to see me, Bella. It's just about work, nothing to do with you. Now you've got your glass of water, haven't you? So you run along and get into bed, because tomorrow we're—" Sophie stopped dead in her tracks. She had nothing planned for the girls the following day except watching TV, eating dry cereal on the sofa and chicken nuggets and chips on the kitchen floor (ketchup required extra saftey measures). "Going to be awake again," she finished lamely.

"Can I finish telling you the story about the flying fairy pony?" Bella asked her. She had begun this story—seemingly one she made up herself—the previous night. It was, surprisingly, quite gripping, but tempting as her offer was, now was not the time for chapter three.

"No, let's save it for tomorrow, okay?—so that Izzy can hear it too. Go on, off you go."

Bella eyed Maria Costello suspiciously before finally padding into the bedroom. Sophie smiled nervously at the formidable looking woman and suddenly felt quite small herself. She had expected Maria for most of the day, finally giving up on her making an appearance after 9:00 P.M. So now Sophie was not prepared. She did not have *her* formidable woman clothes on. She had her Snoopy jim-jams on, and they didn't have quite the same impact.

"Um, do you want a drink?" Sophie offered, thinking of tea, coffee, or hot chocolate.

"Got any whiskey?" Maria asked hopefully. Sophie hadn't got any whiskey. She had two-thirds of a bottle of Baileys that Lisa had given to her at Christmas after drinking the first third of it sitting on Sophie's office floor weeping about some bloke who hadn't kissed her under the mistletoe. Sophie had thought about the bottle of Baileys a lot in the last couple of days, but so far she had not succumbed to it. Now that she was not alone, it was acceptable.

"I've got Baileys," she suggested hopefully.

"Make it a double," Maria said, so Sophie obligingly filled two mugs halfway with the coffee-colored liquor. Of course, Sophie did have glasses that would have been more suitable, but for some reason mugs seemed far more appropriate. Private detectives always drank whiskey (or Bailey's) from cracked mugs on the TV.

"So." Maria settled onto the sofa, kicking off her gold heels and tucking her feet up underneath her. "Did you know your sofa smells of—"

"Yes," Sophie said. "So can you find him?"

Maria nodded and took a large mouthful of the Baileys, holding it over her tongue for a few seconds. "Let me get this straight. The guy leaves his pregnant wife in the lurch and runs off to God knows where to find himself and shag a load of tarts—am I right?" Sophie would have dropped her Baileys in surprise if she hadn't been treasuring it so very much.

"Well, yes," she said. "In principle."

Clearly, Cal had told Maria the details of the case in his own no-nonsense style.

Sophie quickly filled Maria in on the real situation.

Maria's face softened at the news, and she bit her glossed lips. "Oh, the poor little darlings," she said gently.

Sophie just managed not to roll her eyes and say, "Yes, yes, blah, blah, blah. And me, what about poor little me?"

"Yes, I know," she said briskly instead. "Terrible. And you see I can only have them temporarily, and after that they are going into care, so it is rather urgent—"

"Why?" Maria asked.

Sophie looked taken aback. "*Well,* because obviously the less time they spend in care the better," she said, feeling that that was rather obvious.

"No, I mean why can you only have them temporarily?" Maria asked her.

Sophie chose her words carefully. "I'm just not a person who can . . . who is very good with children. It's not fair to them."

Maria scrutinized her as she knocked back her mug of Baileys. "Trust me, you have to be a seriously shit person to be a worse option than some of the care homes I've seen. And besides, you looked like you were doing all right to me."

Sophie held Maria's gaze but said nothing, choosing to skim over the issue of what kind of person she might or might not be. Maria was just one more in a long line of people who seemed to want to know exactly what made her tick.

Sophie was tired of being scrutinized. Tired of people trying to work her out. She didn't want to know the answers to any of these questions, so why should they? At least in this case, she was the customer, and the customer was always right.

Maria shrugged. "All right. You better tell me all you can

about this Louis Gregory then, and I'd better track him down," she said.

"Are you sure you'll be able to?" Sophie asked her. "When the police and Social Services haven't had any luck."

"Amateurs, the lots of them," Maria said, lighting up a cigarette and, seeing the look of longing in Sophie's eyes, handing her one too. "I'll find him, and quick too," she said, blowing smoke out along with her words. "Don't you worry about that, darling. I have *ways*."

After Maria had gone, Sophie sat on the sofa and stared at the blank TV screen. It was amazing, she considered, how quickly humans adjusted to unusual situations. This was only the third night the girls had been sleeping in her bed and she had been lying awake on her sofa, yet this period of quiet reflection and despair had become almost routine.

At least she was doing something that would help the girls and help her, even if it was costing her fifty-five pounds an hour plus VAT and expenses. Once they had found Louis and brought him back to the United Kingdom, the girls would no longer be her responsibility. She would have done the right thing by Carrie and the right thing by them and the right thing all around, and she could go back to work in a nice new pair of shoes and everybody would be happy, especially Gillian. Except, of course, she'd be handing the girls over to a man they hardly knew, a man who had walked out on them without so much as a second thought.

"My God, I love him so much!" Carrie had said the night she rang Sophie to tell her that not only was she pregnant but she was getting married too. "He just looks at me with these incredible brown eyes, and—I'm not joking—he makes my knickers fizz!"

Sophie remembered that description exactly because fizzing

knickers was not something she had ever had firsthand experience of at that point in her life and probably—if she was entirely honest—never had had since.

"You're sure this is love, are you, and not just plain old lust?" Sophie had asked with typical caution. "I mean, are you sure you want to marry him? You hardly know him."

Carrie had laughed. "Oh, Soph, how would you know the difference anyway? You've only ever lusted after people you can't actually have. Besides, I know him, I know everything I need to know about him. He's bloody gorgeous and he makes me laugh. And—I'm having his baby, I'm six weeks gone. When I told him, I was really worried that he'd just walk out on me and that would be the end of us, but he really wants us to have it, Soph. It was a risk, but I somehow knew he would. He grew up without a proper family. He really wants to give that to his children. It's going to be wonderful. We are going to be wonderful. Trust me."

Sophie had trusted Carrie, because for all of her impulsiveness and recklessness, she had this incredible determination to be happy, and Sophie had never heard her sound happier than at that moment. "If you're sure, I'm happy for you, Carrie, I really am," Sophie said, and she'd meant it.

"He's a good man, Soph. Once you've got to know him, you're going to really love him, I promise."

Except, of course, Sophie had never got to know Louis; she'd barely even met him, because he'd left his wife and kids and run away.

"Why didn't you tell me, Carrie?" Sophie said quietly into the half-light. "I would have been there for you, you know. Always, forever, whatever." The three words sounded corny in the empty room, and Sophie felt the fragility of the friendship that had fallen apart without her even noticing, as if it were a spider's web disintegrating in her hands.

Sophie wondered where Carrie was now. Not whether or not she was in Heaven or Hell, or even reintegrating in the marine ecosystem somewhere off the Cornish coast. She wondered where Carrie was inside her, because still, three days later, she had not cried for Carrie. She had hardly had time to feel sad, but even when she did, like now, the sadness was negligible. It wasn't as if she had blocked it out with some grave and protective outer shell. It was more like if there was any sadness inside her at all, there were so many other layers between Sophie's rational thoughts and the core of her missing and loving Carrie that she could barely touch them.

Sophie closed her eyes for a moment and tried hard to feel the grief. She willed herself to cry, but no tears came. Perhaps all of her feelings were muffled by layer after layer of indifferent insulation, because she could not remember the last time she had really felt anything. Except that wasn't exactly true, Sophie admitted to herself. She could remember the last time. It was the day they'd cremated her dad.

Sophie shook her head to clear it. She didn't want to think about her dad now. She needed to stay focused. When all the practicalities were sorted out, that would be when she'd start to feel Carrie's death. She knew it would.

The edge of her bare foot touched something cold poking out from beneath the sofa. Using her toes to slide the object out, Sophie reached down and picked up a book. It was *Dr. Robert's Complete Dog Training and Care Manual.* Sophie looked at the picture of a soppy red setter grinning ludicrously on the front cover and smiled. Only her mum would give her a dog manual to read for helpful child-rearing hints and tips. With nothing better to do, she flicked through the pages until she stopped at the chapter entitled "Puppy Psychology"; a subtitle that read "Puppies and Car Travel" caught her eye.

Sophie shrugged. It was late, and she wasn't going to sleep anytime soon. Maybe a page of two or puppy psychology would help unwind the tightly wound coil of her mind; half a mug of Baileys hadn't worked. It was worth a go.

She was on paragraph two, wondering if you could buy worming tablets for children, when Artemis appeared from the kitchen window and strolled over. The cat took one look at the cover of the book and, Sophie could have sworn, wrinkled her pink nose in disgust before stalking out again in the general direction of the bedroom. Sophie smiled to herself; amazingly, Artemis had seemed to adjust to the girls being in there far more quickly than Sophie had. She had even caught Artemis sitting only three feet away from Bella that morning as Bella studiously attempted to draw her ear, sitting perfectly still as if she were trying to be extra helpful. Perhaps it was because all three females— Artemis, Izzy, and Bella—had something in common. They were all at least half feral.

"Cats and dogs and kids," Sophie muttered to herself as she settled back onto the sofa with the book. "Basically the same principle."

She turned to the chapter on antisocial behavior.

Seven

On Friday morning, Sophie was still hoping that Maria really was going to find Louis as quickly as she'd said she could and didn't yet know that she would be deciding to keep the children much longer than the two weeks she had originally agreed to.

The morning began with Lisa sobbing on the other end of the phone, saying, "I'm sorry, I'm sorry, Sophie. But you've got to come in. I can't stop her. You won't believe what she called me—" Sophie would believe it. She believed Eve capable of doing pretty much anything, but she had to admit she hadn't expected her to stop circling and go in for the kill quite so soon.

"Where's Cal? Pass me to Cal," Sophie told Lisa, who put her through with a snuffle.

"What's the deal, Cal?" Sophie asked him.

"Eve is in your office right now," he said. "She got your leads file and your Rolodex. Somehow she's got your PC password—" Sophie opened her mouth to holler, but hearing her sharp intake of breath, Cal cut her off before she could utter a word. "Don't shout at me, I don't know how she got it—because it definitely wouldn't have been anything obvious like—oh, I don't know— your *name*, would it?"

Sophie, who did suffer from a lack of imagination when it came to passwords, in fact pretty much anything, clamped her mouth shut.

"Anyway," Cal continued quickly. "She says that Gillian has asked her to help you out by keeping on top of things while you are away, being all noble and saintly. I tried to stop her, but she said if I had a problem, speak to Gillian. Well, what could I do? If Gillian says it's okay for her to be in there, then—it's okay, right?"

"No, she's using that as an excuse to raid my clients list and take credit for all of my ideas," Sophie said matter-of-factly. She wouldn't have done the same thing in Eve's position, but she would have wished she had the balls and total lack of conscience to do it.

"Probably," Cal said. "Lisa did try to stop her going in, but she called Lisa a . . . let me see, oh yes, a 'fat blubbering point- less rusty old bike,' and Lisa started to cry, and well, you can guess the rest." Cal paused. "I think you'd better come down," he said.

"I'm on my way," Sophie said, and she hung up the phone. She looked at the girls, who had taken up their newly habitual position on the sofa in their pajamas watching a soap opera with expressions of fascinated horror.

"Right, spit spot, come on, girls—double-quick we're going out." The girls' heads jerked in her direction as if they were pup- pies who'd been told it was walk time.

"Out! Out! Out!" Izzy hopped off the sofa with joy. "Oooh, good. Am I going to wear my fairy dress?"

Sophie shook her head; the fairy dress had gone in the garbage bin and was probably even now being buried in a concrete container in the middle of the North Sea.

"I know," Sophie said, remembering something that the dog book had said about using distraction. "Let's have a race. We'll go and look in your suitcase, and whoever gets dressed the quickest wins a fabulous prize!" Both girls leaped up in anticipation, as if Sophie was about the throw a stick for them to fetch. "Ready, steady, *go!*" she shouted.

And that was how, twenty-seven minutes later, the three girls emerged from the flat blinking in the daylight, one dressed in jeans and a slightly grubby pink Calvin Klein T-shirt and fleece jacket (Sophie), one dressed as a ballerina-pirate fusion complete with eye patch and musical wand and topped off with a sweater and a poncho (Izzy), and one wearing a rainbow-striped hand-knitted sweater that was at least ten sizes too big for her and fell off one shoulder to reveal the graying lace of an aged T-shirt and came down to just below her knees, where her Angelina Ballerina Wellington boots began. All topped off by a lurid pink down jacket.

"Are those wellies comfortable to walk in?" Sophie asked Bella, wondering what her chances were of a bus coming anytime in the next four hours.

Bella furrowed a brow at her. "I wasn't thinking about comfort, Aunty Sophie. I was thinking about speed. I wanted to win the prize!"

Sophie admired her competitive spirit and felt a pang of guilt since technically there was no prize, but as they were all out of the house now, she supposed she could take the girls to the Broadgate branch of H+M right after she had been to the office and confronted the Lady Macbeth of party planning. "And I did win."

"You didn't win, I won!" Izzy shouted as they boarded the 149 bus.

"I won," Bella shouted back.

"I won!" Izzy insisted.

"I won!" Bella repeated.

"I won!" Sophie shouted them both down so that they, the bus driver, and the six or so passengers already on the bottom deck of the bus stopped talking and looked at her. Sophie dropped some pound coins into the driver's change tray and ripped the tickets off the machine. "I won," she repeated as the bus lurched out of the stop and more or less threw all three of them into an empty seat. "I was dressed before either of you, so actually I'm the winner." Sophie squeezed both the girls next to the window and jammed herself onto the end of the seat.

"But you can't be the winner," Bella protested. "You're the grown-up, and anyway you already had your clothes on when you set the competition, so that doesn't count."

" 'S not fair!" Izzy joined in. "Not fair, not fair!"

Sophie looked at both girls and bit her lip. She wanted to say to them that life isn't fair and that it was about time they realized that, but it sounded exactly like the sort of thing Mrs. Stiles used to say to Carrie on a regular basis, and she knew Carrie would hate it being said to her children, even if, quite honestly, right now Sophie thought that Mrs. Stiles was right. But, she wasn't heartless, just rather tired, so she said, "Okay, we'll call it a three-way tie. We all win, okay? After I've sorted out work, we'll all go and get a prize, okay?"

Izzy and Bella exchanged suspicious looks.

" 'Spose," Izzy said.

"I won," Bella said but very quietly and mostly to herself, folding her arms across her chest, her shoulders slumping.

"Er, I think you'll find I won," Sophie said before she caught a woman looking scathingly at her and realized exactly what she was doing. Then she shut up.

Sophie stopped the girls in front of the office building in which McCarthy Hughes occupied the seventh and eighth floors. The children looked upward openmouthed.

"A giant's house," Izzy breathed, awestruck.

"It's a skyscraper, thicko," Bella said. "Giants' houses are much bigger." Sophie thought about the chapter on puppy psychology she'd read last night. Body language, it was all in the body language. You believe that you are in control and in charge, and *they* believe that you are control and in charge—or something like that. Show no fear, that was what the manual said, because they can feel it through the leash. So perhaps it was fortunate after all that it was probably illegal to make children wear leashes. She crouched down on the steps of the building and, putting a hand on each of the girls' shoulders, looked them directly in the eye. "Now listen," she said. "This is where I work. This is my job. It is very *very* important that while you are in this building you do exactly what I tell you. You don't scream or run away or cause a flood or"—Sophie narrowed her eyes at Izzy—"attempt to fix anything just like Bob the Dentist—"

"Bob the Builder!" Izzy said, with a giggle.

"Whatever. Do you understand?" Sophie looked back at Bella, whose attention had drifted skyward once again, and pressed her palm gently down on the top of her head until she was looking in her eyes. "You don't run about, you don't touch anything, you don't talk to anyone, because this is Aunty Sophie's job and it is a very, *very* important job."

Bella screwed up her mouth into a sideways knot. It was an expression that Sophie was beginning to learn usually preceded an impudent and often hard to answer question. She braced herself.

"What do you do for a job, Aunty Sophie?" Bella asked. "Are you a doctor, or a vet or a . . ." The girl searched for an occupation that could be appropriately described as very important. "Are you an astronaut?" she asked. Sophie sighed. There were a lot of people in the world who thought her job wasn't very important, comparatively speaking, and couldn't see why she allowed it to occupy 90 percent of her life that wasn't taken up by sleep, but she hadn't expected a six-year-old to jump on the bandwagon.

"I plan parties," she said quickly, and added under her breath as she stood, "Really, really important ones."

On the way up the lift, Sophie had been planning several types of camouflage to get the children into the office unnoticed. Perhaps she could hide them under her coat, or maybe stick photocopy paper boxes on their heads and edge them along in the shadows. She stopped herself. She didn't have to sneak the girls into the office. Children, unlike smoking, weren't completely banned. Gillian's nanny brought her two in every now and then, during school holidays, for example, and everyone would smile at them and ask them how school was. But Izzy and Bella weren't like Gillian's children. Compared with Gillian's neatly combed and surprisingly sedate offspring, they were like half-wild savages who had previously been raised by wolves.

Miraculously, though, the open-plan part of the office was completely empty, and Sophie guessed that everybody was in Gillian's huge office going over the week's events, with Gillian sitting at the head of the table. Despite her conviction that she wasn't doing anything wrong, Sophie hurried the girls toward her office, and once she had more or less thrown them safely through the door, she slammed it behind her and adjusted the venetian blinds on the interior windows so that no one could see in or out.

"Are you being chased by the feds?" Cal asked, twirling in her chair, looking her up and down. "You look terrible, by the way."

Sophie looked around the office. "Where's Lisa?" she said.

"In the meeting," Cal said. "She said she couldn't go in, because everyone would know that she had been crying, and I said, Well, yes, they would, Lisa, but everyone was used to that by now and she had to go in anyway even if she didn't want to, as it is her job, and you can't just back down from every challenge life throws at you, otherwise you'll never get anywhere. Look at Liza Minnelli." Cal smiled at the girls and winked. Both girls giggled. "And off she went like a trouper. I lent her your emergency mascara, which she put on over her old mascara, so ironically she actually she does look quite a lot like Liza Minnelli now."

Sophie had to admit that Cal's built-in inability ever to answer even a simple question without turning his response into a lengthy monologue did slightly affect her level of affection for him, especially when time was of the essence.

"So what's the damage?" asked, walking around her desk and opening the drawers until she found her spare notebooks. She also took out two pens and a set of highlighter pens, and gave them to Bella. "Sit here in the corner on the floor and do me some lovely pictures, okay?"

Bella took the pens and sat reluctantly on the carpet. "What of?" she asked as Izzy plonked herself next to her.

"Anything," Sophie said impatiently. "Draw the view." Bella looked around her, assessing the view of desk legs, the bottom halves of two filing cabinets, and a wastepaper bin, a deep frown slotted between her brows.

"*I'm* drawing mermaids," she said to Izzy, who shook her head.

"I'm drawing Arsey-miss," Izzy said, and it took a moment for Sophie to realize she meant her cat and was not planning a self-portrait. She returned her attention to Cal, who reluctantly vacated her chair.

"Well?" she asked.

"Same as before—Eve has your Rolodex, your leads book, and your diary," he repeated in a singsong voice, his eyes skyward. "She said Gillian told her to take them. Lisa could hardly contradict her, could she? And she couldn't go marching into Gillian's office asking her what she thought she was playing at, so after the briefest of struggles, we let her take them. What else could we do?" He gave a little shrug and examined his nails.

"Right," Sophie said. She walked back to the internal office window and, prizing open a space between two blind slats, peered through it. Her colleagues were gradually filing back to their desks. She spotted Eve standing by Gillian's office door talking and laughing with their boss as if they were best friends. "The meeting's out. Lisa will be here in a minute. I want you and her to keep an eye on those two. Don't let them out of your sight, okay?" she ordered.

Cal did not have time to answer before Lisa opened the door. "Thank fuck that's over," she said with feeling.

"You're not supposed to say *fuck* in front of us." Bella's voice floated up from the other side of the desk a moment or two before her bangs and then eyes peered disapprovingly over the edge.

"Fuck," Lisa said, jumping and then looking at Sophie. "Oh, f-flip. Sorry, Sophie."

Sophie briefly assessed what Lisa was wearing—a pink button-down shirt—not Sophie's usual style, but it would have to do.

"Never mind that now. Take your top off."

Lisa looked alarmed. "I beg your pardon?" she said.

"I said, 'Take your top off,'" Sophie said impatiently. "I'm not going in to see Eve and Gillian looking like this, am I? You lend me your shirt until I've sorted this out." Sophie seemed confused by Lisa's reluctance, and she peeled her T-shirt off over her head. "You can wear this, all right? Now hurry up." Lisa took the less than fragrant T-shirt gingerly from Sophie's hand and draped it over the back of a chair before unbuttoning her shirt and handing it to Sophie.

"Is now a good time to tell you I lied about being gay?" Cal said. Sophie ignored him, but Lisa's cheeks burned brightly as she pulled the stained T-shirt over her head. Perhaps she had a secret crush on Cal too. Otherwise he'd be the only man on the planet on whom she had not focused her attention at one time or another.

Buttoning Lisa's slightly too tight shirt up, Sophie untied her hair, combed her fingers through it, and twisted it into a tightly knotted bun at the back of her head before securing it with a pen. Cal handed her her emergency mascara, which she applied somewhat haphazardly in the ghostly reflection of the office window. She took out of her jeans pocket the remnants of one of her lip glosses that she had just about managed to salvage from Izzy and rubbed a little onto her lips.

"Right," she said, pulling the shirt down over the top of her jeans. "How do I look?"

"You look like a slightly pudgy Amazon preparing for battle," Cal said, giving her the thumbs-up.

Sophie gritted her teeth and headed for the door. "Right," she said. "I'm going to sort this whole mess out. All you two have to do is keep the kids under control and out of Gillian's sight. Do you think you can you do that?" she asked them.

"Of course we can," said Lisa, smiling down at the busily drawing girls. "Easy-peasy."

Somehow, Sophie did not feel reassured.

As Sophie opened Eve's office door, she was confronted with her colleague's frankly bony arse. Eve was in the midst of committing two cardinal sins. Not only had she opened her office window, thus threatening to send the carefully controlled climate into total disarray, but she was hanging out of it smoking. Sophie watched Eve for a moment kneeling on the seat of her chair, her elbow resting on its back, trying her best to send the smoke out of the window but failing as a passing gust of window blew every puff back in her face. Of course, Sophie could just have pushed her out the window and claimed it was an accident, solving all of her problems in one fell swoop. But it had been almost twenty-four hours since her last cigarette, and Eve was holding her packet in one hand. At that moment, Sophie could have happily murdered Eve, but she just couldn't bear to let the cigarettes suffer too. She contented herself with slamming the door behind her and watching Eve jump before pulling herself in through the window, flicking her cigarette onto the street below as she slid back into her chair, her face a picture of innocence.

"Sophie!" she said, reaching behind her to pull the window shut. "What a nice surprise."

"You're not supposed to do that," Sophie said, nodding at the door and sounding a lot more like a school prefect than she wanted to.

"You're not supposed to do *that*," Eve said breezily, looking Sophie up and down. "Never wear a shirt that gapes in the bra area, Sophie. I thought you knew better."

Sophie knew Eve's tactic better than anyone, but she was not going to be thrown. She sat down with a thud, and one of the buttons pinged off Lisa's shirt. Sophie did her best to ignore it. "What are you playing at, Eve?" she asked bluntly.

Eve shrugged. "How do your mean?" she said, casually.

"What are you doing in my office, taking my Rolodex, my leads book, and my client account info?"

Eve rolled her eyes. "Oh, that. You've raced all the way down here over that, have you?" she said, picking up a pen from her desk and swinging it by its tip. "Gillian asked me to keep on top of your stuff. So I did. What's the problem?" Eve looked genuinely mystified.

Sophie bristled, her inner fury stoked even more by the fact that she wasn't exactly sure what the problem was herself. Cal had rung her, Lisa had cried, and before she knew it she was charging down here like fury. Perhaps there *had* been a slight overreaction.

"Lisa is handling everything," Sophie said, carefully moderating her accusatory tone. "I'll be back in the office soon enough. Just give me back my stuff, okay? You don't need it."

Eve sighed and dropped her chin. "Look, Sophie, really I'm quite disappointed in you. I thought we were supposed to be on the same team. I don't know what you think I was up to, but—"

At that moment Eve's assistant walked in with a pile of photocopying and Sophie's Rolodex. "I've photocopied this, like you said. I'm just about to do the book now, okay?" she said, catching sight of Sophie. "Oh, hi, Sophie. I didn't know you were back in today. Enjoyed your holiday?" Eve gave the poor girl a look sufficiently evil enough to send her scuttling out of the room without waiting for a reply. She was probably off to pick up her severance papers at that very moment.

"I knew it!" Sophie exclaimed, scooping the pile of photocopying off Eve's desk and plonking her Rolodex on top of it. "You're poaching my contacts, my accounts, and my prospective clients." She stared at Eve, who still appeared unfazed, even when caught in the act. "Come on, Eve, don't jerk me around. I know you too well to buy this butter-wouldn't-melt act. Gillian *might* have asked you to check up on Lisa, but she certainly didn't ask you to go through my drawers and do this!" Sophie brandished the pile of photocopying as Exhibit A.

"Okay, Miss Marple," Eve said, holding her palms out. "I was. It's a fair accusation." Eve smirked like a schoolgirl who'd just got caught snogging behind the bike shed.

Sophie was taken aback. She hadn't expected such an easy confession. "Well . . . right," Sophie said. She found the wind suddenly taken out of her sails. "Just don't do it again, okay?" As she turned to the door, she realized that this was exactly what Eve wanted her to do. To leave without making a fuss. She sat down again, and still clutching the papers to her chest, she pulled the chair closer. Eve's face was perfectly devoid of expression.

"It's pretty shit behavior, isn't it? To try to get one over on me when I'm not here to do anything about it?"

Eve raised her eyebrows and twiddled her pen. "The best time to do it, I'd've thought," she said glibly, suddenly switching on her death's-head smile. "Come on, Sophie—you'd have done the same thing."

"Actually," Sophie said with conviction, "I wouldn't have. Let's cut the crap here, okay? We both know that if . . . when Gillian steps back from the office, we want her job. We both know that only one of us is going to get it. We both know that the other one would rather slit her wrists and wear flip-flops than endure the ignominy of staying here and reporting to the other one. I understand that, I accept it. I don't have a problem with competition, as long as it's a fair competition. And shafting me while I'm looking after my dead friend's kids— It's not fair, Eve. It's evil. Seriously evil." Sophie paused for effect. "Gillian would be horrified," she said with the hint of a threat.

"Oh, yes, the dead friend's kids," Eve said bitterly. "How very convenient."

Sophie opened her mouth and then closed it again. Where was the usual poor little mites, oh, how terrible routine that she had become used to? "I beg you pardon?" she said.

"Well, it's all very well going on about it being a fair competition and all that bullshit. But it's *not* fair, is it? It hasn't been fair since you waltzed off to do your Mother Teresa bit. Gillian *loves* you right now! She goes on nonstop about how selfless you are and how rare it is to have the kind of guts it takes to rise to this kind of challenge and how you must have been such a good friend for wosshername, thingy to trust you with her most precious legacy, blah fucking blah. How is that fair? Have I got a dead friend with fatherless kids? No. Therefore, it's not fair." Eve lifted her chin slightly. "I was just leveling the playing field," she finished.

"I didn't ask for this!" Sophie exclaimed, gesturing at the door as if all of her problems were piled up high behind it. "Do you think I'm happy that my best friend is dead?"

"Don't seem too depressed by it, frankly," Eve said.

"Trust me, I'm depressed!" Sophie yelled at her. "I'm sorry if Gillian thinks what I'm doing is the right thing, but do you honestly believe at the end of day that Gillian is going to give me a job over you because of a bit of babysitting?" Oh, God, I hope so, Sophie thought to herself. "She's a tough businesswoman, Eve. She'll give it to the person who's best at her job, and being out of the office is dragging me down enough without you sabotaging me, okay?"

Eve leaned across the desk so that the two women were just a few inches apart. "Okay!" she said. "But just ask yourself one question, Sophie. Ask yourself why do you really want this promotion?"

Sophie shook her head. "Why does everybody keep asking me why?" she protested. "Why this! Why that! No one ever asks *you* why."

"Because we all know that you've been at McCarthy Hughes since puberty, that you've worked you way up the ladder, paid your dues in blood, sweat, and tears et cetera. But seriously, why are you here, why do you *really* want this job, why does it mean so very much to you? Are you absolutely sure that you're not sitting here in my office as a senior accounts manager at McCarthy Hughes by mistake? What if the job center had sent you to a fashion magazine or, or a pet shop?"

Sophie sat back in her chair abruptly. It was a surprisingly tricky question to answer off the top of her head.

Seeing her expression, Eve laughed. "You didn't choose this career, Sophie," she said. "It chose you, and never once in the last ten years have you stopped to think about whether or not it makes you truly happy. You have no idea why you want this promotion other than it's there. It's your Everest."

"That's not true," Sophie said promptly. "Obviously I want it because this is my career," she said. "Because this is what I've been working for for the best part of my life."

"Face it, Sophie—you're so stuck in a rut you can't see past it. But ask yourself, What are you going to do when you've got Gillian's job? Where are you going to go then? What will you have left to work toward, huh? What happened to your childhood dreams?"

Sophie rolled her eyes and thought of Jason Donovan. "He got bald and developed a twitch—that's what happened to my dreams," she said. "Come on, Eve, get real, will you? This is me you're talking to. I don't fall for all your bullshit mind games."

"Oh, Sophie, Sophie, Sophie—" Eve lamented. "You should follow your dreams before it's too late, not joke about them to cover up your true despair," she said, sincerity etched all over her face.

Sophie was unimpressed. "My reasons are good ones," she said. "I put a lot of years into this business, and I want the rewards that I deserve. The same reasons as you, I'm sure."

Eve stood up, and coming around the desk, she sat on its edge, crossing her legs so that one of her shoes dangled balanced on her toes, revealing a fleeting glimpse of a Dolce & Gabbana label.

Sophie seethed. She still had on her now rather the worse for wear River Island flats.

"Not at all," Eve said. "I want this promotion because this is all I've ever dreamed about since I was a tiny girl," She said, completely seriously.

"Bollocks," Sophie replied, and not only because she genuinely doubted that Eve was ever a tiny girl; it seemed more likely she was hatched fully grown from some giant genetically modified egg.

"Well, maybe, but I'm here now, and it's every man for herself, if you know what I mean." Without explanation, Eve took a plastic bag out of her desk drawer, and standing on her chair, she reached up and secured it over the smoke alarm with a rubber band. Sitting back down, she chucked Sophie a much longed for cigarette, which Sophie had to force herself not to scrabble for. After lighting up, Eve paused for a tortuous moment before throwing Sophie her lighter too.

Sophie took her first drag happily, and in that moment of deep satisfaction, she considered Eve, who had tipped her head back and was blowing smoke rings ceilingward.

After a few more puffs, Eve looked Sophie in the eye and sighed. "I'm sorry, really," she said. "Okay?"

Sophie watched Eve through the haze of smoke. "I doubt it," she said mildly. "But just don't think I'm a pushover, okay?"

Eve considered. "Okay," she said, sounding unconvinced. "You know it's nothing personal, don't you? I just get carried away a bit with the whole competition thing. I suppose I'd be quite annoyed if I had to sack you one day. Because, you know, you make me look really good."

Sophie examined her. It was very hard to tell when Eve was joking, largely because with Eve there was a very blurred line between humor and general savagery. "Well, you're on your own for the foreseeable future at least," Sophie said, instantly regretting letting that piece of information slip. "God only knows when I'll spend any decent time in the office again."

"I thought they were going back next week," Eve said with interest. "If I knew you were going to be out longer, I'd have waited for a decent period before raiding your office."

Sophie pursed her lips. Before she could say anything else, Eve's phone rang. She looked at the caller ID unit.

"Gillian," she told Sophie, picking it up while simultaneously opening the window behind her.

"Hi, Gillian, what can I do for you?" she said, hooking the receiver under her ear and attempting to wave the smoke out of the window as she spoke, as if Gillian would be able to smell her cigarette down the phone line. "Yep, yep, okay, I'll tell her. Yep, right now."

Eve hung up the phone. "Oh dear," she said with a tiny, sharp-toothed smile.

"Oh dear what?" Sophie said, handing the butt of her cigarette to Eve, who threw it out the window.

"The little cherubs. It looks like they got out and went exploring."

Sophie leaped out of her seat. "Fuck, fuck! What did they do—what did they wreck?" She braced herself.

"Nothing, they just went for a little wander and made a new

friend—" Eve savored the moment. "They're in Gillian's office right now. She'd like you to go over. Straightaway please."

But Sophie had already left.

"And then after *Neighbours* again, we watched the news, and then we watched *Bargain Hunt* again, and then we watch *Eastenders,* and then we watch—"

"Bella! Izzy!" Sophie forced a laugh. "I thought you were drawing me a lovely picture!"

"We finished," Bella said, holding up a sheet of paper covered in mermaids. "We came to show you, but we couldn't find you. So we showed this lady, who is very nice and gave us a biscuit. We told her we don't eat fruit in case it makes us poo."

Gillian smiled at Sophie, and Sophie smiled back at her, trying desperately to work out if it was a genuine happy smile or an I'm-about-to-rip-your-head-off smile. It was quite hard to tell with Gillian until right at the last moment.

"Sit," Gillian said. Sophie sat. "What lovely girls your godchildren are! Izzy was telling me all about the fun she's been having at your house, including being flushed down the toilet?" Gillian raised an eyebrow.

"Ah, yes, well . . ." Sophie hastily began to explain, but Gillian laughed. Sophie laughed too, slightly hysterically. So did Izzy. Bella stared at all three of them, her mouth as straight as a poker.

"Oh, they are so funny at that age, aren't they—a pure joy from the moment they wake up to the moment they go to bed." Sophie nodded in agreement. She supposed, if you had a nanny and didn't see them for eight hours of the day that they were being "pure joy," that might be true.

"Oh yes," she said. "Joy. Absolutely. Pure."

"You should have said you were bringing them in. If you'd have rung me, I'd have told you not to bother. There's no need for you to come in. Lisa's been doing very well with Cal's help, and Eve's been keeping an eye on her."

"Ah yes, but—"

"So, how have you been coping?" Gillian asked, fixing her with her almost unbearably penetrating gaze.

Sophie struggled to maintain eye contact, a little uncertain of how to respond because Gillian had never asked that question before. Sophie always coped. No, that was wrong. Sophie had never "coped" before because she hadn't had to—she had never struggled with any challenge until now, and "coping" had never been a requirement. Was she supposed to tell Gillian that everything was just fine, or was she supposed to confess that she was finding everything a bit difficult? Which response would make her look better, and which answer would make her more promotable?

"Um," Sophie said.

"Oh, I know," Gillian said, treating her to a conspiratorial little smile that Sophie had never seen before and found slightly unnerving. "It's such a shock, isn't it?" she confided. "Children just change your world completely. And I planned for my two darlings—but I wasn't prepared for them in the least!" Gillian leaned forward a little in her chair. "And you know, I think it's harder when you have them a little later in life, don't you? When you've been used to being your own person for so long and suddenly there's this little being that's . . . that's . . ." Gillian clicked her fingers as she searched for the word she wanted.

"Like a bloodsucking little leech?" Sophie offered.

Gillian's smile faded momentarily before she decided that Sophie must be joking and her rarely heard laugh chimed like broken glass. Sophie laughed too, even though she had missed the punch line.

"I was going to say, this little being is totally *dependent* on you for life," Gillian finished. "But you're really showing guts here, Sophie. I applaud you."

Sophie felt herself straighten in her chair. "Thank you," she said, glancing at Izzy, who was sorting through the contents of Gillian's waste bin, and at Bella, who was listening intently. "They are good kids, bless 'em," Sophie said. Bella probably raised an eyebrow at her, but Sophie couldn't be sure because of the thickness of her bangs. "It's just a case of getting everything settled." Sophie smiled at Gillian, who nodded sympathetically.

"It must be even harder for you, of course, because you didn't plan it. For you it's like they've just fallen out of the sky." Sophie realized that actually that was exactly how it felt, and suddenly, looking into Gillian's kind face, she felt the threat of tears build up behind her eyes. But she couldn't cry, because Gillian would think she was crying for Carrie or the children, and she wouldn't be. She would be crying guilty tears of self-pity.

"Yes," Sophie said, making her voice stay steady. "It does feel a bit like that."

Gillian laced her fingers on the desk and gazed at them for a moment. "Look, Sophie, I think you and I know each other very well by now, don't you?" Sophie nodded. "I know that you're not the sort of person to ask for help. In fact, I know that you're not the sort of person who usually needs any help. But I want to know how you think this will all pan out. Do you think you can keep up your job to sufficient standards in the midst of this upheaval?"

Sophie began nodding even before Gillian had finished asking the question. "I can, of course I can," she said, gesturing at the children. "This is just temporary. Really. Work comes first for me, Gillian. You know how many years I've put into McCarthy Hughes. I've always been loyal. I won't stop now." Sophie found she was leaning forward in her urge to impress her intentions on her boss.

Gillian observed her for a moment longer. "The minute you think you're not handling this. The minute it all gets too much, I need to know, do you understand?" she said.

"Yes," Sophie said, feeling the kind of anxiety in the pit of her stomach she hadn't experienced since the first three times she failed her driving test.

"You know I really feel for you, don't you?" Gillian said, a hard edge glinting under her compassionate tone. "But this is a very important time for McCarthy Hughes. Up until this point, you've been integral to our success. Don't think I haven't noticed that, Sophie, or that I haven't got plans for you." Sophie felt simultaneously pleased and deeply uneasy, a combination that made her nauseated. "But business isn't what it once was for event companies. Budgets are tight; we have to be more competitive and more on the ball than we have ever been before." Sophie got the distinct impression that when Gillian said *we,* she actually meant *you.*

"I suppose what I'm trying to say, Sophie, is that I want to support you in this, I am full of admiration for you. But if you start to feel that you can't manage to look after the children and keep up with work, I'll need to know. I'll need to make other arrangements."

"That won't happen," Sophie said instantly, worrying darkly about what "other arrangements" might be.

"Good," Gillian said. "Look, Sophie, you've heard all the rumors about me stepping down from the office and passing the baton on, haven't you?"

Sophie nodded dumbly. There was no point in denying it. Gillian would only know she was lying.

"Well, I'm telling you and nobody else that that is only going to happen if I feel the people I can trust to take on that responsibility are able to put one hundred percent into this job. Do you understand what I mean?"

Sophie nodded again, wondering if she really did understand.

"Good," Gillian said. And then she began to look through the papers on her desk, a sure sign that your presence was no longer required. For a second, Sophie was too stunned to move. This morning she'd had a life in total chaos, yes, but it had been a temporary chaos, underpinned by the one constant in her life—her job. And now it seemed that Gillian was telling her ever so nicely that if she took her eye off the ball, she could lose what she prized most highly. Sophie looked at the two girls and forcibly pushed back down the ugly resentment she felt rising from the pit of her stomach.

Gillian looked up and flashed her best smile. "Well, off you go then, and take these two to the zoo or something. I'll see you next time you're in for a progress report."

As she stood up and gestured for the girls to leave the room, Sophie looked at the top of Gillian's neatly bobbed head, which was already bent over some paperwork. She knew Gillian; when she had made up her mind something should happen, it happened. But Gillian had scared her. For the first time since getting the children, Sophie realized that there was chance, if she didn't handle this very carefully, that she would never get her old life back. There was, Sophie realized, only one way she could make this work. She had to accept that she was stuck with the children for as long as it took to get hold of their dad—she'd just have to make sure she covered all the bases. Anything she let slip now would take all the work and ambition of the last few years with it. It would be hard and stressful, but she had to remind herself, it wouldn't be forever, just until Maria Costello found Louis.

Praying that Maria Costello was as good as she said she was,

Sophie took the girls back to her office to brief Lisa and Cal. But they were still nowhere to be seen.

"Where did Lisa and Cal go?" Sophie asked Bella.

"Oh, to the ladies', Lisa was crying," Bella said.

Sophie rolled her eyes. "Again?" she asked herself more than Bella. "What was it this time, a broken nail or did some passing stranger chuck her too?"

Bella looked perplexed and shook her head. "No, I think she was pretty upset about Izzy pouring glue in her hair," she said.

Izzy nodded vigorously. "Yes, because it went all sticky and white," she said with a gurgle.

"And because Cal said she should be used to having sticky white stuff in her hair. Why's that, Aunty Sophie?"

"Never you mind," Sophie said. She opened her desk drawer and took out her emergency safety pin, feeling secretly delighted that she finally had a suitable emergency to use it on. She looked at the upturned faces of the girls staring at her with the velvet brown eyes of their absent father as she secured the hole that gaped across her cleavage. "Well, that would certainly set her off. Still, on the bright side, I don't have to tell her about popping a button off her shirt. Come on, let's go. I'll call them later and do a conference call."

"Are we going to the zoo, zoo, zoo, you can come too, too, too, like the nice lady said?" asked Izzy, hopping from one foot to the other.

"No," Sophie said as she led them to the lift. "We're going somewhere even better."

"Where? Where?" Izzy cried.

"Back to the flat," Sophie said.

As Izzy's face crumpled dangerously, Bella's eyes clouded. "But what about our prize?" she demanded. "You said we were getting a prize!"

Sophie paused for a moment. She had forgotten about the prize, and she had rather hoped they had forgotten too, but as the detonator in Izzy's head was only seconds from going off, Sophie rapidly changed her plans. "Of course!" She said with a huge smile. "Let's go to the prize shop!"

"Hooray!" Izzy said, the tantrum abating instantly. "Let's go. Let's go! Let's go!"

Eight

Half an hour later, as Sophie watched Bella trying to decide between faux sheepskin boots and pink suede shoes with hearts on the front, she made a mental note that bribery seemed to date the most effective way of controlling the girls, especially Izzy. She had read about it in the dog book. They recommended liver treats, but Sophie thought clothes and toys were probably more appealing to small girls. The moment she had told Izzy only nice, quiet, happy girls got fairy dresses, the child had transformed into a more sugary version of Shirley Temple and had at least three members of the store's staff in the palm of her sticky hand.

"Oh, what a darling," one of them told Sophie. "Her daddy must be awfully good-looking."

"Wouldn't know," Sophie said absently, which garnered several raised eyebrows.

As for Bella, she had one of each shoe on and was turning in front of the mirror, lifting one foot and then the other, narrow-

ing her eyes as she looked at her reflection and then closing them
tightly before opening them again, as if to get the full shoe effect.

Sophie rested her chin on the heels of her hands and waited.
If she knew anything, it was that you couldn't rush buying a pair
of shoes. She smiled fondly at the expensive thick paper bag with
corded handles that resided by her feet. From the moment she
had seen the new season's pair of Luc Berjen tweed shoes in the
shop window to the moment she had handed over her credit card,
her heart had beat like a drum; now she felt elated and content.
In her admittedly limited experience, shoe shopping was so much
more satisfying than sex, with the afterglow lasting much longer
and leaving behind much less mess. Which was why she jumped
off her stool when her cell phone's polyphonic version of "Love
Lift Us Up Where We Belong" boomed out.

The girls stopped as if they were playing a reverse version of
musical statues and stared at her for a moment before continuing
their activities.

"Good news," Maria Costello said in her ear. "I've found
him."

"You've found him?" Sophie said in disbelief. Bella looked up
at her sharply and, sitting down with a bump, shushed a dizzily
giggling Izzy, who had collapsed on the floor next to her. "You
found a replacement ice sculptor so soon, *Lisa*? Well done,"
Sophie said carefully.

"More or less," Maria said. "At least I think I've found the
country he's in. I'm almost sure. I think he's in Peru. From what
I can tell, he's been there for about two years. That's if he hasn't
moved on since the last time my contact saw him . . ."

"Who's your contact." Sophie asked.

There was a sharp intake of breath. "I never reveal my contacts, love."

Sophie rolled her eyes; she was starting to think that Maria took the whole spy thing ever so slightly too seriously. She was secretly certain that, whoever Maria's contact was, it was nothing more mysterious than one of Louis's conquests, who would no doubt be littered around the world while he lived his life of Riley.

"And so?" Sophie pressed. "Got an ETA? One day? Two?"

"I said I *think* he's in Peru," Maria replied sarcastically. "It's a pretty big place, Peru. I'll try to locate him from my nerve center, but if not, I might have to go out there. You'll have to foot the bill, mind you, and I always go business class on flights over four hours."

Sophie's heart sank. "Maria, Lisa, I mean. Be honest with me, are you going to find . . . my ice sculptor, or am I throwing my money away for nothing?"

"Did you know he was in Peru before I started looking?" Maria asked irritably. "Did anyone?"

"No," Sophie said hesitantly. "But are you *sure* he is?"

"Look, love, I'm a private detective, all right? I'll find him. And I'll call you when I know more."

"There's just one thing," Sophie said. "Do you know what he's doing in Peru?"

But Maria had hung up.

It was then Sophie saw Bella watching her intently. "You have to go a long way to get ice sculptors these days," she told the six-year-old.

What had begun as a quick trip to buy prizes had gone very well and had resulted in both of the girls fully appreciating Sophie: Izzy because she loved her new fairy dress and because Sophie didn't make her take it off when they left the shop but instead made the assistant cut off all the labels and remove the security tag with the child still in it. And Bella because after she had regretfully put back the pink shoes in favor of the more sensible boots, Sophie had gone and bought her the shoes too. Sophie had felt good about herself then, almost as if she would get through the next few weeks with her life intact after all.

This, Sophie had decided, was what being a godmother was all about—although it probably also had something to do with religion. But still—buying presents and being popular was definitely where it was at. Her smugness lost a little of its shine when she realized that she had never made the effort to do even this bit for more or less all of the girls' lives until now. In fact, all she had ever done as their godmother up to this point was to turn up to the christening and send her PA out to buy presents three times a year. Sophie wondered, if Carrie had told her about Louis's leaving her, if she had told her about being on her own with the children and evoked their old promise, *would* she have made more of an effort to see her old friend? *Would* she have had more to do with the children? To be perfectly honest, she didn't know. She would probably have just assumed that she and Carrie were different people now, that Carrie had her own support network down in St. Ives, her own collection of new and different friends who seemed to help her get along very well without Louis until fate stepped in and fucked everything up for her. Until somehow the girls arrived on Sophie's doorstep and all of those girlhood promises and pacts Sophie and Carrie had made to each other seemed vitally important again.

So it was a peculiar mix of guilt and pleasure that led Sophie to take the girls to several other shops and buy them more clothes. And when in one shop they had both stopped and picked up identical orange stuffed cat toys and hugged them as if their little lives depended on them, she bought those too, along with a baby doll for Izzy and a giant drawing and painting set for Bella.

There had been a slight wobble on the way home when, seeing Izzy screw her fists into her eyes and yawn, Sophie had tentatively suggested a taxi. Izzy had been on the point of a total nervous collapse when out of nowhere, exactly like a knight in shining white armor bar the armor, Jake Flynn had suddenly appeared.

"Goodness me, what a beautiful dress," he'd told Izzy, whose mouth had frozen in midwail and transformed into a smile.

"Thank you," she'd said prettily. "I am beautiful, aren't I?"

"Jake!" Sophie had said, managing to sound both grateful and surprised.

"Cal told me you'd been into the office today," Jake had said, with slight reproach. "I would have come and taken you out for lunch if I'd known." Sophie remembered his offers on the phone and realized that in the last few days she'd hardly had time to think about Jake at all. In her real life, she would have been obsessing over every nuance of their conversation for weeks while putting off any chance to find out what it really meant in case it really did mean something. In this life, though, she didn't have time to think about it. It was an unlikely blessing.

"Who are you and what do you want with us." Bella had asked Jake darkly.

Jake had laughed. Bella had not.

"I'm Jake," he'd said. "I'm a friend of Sophie's, and you are . . . ?"

"Bella, and she's my sister, Izzy. She's only three, so she's very stupid, she'll talk to anyone." Bella had looked up at Sophie. "Are *you* her boyfriend?" she'd asked.

Jake had paused and glanced at Sophie, who'd grinned stupidly and shrugged. "Not yet," he had said with a slow smile. "But I'm working on it."

"Her sofa smells of curry," Bella had said helpfully. "And she plucks the hair from her top lip."

Jake had laughed, and Sophie had hoped the chill of the evening would keep her from blushing.

"Well, Bella," Jake had said, gallantly choosing to ignore the girl's revelations, "you look like you've got plenty of booty in those bags. Are you going to get a cab home?"

"No, no, *no, no, NO!*" Izzy had begun to wind up her protests.

"Okay," Jake had said, quickly picking up her bags. "Look, here's the bus now. Come on, guys!" He'd picked up three of Sophie's bags and swung Izzy onto the double-decker, helping Bella and then Sophie hop onboard.

As they'd found their seats, Sophie had stared at him. "You realize this isn't the right bus?" she'd asked him, not sure whether to be enchanted or irritated.

"Really?" Jake had said. "Well, we're off on a little detour then." And Sophie had discovered that she was rather pleased.

Izzy had been charm personified on the ride home. She had not thrown one tantrum between the bus stop and Sophie's front door, and had chatted happily to Jake about everything in her known universe.

As they'd collected themselves and their bags on the pavement, Sophie had smiled gratefully at Jake. "Thanks so much," she'd said, expecting him to catch the next cab back to civilization.

"Not a problem," had responded. "Now which number are you? I'm dying for a cuppa." And Sophie hadn't been able to help but laugh, because *cuppa* sounded so funny in an American accent.

* * *

Jake stood beside Sophie in the kitchen as she made tea and poured out two glasses of milk as if it were the most natural thing in the world for him to be there.

"Am I being too much?" he asked her. "I'll go if you like."

Sophie considered the alternative. "No, please, stay," she said, and Jake fixed her with this long, blue-eyed look that made her feel certain he was just about ready to kiss her.

"One lump or two?" she asked him, holding up the sugar bowl as a shield.

Jake smiled and took a step back. "None," he said, wryly. "I'm abstaining. Apparently."

They carried the drinks back into the living room to find Izzy fast asleep more or less where she had fallen right in the middle of the floor, her arms flung above her head in abandon.

"Shhhh," Bella said, pointing down at her sister. "She's asleep."

Sophie smiled at the little girl, her mouth half-open, the half crescents of her long eyelashes sweeping the tops of her apple cheeks. She could definitely see why people liked their children when they were asleep. Even she felt rather fond of Izzy at that moment. She wasn't *quite* sure, however, how parents managed to love their children for all the time they were awake.

"Here let me," Jake said, and bending, he scooped Izzy into his arms. "Where now?" he whispered.

Sophie led him through to her bedroom and hastily smoothed the unmade duvet, motioning that he should lay Izzy on the bed. As he did so, Sophie drew the quilt up over her, leaving.

"No pajamas?" Jake asked her, trying not to smile.

"No," Sophie said quite seriously. "You see, I've discovered that if you wake her up after even a few minutes of sleep, she thinks that she's been asleep for a whole night and is ready for action again. It's best not to risk it."

The sight she saw when they came back into the living room made Sophie certain that the fragile peace was about to be shattered. Bella was sitting in Artemis's chair, and so was Artemis.

"Don't move a muscle," Sophie whispered to Jake, who stood behind her, his way into the room blocked by her outstretched arm. He looked at Bella sitting with the big gray cat and seemed puzzled. But he didn't know Artemis.

Bella sat with her feet tucked under her, hugging a cushion to her chest. The cat sat on the chair's wide arm, her front paws curled neatly under her chest, watching the interloper intently with a green-eyed stare. Sophie held her breath, certain that at any moment the animal would pounce on Bella with the special fury she reserved for anyone (mainly Sophie) who was in her chair when she wanted to sit in it.

"Don't make any sudden movements," Sophie said, keeping her voice low and even. "Just keep your hands in view and step away from the chair." Bella raised the palm of her left hand hesitantly as Sophie had instructed, but instead of getting off the chair, she reached out ever so slowly and stroked Artemis just behind the ears. Sophie closed her eyes and braced herself for the screaming. "Bloody hell," she whispered to Jake.

She opened her eyes again. And the strangest thing had happened. Instead of ripping Bella's eyes out, Artemis didn't move except to tip her head slightly to one side, clearly indicating exactly where she wanted to be scratched. Instinctively, Bella obliged, and after a beat, the room was filled with a loud, completely unexpected rattle.

Artemis was *purring*. Sophie had only heard the cat purr once before, and that had been with one of the helpers in the shelter, just before she brought her home. She'd been waiting three years for Artemis to purr for her.

"Bloody hell!" Sophie said again, but this time her voice was filled with awe.

"What is going on?" Jake asked her.

"Nothing!" Sophie exclaimed in wonder.

"Yep," Jake said, raising both his brows and crossing his arms. "That's what I thought."

Carefully Sophie eased into the room, sat down on the edge of the sofa, and watched the tableau of cat and girl, a tiny smile turning up the corners of her mouth. "She likes you," Sophie said.

"Cats do like me," Bella answered, still looking at Artemis. "We . . . Well, when we were at home, we had a giant cat called Tango because he was orange, but . . . but when we had to go and live with Grandma, he had to go into a home, because Grandma is allergic to cats, and now I don't know who he lives with." Bella turned her profile a little farther away from Sophie. "So I know that cats like me."

Sophie slipped off the edge of the sofa and knelt on the floor in front of the chair. "But Artemis doesn't even like *me*, Bella," she said without jealousy. "I'm just her landlady. For her to let you stroke her like that after only knowing you for a few days must mean that you are a very, very special person."

"Really?" Bella said, looking at Sophie.

"Really," Sophie said. And because she felt suddenly so grateful to Bella, and because she sensed that she needed her too, Sophie put one arm around the girl's shoulders and gave her a little hug.

"Thank you," she said. "For making Artemis feel safe and happy." She covered Bella's free hand with her own and squeezed it gently. Artemis shot out a paw and scratched the back of Sophie's hand in one fluid movement, giving her a most irritated look before hopping off the chair and running past Jake and into the hallway.

"Ouch," Sophie said, looking at the four red welts that had begun to rise on the back of her hand.

"Sorry," Bella said, looking worried. "I'm sure she didn't mean it."

Sophie laughed. "Oh, she meant it. But you know what? It doesn't matter. I'm just glad she's found a friend. She really needed one."

Bella and Sophie smiled at each other, and Sophie realized it was the first time they had truly connected since Bella had arrived in her life. It was as if she had caught a fleeting glance of the little girl who was in there somewhere, hiding behind the protective outer layer. Sophie felt a curious jump in her abdomen as she watched Bella retreat again; it had felt just for a moment as if she had been talking to Carrie. But Bella glanced at Jake, still standing in the door way and any trace of Carrie was gone in an instant.

"If Artemis liking me after just a bit means I'm a special person . . ." Bella began slowly.

"Yes?" Sophie said with a smile, hoping to coax that other Bella out again.

"Does that mean that her not liking you after three years means that you are a rubbish one?"

Sophie thought for a moment. "Probably," she conceded. She was getting used to Bella's blunt observations, and beside, she didn't have the energy to be offended by a six-year-old.

"Well, I love Artemis, Aunty Sophie, but I think she's wrong. I don't think you're rubbish. I think you're not bad, really. Actually, I like you—you *are* funny." Bella patted Sophie's knee in commiseration. "It's been an awfully long day. Can I go to bed?"

"Absolutely," Sophie said hastily, sounding possibly a bit too pleased.

"Should I brush my teeth?" Bella asked her.

"You'd better," Sophie replied. "At least once every other day is the recommended minimum."

"Is he going home now?" Bella nodded at Jake, who had come into the room and sat on the arm of the sofa.

"In a little bit," Sophie said.

"He'll probably want to kiss you. Bleugh," Bella said, wrinkling up her nose.

"I'll tell you what," Sophie said. "I'll come and brush my teeth with you."

Well, there was no harm in being prepared.

Half an hour later, Sophie offered Jake a glass of warm Baileys.

"Sorry," she said. "It's all I've got, unless you want another 'cuppa'?"

Jake smiled and took the glass from her hand, so that the tips of his fingers brushed hers. "No, I think I need something a little stronger."

Sophie took a bigger gulp of her Baileys than was probably ladylike.

"You know," she said reflectively. "I work sometimes from eight in the morning to ten at night—later than that if we've got an event on. I don't take a break or stop for lunch, I keep going, and at the end of the day I'm tired, but not this tired. I've *never* been this tired before in my life and . . ." She demonstrated her exhaustion quite eloquently by drifting off into silence.

Jake watched her for a second or two before putting his glass down, taking hers out of her hands, and setting it beside his. "You are doing amazingly well," he said.

Sophie looked rather longingly at her glass. "Thank you," she said.

"I mean, from the moment I met you, I got all the obvious

things about you right away," he told her. "I got that you are beautiful and clever and formidable."

"Formidable?" Sophie repeated the word uncertainly.

"I like a challenge," Jake said with a grin. "What I'm trying to say, Sophie, is I like and admire you. I'm really attracted to you. But all this? Seeing you handle it all with such grace and good-will . . ."

"Well . . ." Sophie wasn't sure about that last part.

"You've blown me away," Jake said. "I think I could really fall for you, Sophie Mills."

Sophie froze. "Oh," she said. And then, "Um, how nice."

"I'm going too fast, aren't I?" Jake asked her.

Sophie shook her head. "No, no— I mean— Look, Jake, it's just there's so much going on in my life right now. So much I've got to keep on top of. There's work and that's so important and the girls of course I've got to get their dad back otherwise they'll go into foster care and that would be wrong. I don't think that now is the right time to start anything . . ." Sophie was almost unable to believe what she was saying. For the last few weeks, whenever she had thought about Jake, she had imagined what it would be like to hear him saying these words or something very like them to her. Now that he was, she felt like leaping up and opening all the windows and washing the kitchen floor. Maybe Cal was right about her. Maybe she *did* have intimacy issues, whatever intimacy issues might be. Maybe she did like the idea of Jake falling for her much more than she liked the reality.

"I understand that," Jake said gently. "But can I ask you, Sophie—is it just that? If it's just that, I can wait until you're ready. But if you don't think you're attracted to me at all, then you'll tell me, won't you?" He laughed. "Usually I can tell what a woman is thinking just by looking at her. You're not at all like that. You're a genuine enigma. I can't figure you out at all."

Join the club, thought Sophie as she looked at Jake's lightly tanned face, his blue eyes and dark blond hair. He was indisputably attractive. If you looked up the word *attractive* in a dictionary, it would probably say in italics *"See Jake Flynn."*

"I am attracted to you," she said, and she was—it was impossible not to admire a man who was so pleasing.

Suddenly Jake leaned forward and picked up her hand, pulling her closer to him. "Well then," he said, his voice low. "Would you mind if I kissed you? Just so I've got something to dream about while I'm doing all this waiting."

"Okay then," she squeaked. Jakes arms moved around her waist and pulled her body tightly against his, and he moaned in the back of his throat as he kissed her. Sophie opened her lips under his and closed her eyes. It was a nice kiss, a nice warm kiss, and it did feel good to be that close to another human body. She tightened her arms around his neck, and he slid his hand under the hem of Lisa's shirt and—

"Izzy's been sick." Bella's voice boomed in Sophie's ear. She and Jake sprang apart in one movement to opposite ends of the short sofa.

"Your cheeks have gone red," Bella said, screwing up her mouth as she looked at Sophie. "Anyway, Izzy's been sick in the bed. I tried to get her to do it the bin, but she couldn't wait. But at least she missed most of your shoes."

Sophie brushed the back of her hand unconsciously across her mouth and looked at Jake. "I'm sorry," she said.

But he just shrugged and smiled. "No, I'm sorry," he said. "I *knew* there was a reason why we were waiting." He laughed sweetly. "Come on. I'll help you clean up."

Later on, when bedclothes and pajamas had been changed, baths had been had, and an overwrought three-year-old had finally been cajoled back into bed, Sophie shut the door on Jake

Flynn and sat on the sofa, looking at the blank screen of the TV again.

It had been a nice kiss, she concluded. And it had felt good to be in someone's arms again. Sophie had begun to wonder if that was as wonderful as kissing ever got when exhaustion finally overtook her, and she slept on the sofa sitting up, fully dressed and entirely unwashed.

Nine

Maria Costello called Sophie again at 9:00 A.M. exactly on a Saturday morning two weeks later.

"I've nailed him," she said.

Sophie had to pause for a beat until her brain managed to tell her who was on the other end of the phone. In the last couple of weeks she had become so locked into her strange new life of juggling the children, work, and Jake that she had almost forgotten there was a possible end in sight. A time when she might just get her ordered, quiet, peaceful life back.

"Really?" Sophie stood up, feeling a rush of blood and adrenaline to her simultaneously overstretched and shrinking brain. She left the table, where she had been trying to update her month-end figures in the midst of a cat's tea party, and took the phone into the kitchen. "And have you found out *exactly* where he is?" She asked.

"Exactly," Maria said triumphantly. "I've got his phone numbers, his address. I'll give you his inside leg measurements if you want me to."

"The address will do," Sophie said, scrabbling about in her pen drawer, which always seemed to contain everything except pens. Finally she found one pen at the back and ripped off a piece of paper towel to write on.

"Go on," she said.

"Here's the number of the school he works at." Maria read out the phone number and address with brisk efficiency, spelling the Spanish words at staccato speed. "The bill's in the post, okay?" she concluded.

"Hang on," Sophie said hurriedly. "Did you say he works at a *school*? What kind of school? Can't you tell me a bit more about him? I mean, I had him down as an international drug baron."

Maria laughed, but she didn't sound amused. "More of a male Mother Teresa," she said. "He's been working as a volunteer for a street kids' charity for the last couple of years."

Sophie processed that bit of information. A man who leaves his wife with a newborn baby didn't seem the type to devote his life to a children's charity. Probably, she decided, it was the guilt, but being a coward as well as a bastard, he had tried to salve that guilt a few thousand miles away instead of facing up to what he had done at home.

"And it's definitely him?" she said.

"Definitely," Maria said firmly.

"Thank you, thank you, Maria."

"I want payment by overnight mail," Maria said, and she hung up.

Sophie put the phone down and looked out the kitchen window, to where Artemis sat on the top edge of the neighbor's fence, poised to eviscerate the next passing vole or other unfortunate mammal. Sophie ran her palms over her cheeks and crossed her arms under her breasts.

So Maria had found him, and now she had to think about what that was going to mean. Two weeks ago Sophie could not have thought of anything beyond finding Louis. Now she realized she had to; his return would have consequences for everyone involved. She thought of the expression on Mrs. Stile's face when she had mentioned Louis. She thought of Carrie alone with her children, too proud or embarrassed or maybe too distant to tell her that Louis had gone.

Sophie hadn't considered the consequences for anybody besides herself. It was very likely now that she had found Louis that her life would improve and the burden of the children would pass from her to him, which after all was only right. But what if his coming back wasn't the best thing for the girls?

Two weeks ago, Sophie wouldn't have thought twice about dialing that number and getting Louis back here as fast as humanly possible. But in the fourteen days that had passed since Maria's first phone call, something had changed. Something that Sophie could hardly put her finger on until that moment.

She realized she had actually started to care for Bella and Izzy.

It wasn't like being in love or anything as grand as that. She hadn't suddenly felt compelled to adopt them and call them her own. After all, she hadn't really kissed or hugged either of them since they had arrived. But gradually Sophie felt she had come to respect them coping as bravely and as stoically as they did with all that had happened to them, a fact she was grateful for, as she was certain if they had worn their grief on their sleeves, she would never have been able to handle them. And besides that, she had got unexpectedly used to the new rhythm of her life and having the girls in it.

In fact, Sophie reflected, the hardest hurdle to overcome had been not the children but working her job around them. Somehow she had expected it to stretch and give way like a fast-flowing river rushing past boulders. She had thought that Gillian's motherly compassion for her dead best friend's kids would be endless and that her need to keep Sophie on would be essential, but in fact Sophie had learned something in the last two weeks that she would rather not have discovered: as far as work was concerned she was expendable. It was a cold and sobering lesson to realize that the ten years she had devoted to McCarthy Hughes had not earned her any security to speak of. But even so, she was more determined then ever that she should not let all she had worked for slip away.

So they developed a routine.

Every morning Izzy would wake Sophie up at just after six. The two of them would wake Bella, and then all three would eat cornflakes and toast on the kitchen floor. Sophie would suck down a cup of boiling hot instant coffee as if it were the elixir of life, and Bella and Izzy would drink a pint of low-fat milk between them.

The three would then wash together in the bathroom. Sophie would fill the sink with warm water, hand the girls a sponge each, and do her best in between their splashes and soakings to get herself clean. She would look at the bath and dimly remember a time when she used to have an hour or so to lounge in it, but the best she managed now was a swift shower after the girls were in bed. Dressing was relatively easy, mainly because Izzy wore only one thing, which worked out fine since Sophie had begun to use her washing machine regularly and then dry the fairy dress on the radiator every other night. Sophie supposed there was some kind of unspoken rule that you should not allow a child out in public in a dress that had caked tomato ketchup encrusted down its front, but she refused on principle to wash it every single day.

Bella was even easier to manage, choosing items out of her meager wardrobe every day with an élan her mother would have been proud of. There had been an incident when she had helpfully put in a load of wash and transformed all Sophie's pristine white underwear into a sort of brothel pink, but Sophie had been surprised to discover she didn't care. Her pants may be pink, she reasoned, but at least they were clean. Sophie herself managed to keep up her appearance of groomed neatness, which hid the lesser parts of personal grooming that she had had to let go, so that the stubble grew on her legs and under her arms and her fair brows thickened slightly. No one was going know, after all, and whether she realized it or not, it gave her another reason to keep Jake Flynn at arm's length.

And then Sophie would take the girls to the office every morning between nine and one. The first day she did this, Gillian had suggested in a kind but resolute manner that she organize some part-time child care because an office was no place for small children. Of course, Gillian was absolutely right, but at that point Sophie had felt like she was in one of those fairy tales when the prince has to achieve three impossible tasks to win the hand of the princess. She felt like she had to solve all of these impossible tasks, only at the end she didn't get anything like a prince; in fact, if she was very lucky, all she would get would be her old life back intact.

But Sophie had nodded politely and asked Cal to find the number of a day-care provider in her area, confirm that she was registered, and double-check her references. She had taken the girls around to meet Alice Hardy that very afternoon. Bella and Izzy had seemed to like Alice's friendly, sunny ground-floor flat with a playroom, and while Bella read a book seated at a mini table and chair set as Sophie talked over terms with Alice, Izzy went as far as to play shop with a little boy that Alice had that day.

So it had been a bit of a blow the following morning when the girls realized Sophie was leaving them with Alice and both collapsed into inconsolable tears. Sophie had felt that Izzy's tears were more a reaction to her sister's distress, but Bella's reaction had taken her aback. She hadn't seen any emotional outbursts from the uniquely even-tempered child and so had supposed her placid exterior was the norm. But as Sophie had waved good-bye, Bella's face had crumpled and she backed away from Alice and turned in to Sophie's leg, clinging to her thighs.

Sophie had crouched down to try to untangle Bella, and Izzy launched herself at Sophie's back and flung her arms around her neck. Briefly, Sophie had thought it was like being wrestled by two man-eating crocodiles.

"Come on, girls," she'd said briskly. "Let's be reasonable."

"Please don't leave us here," Izzy had begged. "Please don't leave us!"

"It's only for a couple of hours!" Sophie said, irritated at first. "I'm coming back!"

"*Please* don't leave us again, Aunty Sophie," Bella said. "We don't know these people, and please don't make us live with people we don't know—please, *please*! We'll be so quiet. We will be so good, and I won't let Izzy be naughty, please, *please*!"

"I won't, I won't, I won't," Izzy had wailed right in Sophie's ear.

It had taken a moment for Sophie to decipher the words from the sobs, but once she did, she'd thought she understood. "This is just while I go to work," She'd attempted to explain. "Like school or nursery. It's not a foster home or anything like that." Sophie had sensed Bella wanted further reassurance, but she hadn't known what else to say.

"If we are with you, we know we're safe," Bella managed to say, her dark eyes made liquid by the tears in them.

A strange look had passed between Sophie and Bella then. Sophie had suddenly realized that somehow Bella had come to trust and need her, clinging—Sophie guessed—to the one thing in her life that seemed relatively stable. It was another hint, another glimpse of the real girl who was hidden so carefully away. It made Carrie's death suddenly seem all too real, in that sunny basement flat over half a year later, and for a second Sophie had felt the threat of tears prickle behind her eyes. She wasn't the only one who locked her emotions tightly away.

Since the moment Tess Andrew had walked into her office, Sophie had barely allowed herself a moment to think about Carrie, partly because she felt she didn't have the room or time yet to grieve or to miss Carrie but also because she was afraid that, when the dust had settled, she might find out she felt nothing at all, or else not nearly enough, about the death of a friend who had once meant everything to her. But in that moment Sophie had felt everything that Bella was feeling, and she knew that somewhere inside of her, feelings for Carrie must still live. And knowing that connected her attachment to the children with one more fragile strand, because Bella was showing her a reflection of herself. A picture that made sense.

"Okay," she'd said with a shrug. "You're coming with me."

"Children often cry like this at first," Alice told Sophie kindly. "And they nearly always are putting it on. They're happy as soon as Mum's gone. They'll get used to it."

Sophie had looked into the other woman's open, well-meaning face. "You're probably right," she'd said. "I just think that these two have got enough to get over already."

And the moment Sophie had walked into the office with the children that morning, she had gone to Gillian's office and played her in a way she would never have previously dreamed of.

She'd told Gillian she had tried to leave the girls with a care giver; she'd told her how they had reacted. "They just lost their mother," she'd said. "They are terrified of being abandoned again." It was a direct challenge to Gillian, daring her not to show compassion for the children's plight. "I know this is no place for kids, but I'll make sure they are kept out of the way, and I won't let them interfere with any of my work. The minute they do, I'll think again."

"It's not just what I think," Gillian had said cautiously. "There's health and safety and insurance and all sorts of other things to consider."

"It's only temporary," Sophie had pressed her. "Their dad will be back soon."

"Well, you'd better make sure you're only in the office for as short a time as possible," Gillian had said. "And I want to see updates for all your accounts before you go."

Sophie had had a long talk with the girls, explaining why they had to be extra good, and they had stared at her blankly. The connection she had felt with them at Alice Hardy's seemingly lost again.

And then Cal had produced a huge box of building blocks. He'd unrolled a colorful rug and set it down in one corner before tipping the blocks out. Izzy had hopped with anticipation.

"And here are crayons, and pens and paper. And here's two Barbies and a Barbie car. Now"—he'd looked sternly from one girl to the other—"these are *my* toys, and I am *very* kindly letting you play with them, so I expect you to play nicely, and share and not take them out of this office, or I will have to take them back. Now do you promise?"

"Yes, Cal!" the girls had chorused before descending on the rug.

Cal winked at Sophie. "It's sort of like learning another language," he'd said. "Once you let yourself go enough to get hold of the accent, you'll be fine."

"Well," Sophie had replied. "Fortunately I'm only on a short trip, so all I need is a phrase book. Anyway, where did you get all those toys from?" She'd asked, full of gratitude and admiration for her PA.

"I told you," he'd said. "They're mine. From when I was a kid."

And Sophie had decided she believed him.

It was in the middle of this gradual buildup of routine that Tess arrived one evening at the flat.

Sophie squinted at her as she held the front door open. "I'm sure I know you," she said sarcastically. "Oh yes! That's it. You're the one who told me I wasn't alone and that I could expect regular visits."

"Well, you weren't," Tess said, bustling into the flat. "I've called you every day, and every day you've said that things have been going well. I've had this awful neglect case to deal with. And sometimes there aren't enough of us to go around. We have to prioritize."

Sophie shrugged. Tess did phone her every day, it was true, and she supposed that she had only herself to blame that her tiredness and slowly decreasing powers of communication had led her to tell Tess what the social worker wanted to hear in order to get her off the phone and allow Sophie to go to sleep in front of the TV. But then again, as over two weeks had passed since the girls arrived and all three of them were still alive, she supposed she hadn't actually been lying. It gave her an unexpected sense of achievement and satisfaction. All this moaning from parents about how hard it was to bring up children was a load of overblown self-pity in Sophie's eyes. All you needed was a routine and a freezer full of chicken nuggets.

"How's it really been?" Tess asked her once she had a mug of tea in her hands.

"It's really been really hard," Sophie said. "My job's been the worst part. But I think I'm on top of that mainly. I even landed a new client this week. It was quite funny, because Izzy had just felt-tipped some stripes on my linen skirt, but I had to go into the meeting anyway, and the woman asked me where I got it—she said she thought it was fabulous! It's ruined, of course. I've added it to the bill. And I suppose I haven't been sleeping well or eating the way I used to, and my skin's gone—"

"How has it been for the girls?" Tess interrupted her, and Sophie remembered belatedly that she wasn't the most important person in her life anymore.

She thought for a moment. "Okay," she said. "I mean, I get the feeling that most of the time they are living in a sort of suspended animation, waiting for when they know exactly what's going to happen to them, waiting for when they can *feel* what *has* happened to them. I guess we're all like that," she said, realizing that was the way she felt too.

"I've had them for over two weeks now," she continued. "Have you found Louis yet?"

Tess dropped her gaze to look at her bangles. "No," she said evenly. "But we've only been looking for a month, remember. We know he went to the States right after leaving here. It's the red tape, you see, dealing with government bodies overseas. It makes everything so slow." She looked back up at Sophie. "But I know we set a time limit on this. I've found a foster home that will take them together. They could go tomorrow if you like."

It was a pivotal moment. A moment when Sophie could have let all her worries go and passed the buck, passed the children on to someone else. But she remembered the look on Bella's face that morning at Alice Hardy's too clearly, and she remembered that flash feeling that had burned across her chest too. She just couldn't do it, even though a large percentage of her still wanted to. She couldn't do it to the girls, who had been through too much already and still had so much more to face. And although she wasn't conscious of the thought, Sophie couldn't do it to herself. Slowly the instinct and intuition that she claimed never to have had was awakening. And that small, sleepy part of her dimly sensed that she needed the children just as much as they needed her.

"They can stay with me," she said.

Tess looked genuinely surprised. "Really?" she asked.

"Yes. Like you said, there's still a good chance Louis might turn up, and I just don't think it would be right to move them again now. We've got a routine and everything."

"But if it's affecting your job . . . ," Tess said uncertainly.

"I'm coping," Sophie replied firmly. She had always liked a challenge.

And among all the distractions, obstacles, and challenges that had suddenly sprung up on a previously tranquil horizon, Jake positioned himself firmly in the middle.

He had called Sophie the morning after they had had the perfectly nice kiss.

"I've got to tell you," he'd said. "I couldn't stop thinking about that kiss."

"Lovely," Sophie had said, for want of anything else to say.

"It was lovely, wasn't it?" Jake had laughed. "That's such an English word, *lovely.*"

"I think you'll find most of the words you speak are English," Sophie had said.

Jake had laughed again. He had a sweetly unself-conscious laugh, like that of a sort of delighted little boy, which didn't quite match his suited and booted hard body. "When can I see you again?" he'd asked.

Sophie had thought. "Well, we've got to meet next week to sign off on the last batch of invoices for your party . . ."

"So lunch after that?" Jake had asked. "I know you'll have the kids, but we could all go maybe?"

"Jake, I don't know," she'd said. She didn't want any misunderstandings between them. "Remember what I said before about waiting awhile? There's so much on at the moment. I just— I can't really see you in that way. I haven't got any time or space to think about you, to really know what I'm feeling. It wouldn't be fair to you."

Jake had paused for a moment. "Well," he'd said. "I knew exactly how I felt about you before you even uttered one word, but I guess that maybe that's the difference between us. You're an instant smash hit, while I'm the type who grows on people. Look, why don't you just let me be your friend? You need a friend right now."

"I do," Sophie had conceded.

"So I'll bring over some wine and Chinese tonight," Jake had said. "No strings, okay?"

"Okay. And Jake, thank you. I really appreciate all this."

"Of course you do," he told her. "And that's why, sooner or later, one way or another, you're going to fall in love with me."

Jake had come that night and twice again since, sitting and talking over work and children with Sophie until she'd yawned extravagantly and he'd taken the hint. She'd enjoyed his company and the way he looked at her, but never once had she felt the urge to throw caution out the window and let him kiss her again.

"I will," she kept telling herself. "When the time is right. It's just that the time isn't right yet."

Ten

Clutching the piece of paper that might hold all their futures on it, Sophie went from her bedroom to the living room to check on the girls. They were lying on the floor with two of Cal's Barbies, which he had graciously allowed them to bring home, acting out some kind of intense drama, which—from what Sophie could glean—was based on a recent episode of *Coronation Street*.

"All right?" she asked them casually.

They ignored her, which was usually a good sign—when it didn't mean they were in the midst of extreme naughtiness. This morning Sophie didn't care either way.

"I'm just going to tidy the bedroom up," she lied. "So don't go swallowing any choking hazards, okay?"

There was no response again except for the high-pitched chatter of Barbie Ken Barlow telling Barbie Deirdre he'd never trust her again.

Sitting on her bed, Sophie looked at the numbers.

She wondered if it might be an idea to actually tidy up her bedroom before phoning, but then she made herself look her reflection right in the eye. "You have to do this," she said. "There is no alternative."

She dialed the number and heard a series of clicks on the line before the long foreign ring tone sounded.

Sophie put down the phone.

"What am I *thinking*?" she said out loud and with some relief. "They'll speak Spanish, or Peruvian or Inca or something. I need a phrase book at least, or . . ." An idea popped into her head. "I'll phone Cal."

Sophie had done the bedroom and changed the sheets by the time Cal arrived.

He looked her up and down as she opened the door still in her pajamas. "You should just dread you hair and be done with it," he said.

Sophie said nothing because she knew he was seriously pissed off with her for dragging him out of the bed of an Italian chap called Mauro, who apparently not only was drop-dead gorgeous but also made the best spaghetti carbonara in the whole of London.

"You never eat food unless it comes in the form of a canapé," Sophie had reminded him half an hour earlier as she tried to persuade him to give up his Saturday morning for her. "You don't even like pasta."

Cal had bitched and sniped at her via his cell phone for most of his trip over, but Sophie had taken it all on the chin because, after all, he was right. He *didn't* have to come over to her flat and help her on a Saturday morning. It *was* above and beyond the call of duty. She *would* have to grovel to him for weeks, take him to lunch and sign him off for as many Friday afternoons as he wanted for six months.

"Hello, girls," Cal said to Bella and Izzy as he passed the living room. They were now lying in front of the TV, but miraculously they didn't appear to be watching it, perhaps because what was on was some undetermined sport. Bella was drawing yet another mermaid-strewn coastal scene with her new set of felt-tips, and Izzy was feeding her new baby doll.

"Come on, baby," Izzy said, sounding rather impatient. "Let's have some nice chips for tea on the kitchen floor and then we'll watch TV all day!"

Cal raised an eyebrow at Sophie. "And to think they are all saying you're a natural with the kids at work," he said tartly.

"Yes well." Sophie coughed. "It's a learning curve. So, anyway, follow me to the bedroom."

Cal followed her with a derisive snort. "That's exactly what Mauro said to me," he said mournfully as she closed the door behind her. "So come on then, tell me what this is all about. Although why you couldn't tell me on the phone, I don't know."

"Because your cell phone signal wasn't very good and I didn't want to have to shout out what this was all about in case *walls have ears,* if you know what I mean."

"I don't," Cal said sharply. "So speak English. You're being annoying."

"I know," Sophie said. "I'm sorry. I had to call you over because of your language skills. I had to think for a moment if Spanish was one of them, but then I remembered in your interview when you told me you'd been traveling all around the world and that you'd worked in Barcelona for a year for a law firm and spoke fluent Spanish."

Cal pursed his lips and looked out the window. "Yes, I do recollect that," he said, carefully.

"Well, Louis Gregory is in Lima, so I need you to call and

speak Spanish to whoever picks up the phone so we can get hold of him, okay?"

Cal bit his lip. "And you don't speak Spanish at all?" he asked.

"Nope," Sophie reaffirmed with a nod, her hands on her hips. "You know me!"

"So you'd have no idea what the Spanish person or indeed *I* was saying, for example?" he doubled-checked, crossing his arms over his lucky shag shirt, a pale blue one shot through with subtle silver pinstripes.

"Not a sausage," Sophie said, honestly.

"Okay, I'll do it," Cal said. He took the piece of paper with the number on it from Sophie, sat on the edge of the bed, and looked at it.

"This is important, isn't it?" he said, with an edge of reluctance.

"Just a bit!" Sophie said, laughing nervously. "Like the lives of three people depend on its outcome!" She put a hand on his shoulder. "That's why I really do appreciate you coming over, Cal. You're totally saving my life here, even if you are pretending to be all flippant about it. You really are wonderful, you know."

Cal nodded. "I'm sorry, Sophie," he said, unable to look at her. "I lied on my CV. I lied in the interview. I didn't go around the world. I went skiing in Aspen for two weeks once, and I didn't work for a year in Barcelona for a law firm. I stayed there for a month with an old boyfriend and worked in an English bar until we broke up. I can't speak fluent Spanish. I can barely speak tourist Spanish. I can't actually speak fluent anything. When you ask me to tell you what to say to overseas clients, I look it up on the Internet. There's this amazing site that gives you pronunciations and everything." He dropped his head and braced himself, although he didn't know why. He should have known by now that she was terrible at losing her temper—doing so required far too much abandon.

Sophie just stared at him. She didn't know what to be more cross about, the fact that he'd lied his way through his job interview, the fact that she had fallen for it, or the fact that he was about as much use to her now in practical terms as he was as a lover. And then she remembered, at least he was here. He had come, and he had told her the truth when it mattered.

"Bastard," she said, but in general rather than directed straight at Cal. "Look, you must remember some basic phrases if you lived there for a month, and we did that Spanish fashion label a couple of months back. You must remember something from then?"

Cal shrugged. "I guess so," he said uncertainly before catching Sophie's look of anxiety. "Oh, what the hell? Okay, I'll do it."

"Well, go on then," Sophie said, nodding at the phone, as unaware that she was twisting her fingers as she watched him.

"But what's the time difference?" he said. "There might not be anybody there."

Sophie sighed and sat down on the edge of her bed beside him. "I don't know," she said. "I forgot to look that bit up. It's five hours to New York, isn't it, and it's at least as far away as that." She looked at her watch. "So assuming it's about the same, it's just gone eleven now, so it's either four o'clock in the afternoon there or . . . six o'clock in the morning. I think it's six o'clock in the morning. Maybe earlier. . . ." Sophie sighed. "There'll be no one there, will there? I was really psyched up for this too."

Cal looked at her profile, her chin dropping to her chest. "What the hell, let's do it now anyway. You never know, we might be lucky," he said. He dialed the number, and they waited. The passing seconds seemed to stretch on for hours.

"Ah, hello . . . Um, *Buenos dias* I mean." There was a pause, during which Cal nodded at Sophie and winked. "*Arrepentido* about the, er—*hora*. It's an emergency a . . . *urgencia?*" Sophie gave him a worried look. His Spanish sounded all made up to her, and the faint voice of the person on the other end of the line sounded less than thrilled to be talking to Cal at six o'clock in the morning. But he pressed on, smiling as he spoke, as if his charm might somehow work long-distance too. "*Me llamo Cal,* and I am trying to speak, um, *hablar?* To Louis Gregory. *Louis Gregory, por favor? Urgencia.*" Sophie heard the faint rattle of a voice on the other end of the line. "*Sí . . . Sí . . . Sí. Gracias!*"

"What are they saying?" she whispered.

"Not the foggiest," Cal said happily. "But hopefully they've gone to get someone who can speak English. I think they got the emergency bit," he said proudly. "I learned that after my boyfriend broke his ankle coming off a moped and I had to call an ambulance." Cal listened intently to the echoes on the line. "If I'm not very much mistaken, somebody in Lima likes listening to Justin Timberlake in the small hours of the morning—and who can blame them?"

They waited for what seemed like an age, and then Cal looked at Sophie as he heard the clatter of a receiver being picked up.

"Oh, hello," he said after a pause. "Right then, hang on a moment." He held out the receiver to Sophie, who stared at it in horror.

"But, Cal, I can't speak Spanish," she said.

"You don't have to," Cal said. "It's him. It's Louis Gregory."

"So," Cal said urgently, as Sophie put the phone down. "What did he say, how'd he react, did he cry?"

Sophie shook her head and replayed the conversation she had just had, because it had happened so quickly she wasn't exactly sure if she understood it.

"Listen, babe, do you know what time it is? You've woken the whole place up! Look, before you say anything, I meant to call you, but I've just been up to my eyes in it . . ." This had thrown Sophie. She had not expected Louis to be expecting a call from another Englishwoman whose male secretary put the call through with the world's worst Spanish in the early hours of the morning—or indeed another English-speaking woman at any time, full stop. She'd thought that perhaps Cal had made a mistake and it wasn't Louis at all.

"This is Louis Gregory, right? Formally of St. Ives, Cornwall?" There'd been a short silence, and Sophie almost physically felt Louis tense up.

"Yes?" he'd said, and he laughed, probably a nervous reaction Sophie decided in retrospect, but one that had made her feel even more nervous.

"Hello, it's Sophie, Sophie Mills? Do you remember me?" There'd been an echo on the line, and after Sophie had finished each word, she'd heard it repeated in her ear, her voice sounding thin and girlish and not at all like a voice delivering serious news. "Sophie Mills, I was at your wedding. Carrie's friend. Carrie Stiles's friend—I was a friend of your wife." The echo had continued for another beat, and suddenly Sophie had been able to sense the change in him, thousands of miles away. She could picture him sitting up a little straighter, the smile fading from his face as moment by moment he realized what her call meant. It meant something bad had happened.

"Where are the girls, are they hurt? Is one of them hurt? What's happened?" he'd said quickly, and Sophie had found herself stumbling to reassure him—this absentee father and wife leaver whom neither girl seemed to know existed—that both of his children were okay.

"They're okay, they're here with me," she'd said quickly. "They are not hurt." She had heard him breathe out a sigh and almost felt it in the shell of her ear.

He'd taken a deep breath. "What's happened, Sophie?" he had asked, but Sophie somehow had known the question was a formality. Somehow, she'd realized that he already knew the answer, so she'd just told him outright.

"Carrie is dead," she'd said.

"Carrie is dead," the line had echoed, and Sophie had breathed in sharply, as if she was hearing the news for the first time too. But then her fledgling intuition had faltered. She had been bracing herself for an emotional outburst, questions, tears even. But there had been nothing—just silence. Sophie had remembered how she'd first reacted when she'd first heard, how she still felt—as if her heart was a thousand miles away—so she'd gone on filling the void with details. "It was a car accident, almost seven months ago." Still Louis had said nothing. "She was killed outright. The girls went to live with her mother and then Mrs. Stiles couldn't cope and called in Social Services about a month ago. They were sorting out the house and found a will. I was in the will, as guardian. So the girls came here." She had taken a breath. "Social Services have been looking for you for the last month, but they had all the red tape to get through, so I hired a private detective to find you and she did." This time it had been Sophie's nervous, inappropriate laughter that had echoed on a second's delay in her ears. "Look, Louis, I know you haven't seen them in a long time, maybe you don't want to but—"

"I'll be on the next flight I can get on," he said out of the silence.

Sophie had been taken aback by the sound of his voice, hardened with urgency.

"Oh, right, okay then," she'd said slowly, supposing that she had the result she wanted. "Let me just give you some details . . ."

She'd heard Louis scrabbling for a pen as he took down her address and number.

"Thank you for everything you've done," he'd said. "But I'm coming to get them, now."

"Do you know when—" The dial tone had buzzed in Sophie's ear. "We can expect you?" She'd finished the sentence into thin air.

Sophie had learned very little about Louis from that phone call. He had hardly reacted to the news that the mother of his children was dead, and he had just more or less assumed that he could waltz back into the girls' lives after three years away and take them off to God knows where to God knows what kind of life without so much as a by-your-leave. She experienced yet another unfamiliar sensation, a sharp protective pang in her gut, followed by a surge of unexpected fierceness. She found herself thinking, Over my dead body, and then she smiled to herself as she realized just how apt and inappropriate that phrase was.

She looked at a bemused Cal. "He says," she told him, "he's coming. Not big on details like how or when, but he's coming apparently."

Cal rested his lightly stubbled chin in the palm of his hand. "*And*—what's he like?"

Sophie shrugged again and felt a worm of worry begin to insinuate its way into her chest as she contemplated all the possible consequences of the chain of events she had just set in motion. She bit her lip and looked at Cal. "I don't know," she said. "I just don't know."

Eleven

The girls were delighted to see their grandmother. Izzy twirled and pranced around the small front room of Mrs. Stiles's new ground-floor apartment, bumping happily into the crowd of old furniture, and Bella, although less showy than her sister, did quite a lot of discreet toe pointing and heel lifting in a bid to show off her new shoes to their maximum advantage. Unfortunately, in the midst of Izzy's balletic craziness, only Sophie, a fellow toe pointer, noticed, so she bent down and whispered into Bella's ear. "Your shoes look fabulous." Which made Bella smile.

"Calm down, Izzy!" Mrs. Stiles ordered as Izzy threw her arms around her legs and buried her face in her skirt, declaring, "I love to see you, Grandma!" at the top of her voice.

"I love to see you too, darling," Mrs. Stiles said, looking flustered but pleased by the sign of affection. "But I'd also love to keep my knees in one piece. This arthritis—it'll be the death of me if the blood pressure doesn't get me first," she said, patting Izzy on the head.

"Or the cancer," Bella reminded her.

"Oh yes, well, you're right. It might be cancer, bowel probably, I've got terrible constipation," Mrs. Stiles said matter-of-factly, and Sophie realized that the children must have discussed the exact nature of Mrs. Stiles's demise quite often during their stay with her, which she found rather disturbing. A philandering father or a morbid grandmother—there wasn't much of a choice when it came to close relatives.

"Oh, you'll outlive us all," Sophie said with forced joviality.

"I sincerely hope not," Mrs. Stiles said bleakly. Her face took a downward tumble, as if somebody had just switched the gravity back on, and Sophie realized exactly what she had just said.

"I'm sorry, I only meant . . ." She sighed. "Oh, look, I don't know what I meant," she said with a vague gesture to back her up. "I'm sorry."

Mrs. Stiles ignored her. "Do you two girls want some lemon barley and a French fancy?" she said. The girls nodded, and Sophie followed Mrs. Stiles into the small kitchen and stood in the doorway watching Bella and Izzy lean up against the window of the living room and breathe hard against the glass, drawing faces in the mist before it faded, and then, flinging open the patio doors, they ran out onto the small shared courtyard and began marching around the central bird bath with apparently motiveless enthusiasm.

"I've just cleaned those windows," Mrs. Stiles said to Sophie, pressing her lips together. It wasn't that she didn't want the girls here, Sophie decided, it was rather that she didn't like them turning up unexpectedly. She didn't like any unannounced pebble rippling the calm surface of her routine. Sophie didn't blame her; she supposed that two sudden if minor strokes and the death of your adult daughter would make you cling to the belief that every to-morrow was much better off being exactly the same as yesterday, because at least then you knew where you stood. This was why it was a shame really that Sophie was about to throw a bloody great big brick into her pond, so to speak.

Once again Sophie had cause to reflect on the fact that she had been so keen to find Louis, so certain that his arrival would be the answer to everyone's problems—mainly her own—that she hadn't stopped to consider the implications of him turning up for anyone else. Not for Mrs. Stiles, not for Tess Andrew, and not for the girls. However, Louis was coming now, and there was nothing she could do to stop that, so she had to tell her, and if there was one thing that Sophie had learned over the last few days, it was that if you had to tell somebody something she didn't want to hear, there was no way to dress it up.

"Louis is coming back to London. He's coming to see the girls," she said. Mrs. Stiles poured water into the two cups of lemon barley she had prepared and set the jug down on the counter before turning to look at Sophie.

"They found him then," she said. "I had hoped they wouldn't; I told that Tess not to bother. She more or less told me it would take months. I'd hoped for the girls' sake that she was right."

Sophie didn't know how to react to that piece of information, so she said nothing but watched Mrs. Stiles shake her head and twist her swollen, knotted fingers, her left side slow and heavy.

"Well, now he'll be happy, won't he?" she said bitterly. "Now he'll get everything his own way, won't he? My daughter's dead, out of the way for good, and he can come waltzing in like some kind of hero and drag them off to God knows what kind of life." She shot Sophie a red-hot look. "I certainly won't ever see them again, once he's got them. He won't let me."

Sophie tucked her loose hair back behind her ear and chewed her lip for a moment. She had to be straight with her. "It wasn't Tess that found him," she said. "It was me, sort of. I spoke to him earlier today." Sophie remembered the sense of unease the conversation had left her with. "He sounded really worried about the girls. He said he'd come straightaway." But her uncertainty sounded in her voice, and Mrs. Stiles looked skeptical. "Look, I can't suddenly have two children, Mrs. Stiles. As much as I . . . like the girls, none of us can go on the way we are. It's not fair to them or me, and what's the alternative? I thought that this was what Carrie would want."

Mrs. Stiles looked over Sophie's shoulder and out the window to where the girls continued to circle, the winter sun blanching all the color out of her skin.

"Carrie wanted you," she told Sophie pointedly. "That's why your name was in her will. Besides, you hardly knew her at all when she died—how would you know what she would want now? Well, I'll tell you what she didn't want. She didn't want a husband who ran out on her and her children at the first sign of trouble. And she wouldn't want him taking those two girls, she wouldn't." Mrs. Stiles narrowed her eyes. "Oh, he might play at being a dad for a while—but for how long? How long before the novelty wears off and he's bored again? What will happen to them then?" She took a deep, shuddering breath. "I just wish, I just *wish* I was twenty years younger and I could look after them myself. If I could, I'd fight tooth and nail to keep them from him, to do *something* for Carrie at last. To be able to help her. She would never let me help her, she never wanted it. Sometimes it felt like she hated me, but I don't know why, Sophie, I don't . . . Because I loved that child *so* much. She was my *life*."

Sophie was appalled to see a tear track its way through the

powdery surface of Mrs. Stiles's skin. She reached out a hand and touched the older woman's thin shoulder.

"I'm all right," Mrs. Stiles said, taking a step away. She reached for the kettle with her right hand and filled it at the tap.

"Look," Sophie said. "Tess won't let him just walk off with them. I won't let him, I promise you. He can't anyway. There's all sort of orders and things protecting them."

Sophie looked toward the living room as the girls marched in through the double doors, around the ancient coffee table, and back out again. "They don't even know he's coming yet." She lowered her voice. "Do they even know who he is?"

Mrs. Stiles put two tea bags in a pot and watched the boiling kettle.

"All they know is that he had never been there for them, not even when they needed him the most," she said, picking the kettle up the moment it boiled and filling the pot to the brim. "Carrie would never have a bad word said against him, but I told her—they should know. They should know what kind of man he is."

Sophie hesitated for a moment before asking Mrs. Stiles the question she'd really come to ask. "Did Carrie tell *you* straight-away that Louis had left her? Because, well . . . I didn't know."

Mrs. Stiles looked sharply at her. "She never told you?"

Sophie shook her head.

"No," Mrs. Stiles continued. "She didn't even tell me after the christening. I daresay she never would have told me at all if it had been up to her. But she started having money trouble. I know she didn't want to ask me for help, but she had no choice. She needed some money to keep going with the mortgage payments until she could start this new full-time job she'd got. Of course I asked what Louis was doing to get them out of trouble, and that's when it came out. He'd been gone nearly a year before she told me."

Mrs. Stiles gazed into the distance as she reflected on the memory. "When she was a little girl, the age of those two out there, we were such good friends. So happy, you know. I wish . . . I wish I hadn't let everything that happened between me and her father come between me and her. After he went, I was so hurt, so angry. Not just at him but at everything. We were never that close again. I knew I was pushing her away, but I couldn't seem to stop myself. I always thought there'd be time to make things right one day. I was wrong. And now these two will be off with Louis and I won't have any time with them either."

Sophie reached out and squeezed Mrs. Stiles's thin arm. "Please," she said. "Try not to worry. Look, I'll pop out the front now and call Tess. Once I've told her, she'll know what to do, okay?"

"Don't be long," Mrs. Stiles said stiffly, pouring milk into a jug. "Your tea will stew."

For some reason, Sophie had assumed that social workers should be on call seven days a week, but it appeared that Tess was not available on a Saturday afternoon after all. Her cell phone was switched off, and her work number rang off the hook. Unable to produce anything to reassure both Mrs. Stiles and herself, Sophie sighed. Noticing her breath mist in the cold air, she took a surreptitious look left and right and reached for the packet of Marlboro Lights she had managed to buy on yesterday's shopping trip at the same time as buying the girls a king-size Snickers bar each and smoked it quickly, stubbing out the butt under the toe of her shoe and bending to scoop it up, slipping it into her pocket and taking a few more deep breaths of cold air before she went back in. Her temples throbbed as she tried to work out all the implications of what might happen next, and she felt a kind of hollow worry gnawing at her from the inside out.

Sophie had the strangest sensation that she had felt exactly like this once before, standing in the cold watching the heat of breath cool in the air, letting the tips of toes freeze rather than move her body on to the next moment and the moment after that, when things would never be the same again. It was a sense of déjà vu that was as strong and as jolting as the memory caused by a smell or a photo.

It didn't take long to place the memory. It had been at her father's autumn funeral. Sophie standing in her best black shoes by the little pile of flowers the crematorium had arranged for him in one corner of the courtyard. Friends and family had milled there for a while, shaking hands and avoiding eye contact, not really knowing what to say to one another until the modest crowd had drifted back toward the cars in preparation for the wake. That empty, worrying sensation had come to her just before Sophie finally realized what had happened. She had been standing beside a wreath of flowers with a card that read "To Dad, miss you so much" when abruptly the pain, the shock, and the horrific knowledge that loving her dad wouldn't mean anything ever again had engulfed her.

She had been unable to move. She had stood watching everybody else leave. After a few seconds, Carrie had noticed Sophie was not among the group and had come back to fetch her. "Come on," she'd said, her cheeks rosy in the cold. "It's freezing."

"He's gone," Sophie said, staring at Carrie. "Nothing's ever going to be the same now."

"That's not true," Carrie said, hooking her arm through Sophie's. "We'll stay the same, you and me. We will always stay the same, I promise. Always. Forever. Whatever. Right?"

So Sophie recognized the way she was feeling at that moment. She knew it was exactly the same way she had been feeling on the day she had said good-bye to her dad just before the pain became too much and the walls came down between her and the hurt. And Sophie had known at last that Carrie had been wrong and she had been right.

Nothing ever stays the same.

When Sophie finally went back inside, she was entirely unprepared for what she saw, but at least it lifted her from the complicated coil of her thoughts.

Actually, it wasn't so much what she saw, which was Mrs. Stiles sitting on the sofa flanked by the two girls, their respective heads leaning sweetly on each of her shoulders as the ensemble rocked from side to side. It was what she heard. The old lady and two small girls were singing "Motorcycle Emptiness" by the Manic Street Preachers as if it were some kind of raucous lullaby, with Bella and Izzy filling in for the thunderous guitar solo with enthusiastic "Nee, nee, nee-nee neeeows."

Certainly Sophie thought she would never live to see the day that Mrs. Stiles sang hardcore political Welsh rock, although the girls' grandmother did change some of the more controversial lyrics for propriety's sake. Still, as unorthodox as the rendition was, it sparked an unexpectedly vivid memory, which came thundering back to Sophie just as the girl's version of the guitar riff suddenly became real again in her ears.

It was summer. She and Carrie were more or less eighteen. Still so close that they felt they would always mean as much to each other as they did on that day, that it would be impossible for them to drift apart. It had been just a few weeks before Carrie was due to leave for university, and it would be another week or so before Sophie would get her entry-level job at McCarthy Hughes. In reality they were just about to take their first steps in completely opposite directions.

They were in the park, Sophie with her brand-new portable

CD player that weighed ton. They'd just bought the new Manic
Street Preachers CD, and they were sitting on the grass listening to
it, turning up the volume as loud as it would go—which wasn't
very loud. Dressed entirely in black, they looked especially cross
and sullen as they listened because that seemed the most appropriate expression for listening to the Manic Street Preachers, who
were, it seemed, quite cross and sullen about most things. But
when "Motorcycle Emptiness" came on, Sophie had been unable
to stop herself from humming along under her breath and tapping
her bare toes against the rough grass in time to the catchy tune.

Carrie maintained her scowl as she studied the CD's sleeve.
"Yeah, too fucking right, Sylvia," Carrie said.

"Sorry, who?" Sophie asked, looking over her shoulder, a little
slowly because just at that moment she had been wondering what
the chances were of her getting James Dean Bradfield to sleep
with her, and if he did what the chances were of him being
cheered up by it, and if he was would she still fancy him so much,
as his sullen good looks were at least half of his appeal.

"Sylvia Plath, dummy," Carrie said, rolling her eyes. "On the
cover under the title 'Motorcycle Emptiness' there's a line of her
poetry, about God. About there being no God to be precise."
Carrie read Sophie the line, which she couldn't quite remember
now but which she knew she hadn't really "got." Sophie had
blinked at her friend from behind her shades.

"You are such a plebe," Carrie said, rolling her eyes. "And anyway, James Dean Bradfield wouldn't sleep with you, you're too
middle-class."

Carrie sighed and flopped back onto the grass. "There is no
God, Soph," she said. "There is no order or truth. Nothing in the
world is fair or just. You just have to fight, you have to fight for
everything you want in this world, because no one, no one will
give it to you. Not even God. Especially not God."

Sophie sat up and looked closely at Carrie. She realized that her usually effortlessly cheerful friend wasn't feigning anger. She was genuinely furious.

"What's up?" Sophie said simply.

"It's Mum, isn't it? It's always Mum. Nothing I do is good enough for her. She's never just proud of me. She's never just happy for me. And now this course I'm starting—even that's not good enough. Never mind it's one of the most competitive art courses in the country. She wants me to change to something more academic, like history. It's like she's my mum and she doesn't know me. She knows nothing about me. Why can't she just support me for once instead of throwing flipping God in my face every five minutes and trying to control everything I do? I just want to be me. I can't wait until I can get as far away from her as possible and have my *own* life, a normal happy family life, and be free of her for good." Carrie shook her head as if an angry wasp had somehow got inside.

"She's not that bad," Sophie said. "I think she's going to miss you. I think she's scared about you going."

"I know," Carrie said. "So why is she doing her best to make me so keen to leave?"

Sophie shrugged. "I don't know, Carrie," she said. "Your mum is even weirder than mine."

"Well, I'll tell you one thing," Carrie said. "From this moment on, I'm never going to do a thing I don't want to do. I'm never going to miss another chance, another experience or feeling. I'm going to take everything I can out of life, and whenever I forget or feel like I can't be bothered or look like I might be turning into Mum—God forbid—I'm going to play this song to remind me. A song about living life to the fullest."

They both paused and listened to the exhilarating guitar riff once again.

"Actually, I think it's about political apathy and oppression," Sophie said.

"Yeah, I know," Carrie said, winking at her. "But it's got a rocking good chorus."

It took a few more seconds for the trio to repeat to fade, but when they had finished and Izzy had covered her face and giggled and Bella had kissed her grandma's cheek with no-nonsense firmness, Mrs. Stiles did seem to be a little happier and more calm.

"You should be on TV," Sophie said, applauding gently.

"It was Carrie's favorite song," Mrs. Stiles said. "A load of old rubbish, of course, but she and the girls sang it all the time."

"Not all the time," Bella corrected her, with her usual passion for total accuracy. "It's our cheering up song. I don't really know what it means but . . ."

"It's got a rocking good chorus?" Sophie said. Bella nodded and smiled.

Sophie felt more or less in control as she walked the girls to the bus stop. Her equilibrium was restored after the gathering tide of feeling that had threatened to breach her defenses at Mrs. Stiles's house. She felt as if she knew how to deal with Louis now, as if somehow Carrie had told her. She knew she couldn't shut the door on him, because after all, she had been the one to open it. She knew that she had to let him in for the girls' sake, and that what was best for them was what was important, no matter who else it hurt. This might be their only chance to know their father; she couldn't stand in the way of that. But she also knew that they needed someone to guide them and support them as they got to know him and as the possibilities of a future with him opened up. They'd need someone if, as Mrs. Stiles predicted, fatherhood was too much for him and he decided he couldn't take the children on after all. They'd need another option.

For some reason, ever since Sophie had spoken to Louis on the phone, she had felt doubly angry with him. She was angry with him for going, she was angry with him coming. It was an impossible way to feel, but she couldn't let it go. None of this should have been her responsibility. If he had been where he should have been, looking after his family, then maybe none of this, *none* of this would have happened. Maybe Carrie would still be alive a few hundred miles and just a phone call away.

When Sophie tried to imagine what effect Louis's return would have, there were all sorts of obstacles, all sorts of corners that she couldn't see around, but she knew one thing. The girls' atheist mother had made her their godmother for a reason, to stand by them in times of need, and Sophie was going to do it. Not because she had to, she discovered as they waited at the bus stop, but because she wanted to. And she wanted to not only for the children, whom she had gradually started to admire and even like, but for Carrie, whom she was slowly beginning to miss from the outside in, like a spring thaw. Sophie was missing her friend—fierce, strong, and independent Carrie, who had been her best friend once, on that sunny afternoon in Highbury, lying on the grass, playing the air guitar.

Carrie, who was more alive to her now that she had been for years.

It was almost dark when they got back to the flat. The pale winter sun had sunk beneath the bare tree branches that laced the horizon, leaving the cold gray sky with a faint amber glow. Sophie stopped by her much missed black VW Golf with cream leather interior and patted it fondly. And then she had an idea. She thought about the dog book and the chapter she had read on puppy car sickness. She thought about her CD collection, which was spread mostly over the floor in front of the passenger seat and contained the Manic Street Preachers' greatest hits.

"This is my car," she said to Izzy. Izzy looked at the car.

"She's got a name—can you guess what it is?"

Izzy blinked and looked at it. "Car?" she said after a moment. Sophie shook her head. "It's Phoebe," she said. Of course the car hadn't ever had a name in its life. Sophie loved her Golf because it went very fast on the highway and still felt like it was cruising. "She told me last night that she's lonely, and she knows you don't want to go for a ride in her or anything like that, but she wondered if you fancied just sitting in her for a bit because it would really cheer her up."

Izzy's face became deadly serious. "No thank you, Phoebe," she said.

The main difference between three-year-olds and dogs, Sophie realized, was that three-years-olds-talked back. "Never give up until you've cleared that first hurdle," the dog book said, so Sophie persisted. She opened Phoebe's rear passenger door and nodded at Bella to get in. "Well, how about if Bella sits in the back and I sit in the passenger seat here, like this"—Sophie opened the front passenger door and perched on the seat sideways—"with my feet on the pavement, and *you* sit on my lap? That would cheer Phoebe up no end."

"That's a good idea," Bella said, climbing in and sitting on the edge of the seat, her legs dangling over the side. Izzy remained motionless on the pavement, and although she was less than a foot away, she suddenly seemed almost out of reach.

"I was in the car with Mummy," Izzy said in a low voice. "And there was a big bang and I was a bit shaken up, wasn't I?"

Sophie bit her lip. "I know," she said.

"And Mummy went out of the car," Izzy said. "And she hasn't come back yet. Is she coming back?"

Sophie felt the waters close over her head and suddenly realized exactly what the expression *out of your depth* really meant. She had been prepared for crying and tantrums and holding of breath, but she hadn't been prepared for this. She looked over her shoulder at Bella, who sat perfectly still, her mouth and chin tucked into the neck of her coat, her eyes downcast.

"No, Izzy," Sophie said after a moment, because there was no other answer. "Mummy isn't coming back. Not because she doesn't love you or Bella or want to be with you but because she's gone now to be in the sky and the stars—" Sophie stopped, because she realized that Izzy took everything she said quite literally. She was now squinting up at the sky, looking for stars that had been blotted out by the city's orange glow.

"But I know one thing," Sophie said, regaining Izzy's attention. "Mummy wouldn't want you to be scared of anything, because you are such a very brave girl, and I know you don't want Phoebe to be sad, do you? So why don't you come and sit on my lap, and we'll sing 'Motorcycle Emptiness,' okay?"

Izzy looked confused.

"She means the little car song," Bella said out of the half dark. "We used to sing it a lot in the morning in our Mini on the way to school."

"The little car song," Sophie repeated.

Izzy took a step forward and climbed awkwardly onto Sophie's knees, winding her fist into Sophie's hair for support. She looked around the interior or the car. "Ready, Phoebe?" she asked the car.

"Vroom, vroom, ready," Sophie said in a gravelly voice out of the corner of her mouth.

Izzy started humming first, and then Bella, who was the only one who knew all the words—or at least Carrie's version of the words—chimed in. Awkwardly at first, Sophie joined in here and there. Gradually the mumbles and humming grew louder and louder until they finished the song on a rowdy crescendo.

"Yay!" Sophie said, applauding with her arms still around Izzy's middle.

Izzy smiled. "Did you like that, Phoebe?" she said. "Do you feel all better now, Car?"

"Vrooom, yes I do," Sophie said in her newfound car voice. And to think only a few weeks ago she was chairing meetings of international import in boardrooms. Still, you did what you needed to do. "Do you want to come for a ride with me next time? Um . . . vrooom?"

Izzy climbed off Sophie's lap and hopped back onto the pavement. "No thank you, Phoebe," she said. "But I will come and see you again soon. I promise."

Sophie's downstairs neighbor emerged from the communal front door and walked briskly down the steps just as Izzy chimed, "Please let us go in now, we are ever so cold," with Dickensian feebleness. The neighbor cast Sophie a chilly look over her shoulder and headed off to her Saturday night yoga class.

Izzy was already in bed waiting for Bella to tell her the next part of her story when Bella came into the kitchen with her glass for some fresh water. Sophie took it, tipped the old water away, and refilled it.

"That was a good idea today, Aunty Sophie. With the car, I mean. I think you helped Izzy a bit," Bella said.

Sophie looked at Bella and, with a surge of newfound confidence concerning child/dog psychology, asked her a question. "Listen—are you okay? Because, you know, if you wanted to talk about your mum . . . or your dad even . . ."

"I'm fine," Bella said, taking the glass carefully out of Sophie's hand, her expression completely neutral.

"Look, Bella," Sophie began. "All I'm saying is that—"

"I'm fine, Aunty Sophie," Bella said, smiling just to prove it, with a wide-toothed mirthless grin. "Come on, it's the pen-ult-i-mate part of my story tonight." Bella used the word she had heard the BBC announcer use about half an hour before with consider-able care.

"Okay." Sophie said. "That sounds exciting."

Later, thrilled and relieved that Blossom the fairy pony looked like she would make it back to her home with the mermaids by the sea after all, Sophie went back into the living room and fished the dog book out from underneath some cushions. Artemis came out of the kitchen and gave her a passing glance before curling up on her chair and turning her back on Sophie just to make sure she didn't make any more reckless stroking attempts.

"What do you reckon, Artemis." Sophie asked the cat's back as she flicked through the pages. "Do you think there's anything in here about telling your abandoned puppy that Daddy's com-ing back?" Of course there wasn't, so Sophie threw the book on the floor and stared up at the ceiling. He was coming, so she had to tell them. But how? Then Sophie had, in her opinion, a quite brilliant idea.

Tess could tell them.

When that was settled, Sophie began the chapter on nutrition. It told her that chocolate can be fatal to dogs.

"Thank God we're not dogs, hey, Artemis?" she said to her cat. Artemis did not dignify the comment with a response.

Twelve

Tess sighed and looked out the window. Sophie, who usually enjoyed the winter because it was much more sensible than the summer and gave a girl opportunities for much better clothes, was not enjoying the end of January because the sun persisted in shining in crisp blue skies day after day. Sophie was not a fan of sunshine. It seemed to give usually normal people an excuse to wear far fewer clothes than suited them, turn up late for work, take weeks and weeks off, and dawdle about being wistful over some romantic liaison or another. She had hoped for a typical wet and gloomy English winter. But no, the sun kept shining, interfering with people's moods and, worse still, their daytime TV viewing. Sophie was glad she had blackout curtains, because she didn't know what she would have done without the TV in the last few weeks. TV, Sophie had decided in the small dark hours of the night, was the world's greatest invention, superseding the wheel, antibiotics, and, yes, even the open-toed sandal.

Tess sighed again.

"You seem a bit pissed off to be here, actually," Sophie said with an edge of recrimination.

Tess pursed her lips. "Well," she said, "it *is* Sunday. A day recognized in many cultures to be one of rest. But as the many messages you left me were so adamant that you had to see me, here I am. At your service." Tess was making no attempt to hide the irritation in her voice, which frankly, Sophie thought, was just plain unprofessional.

"Yes, well, you want to try having two kids in your house. Rest? What's rest? There are no days of rest around here," she said, raising a now rather bushy eyebrow. She backoned Tess into the kitchen and closed the door.

"So you'll want to know why I've asked you here today," Sophie said.

"I can hardly bear the tension," Tess replied dourly. "Look, if you want to tell me you've changed your mind about keeping the girls until we get Louis, then just tell me. That foster place has gone now, so I'll need all the notice I can have to—"

"How long did you say it would take your lot to find Louis?" Sophie asked, regretting the absence of a spotlight to shine in the social worker's eyes.

"Well, you know." Tess looked uncomfortable. "A couple of weeks—three or four at the most."

"Yes, that is what you told me," Sophie said. "Funny that, because you told Mrs. Stiles it would take *months.*"

Tess was momentarily flustered. "Ah well, yes. Because that was what *she* wanted to hear. I promise you, we have done our best," she protested feebly. "As much as resources and time will allow. And you know . . ." She faltered under Sophie's stony glare. "I can assure you that every possible undertaking has been . . . er . . . undertaken to—"

"So," Sophie interrupted her. "You are in the business of telling people what they want to hear instead of the truth, are you, Tess? You tell Mrs. Stiles it will take months so she doesn't have to worry about Louis stealing her grandchildren away and me that it's a matter of days so I'll be your free babysitter. How is that ethical?"

"Look . . . ," Tess began. "It's a question of priorities, and I genuinely did think it might be very quick to find Louis—but all things being equal, allowing for administration difficulties and intergovernmental authorities' communication—"

"It's all right. You can cut all the social worker speak. You don't have to look for Louis Flipping Gregory," Sophie said, enjoying her moment.

"I don't?" Tess asked, blinking.

"No, you don't, because I found him. Or rather, a private detective I hired did. It took two weeks. It was easy, actually." Sophie found that she had to press her lips together in order to prevent herself from sticking her tongue out and going "na-na-na-na" at Tess, Izzy style. "He's coming back to 'get his girls' apparently." Sophie did a passable impression of his deep and slightly gruff voice. "As if he owned them or something."

"Oh," Tess said again, sounding ashamed. "Well, that changes things."

"Yes, it does a bit, doesn't it? So do you want to tell me now why you lied about finding Louis, or shall we save it for another time? Perhaps for a formal complaint hearing?" she said icily. "Because I don't mind telling you I thought you were supposed to tell the truth. I thought it was in your job description?"

Tess screwed up her mouth into a tight knot. "I did tell you the truth, mostly. Look, they needed a place to stay and you seemed to think it was important that Louis might be back on the scene soon—so I let you draw your own conclusions. The point is—"

"My own conclusions!" Sophie raised her voice and then, re- membering the children in the room next door, took a deep breath and forcibly lowered it again. "You lied to me. That's mis- conduct probably."

Tess paused before answering. "The point is I did what I thought was best for Izzy and Bella. And I didn't lie. Not exactly." She tested a half smile on Sophie. "Look, I know you want what's best for those children as much as I do. Don't you?"

Sophie considered the question and found somewhat to her surprise that she did. "Of course I do," she said, glancing out the window and over the row upon row of rooftops and TV antennae that made up the cluttered horizon and wondering exactly when that had happened. She looked back at Tess and gave her a con- ciliatory half smile. "Okay," she said. "Let's forget that—for now. What is important is that you do your job."

"Of course it is," Tess said, sounding mildly offended.

"You have to vet Louis, make sure that he's fit to be father to those girls. You have to check and double-check everything he's been up to for the past three years."

"Of course," Tess said. "It goes without saying."

"And what if they don't like him—what then?"

Tess didn't waver. "We have to try our best to reconcile them, we will reconcile them."

Sophie nodded. There it was again—that absence of a decent Option B.

"And I thought it would be better coming from you," she said quickly, breaking eye contact.

"What would?" Tess asked her.

"The news—you know, about Louis coming home." Sophie glanced sideways at her. "You're trained to do that kind of thing, aren't you? Explain stuff like absent fathers and all that."

Tess sighed. "Right," she said. "Will you be there too?"

Sophie rolled her eyes. "Obviously." Admittedly, it had only just become obvious to her.

A strange thing had happened to her in the last twenty-four hours, something she hadn't expected. When she thought about the girls and what the future might hold for them, her stomach churned and she felt a deep sense of unease, as if the world she had once stood so firmly on was tilting and swaying. She wondered if for the first time in her life she was having an actual gut feeling, about Louis Gregory. If her rarely utilized woman's intuition existed deep within her after all, and now it was kicking in, telling her to be cautious.

So before Tess had arrived Sophie had sat on the loo for a long time (just in case it was indigestion) and concentrated on the feeling. It had, she realized, taken her an amazingly short time to feel totally responsible for Carrie's children. She concluded that the churning of her stomach was genuine fear. She knew that somehow she would have an impact on how they were going to live the rest of lives and that it would be up to her, at least partially, whether they were happy. Sophie closed her eyes and tried to visualize Carrie the last time she had seen her, getting that train at Paddington Station, until she could see Carrie smiling at her. Sitting on the loo with her eyes shut, Sophie smiled back at her.

She couldn't say she loved the girls exactly, because she wasn't exactly sure what that felt like. But she realized that gradually she had begun to feel something for them, an almost new emotion that she had only experienced once before, when she saw Artemis alone in a pen at the shelter. It was a strong and immovable impulse to protect them from anything harmful. She knew then that she had to make sure they were going to be okay, that she would have to do whatever it took to ensure their happiness.

"Look," Tess said. "I promise you absolutely that I won't let you or the girls down. I'll put Louis through every mill going, and until then—"

"Until then," Sophie said almost casually as she directed her gaze back to the urban horizon, "those girls aren't going anywhere."

Thirteen

I need a couple of minutes," Sophie said to Tess, patting her cheeks, which she knew had flared up during their conversation.

"Okay, you go and take some deep breaths, and then— Well, we might as well tell them, hadn't we?" Tess said, biting hard on her lip.

Sophie nodded and slipped past the girls, who had lost interest in the *EastEnders* omnibus and were in the process of making camp out of the sofa and the chair and Sophie's full-length leather coat. They both paused as she passed them, standing stock-still like a couple of meerkats expecting to be pounced on at any second by an enraged predator, but Sophie barely even glanced at her coat and offered them only an absent half smile as she headed to her bedroom.

"Right, now all we need is some tent pegs," she heard Bella say as she shut the door. She sat on her bed for a moment and stared across at the dressing table mirror. She thought about using her red-patches-green-cover-up-stick thing, but it had disappeared recently, quite probably another casualty of Izzy's apocalyptic attack on her makeup bag. Instead, she picked up a spray can of deodorant and held its cool, smooth surface against first one cheek and then the other.

As she sat on the bed, Sophie noticed a corner of pale pink material peeping out of her tightly shut closet. She opened the door, still clutching the deodorant to her face, and pulled the trapped garment free. It was a new dress that she had brought in the no-man's-land between Christmas and New Year's. She had bought it at the full price, 359 pounds, even thought she knew that less than a week later it would inevitably be half the price, because she had fallen in love with it instantly and because there was only one in her size. And she'd made a mental note not to go back to that shop until at least April so she wouldn't see how much the reduction was. Sophie didn't normally spend that much money on dresses—although, to be fair, she needed party dresses a lot more than most people—and she had never even heard of the designer, Shelli somebody. But for some reason that dress, with its twenties-style soft pink chiffon shift sliding over its deep pink silk underslip, had appealed to the closet romantic in her. She loved the four tiny velvet-covered buttons at the scoop neck and the extravagant beadwork, hundreds of beads on the fabric that radiated from the princess waist and flared into a handkerchief hemline. It was the kind of dress girls wore in musicals when dancing with their true loves for the first time under the light of the silvery moon. Plus, it was very flattering around the hips.

Sophie had been secretly looking forward to wearing it this week, at the Madison Corporation's New Year's party, which she had been so painstakingly organizing for Jake, and before Jake had announced quite plainly that he was attracted to her, she had been looking forward to him seeing her wear it and wondering whether it would make him notice her as a *woman*.

Unlike most corporate seasonal parties, it didn't fall on or as near to the actual holiday as possible, when nobody would really want to come anyway, but had been scheduled, rather cleverly Sophie thought, mainly because it was her idea, at almost the end of January. For exactly the time when all everybody could see was another long gray year exactly the same as the last year stretching out remorselessly ahead of them and a party was just what they needed. Jake had wanted it to be extravagant, a flagship event, and Sophie had made sure that it was going to be. It was Cal, though, who had found a venue which could make that requirement literally come true; a first-class ocean liner that was docked at Tower Bridge for a week every two months with a full-scale ballroom and top-notch catering staff that were occasionally available to hire for the right price. Guests could even book a berth for the night.

Ever since Cal had discovered it, they had both been waiting for the right client with the right schedule and the right budget to book it, too afraid to tell anyone, even Lisa, in case the idea somehow got leaked and someone else got the credit. The Madison Corporation was that client, and the event was going to be magical. It was the first party in ages that Sophie had actually been excited about.

Unconsciously, she marked the passing of time by the events she created and by what she wore to them. That dress had been hanging in her wardrobe silently ticking like a kind of alarm clock, counting down the routine days until something different and mildly thrilling happened.

Now, Sophie realized, the party, the bright pinnacle in her diary for weeks and weeks, didn't really matter anymore. It might boost her promotion chances. Jake would still be impressed by her looking blond and lightly fake-tanned in dusty pink. But the excitement a of wearing a floaty dress and matching satin shoes had somehow faded. Sophie fingered the edge of the material and took a breath as she hung the dress back in her wardrobe.

"Never mind," she told herself, patting her considerably cooled cheeks. "It won't be long before frocks and parties are the highlight of your life again." Except that, as Sophie padded back to the living room, where she heard Tess and the girls laughing, she had to admit she wasn't exactly sure if she wanted that to be true.

Tess had positioned the girls side by side in Artemis's armchair, where they sat wriggling and elbowing each other reflexively. As Sophie left her bedroom, Artemis had appeared through the open window and slunk past her, taking up her new favorite position on the arm of the chair by Bella's side. She ducked and tilted her head for Bella, who scratched her ears obligingly, and gave Sophie her usual glare.

"Well, here we are," Tess said, beaming at the girls.

It was exactly the same smile that she had offered to Sophie just before announcing Carrie's death. She really had to work on her delivering-important-news face, Sophie thought. She made it look like you were about to find out that you'd somehow won the lottery even though you never play, not that your world was about to be tipped upside down—again. Bella knows, Sophie thought, watching the girl narrow her dark eyes at Tess. She recognizes that smile.

"You two have had a lot to cope with, haven't you in the last few months?" Tess's smile widened.

"Yes, we have!" Izzy sang in agreement, assuming her grown-up face.

Bella nodded and crossed her arms.

Sophie looked at each girl's expression and felt an unfamiliar tightening in her chest.

"I know you've been moved about a lot, one place to another, and I know that . . ." Tess paused and rubbed her knees with her palms, making a rasping noise over her tights. "I know that you must miss Mummy very much."

"I do," Izzy said sadly, her narrow shoulders slumping. "I do, but she can't come back, because Aunty Sophie said she was in the sky, which is very far."

Bella put her spare arm heavily around Izzy's shoulders, pushing her slightly deeper into the cushion of the chair with the weight of her embrace.

"And you both have been very brave and very good. Aunty Sophie has told me how *especially* good you have been since you came to stay with her."

Sophie, Bella, and Izzy all looked at Tess with openmouthed disbelief.

"Well, mainly good, anyway," Tess said, hurrying along. "And you like it here, don't you?"

"I like the telly," Izzy said, brightening a little bit. "And I used to like chicken nuggets, but I don't anymore. I think I'd like fish fingers next and carrots. We used to have carrots, didn't we, Bella?" Bella nodded. "We had loads of butter on them so they wouldn't be too yucky." Bella nodded again. "Orange food is my favorite actually," Izzy finished.

"Tess," Sophie said, sort of under her breath, "just get to the point."

"So girls," Tess said, reinstating her beam. "Do you remember your daddy?"

"No," Bella said quickly. "We don't."

"I don't," Izzy agreed. "I haven't got a daddy, have I?" she asked with genuine curiosity. "Or a grandpa? Or . . . a dog?"

"Well, actually, Izzy you have—got a daddy, I mean."

Izzy's face transformed into a picture of pure delight and surprise, which Sophie would have been moved by if she hadn't seen her use exactly the same expression when she was confronted with a pair of her damp pants that she had cunningly slipped behind one of the last remaining sofa cushions the last time she hadn't quite made it to the loo.

"Oooh, Bella—we're getting a daddy!" she said, drumming her heels against the base of the armchair.

"No, we're not, Iz. Our dad's not around anymore. He left home when *she* was a baby," Bella said carefully to Tess, jerking her head sideways at her sister.

"Well, yes, I know, darling," Tess said. "But guess what? Your daddy is coming back to see you! And *maybe,* if you want it, girls, you might go and live with your daddy!" Tess clapped her hands together, and Izzy jumped off the armchair and began spinning. "Hoo-*ray*! Hoo-*ray*! Hooo-*ray*!" she shouted as she pirouetted.

"No he is not!" Bella stood up and shouted over her sister so that the younger girl stopped and stood stock-still. "He is not coming back here and I don't want to see him and she doesn't want to see him and we don't want him so if he comes here you can just tell him to go away again because nobody likes him or wants him!" She ran out of the room, slamming first the living room and then the flat door behind her.

"Oh, fuck," Sophie said, leaping over the back of the sofa after her with an athleticism she hadn't known she possessed.

Tess looked at Izzy, who returned her gaze standing perfectly still. After a moment, she unfroze herself by sheer force of will and crossed over to Tess, putting her hands on the social worker's knees. "She's not supposed to say *fuck* in front of us, is she?"

Mercifully, Bella had not opened the door onto the street and run under a bus, as Sophie had momentarily feared. She breathed a sigh of relief when she saw the girl huddled at the bottom of the stairs and walked slowly down to join her.

"Are you okay?" she asked.

"Yes." Bella lied badly, her voice slightly muffled through a layer of purple fleece.

Sophie brushed a locked of Bella's black hair away from her cheek and tucked it behind her ear. "I'm sorry, I knew it would be a shock and everything, but I really thought you'd be pleased . . ." This was true. She had just assumed the girls would leap into Louis's arms whether or not he was decent father material. It had never occurred to her that they might not want him.

"I'm not pleased," Bella said, turning her face a little so that Sophie could see one eye and half of her mouth.

Hesitantly, Sophie reached out her palm and rubbed Bella's back. "I can see that," she said with half a smile. "But, well, do you remember your dad at all, Bella?"

Bella sat up and brushed her hair out of her face a few times. "Yes," she said darkly. "I was a bit older than Izzy when he . . . he just went."

Sophie tried to frame the million or so questions she had into one that was manageable for a girl of six and a bit. "Well, was he unkind to you or to Mummy, was he mean? I mean, did he ever . . . hurt you?" she asked carefully. To her huge relief, Bella shook her head.

"No," she said. "But he went away, didn't he? He left us all alone. He didn't come back. He didn't even say good-bye to me, and I thought . . . I thought he was my friend. He used to say I was his best friend. After that, Mum said we didn't need him. We didn't need any man to look after us because we looked after each other—we were the Three Musketeers." Bella stared at her knees.

Sophie tried again. "I know that this must be hard, Bella, but well . . . he is coming all this way to see you—that must mean something. And when I told him—"

"*You* told him?" Bella said quickly, looking up at Sophie.

"Yes," Sophie confessed. "When I told him what had happened, he said he'd come straightaway, as soon as he could." Sophie pushed her own misapprehensions to one side. "So he must care about you to do that, musn't he?" Bella did not move, so Sophie continued. "And well, you are going to need a proper place to live soon, and I just thought it would be better if it was with—"

"We've *got* a proper place." Bella stared at Sophie with a deep furrow between her brows.

Sophie blinked at her and winced internally. She hadn't expected this.

"We live here, don't we?" Bella said. "With you? You said at that day-care place we could stay with you."

Sophie took her hand away from Bella's shoulder and dropped her head. It hadn't occurred to her that Bella might have thought her stay in the flat was anything other than temporary, and that her promise at the childminder's was more general than specific.

"Aren't we staying here with you?" Bella said, looking worried. "Have we done something wrong again? I know we're naughty sometimes, but it's usually by accident and—"

Sophie shook her head and felt her chest tighten again. "It's not because you're naughty," she said gently. "Look, Bella, right now I don't know what's going to happen next because so much has happened already that I never expected. But you have to know that when you came here it was only supposed to be for a week or two . . ." Sophie stopped. "You're not supposed to live with me forever. You wouldn't want to in my silly little flat with no garden now, would you?"

"I wouldn't mind," Bella said. "Will we have to move again?" Her voice dwindled away to almost nothing.

Sophie looked at her tiny frame, so stiff and resilient, and she wanted to say something, anything to make Bella feel happier and more secure. But she couldn't lie to her, not now, even if comforting lies were what the girl wanted to hear. She and Izzy deserved the truth.

"Yes," Sophie said softly. "I'm sorry, Bella."

"With who then?" Bella's face was ashen under the bright hall light, her voice small and feather light. "With Dad? Strangers like the childminder?"

Sophie cursed herself inwardly. Just as she thought she was getting the hang of communicating with Bella, she went and put her foot in it. She felt her ineptitude all too keenly.

"All you've been through—it must be so hard for your, Bella," she said eventually, sidestepping her question. "I think you're amazing. You cope so well when you must miss your mum so much—"

"I don't miss her," Bella said. "I can't miss her. I haven't got time, you see, because since she went away everything keeps changing and just when I think it's going to be okay it changes again and I have to get used to all new things and I have to be in charge of worrying about what's going to happen to us. Mummy told me that I was in charge when she wasn't around, of looking after Izzy I mean. I think . . ." Bella paused for a long moment. "If I start thinking about her and missing her, I'm afraid I won't be in charge anymore. I'll be too sad and then I'll forget to do anything else."

Sophie pulled Bella to her, impulsively wishing that she could draw all the pain out of her small body and absorb it. It was the first time she had really hugged her goddaughter.

"I do see," she said, thinking about the first months after her dad died. "I really do. But you know what? You don't have to be in charge. I know that you feel like you do—but you don't. You've got Tess and Grandma and me and even Artemis to do all the worrying and the looking after for you and Izzy. If you want to be sad, you won't be letting anyone down. Your mum wouldn't think so, not for a second." Sophie paused for a moment and thought very carefully about what she was about to say. "I don't know your dad, Bella. I don't know why he went and I don't know why he didn't keep in touch with you, but I do think you sort of have to give him a chance. Because he is after all your dad, and you said he did used to be your friend."

"But what if he's horrible to us?"

"Well, if he is, then you don't have to live with him. You don't have to do anything you and Izzy aren't happy with, okay? Everyone is here to make sure that you and Izzy are happy and safe."

Bella looked up at Sophie, her dry eyes burning. "But what will we do then?" she asked. "If we can't stay here?"

There had to be a moment like this, Sophie thought, in everyone's life, when the very next thing you say might change you and the world as you knew it forever. She felt her stomach dip and churn as if she had just run headlong at a cliff edge and brought herself to a stop at its very brink.

"Then we'll work out what's best," she answered, feeling like a coward unable to deliver the promise that Bella wanted.

"What's best?" Bella said dimly, staring down at her feet again.

"Yes," Sophie said.

Bella sat up a little and lifted her chin to look at Sophie. "Okay," she said with a look of weary resignation that should never have visited her young face. "Okay, Aunty Sophie."

There had to be something, Sophie thought, some promise she could make to Bella and Izzy that she absolutely knew she could keep. Some promise that could give the children something solid to rely on.

"Bella, I've been flaky, I know I have," she said. "Dragging you to the office and back. Making you watch TV all day long, not knowing what to feed you and then just feeding you one thing, but please believe me when I say I want you to have the best and happiest life you can. I really, really do. And you just wouldn't have that with me—would you?" Bella blinked at her and said nothing. "But I promise you—whatever happens, I'll be on your side. I'll stick by you and Izzy. I'll never let you down. I promise. Always, forever, whatever." Sophie said the three words on an impulse and sat back a little as Bella's eyes widened.

"How did you know?" she asked, resting her cheek against Sophie's arm with a sudden touching display of affection that Sophie had not expected. She felt Bella's breath on her skin and kissed the top of Bella's head, and for a moment it felt as if there was something physical connecting them, a new closeness created on this bottom stair. She would never have known how to kiss Bella before that moment, and suddenly it seemed perfectly natural.

"Know what?" Sophie said to the top of her goddaughter's head.

"That's Mummy's special promise to us. Whenever she said 'Always, forever, whatever,' we knew—we knew that things were really, *really* true."

"Well then, you know that you can trust me," Sophie said, and Bella tightened their embrace.

It happened then, like a slow-turning circle finally completing itself. Sophie found that she was beginning to care more about what happened to Bella and Izzy than she cared about what happened to herself.

Fourteen

W hat, nothing at all?" Tess said, attempting to stir some life into her forlorn cup of coffee as she sat at her desk.

"Nothing. Not a word," Sophie told her over the phone, sitting on what used to be her bed. "I mean, it's been . . ." She unfurled a finger for each day since she had spoken to Louis. "Saturday, Sunday, Monday, Tuesday, Wednesday. Five days if you count today. Five days. It doesn't take five days to get anywhere anymore unless you're walking. I mean, it's not as if he was in deepest, darkest Peru. Well, anyway, it doesn't take five days, does it?"

Tess sat back in her chair. "No, I wouldn't have thought so," she said. "But I suppose there are other considerations. Maybe he had to give notice at the charity—" Sophie barked a short laugh at the word *charity*. Tess waited for a moment to continue. "*Maybe* he couldn't get a flight or get the money for a flight. Have you thought about calling him again?"

Sophie glossed over that rather obvious idea. She didn't want to dial that number that had cost her fifty-five pounds an hour plus VAT and talk to him, because that would mean that he was still in deepest, darkest Peru which had implications she was aware of but not quite ready to think about yet.

"He said he was coming right away. He made it sound like he was going to leave right at that minute and get on a plane. And the girls are on edge. Bella is really upset about the whole thing, and Izzy goes mental every time the phone or doorbell rings. It's been a nightmare keeping them occupied."

"Well, TV does wear a bit thin after a while," Tess said.

"We haven't just been watching TV actually," Sophie said resentfully. "We've been to the park twice, the corner shop, Grandma Stiles's, *and* we sat in the car with the doors open and played CDs for a couple of hours."

"Izzy too?" Tess asked, genuinely impressed.

"Yes," Sophie said with more than a hint of pride. "Next time we're shutting Phoebe's doors, and the time after that I might turn the engine on. We'll be on road trips before you know it."

"Phoebe?" Tess inquired.

"Yes, Phoebe—that's the car's name," Sophie said a little sheepishly.

"That's a really good idea," Tess told her with naked astonishment.

"Thanks for your unwavering belief," Sophie said wryly, neglecting to mention she got the idea out of the dog book. "And they really like shopping, so we've done quite a lot of shopping. I rebought all of my makeup, so Izzy owes me all her pocket money for the rest of her life, and we found them some really cute shoes, bought me some ugly sensible ones and some more jeans, and—we even went to the supermarket."

"And I bet it was better than last time, right?" Tess said.

"No, it was a god-awful nightmare, but you *see*," Sophie explained seriously, "at least this time I knew what to expect, so it wasn't so bad. I think I'm building up a resistance to the horror. It's sort of like when you become an alcoholic and after a while it doesn't matter how much vodka you drink it doesn't make you drunk anymore?" Tess decided to leave that part out of her next report. "All in all," Sophie concluded. "We've had a pretty good time."

"That's really great," Tess said. "But listen, we have to give the man every chance to do the right thing. I mean, that was big news you gave him. He might have needed a day or two to come to terms with it."

Sophie rolled her eyes. "Oh, what, like I got, you mean?" she said sulkily.

"You weren't married to Carrie," Tess admonished her.

"No, and neither was he for very long!" Sophie said. Just at that moment the doorbell vibrated through the flat with its insistent electronic rattle.

"It's the door, it's the door, it's the *door*, IT'S THE DOOR!" Izzy's cries grew louder as she made her way from one side of the flat to the other.

"Oh, shit," Sophie said. "I've gotta go. Izzy, don't open the flat door!" The sound of the flat door banging hard into the hall wall echoed in Tess's ears. "Izzy, don't you dare open the front door!" Tess heard Sophie call out.

"If it's him, ring me," Tess said. But she realized she was talking to a dial tone.

"Oh, it's you," Izzy said, looking up at Cal. Sophie arrived 0.01 seconds after Izzy had opened the main front door, streaking past Bella, who stalked into the bedroom and shut the door firmly behind her.

"What did I say about opening the front door?" Sophie asked Izzy, ignoring Cal for a moment.

"You said don't open the front door," Izzy replied, looking up at her sweetly.

"And what have you just done?" Sophie asked.

Izzy gave Sophie a look that implied she thought Sophie was a bit of an idiot. "I opened the front door!" she said slowly and carefully, because it was obvious.

"But I said not to!" Sophie said, raising her voice a little and stamping her foot a little bit.

"I know!" Izzy said. "But it's not him anyway, it's just *him*." And she flopped facedown on the doormat and lay there perfectly still in mercifully silent protest. Sophie, who had become used to this particular maneuver, had stopped worrying that Izzy was suffering from blackouts and looked up at Cal.

"Aren't you supposed to be individually testing thirty-eight thousand fairy lights for the Madison party?" she asked with a tight smile.

"Couldn't be arsed," Cal said drily. He looked down at Izzy. "I have to say, Izzy, I thought you'd be more pleased to see a man with an Animal Park play set."

Izzy did not move.

"Animal Park doesn't match up to her daddy," Sophie told Cal, worrying about how much the three-year-old had invested in the appearance of her father. She had thought Izzy might just forget about it after it was mentioned. But she didn't; the arrival of Louis seemed to be the subject of her every thought and question. "But why are you here, Cal? You really should be at the ship, you know—marching about with your clipboard giving all the workmen a hard time!"

Cal looked skeptical. "I've already done that," he said. "Even though it's not in my job description. I need you to check some final details with me and sign off some invoices. I'm not author-ized."

Sophie nodded. "Come on then, Iz," she said. "Upsadaisy."

"I wanted it to be the daddy man, not the flowery smelling man!" Izzy wailed. Sophie scooped her up, flung her over one shoulder, and began staggering up the stairs.

"I feel strangely rejected," Cal mused as, back in the living room, Sophie deposited Izzy on the armchair and looked at her. She wasn't really crying; it was this other type of crying she did—a sort of dry, repetitive whining, usually when there was a remote danger that she might not be the center of the universe for five seconds.

"How about you take a chocolate biscuit to Bella to cheer her up?" Sophie suggested.

Izzy's face instantly transformed into a radiant smile. "And me as well?" she said. "Can I take me one too?"

Sophie nodded and handed Izzy two cookies. "Go on then, and don't eat Bella's on the way!" Izzy giggled and ran out of the room. Sophie looked at the packet of chocolate biscuits and then at Cal. She took one out and put it entirely in her mouth.

"So what's the problem?" she asked him through a haze of crumbs.

"Oh, if only Jake could see you now," Cal said, observing her with some distaste. "If you had a sex life, you know, you wouldn't be bulimic. Anyway, there are no problems. I just wanted to check a few details with you, like you have confirmed the menus with the caterers . . ."

"Check," Sophie said breezily.

"You have okayed the pyrotechnics with Health and Safety chaps."

"Check," Sophie said, as if there would be anything that she, the queen of perfection, would overlook.

"You have arranged a babysitter that won't send the girls into hysterics?"

"Che——- Oh, fuck," Sophie cursed and took another biscuit from the packet.

"I knew it," Cal said. "Well, you have to be there. All the big cheeses will be there, including Gillian. The Madison do is possibly the biggest party McCarthy Hughes has ever thrown this side of the Atlantic. It's going to be fabulous, and you'll be there in the spotlight, everybody looking at you and thinking how wonderful you are."

"I know!" Sophie wailed. "But the girls don't like anyone but you. Will you do it?"

"I'm not doing it," he said. "I've worked my butt off for this party. I'm going to be there to enjoy it."

Sophie nodded. Cal was right. Besides, he was the master at making sure people were mixing and at troubleshooting any incipient problems. After all the help he had given her, he was the one who deserved the credit most of all.

"Right," she said.

"So . . . ?" Cal waited.

"Well, I mean, that's it, isn't it? I can't go," she said, nodding in the general direction of the bedroom. "I can't take those two to a grown-up party. There are too many choking hazards for one thing. Plus, practically everything is flammable. Imagine the insurance costs if we sank it!"

"There's got to be someone," Cal said, thinking furiously. "Someone that they know you won't leave them with forever. Someone strange enough for them to feel at home with—"

"Thanks," Sophie said.

Cal clicked his fingers. "How about their grandma?" he suggested.

"Nope, she'd never get up those stairs," Sophie said.

"No, their other grandma—your mum, I mean," Cal added, as if it were obvious.

"Well, technically, she's not their grandma, *but . . .*" Sophie considered the prospect of her mum in charge of Bella and Izzy for a couple of hours. She had not heard from her mother since the night she had come around with the dog book, not unless you counted one phone message, which consisted entirely of yapping dogs, and that was probably more to do with Scooby messing with the speed-dial button than her mum trying to call her. Anybody else's mother would have been here helping out, taking an interest, interfering at the very least. Still, it did seem like her mum was the last—no, only—resort.

"Would they like her, do you think?" Sophie asked him.

"They'll love her. She's bonkers," Cal said. "Plus, she can come here and they'll feel safe."

"What the hell?" Sophie said, picking up the phone and dialing her mum's number.

After the usual dog-related pauses, her mother came to the phone. "Hello?" she said.

"Mum, it's me," Sophie told her. "Listen, I've got a favor to ask you, and I really need you to do this for me, no arguments."

Sophie kissed Izzy and then Bella on the tops of their heads.

"Those pajamas are fab," she told them. "Total princess jammies."

Izzy giggled. "You look like a *real* princess," she said. "All sparkly and lovely, and you don't smell. I quite love you when you look nice, actually."

Sophie glanced down at herself. Thanks to her mum's early arrival, she hadn't scrubbed up too badly. She'd even managed to shave her legs and wax her top lip, as well as shower and wash her hair. She hadn't had time to straighten it, though, so it just sort of wafted about, like a cloud of gold as Bella had poetically put it. More like a flyaway mass of static, Sophie thought, but she preferred Bella's description.

"It's not bad, this dress, is it?" she said, delighted that after mountains of chips it still fitted her.

"You do look pretty," Bella said solemnly. "But you are coming back, aren't you?"

"Of course!" Sophie exclaimed, crouching down with some difficulty in her heels. "Now you two be good for my mum, okay? Go to bed and go to sleep, and I'll see you when I get in."

"You'll definitely come in our room and see us, won't you?" Bella insisted.

"Yes, I definitely will," Sophie said. She stood up, using Izzy's head to steady herself. "Right, I'll be off then."

Sophie walked down the steps to the street door with her mum. "Now you know what to do, don't you?" she asked her.

"Yes." Iris nodded. "Watch telly and get drunk."

"Mum!" Sophie protested. "I'm serious!"

"So am I, darling. Okay, don't let them play with matches, don't give them any sharp objects, and don't let them run under a bus," Iris recited the list of concerns that Sophie had given her verbatim, although she considered most of them unlikely since both the girls were going to be asleep. "Look, you've been doing this for a little over three weeks. I've been doing it for thirty-five years—"

"Mum, I'm twenty-nine!" Sophie said, appalled. "And I'm not joking about the bus thing. The latch on the door downstairs is, well, dodgy—"

"They'll be fine. I've got your cell phone number. I'm just glad you asked me to help you at last."

"What do you mean? I was waiting for you to offer to help me!" Sophie exclaimed.

"Oh no, dear," her mother said mildly. "I learned a long time ago never to offer to help you. It just annoys you, because you usually know best. I've been waiting years for you to need me for anything. Now, off you go and have a good time." Iris gave Sophie a look of approval, and Sophie smiled warmly at her mum.

"You've really helped me out here, you know," she said.

"I knew I was good for something," he mother told her. "And you look lovely. I'm sure you could get a boyfriend if you tried."

"Yes, but do I want one?" Sophie mumbled as her taxi pulled up, thinking of Jake waiting for her aboard the ship.

Fifteen

It looks incredible, doesn't it?" Cal said with quiet pride in the party he had contributed so much to as he leaned next to Sophie looking over the golden balustrade that encircled the ballroom. "Exactly like *Titanic,* the movie."

Sophie nodded and sipped her martini. "Yes, it does," she said. "But hopefully without all the sinking and drowning and Celine Dion."

Cal gave her a disapproving look. "Don't diss Dion," he told her. "She gives me hope that somewhere out there I might one day find my very own Leonardo to float about on a piece of wood with and then watch freeze to death."

Sophie looked surprised. "Really?" she said. "One day you want to get that committed to someone?"

Cal thought about the prospect for a moment and then shrugged. "No," he said. "Probably not. At least not with any of that lot down there." He sighed and flicked his imaginary hair out of his eyes. "I don't know. Why are all the sexy men either married or straight?" he asked woefully.

Sophie looked bemused. "You *are* joking, aren't you?" she said, looking at the motley crew of suited doppelgängers dancing like their dads below.

"Of *course* I'm joking," Cal said. "God, considering you're my boss, you're pretty dim sometimes." Sophie watched a parade of waitstaff emerge from the kitchen in perfect unison with tray after tray of canapés and spread out among the ravenous crowd. It was sort of like watching feeding time in an incredibly well-dressed tank of piranhas.

"Actually, Cal, I've been thinking about that today," Sophie began. "You know when you came around this morning, I had this sort of revelation . . ."

Cal finished his martini and looked at the empty glass regretfully. "Oh, God, not another lipstick lesbian—it's like a plague!" he said. "Still, I always suspected."

Sophie ignored him. "I was thinking that you've more or less organized this party by yourself and, well, I wondered why it was you never pushed me to promote you. I mean, you've been my PA for years—a brilliant one. You've never asked to have a shot at organizing your own event when the chance is thrust upon you, and yet, well, Cal, you're brilliant at it."

"I know," he said. Sophie looked at him. "Look, I like working for you, my salary goes up every year and I get a good bonus. My job is seriously easy, and I'm only twenty-five. I like coming into work at nine, swanning around until five, and then going out to blow my wages. It does get to be a bit of a drag when your boss's dead best friend's kids turn up and then suddenly that bit in your contract about performing extra hours as and when necessary becomes all too real. But, well, don't let this go to your head—but you're a good boss."

Sophie glowed with pleasure. She'd always *thought* she was.

"Cal, I want to promote you," she said.

"Oh, God," he said. It wasn't quite the grateful reaction that Sophie had been expecting.

"It's just that I realized today exactly what it is you do. You're right, you do much, much more than your job description."

Cal rolled his eyes. "I could have told *you* that," he said.

"Well," Sophie persisted, "if you want it, you've got it."

Cal blinked and looked at her. "Got what?" he said, looking bemused.

"The promotion!" Sophie exclaimed. "I've talked to Gillian about it already, and she thinks it's a great idea. We both think that you'd make a fantastic account manager. You are brilliant at your job, Cal—God knows how, considering you spend most of the day surfing the Internet for vintage Galliano—it's only fair you get recognized for it." Sophie watched Cal watching the heaving crowd below in unexpected silence. She watched the ever-changing disco colors light and relight the halo of his profile with pink, then blue, and then gold.

A small, sweet smile turned up the corners of his mouth. "Really?" he said, his habitual urbane chic guard slipping just a little. And then, "I don't know, Sophie, it's hard work, isn't it? And I'm not keen on change, I'm a Cancer."

Sophie shook her head. "I just think you can do more in the company," she said. "I'm offering you a chance. If this was the other way around, you'd tell me to get out of my rut of insecurities and paranoia and start living my life for once, and anyway you're almost doing all of it already. You'd only notice the change in your pay check."

Cal glanced at Sophie. "That's my kind of change," he said. He looked at her for a moment longer. "All right then. As you're begging me, I accept." Sophie offered him her hand, and they shook on it. "I want more money, of course, and I still won't sleep with you, though you realized that, didn't you?"

Sophie sighed. "That is definitely not in the job description," she said emphatically.

Sophie wondered how she could look at her watch without offending Jake, who had found her forty minutes ago and had her pinned in a corner.

"My God," he'd said, looking her up and down with naked interest the first moment he saw her. "You look stunning."

And he had stared at her for a moment longer, making Sophie squirm a little.

"Sorry," Jake had said. "It's just— Well, you look incredible." He'd smiled, and it was a sweet, boyish smile. That had made Sophie smile and blush too.

And she had enjoyed standing here in Jake's company. He'd listened with real interest to her telling him the latest news about the children and her concerns and hopes about finding Louis. He'd laughed at Sophie's oddly proud tales of Izzy's antics and looked genuinely touched when she told him about her and Bella's heart-to-heart.

"You really care about those kids, don't you?" Jake had said to her a few minutes ago.

"Well," Sophie had replied, "I suppose I do—in a way."

Jake had looked at her with a renewed intensity that made her take a step back from him. "You'd make an incredible mother," he'd said, smoldering at her.

"No, I wouldn't," Sophie had said reactively, scared by the comment.

"You would," Jake had asserted.

"I wouldn't," Sophie had insisted, and then she had clamped her mouth shut, realizing that the exchange was sounding dangerously close to a playground spat.

Jake had cast an embarrassed glance at his toes before looking at Sophie again. "I scare you, don't I?" he'd said.

"You don't," Sophie had lied, shaking her head firmly so that her hair flicked over her shoulders.

"Why do I scare you?" Jake had asked himself more than Sophie. "I think it's because I wear my heart on my sleeve and I show you how much I like you. I'm too straightforward and should be more mysterious and cool, right?" Sophie had shrugged. "I apologize, Sophie," he'd said, and he had looked so sad that impulsively Sophie had closed the space between them and put her hand on his arm.

"Don't be sorry," she'd said. "I'm just a bit rusty, that's all. I haven't done this for a while, and I'm English, you know. Reserved and all that." Jake's smile had faded as he looked into her eyes, and Sophie had felt sure that at any moment she would be swept away by his sexual magnetism and charisma, because if she wasn't, then seriously, she had to be clinically dead.

But to her amazement and dissatisfaction, even as Jake's soft, firm lips had closed in on her in the shadows, she'd discovered she was worried that she should be mingling more. That she should be networking, exchanging business cards and building contacts. She should have checked that the second wave of canapés were ready to go and that the drinks were still flowing, and, most important, that the pyrotechnics people had everything ready for the fake New Year's countdown that was due to take place at 10:30—well, it was a school night.

Jake's fingers were entwined in the hair at the nape of her neck and his hand pressed firmly into the small of her back until finally, nudged out of her detached reverie, Sophie returned his kiss. She felt his reaction with a physical jolt. She broke off the kiss and took a step back.

"You're incredible," Jake said, his voice dark with longing. "Let's get out of here. I've got a room onboard tonight."

Sophie looked at him uncertainly. In the last few moments of that embrace, she had wanted to kiss him, she had wanted his hands on her, or at least her body had wanted him.

"I don't know," she said. "I mean the canapés and the fireworks . . ."

"Come on," he said, brushing aside her protest as he took her hand and started to lead her through the crowd and back to the cabins. Sophie let him lead her because part of her wanted to go, part of her wanted to know what it would be like to be undressed by Jake in the state cabin of a luxury cruise liner, but a much bigger part of her knew with some relief that it wasn't going to happen. Not here, not tonight anyway, and especially not with her brothel pink pants on.

"Jake," Sophie said, pulling him to a stop and then letting go of his hand. She lifted her chin and took a step back, conscious of the crowd around them.

"I can't," she said, shaking her head. "I'm at work here! Gillian would kill me." She laughed awkwardly, but Jake looked disappointed.

He sighed. "*I'm* sorry," he said. "A little too much good champagne and not enough beautiful you. It's made me a little crazy. Of course you're right."

Sophie smiled at him gratefully. "I have to go," she said, gesturing at the party that was simmering all around them. "I've got to check the last lot of arrangements, and then I've got to get back to the girls before they burn the house down or something."

Jake grinned and shrugged. "One day I'll get you to myself," he said.

"You will," Sophie said, wanting to give him something.

"I could take you home," he offered hopefully.

"No," she said. "This is your party! Stay and have a good time."

She turned on her heel and walked quickly into the crowd without looking back, knowing that Jake would be watching her.

"God, you are shit," Eve said, appearing at her elbow with barely a rustle of her long, extremely clingy green dress. Sophie thought she looked like the snake in the Garden of Eden.

"Thanks," Sophie said, drily. "And how are you?"

"I mean with Jake there—the poor bloke's been trying to shag you all night." Eve squinted at a shocked looking Sophie. "Can you really not tell, or is it all an elaborate hoax to make you more elusive and alluring?"

Sophie shook her head. "There is nothing going on between me and Jake," she said firmly. She could trust Cal, but it would be disastrous if any gossip found its way onto the office treadmill. Not that Eve needed any hard facts. In this case, Sophie's reputation as an oblivious ice queen seemed to be standing her in good stead.

"Good God, woman," Eve said. "He's so hot for you they practically had to raise Tower Bridge to accommodate his hard-on!"

Sophie shrugged. "It's been lovely chatting with you, Eve," she said. "But I've got a few more details to sort out for *my* party."

"Bitch," Eve said as Sophie glided off toward the kitchen, and Sophie knew that, even though Eve had had the last word, *she* had won. The event had won for her. It was truly brilliant.

And somewhere out there in the crowd, Gillian would be thinking exactly the same thing.

The tramp sitting on her doorstep took the shine off Sophie's triumphant glow. When she saw him, she sighed and considered walking past her own home and lurking about around the corner for a bit in the hope that he would get bored and move on. She watched him for a second from behind a plane tree. He was a hulking big man with one of those seriously suspect beards that look as if they might harbor mini-ecosystems all their own. He was leaning back, resting his elbows on the steps, looking for all the world as if he were enjoying the view from his balcony across the Italian Alps.

It wasn't that Sophie didn't have sympathy for homeless people, she did. After all, she gave five pounds ninety-nine a month to Shelter and ticked the box about the tax refund bit, so she knew that she cared. She just didn't care for one of them being on her doorstep. Nevertheless, he looked like he was there indefinitely. There was no way around it, Sophie decided. She'd just have to go over there, ask him very politely to move, and hope he wasn't the belligerent type. She scooped up the loose change in her pocket and held it in her fist.

"Here's three twenty-eight," she said, holding out the change. She was alarmed to see that she made the tramp jump, which she thought could never be a good tactic. "Move on, please, my husband's a policeman. He'll be home in a minute."

The tramp looked her up and down with a distinct air of bewilderment. "Fuck," he said, half-laughing. "You really startled me. But anyway, you're here now, thank God. I'm freezing."

Shit, Sophie thought, he isn't belligerent but he's delusional. And he sounded younger than the average tramp, although, to be honest, Sophie had no idea what the average tramp age was.

"Look," she said, wondering if he looked yellowish because of the streetlight or if he was in fact yellow. "I understand that it must be hard being homeless and everything, but . . ."

The tramp stood up abruptly, causing her to stumble backward down the step and lose her balance momentarily. She felt

the man's arm encircle her waist and steady her before withdrawing to a respectable distance. It was then that she realized he
smelled rather nice for a tramp.

Sophie took a step back and squinted hard at the vagrant in
the glow of the streetlamp. "Oh," she said bluntly. "It's you.
Hello, Louis."

He looked older than Sophie remembered, which would be
partly because of the beard and partly because of the fact that he
was older, six years older, as was she.

"Your mum wouldn't let me in at all," Louis said amiably as
they stood in the shared hallway. "She said you'd kill her if she
did and that I'd better wait until tomorrow to talk to you. But
I've waited so long—I couldn't wait until then. So I sat here until you came back. At least it's warm in here. It's freezing outside." He looked her up and down once again, with the benefit
of electricity.

Sophie blinked at him in the bright hallway. The lights in this
communal part of the converted house were set to stay on for
only five or so minutes at a time. In two or three minutes, they
would blink out, and she found herself hoping that when she
turned them back on, he'd be gone. Now that she could see him
clearly, it was obvious that he wasn't a tramp, he was just rather
travel-worn and scruffy. He had a sort of red quilted parka on
over a thick sweater, and until he had taken it off a moment ago,
a cap pulled down over thick, longish black hair. And his beard
wasn't initially as bushy as Sophie had first thought—at least a
third of it was actually just the fringe of his black scarf tucked up
under his chin against the cold.

"I didn't think you were coming," she said, glancing up the
stairs to the front door of her flat and suddenly wishing that she
was on the other side of it. "I mean, you said you were coming
right away—about a week ago."

It seemed unreal to be standing here in the hallway with Louis. She had almost stopped believing that he was real, and now that he was here, now that his physically imposing presence was making even deeper ripples in her previously tranquil life, Sophie found she did not know what to say to him. She had totally and uncharacteristically failed to prepare. Besides, she was irritated with him for being so relaxed. She unwound her pink beaded scarf from her neck and slipped off her faux fur coat. She suddenly felt very hot.

"Wow," Louis said, and then, seeing Sophie's expression, added, "Really nice dress I mean. I like pink."

Sophie raised an eyebrow, gratified to see him unsettled at last by the oddness of their situation. "So what now?" she asked, sweeping her hair back over her shoulders, a haughty gesture Carrie used to tease her about endlessly.

"Well," Louis said, looking around the hallway and showing a great deal of interest in the cornicing, "you know, just, right then, let's . . . get on with it?" He clapped his hands and rubbed them like a classic silent movie villain. "Look, I'm sorry I didn't get here right away, but I couldn't leave the school totally in the lurch. I had things to sort out. I had to get money together for a flight. Luckily, I already had most of it saved up. Look, I know I hung up on you—that was stupid and rude. I don't think I really knew where my head was at just then, if you know what I mean." Sophie supposed she did. "Anyway, I'm sorry about that and sorry it took me so long. It's been a nightmare getting here, believe me." If Louis expected any sympathy, he was disappointed. "So, like I say, I couldn't just leave people in the lurch," he finished.

"Couldn't you?" Sophie heard herself say, her voice crisp with frost. "I rather thought that was your forte."

Louis's open, friendly smile froze and wilted. "Look, I'm here now, and I want to see my girls. My daughters. I've come a very long way, and all I've been thinking about is this moment. Let me see them, please."

Sophie studied Louis, standing casually in her hallway. He looked perfectly comfortable with the situation. He didn't look anything like a man whose ex-wife had recently died, leaving his abandoned children virtual orphans. Sophie had not expected him to come tonight, but now that he was here, she had at least expected him to be nervous, full of regrets and remorse, and sort of guilty-looking. He was none of those things, and that made her furious.

"The girls are asleep," she told him briskly, stepping onto the bottom stair so that she was almost equal with his height. "Surely you must realize that you can't just walk back into their lives, wake them up, and say, 'Hey, girls, Daddy's back!' after three years!" She found she wanted to say something, anything to shake his almost indecent composure. "Besides, Izzy doesn't really know who you are," she told him bluntly. "And Bella doesn't even want to see you."

Louis's face did not move a muscle as he returned Sophie's direct look. "Listen," he said in measured tones. "You are the one that found me. I thought you'd be glad to see me. And anyway— they are my children. And if I want to, I can go up those stairs and take them out of here tonight. You can't stop me."

Sophie moved up another step. She knew that he was right, at least about the first part: she had been the one to find him and should be glad to see him, but still, she had to will her simmering fury not to manifest itself by igniting her skin. She didn't know why she was reacting to his arrival the way she was, perhaps because she was unprepared to find him on her doorstep, perhaps because all of the emotions she had been battling over the last few weeks had reached a critical mass. Sophie felt that *somebody* should be angry with Louis Gregory for leaving his family behind, and as she didn't see anybody else available to do the job, she felt that it might as well be her.

"Actually, no, you can't take the children," she said, taking one step at a time. "And yes, I can stop you. I have been granted a residency order, *and* in the eyes of the law I'm their legal guardian. You'll need a court order to take them anywhere." Sophie stretched the truth a little, gambling that Louis knew as little about the legalities as she did.

"But I'm their father!" Louis looked crestfallen, and Sophie saw that he was not as bullish and confident as he had first appeared to be. She took a breath and evened out the tone of her voice. She realized she wanted something rather complicated from Louis. She wanted him to feel guilty and contrite, to show the level of remorse she thought appropriate for his crime. But she didn't want to scare him off completely; she couldn't afford for him to leave and never come back. She had to push her own emotional reaction to him to the back of the queue and remember the girls.

"Louis," she said, "this is what I suggest you do. I suggest you go away and find a place to stay. And in the morning, when you look less like an escaped convict, you can come back." She reached the top of stairs and looked down on him. "I'll tell the girls you are here in the morning. We'll take it from there, okay?"

Louis stood stock-still, his eyes locked on Sophie's for a moment, and then shrugged. "I don't have much choice, do I?" he said, heading for the door. "I'll be back first thing."

Just at that moment, the lights blinked out. Sophie stood at the top of the stairs in the darkness and held her breath. But when the light returned, Louis was still by the front door. Sophie watched as he unlatched it and zipped up his parka against the cold air.

"Oh, by the way," she said, "the girls are coping really well, considering they've lost their mother. Thanks so much for asking."

Louis's face flashed with anger as he slammed the door behind him.

Sophie took a deep breath and found that she was shaking. Not once while she had been waiting, hoping for Louis to turn up had she considered that her reaction to him might be so physical, so visceral. Bright red blotches had already begun to blossom on the skin under the thin material of her dress, and her blood was ringing in her ears. Sophie knew that speaking to him the way she just had wouldn't solve anything. But the moment he had stood in her hallway, his presence filling every corner, it had been as if he had ignited a spark in Sophie. She couldn't just stand by and make this homecoming easy for him. She had to stand up to him for Carrie and her children.

Sophie let herself into the flat and found her mother standing in the hallway. "Has he gone?" she asked in a whisper.

"Yes, Mum, thanks for making him wait," Sophie replied, following her mother back into the living room.

"How did it go?" Iris asked her. "He seemed like a very nice young man. He was disappointed when I said he couldn't come in, but he didn't make a fuss."

Sophie thought carefully about her five minutes with Louis. "I don't really know," she said. "But your're right—he seems normal, nice."

And then Sophie realized. That was it. That was the reason he had made her so angry.

If he was so normal and nice, then why did he run away?

Sixteen

*I*zzy had chosen to wear her new party dress for the occasion, over an orange jersey top with her favorite green and black striped tights, which had once belonged to a Halloween outfit. She was sitting on the edge of Artemis's chair, drumming her heels against the leather-clad base with infuriating regularity, utterly unaware of the murderous looks she was incurring from the cat, which was balanced on the back of the chair just above the girl's left shoulder. If it had been anybody else—apart from Bella—Sophie was fairly sure Artemis would have dealt with them by now with her usual violent efficiency.

"Is it time *now*?" Izzy asked, exactly thirty seconds after the last time she had asked when the man who was her daddy was coming.

Tess, who had arrived over an hour earlier, shook the silver bangles on her wrist until she could get a clear look at her watch. "No, darling. We'll just have to wait a bit longer." She raised an eyebrow at Sophie, who was standing in the small kitchen cradling a cup of coffee more for its warmth than for its contents.

"Okay, Bella?" Sophie asked the girl, who was lying on the floor where the rug had once been, staring blankly at the ceiling. She nodded and blew out a puff of air angled upward so it fanned out her thick bangs. Somehow, she had managed to dress herself entirely in black, quite a feat considering that black wasn't exactly the color of choice in most six-year-olds' wardrobes. Of course, when Sophie had looked closely, she'd noticed that Bella had committed a cardinal sin and gone into her wardrobe without permission. There she had found a black shirt, a black sweater, and a black belt, and had used the belt to adapt the other two items into a sort of dress, which she was wearing over a pair of Sophie's black woolly tights, which even though they must have been pulled right up to her armpits, still wrinkled around her ankles. Bella must have judged that the gravitas of the occasion would prevent Sophie from being cross with her. She was right, of course, and also it was hard to be cross with someone who had shown such initiative and managed to look so funny when she was trying her best to look foreboding and cross. Perhaps it was the one small detail Bella hadn't quite managed to cover that made her so sweet instead of surly. Her boots were still pink.

"We're not going anywhere with him, are we though?" Bella asked after a while, her voice anxious despite her defiance.

"No," Tess said, giving her a little pat on the shoulder. "Not today."

Sophie put her mug down on the kitchen counter and, walking into the living room, knelt on the floor next to Bella and looked at her. Bella returned the look with her much practiced scowl.

"Are you going to be okay?" Sophie asked her.

"I said I was, didn't I?" Bella replied.

It was true, Bella had said that at just after three that morning. About two-thirty she had padded into the living room and, kneeling by the side of the sofa, had stared at her godmother until finally Sophie's sluggish and underused sixth sense had kicked in and she'd opened her eyes.

"Oh, good," Bella had said. "You *are* awake."

It had turned out, probably inevitably, Sophie concluded, that she had not had to break the news of Louis's imminent arrival, not to Bella at least, because Bella already knew. She had overheard Sophie talking about him to her mother when she came in and heard her say that he would be back in the morning. Bella had tried to go to sleep and pretend she didn't know about Louis, like she'd had to at Christmas, when she'd pretended she didn't know that it was Grandma who put the presents at the bottoms of their beds and not Father Christmas. Obviously it wasn't Father Christmas, because no one had told him where they had moved to, and she knew for a fact that Grandma hadn't posted their letters to him because Bella had found them in her knitting basket. And anyway, even if she hadn't seen Grandma doing it, she would still have known, because Father Christmas would have got her a *real* Barbie and not a fake one, whose head fell off almost right away. Sophie had nodded and rubbed her eyes, trying to keep up with six-year-old logic.

"But then," Bella had told Sophie gravely, "I realized that I had only pretended about Christmas so that Izzy wouldn't find out and get upset, but as Izzy is going to know about *him* in the morning anyway, I thought it would be better to get up and come and see if you were awake than to worry about it all by myself. And luckily you were," Bella had finished. "After a bit."

Sophie hadn't known whether to be touched or terrified, but she'd somehow made room for Bella, who had clambered over her and tucked her feet under Sophie's duvet.

"What worries you the most?" Sophie had asked her, imagining that she had to try to talk to Bella about her worries.

"Everything I can think of," Bella had said, lifting Sophie's arm so that she could wriggle under it. "We don't have to go anywhere with him, do we?" she'd asked when she was positioned comfortably.

"No," Sophie had said, adjusting to the warmth and weight of Bella's small body against hers. She had expected to feel tense and awkward as Bella snuggled closer to her, but instead she'd felt a new kind of still calm. "Not at all. I don't think anything much will happen tomorrow. I think you'll all just say hello. Get to know each other again." Sophie had moved her neck to an obtuse angle in order to look at Bella. "Look, I know how you feel, being worried about your dad coming back. It must be huge, not having seen him for so long. You must feel so nervous. But there are some things that, no matter how much we worry about them, we just have to face them, and most of the time they turn out not to be nearly as bad as we thought they would be. And *sometimes* they turn out to be wonderful."

Bella had yawned, nestling deeper into Sophie's body, and they had watched the headlights of the relentlessly passing traffic beam momentarily across the ceiling, minute after minute.

"We could hear the sea in my old house, sometimes," Bella had said after a while. "You couldn't see it, because it was sort of on the side, but in the summer when the windows were open, you used to be able to hear it. *Whoosh, whoosh, whoosh.*" Bella had swept her fingers back and forth to mimic the motion of the waves. "A bit like the cars going by outside your house."

Sophie had listened for a moment longer. "Yes," she'd said. "A little bit." She'd doubled her chin in order to get a look at Bella. "Look, you'll be all right tomorrow, won't you?" she had asked

Bella, when she should have been reassuring her. Selfishly, she'd wanted the little girl to say yes.

"I will be," Bella had said, her answer distorted by a lengthy yawn. "Because I have to be, don't I? Like you said."

Sophie had fretted for a few minutes about what she had actually said. Had she really told a six-year-old to stop worrying and pull her socks up? That was how Bella had made it sound, but it wasn't what Sophie had meant to say.

"Listen, Bella?" Sophie had wanted to try again. "Bella?"

But somehow, despite her anxieties, Bella had been sound asleep, something that Sophie had not quite managed to achieve for the rest of the night.

Which was why, on the following morning, she had a shooting pain from the top of her head into her left arm. Sharing the two-seater sofa with Bella had given her a very painful crick in her neck. Either that or she was having a heart attack. The latter option seemed to her entirely possible.

Tess jangled her bangles again and squinted at her watch. "He definitely said this morning?" Tess asked.

"Yep," Sophie said. And he had seemed so adamant that Sophie had assumed he meant first thing in the morning, which was why she had called Tess on her cell phone at just after seven and got her over to the flat by eight. It was now almost ten. That was three hours of Izzy racing around like a demented tree fairy. Three hours of Bella sulking around like a kindergarten beatnik, and two hours of Tess jangling her bangles and squinting at her watch. Obviously, Louis Gregory's concept of time was entirely different from the rest of the world's. He seemed to think that "coming now" meant five days later and "first thing in the morning" could be any old time before midday.

"In my experience," Tess said, "it's a good idea to get a set time, so that everyone knows exactly what they are doing. I have several other cases I need to attend to. I really can't stay much longer."

Sophie was just about to complain that it was no good lecturing *her* when the doorbell sounded and all four females jumped.

"He's here!" Izzy shouted, scrambling off Artemis's chair and shooting out into the hallway, sending the cat flying in the opposite direction.

"*Izzy!*" Sophie yelled, in hot pursuit. "Don't you dare open—" The flat door slammed open farther, deepening the Izzy-manufactured dent on the corresponding wall. "Izzy, wait there! I mean it!" Sophie shouted. She wanted to close her eyes as she watched Izzy half-scramble, half-tumble down the communal stairs, but she was too busy chasing her to do either. Izzy made it to the front door and was jumping up to open the old-fashioned latch, which was halfway down the door and easily within her reach. It swung it open. Sure enough, Louis stood on the other side of the door and looked down at her. Sophie reached them a second later.

"Is that him?" Izzy said, looking upward openmouthed until her eyes reached Louis's lofty head. Sophie put her hand on Izzy's shoulder. It was unfair, she knew, but she somehow wished the three-year-old had been a bit less awe-inspired by her admittedly very tall and, objectively speaking, rather handsome long-lost father.

"Yes," Sophie said. "Izzy, this is Louis. Louis is your daddy."

Father and daughter regarded each other with equal hesitation until Louis held out a hand, presumably for a shake, and turning on her ballet-shoed heel, Izzy flew back up the stairs with the same haphazard technique and breakneck speed as she had descended them. A moment later the flat door slammed shut.

Sophie looked awkwardly at Louis and shrugged. At least he

had spent the part of the morning that he was not here ridding himself of the last vestiges of tramphood. His hair, though still touching his shoulders, was washed and pushed back from his face, and he had shaved off his beard, revealing a clean, smooth jawline and generous mouth, his children's mouth. Without the hat and the scarf and the facial hair, he looked much better, Sophie supposed with oblique regret.

"So, you finally made it then?" She was struggling not to sound bitchy, but somehow she did. She stepped aside and gestured for Louis to enter.

"Yes, finally," he said, his tone carefully measured. Sophie shut the door behind him, and he took a breath. "Look, can we start again? I'm really sorry about last night. You were right, I was out of order. I don't know if it was the jet lag or the shock, but I just didn't want to wait. I didn't even think I'd have to. But I was stupid coming over. I'm sorry. I didn't want to piss *you* off." He smiled at her. "Definitely not part of my plan after everything you've done for the girls and for me . . ."

Sophie was not surprised by the charm of his follow-up smile or its effect on her. It made her want to like him instantly, which in turn made her feel cross again. She couldn't just go around liking people willy-nilly, not Louis anyway. Not when there were questions to be asked and serious arrangements to be made. It was all very well being likable, but was he responsible? Was he serious about being a dad again? Was he suitable? Instead of smiling back, Sophie nodded stiffly.

"And I know," Louis continued after a moment, "I know I should have been here earlier, a lot earlier, but I— Oh, fuck—to be honest, I've just been walking up and down outside for about an hour. I'm so nervous . . ."

"Look," Sophie told him, lowering her voice. "If you're going to freak out, now is not the time to do it." She sighed with exasperation. "*You* are the grown-up here. All *you* have to do is to get up those stairs and say hello to your daughters. *Apparently,* you've been working with children for years. You must know *something* about how to talk to them by now," she told him with open sarcasm, neglecting to mention that her own experience was limited to a couple of weeks. "And anyway, how can *you*"—Sophie looked up at Louis and guessed he was about four inches over six feet— "be scared of that tiny girl and her slightly bigger sister?" She also conveniently forgot her own very real five-foot-six-inch terror of Izzy, which still reared its ugly head whenever the warning signs of a tantrum began going off.

Louis swallowed and nodded purposefully. "You're right," he said. "You're right."

"Obviously I am," Sophie said, slightly imperiously, which for some reason made Louis smile his irritatingly nice smile again.

Tess was the only person directly visible when Sophie showed Louis into the living room. She stood up and smiled broadly at Louis, delivering her extra-special all-purpose disaster-celebration smile with her usual warmth.

"Hello, I'm Tess Andrew," she said, extending her hand. "The children's social worker."

Louis's already hesitant smile faltered, but he shook her hand anyway with reasonable firmness and looked around the room. Like Sophie, who was leaning in the doorway, he spotted Izzy's special fairy scrunchie, an extravagant affair made up of layers of white and pink net and sparkly bits, which was just visible over the back of Artemis's chair.

"Oh dear," Louis said loudly. "It looks like that fairy must have made herself invisible." Sophie and Tess exchanged a look behind his back, Sophie rolling her eyes and Tess dimpling and twinking. So much for Tess's being objective; she looked like she was in love already.

"That clever fairy must have made herself invisible and flown all the way back to fairyland," Louis continued. "What a very clever fairy."

"I *am* a clever fairy!" Izzy sang, jumping out from behind the chair in a mass of glittery substances. "Here I am!" she cried.

"Oh my!" Louis said, clasping his hand to his chest and sitting down on the sofa abruptly. "You gave me quite a shock!"

Izzy giggled and hopped over to him.

Louis's long and large frame seemed to fill the small room in a way that two girls, a woman, and a social worker didn't. "I'm a fairy because I've got my fairy dress on, haven't I? And yesterday I went to the shops and the café with Aunty Sophie and also there's my cat over there except she's gone now because she doesn't like you but she doesn't like anyone much except for me and Bella, me the most, and I was in the car and a big van made it go *bang* and I don't like cars now." Izzy paused for breath. "Except for Phoebe who I don't mind and sometimes Phoebe gets lonely so we sing to her." Louis's smile did not waver as Izzy related to him the story of her life in twenty seconds, but Sophie thought she had seen something in his eyes when Izzy described the car crash, a fleeting shadow perhaps.

Sophie had formulated a theory that Izzy's seemingly flippant recounting of the accident that killed her mother didn't mean she didn't understand it or wasn't hurt by and afraid of it. She had to talk about it to everybody she could because somehow saying it out loud made it real for her. Sophie hoped that Louis would see some of that in Izzy, that he'd understand she was still fragile despite her resolute chirpiness.

"You are a very, very brave little girl, aren't you?" he said gently.

Izzy hopped one step nearer to him. "Yes, I am," she said. "*And* I can do ballet, because it's easy, you just go round and round and do pointing. Are you my daddy?"

Louis bit his lip and nodded. "Yes," he said, as if the fact was somehow news to him. "I am. I am your daddy, and I'm very, *very* pleased to meet you."

Izzy cocked her head to one side and examined him. "Do I like you?" she asked him, spreading her palms upward, her habitual gesture of a question.

"I don't think you know yet," Louis told her. "I think you'll decide when you're ready. But I like you, very much, already."

Izzy nodded. Tess beamed, and Sophie resisted the urge to shove her fingers down her throat.

"I am lovely," Izzy agreed. "I'll make you a cup tea for now." And she raced off into the bedroom, where her plastic teaset was stored under Sophie's bed, where Bella no doubt was languishing. Sophie wondered if she should go and pull the older girl out from underneath the duvet, but she decided against it.

This of all things Bella had to do at her own pace, and if she felt anything like Sophie did at that moment, she felt as if she had just stepped off a tall building and was watching the world come rushing up to meet her. Sophie couldn't help but think that everything was happening too fast, that after what seemed like a lifetime of wanting this to happen, now it was too soon. She wasn't ready.

"She looks like me, doesn't she?" Louis said to Tess.

Vain and a megalomaniac, Sophie thought as she retreated into the kitchen to make real cups of tea.

"They both look like you," Tess said pleasantly. "Of course, I never had the pleasure of meeting Carrie, but I've seen photos of her. She was always laughing. It's easy to see where the girls get their spirit from. But as for their good looks, definitely you." Tess actually giggled, which Sophie considered most unseemly at her age and for her professional role.

She emerged from the kitchen and handed Louis a mug of a tea.

"Oh right, thanks," he said. He set the tea carefully down on a coaster on the coffee table, ironic considering the coaster was positioned directly above one of Izzy's permanent marker pen masterpieces. There was a moment of silence.

"Is Bella here?" Louis said. "I mean, will I see her today too?"

Before Sophie could say anything, Izzy flew back into the living room and threw a plastic teacup into Louis's lap. "There you go!" she shouted, out of breath and excited. "Drink it, drink it up!"

Louis retrieved the cup from between his legs and took a long, noisy sip. "Ahhh," he said, before handing the cup back to Izzy. "Deee-licious. But mind the real hot drinks, won't you? You don't want to get burned."

"Okay," Izzy said. "Would you like more tea?" Louis nodded, and Izzy edged her way carefully past the coffee table on her way out, beaming at Louis as she went.

Typical, Sophie thought. If I'd have told her that, it would have been third-degree burns all round by now. She glanced at the doorway. Bella was standing on the threshold. Sophie caught Louis's eye and nodded at the door. He turned around and saw his older daughter.

"Bellarina!" he said, holding out his arms. For a second Bella did not move, and then she walked around the sofa and stood beside Sophie.

Louis dropped his arms, but his smile remained steady. "It's so good to see you," he said, shaking his head as he took in the sight of her. "You've grown into a big, grown-up girl." The natural ease with which he had engaged Izzy seemed to vanish. For a moment Sophie could not understand why, and then she realized. He had never met Izzy before. They had no history, their relationship started with a clean slate. But he had been a father—a wonderful father, according to Carrie—to Bella for three years. Seeing her again must have been much harder, because with Bella there were so many loose ends.

A few weeks ago Sophie would not have believed that Bella would still carry around the memories and feelings of her three-year-old self, but then, until a couple of weeks ago, she supposed that if she had thought about it at all, which she didn't, she would have thought that children didn't really feel or think anything at the ages of three or six and a half. She would have thought that their emotional sensitivity and intellect didn't really kick in until they were at least thirteen and properly human. But now Sophie knew Izzy and Bella. And now she knew different, and she knew absolutely that the three-year-old girl Louis had left behind along with his wife was still there, still part of Bella, still furious, frustrated, hurt, and confused.

Louis leaned forward and looked at Bella, who looked at her toes. "I'm so sorry, Bella, about Mummy, I really am. I really wish that I had known about it sooner so that I could have come and been with you. When I found out, I came as quickly as I could and—" Louis studied Bella's face for a moment. "You're angry with me. It's okay, you should be. I have a lot to explain to you. A lot of things to say I should have said before. But please believe me when I say I really have missed you. I really have thought about you every single day."

Sophie sensed the tense lines of Bella's body and noticed her hands clenched into fists at her side.

"I came to see what you looked like," Bella said. "You look the same." She glanced up at Sophie. "I am very tired. I think I'll have a nap."

Sophie nodded.

"I don't have to talk to you," Bella told Louis. "Aunty Sophie said."

Louis pressed his lips together. "No," he said. "You don't—"

"I know," Bella said. "Good-bye."

"Good-bye, darling."

Bella walked out of the room without looking back.

"Are you okay?" Tess asked Louis gently.

"Shouldn't you be asking Bella that?" Sophie said scathingly, as if Louis weren't present.

"I will," Tess said. "But as my job is about reuniting the family as a whole, I have to consider the feelings of all parties. The girls have got you fighting in their corner. Louis has no one."

Sophie was about to voice her protest when, ignoring her completely, Tess turned to Louis and asked him again, "Are you okay?"

"I suppose I should have expected that," he replied, glancing warily at Sophie, as if she might pounce on him the moment he opened his mouth. "But to be honest, I've been thinking about seeing her for so long that I didn't think about what would happen when I actually did."

Sophie sat down in Artemis's chair and crossed her legs. Why, she wondered, wasn't the social worker grilling him like she was supposed to? She stared meaningfully at Tess.

"These times are always difficult, dear," Tess told Louis. "There are many adjustments to be made, many hurdles to overcome. Think of what the girls have been through recently, losing their mother at such a young age, when they needed her the most. Moved around from one place to another. Their little lives have been a real roller coaster for the last seven months. There's been no security or stability. That's why it was such a godsend when we found Sophie. They've blossomed here."

Sophie's head snapped up at that comment. Had they? she wondered.

"They are different children, and that's why for the foreseeable future we don't want to give them any more upheaval than is necessary, do we? That's why it would be better for them to stay with Sophie while you are all getting to know each other."

Louis looked up sharply. "But they're *my* girls," he said stubbornly. "I'm their dad. I can take them now if I want to—you can't stop me."

Tess shook her head. "I think Sophie already explained that I can stop you. Look, Louis, we didn't know if you were coming back until a few days ago. We have yet to make any further decisions on the next step for the girls. We certainly won't be changing their current situation until a few things have been clarified."

Finally, Sophie thought, she's playing hard ball. She felt relieved by Tess's statement, relieved to know that the girls wouldn't suddenly just be gone.

Louis looked dumbstruck. "What sorts of things?" he asked Tess, who smiled at him reassuringly.

"Well, why don't you come to my office and see me this afternoon and we can talk over the details?" she said, reaching out and patting his knee. "It's nothing to worry about, but I'm sure you would want us to check and double-check anyone who the girls might live with one day. Even you." She went on before he could respond, "Now how about two—can you make that?"

Louis's shoulders dropped, but he did not argue. "I suppose so," he said, taking the card that Tess held out to him.

"Excellent." Tess jangled as she rose to her feet. "Well, I'll be off now, but can I suggest that we agree on a visiting strategy? First of all, it's very important that you agree to a time and stick to it, so that the girls know they can rely on you. Second, I suggest you extend each visit a little bit. Don't try to rush it. These things take time. I'll see you later." She grinned at Sophie. "Don't worry, I'll see myself out."

But Sophie followed Tess out and down the stairs anyway.

"Um, excuse me," she said. "But you can't just leave him here with me. What if he goes berserk, ties me up, and runs off with the girls? What if he's a loony psycho killer?"

Tess smiled. "When you've been in my job as long as I have, you just know whether someone is the loony psycho killer type or not. There are a lot of things we have to find out about our Mr. Gregory. But I'm fairly sure that is not one of them."

Sophie rolled her eyes. "Yeah, well, that's what they said about Ted Bundy," she replied scathingly. "Anyway, let's not forget that it was *you* who was fairly sure it would be okay to leave two small children in *my* care, shall we?" Sophie frowned, confused by how she had managed to insult herself when Tess had been her target.

"Exactly." Tess reached out and caught Sophie's hand. "You're really good at this, you know. Much better than I thought you'd be."

"Right," Sophie said crossly. She didn't know whether to be touched by the compliment or to give in to an urge to hit Tess over the head with the nearest blunt instrument for manipulating her so successfully. Still, she supposed that probably made *her* the nearest thing to a loony psycho killer in the place right now.

Sophie paused as she closed the flat door behind her. She looked at the entrance to the living room and at the back of Louis's head, which was bowed slightly. Neither girl seemed to be in the living room, so Sophie took a detour via her bedroom and stuck her head around the door. Bella was lying on the bed playing with Artemis and what once had been a pair of Sophie's control-top satin sheer tights.

"Okay?" Sophie said. She had long ago given up wasting energy mourning the gradual demise of her wardrobe.

Bella nodded.

"Where's Izzy?" Sophie frowned—she couldn't see the three-year-old.

"Baking," Bella said, pointing downward. "At least she was, but it all went a bit quiet a few minutes ago."

Sophie walked around the bed, where sure enough, Izzy's lower half was protruding from underneath. Sophie crouched down and peered at Izzy's top half. The excitement of the morning must have overcome her—she was fast asleep. Carefully, Sophie fished her out from under the bed and laid her on top of it, as far away from Artemis as possible.

"Do you think she's got narcolepsy?" Sophie asked Bella.

"No," Bella said, as if she had the first clue what narcolepsy was. "I think she's three."

"Of course," Sophie said with a smile. "Silly me. Well, look, I think Louis will be off soon. Do you want to say good-bye."

"He never said good-bye to me," Bella said bluntly. She laid her head down on the pillow and ran her palm along Artemis's back. "Besides, I'm having a nap anyway."

Sophie nodded and closed the door quietly behind her.

"They're both asleep," she told Louis. "Izzy's funny like that. One minute she's all go, and the next she's snoring."

Louis smiled. "Bella used to be the same way."

He and Sophie looked at each other for a moment, neither one knowing exactly what to say next.

"Right," Louis said, standing up suddenly. "I'll be off. What time do you want me tomorrow?"

Sophie felt herself blush inexplicably and cursed her unpredictable complexion. "Well, early's good. They get up at six. So, eight?"

"Okay, eight it is." And Louis was gone as suddenly as he'd arrived, leaving her small flat feeling positively palatial.

Sophie sat down in the unusually quiet living room and rubbed her eyes as she thought about Louis. He didn't seem like an ogre; he didn't seem like a thoughtless womanizer with a string of kids stretching around the world. He did seem like he was truly delighted to see Izzy and Bella again and anxious that they like him. But none of those things fitted with the picture she had built up from the bits and pieces of information she had gleaned about him. If he had just callously run out on Carrie, why would she have kept his absence a virtual secret from Sophie? If he was so concerned about his children, why did he go as far away from them as he possibly could? If he was such a good father, the kind of father who had a cute pet name for his elder daughter, and if he was such a good person, this selfless charity worker, then why did Mrs. Stiles hate him with a passion? And why was Bella still angry with him?

Somewhere in all this lay the truth about Louis Gregory. And Sophie knew that it was up to her to find it.

She was still trying to puzzle it out when Jake phoned.

"I called you at the office. I was sure you'd be there enjoying your success," he told her. "You should have about a hundred people calling today, all wanting the same party!"

Sophie grimaced and tapped her forehead with the heel of her palm. She had really been looking forward to going in today, to taking all the glory and capitalizing on her success. But the moment Louis turned up, she had completely forgotten about it. She hadn't even called Gillian, which meant that she had let slip a crucial moment to consolidate her position. She swore silently.

"Louis was here when I got back last night," she told Jake by way of explanation.

"Ah, the prodigal father," he said. "How'd that go?"

"Hard to tell really. I don't know how to be with him.

Whether I should be angry and cross and protect the girls from him. Or whether I should be nice and helpful and try to get them to like him. I mean, he got Carrie pregnant and ditched her. Maybe he's not the sort of man who'd make a decent dad."

"Oh, I don't know," Jake said reasonably. "You don't know what happened between him and Carrie. Maybe you shouldn't cast him as the bad guy until you know the facts."

"That's just it," Sophie said. "I don't know. I wish I knew."

"Then ask him," Jake told her, as if it were obvious.

"I can't ask him!" Sophie said, sounding horrified.

"Why not?" It was good question.

"I hardly know him," she replied, knowing her answer was inadequate.

"But you've been caring for his kids," Jake pointed out. "You were once close to his wife."

"I just . . . I can't ask him outright," Sophie said.

Jake laughed. "Then be nice to him, let him trust you. Soon enough he'll relax and tell you what you want to know."

Sophie nodded. "That *is* a good idea," she said hesitantly. "I know I should try to do that, but when I think about what he's done, I just want to punch him."

"Don't do that," Jake said. "Play the long game, it works every time. Or at least I hope it does."

Sophie smiled. "I'd better call the office," she said. "Check that everything's okay. At least Gillian will be glad to know Louis's back, although I'll have to take a few days off completely until the girls get used to him, if they ever do."

"I wouldn't worry about Gillian," Jake told her, a smile in his voice. "I spoke to her this morning. I told her that I was thrilled with the job you had done and that I would be signing a long-term contract with McCarthy Hughes based largely on you."

Sophie took a moment to absorb that piece of information.

"Jake . . . ," she began uncertainly. She supposed she ought to be pleased. After all, the seal of approval from her biggest client could only help show Gillian how well she had dealt with work under the circumstances—that in fact she had excelled herself even when the going was tough. But somehow Jake's having talked directly to Gillian made her feel uncomfortable. After all, they hadn't exactly been discreet last night. Anybody could have seen them kissing. And what would Gillian think if she heard about that?

"Jake, thank you. But I don't want people to think that you're putting a word in for me because of . . . 'us,'" she said uneasily.

Jake laughed, but she could tell she had somehow wounded him.

"Sophie." His voice hardened. "You might remember that before I started mooning around you like a lovesick schoolboy I ran the U.K. operation of the Madison Corporation, the world's third largest private asset management corporation. I know my business, and I promise you, no matter how much I want you, I would *never* compromise my position just to impress a woman."

"Of course you wouldn't," Sophie said hurriedly. "I know that. Oh, Jake, I'm sorry—"

"You are good at your job, Sophie," Jake interrupted her. "And I'll be sticking with McCarthy Hughes for our event management because of that and that alone—whether or not anything happens between us."

"I'm sorry, Jake. I'm just a bit tired, and there's so much going on—"

"You know what?" he said, clearly not wanting to hear Sophie say that line again. "You need to take some time off from work completely, and perhaps you should take some time off from me. Try to figure out what you want and call me when you do, okay?"

"I will call you," Sophie said, feeling anxious that he was withdrawing from her so abruptly. "Jake, you've been great these last few weeks. Thank you."

"It's no big deal," he said, his voice melting a little.

"And I'm so sorry about last night," she said.

"Oh, baby," Jake said warmly. "Not as sorry as me."

Seventeen

By the next morning Sophie had formulated a plan which she considered to be a work of Machiavellian genius that would rival any of Eve's concoctions.

She was going to take Jake's advice and be nice to Louis. It was a simple plan but one that invariably worked when she was hooking a difficult client. She would be really encouraging. She'd be perfectly pleasant and nonconfrontational, and gradually he'd let his guard down. When he was relaxed with her and trusted her, then she'd find out exactly what he was up to and exactly who he was. And when the time was right, she'd be able finally to ask him—what *did* happen between him and Carrie?

Sophie had thought she actually didn't know very much about Carrie's relationship with Louis or her feelings for him, other than the brief descriptions of general contentment that Carrie had given in passing during their rare conversations over the years—even, it seemed, after he had left. But the more Sophie thought about it, the more she realized that she did know. There were tiny clues slotted inside memories that Sophie had rarely, if ever, accessed until now. And now another puzzle piece had come back to her.

Carrie had sent her some photos after the wedding. Sophie remembered that the film must have been rarely used, because it showed Carrie throughout the developing stages of her relationship with Louis right up until the so-called honeymoon, when she sat on the beach at St. Ives looking, according to Carrie, who had inscribed the back of each picture, "like a big fat whale."

Sophie reached over and switched on a light next to the sofa. She looked at the video clock; it was nearly seven-thirty, which was sleeping late when Bella and Izzy were in your life; the excitement and drama of yesterday must have worn them out. It didn't take her long to find the photos, she knew exactly where they were—in a shoe box on top of one of the kitchen units. Sophie retrieved the box and sat down on the edge of the sofa, praying that the girls would stay in bed for a few moments longer. She didn't want Carrie's photos to upset them.

The first four or five were all taken on the same beach. It must have been right at the start of the relationship. Carrie was smiling and radiant, her brown curls blown about by the breeze. They had taken photos of each other. In one of Carrie's, her arms were outstretched as if begging for an embrace, and in another she was blowing a kiss right at the photographer. Louis looked less comfortable in his photos, his hands shoved in his pockets, a shy half smile on his face, and his shoulders shrugged against the cold. But in one image Carrie had caught him unawares gazing out at the horizon, looking relaxed and, yes, quite attractive if scruffy and unkempt were your type. Sophie turned over the photo and smiled. "Mine, all mine!" Carrie had written on the back triumphantly. The last photo of the set was of them both. Sophie guessed that Carrie must have held the camera at arm's length to take them together because the photo was blurred and out of focus. It was easy, however, to make out the width of their smiles, even though Carrie's hair had flown over most of Louis's face.

There were a few snapshots of the Cornish countryside, each inscribed with the location, time, and date, and after those came two photos of what had become Carrie's house. A tiny terraced house that seemed to perch precariously on one of the steep lanes that led up away from the beach. Virgin Street it was called. Carrie had laughed and laughed when she told Sophie her new address, delighted that she of all people was going to be living on such a chaste road. It had cost much more than they could afford, and Carrie had had to swallow her pride and beg her mum for a deposit, and Louis had had to take on a second job to make the payments on the mortgage, but Carrie had known from the moment she set eyes on the run-down little house that she had to have it, and she got it. Which, Sophie reflected, was just like Carrie—she always got what she wanted in the end.

Then came the wedding photos. Clearly whoever had taken these photos was more than a little worse for the wear; the subject of each print was tilted and skewed, as if the wedding had taken place during an earthquake. The only straight and fully in focus picture was of a rather nice fire extinguisher. But mainly they were of Carrie and Louis, holding hands and laughing. Louis was flushed, and Sophie remembered that he had been quite drunk and had stumbled through the vows. Carrie, who was very pregnant by then, was also flushed but not drunk. She looked so happy. She looked almost victorious. As Sophie looked at the next photo, she saw herself—or at least half of herself—her face obscured by her hair. Carrie had reached out a hand to her and pulled her close, and as Sophie looked at the photo she suddenly remembered what Carrie had whispered in her ear in that moment so vividly that she could almost feel her friend's breath on her neck. "I've finally done it, Sophie," she'd whispered. "I've got everything I wanted. I'm free."

Sophie remembered thinking that being married to a drunk surfer and saddled with a baby at not quite twenty-three was the very last thing she would call free, but Carrie seemed to believe it. Then Sophie came to the final photos: Carrie on the beach, in a big, loose white cotton shirt propped up on her elbows, a plate of sandwiches balanced on her bump. In the background, Sophie saw something she hadn't remembered. She had always assumed that Louis had taken these last few photos, which Carrie had captioned. "The Gregorys honeymooning at home," but he couldn't have, because he was in them. Not in the foreground but much farther back, just above Carrie's left shoulder.

Sophie peered at the photo. Yes, it was definitely Louis, messing around with someone else, another girl. A slender blonde. He had his arms around her waist, and she had her head tipped back and was smiling up at him. Sophie bit her lip. If she had been about to give birth and was sitting on a beach with her brand-new husband frolicking with some hussy a few feet away, she would have been livid. But would Carrie? Probably not, Sophie concluded. Carrie had an amazing self-confidence. She would never have believed that Louis would do any more than flirt with the girl because he absolutely loved her. She had told Sophie that often enough in the years before Izzy. It must have been devastating for her when he left—she would have been totally unprepared. It must have hurt her pride just as much as her heart. Maybe that was why she hadn't told Sophie about it.

Sophie ran her thumb along the edge of Carrie's face and smiled back at her, and she was surprised to feel a rush of tears build up behind her eyes. She closed her eyes and took a deep breath. She hadn't cried for Carrie yet—she hadn't had time to—and in all the chaos and confusion, she had almost forgotten that she still loved her, that despite their distance, she knew if she had walked into a room and found Carrie there, not only would she have been delighted to see her but they would have never stopped talking and laughing until it was time to go. Sophie had taken the depth and longevity of their friendship for granted, and now she realized she would never again walk into a room and see Carrie there.

"Mummy!" Sophie jerked her head up and saw Izzy peering over the side of the sofa.

"That's Mummy!" Izzy said, delightedly pointing at the photos that were laid out on the sofa. She ran around and sat next to Sophie, who gathered the photos into a loose pile.

She looked down at Izzy's expectant face and, uncertain that she was doing the right thing, handed her the first photo on the pile, the one of Carrie blowing a kiss.

"Oh, Mummy," Izzy said, chuckling fondly, and she planted a kiss on the photo.

Silently Sophie handed Izzy photo after photo, and each one seemed to thrill her even more.

"That's that man who is my daddy there!" she exclaimed at the first image of Louis. "With my Mummy!" Izzy seemed to think it was incredible they should be together, and Sophie realized Izzy probably didn't understand that they had once known each other. Izzy cooed over the wedding pictures and laughed and laughed at Mummy with the sandwiches balanced on her tummy.

"Mummy," she said. And just as Sophie had done, Izzy ran her finger gently along the side of Carrie's face.

"Mummy," she said, more softly this time.

Sophie put her arm around the little girl and held her own re-actions tightly in her chest. "You can keep these if you like," she said. "And then you can look at Mummy whenever you want." Izzy nodded and gathered up the photos. "Where is Mummy again?" she asked after a while.

"She's in the sky, Izzy, and the stars and the sun," Sophie said, carefully making sure her voice stayed steady.

"And in the moon and the trees and the lampposts and the, and the—houses?" Izzy asked her.

"Yes," Sophie said. "Mummy's all around you. Watching over you and loving you and keeping you safe." More than anything, Sophie wanted to believe her own words; she wanted to recapture some of the childish faith that Izzy had.

"But I want to see Mummy properly," Izzy said, her voice very small now and her eyes welling with tears. "I want to cuddle her up."

At that moment Bella, already washed and dressed, appeared on the other side of the sofa and, pulling herself onto the seat, put her arm around Izzy too, so that it crossed over Sophie's.

"See that bump?" she said, pointing at the photo. Izzy nod-ded, her bottom lip still quivering. "That's me in there," Bella said.

"That's not you in there," Izzy said with a tiny smile. "You couldn't get in there!"

"I could when I was a tiny, tiny baby and not even born yet."

Izzy examined the photo again. "Where's me?" she demanded, but with a fraction of her usual imperiousness. "Where's me in a bump? I had a bump too, didn't I?" Fortunately, Sophie did have a photo that Carrie had sent her just before Izzy was born. It had ar-rived in an envelope with no note, only a quick message scrawled on the back, "Thought you'd like to see how fat I'm getting!"

Sophie quickly flicked through the remaining contents of the shoe box and took the photo out. Carrie was smiling, although she looked a little thinner in the face and paler in that photo. Now that Sophie compared the two photos, she saw that Carrie's initial radiance was gone. Still, she handed it to Izzy.

"Here," Sophie said. "That bump is you."

Izzy laughed again, even as the tears dried on her cheeks, and as Sophie relaxed, she discovered that she had been holding her breath. She glanced up at Bella, who was looking at the last photo of Carrie, her lips pressed into a thin line, her hands folded in her lap.

"Are you okay, Bella?" Sophie asked. It was a question she found herself asking routinely, never receiving a satisfactory answer. Whereas Izzy was beautifully transparent, her sister could be like a tightly closed book.

Bella nodded and hopped off the sofa. "I'm getting Cheerios," she said, and she trundled into the kitchen.

"And me, and me as well!" Izzy shouted, scooting after her, leaving the photos scattered across the sofa. Sophie gathered them up and put them back in the shoe box.

"I'll leave these on the table," she called out to the girls, who were doing their best to scatter cereal all over the floor. "Better get a move on, because Louis will be here any minute." And just then the doorbell sounded. Sophie looked at the clock. It was right on the dot of eight.

If there was one thing that Sophie decided she was never, *ever* going to do ever, *ever* again it was to answer the door to a handsome man in her cartoon pajamas.

"You did say eight, didn't you?" were Louis's first words to her as she ushered him up the stairs, hoping that the length of her hair would be enough to prevent him from getting the full Snoopy effect of her nightwear combined with her blazing hot cheeks.

"Yes, yes, I did," she said, trying to keep the brisk tone out of her voice and to remember Plan Nice. "We found some old photos, and we got held up looking at them."

Louis stood back at the flat door and waited for Sophie to go in first. "Suits you," he said drily, with half of that infuriating smile. "Snoopy style, I mean."

"Ha-ha," Sophie said without mirth, narrowing her eyes at him. When she walked into the living room, Bella was ensconced in Artemis's chair eating her Cheerios and watching TV, and Izzy was on the floor doing the same thing, only a lot less tidily.

"Hello, the man who is my daddy!" Izzy said, waving her spoon at Louis. "I saw you today!"

Bella said nothing, only glancing at Louis, who loomed awkwardly in the corner.

"Look," Sophie said. "Can you make yourself a drink if you want one? I need to get dressed."

Louis smiled again.

"What?" Sophie demanded of him.

"It's just that—Well, you're a lot less scary in pajamas," he said quickly and headed for the refuge of the kitchen.

Swallowing her irritation, Sophie looked from Bella to Izzy. "Be good," she said. "I'll be ten minutes." But she took at least twice that long because she felt compelled to have a shower and give her hair a quick wash as well, applying extra concealer and mascara to make up for the whole pajama incident. While it obviously didn't matter at all what Louis thought of her, Snoopy pajamas did not put her in the best light, and if he thought of her as the kind of person who wore cartoon characters to bed, then it would be much harder for her to get him to take her seriously. And she didn't like the way he had seemed to relax in the situation before she had. Yes, it would make implementing Plan Nice much easier, but why should Louis—the one who was utterly in the wrong—have the way made so smooth for him that he could easily forget he'd had at least some part in creating this tragedy? The thought of it made Sophie edgy and defensive.

When she returned to the living room, her damp hair preparing to frizz around her shoulder, Louis handed her a cup of coffee. "You look great," he said, quite naturally and easily.

"Er, thanks," Sophie said, thrown off-kilter by his casual cunning.

She looked at the children. Bella seemed engrossed by some woman's account of a botched hysterectomy, while Izzy had abandoned her cereal and was showing Louis the photos. He looked at them exactly as Bella had done, all expression carefully tucked away and his hands folded in his lap.

"And that is *you*!" Izzy told him, pointing him out in case he didn't realize.

"Yes," Louis said, producing a smile as Izzy looked up at him, smiling. "It is." He turned to Sophie. "I thought I could take them to London Zoo. It's quite mild out and dry." He opened the plastic bag he had been carrying and brought out two hat, scarf, and glove sets, a pink one with gloves attached to the hat and a lilac one with mittens. "I got them these just in case it was a bit cold."

"Mittens and kittens!" Izzy said, grabbing the lilac set and trying to put it on despite the fact that all the pieces were still attached to one another with plastic tags.

Sophie hadn't thought about actually taking the girls out but remembered her plan and Tess's initial assessment of Louis as not the child-snatching type. That was backed up by a long phone conversation she had had with the social worker late yesterday afternoon. Tess had told Sophie that Louis was cooperating fully with her and that he seemed to be genuine about his commitment to his daughters. Sophie decided that actually it would be good for the girls to get out, and it might be easier for all of them when they weren't in such a confined space.

"Okay, but, um, well, can I come too?" she said, remembering Tess's stipulation.

Louis seemed slightly taken aback. "Why? I mean, that's great, I'd like you to come along, but I'm not planning to smuggle them abroad or anything."

Sophie nodded. "I know that, but they don't know you, do they?" She shrugged. "Look, I'm sorry, but Tess told me I should stay with them for the first few visits. If you don't like it, you'd better call her."

Louis sighed. "No, no," he said. "If that's what Tess wants. Right then." He winked at Izzy. "Want to go to the zoo, Izzy?"

"Yes, I do, I do want to go to the zoo! I want to see the penguins and the spiders," Izzy shouted, her new hat jammed on her head, the mittens flailing off the sides like demented antlers. Louis and Izzy laughed together, their eyes dancing.

"I'm not going," Bella said flatly, without taking her eyes off the TV.

"You *are* going," Izzy said. "You're coming with me and the man who is my daddy to the zoo to see penguins and spiders, aren't you?"

Bella shook her head and glared at Izzy. "I am not," she said emphatically.

Sophie saw Izzy's lip begin to quiver and quickly knelt beside her. "It's okay, darling," she said, putting an arm around Izzy. "Hang on a minute." She gave Izzy a squeeze and walked the short distance over to Bella on her knees. "Bella, I know this is hard for you, but please don't make it hard for Izzy too. She wants to go to the zoo. And I bet you do too, really, don't you? I'll be there, and if you don't go, none of us will." Bella stared blankly at her.

Izzy came over and put her hand on Bella's knee. She was sobbing, deep, dry, ragged breaths that sounded painful. "Please, Bella," she begged. "Be happy!"

"Come on, Bella," Sophie said. "Show Izzy what a grown-up big sister you can be."

Bella sighed and looked at Sophie. "I *am* only six, you know," she said glumly, and Sophie felt terrible.

"I know," she said. "I keep forgetting you are such a little girl because you are so clever."

"Okay, I'll come to the zoo, I suppose. But I shan't enjoy it," Bella said reluctantly.

Eighteen

There was a debate about how to get there. Probably in an early attempt to scupper the whole expedition, Bella had refused to go on the bus because "buses smelled." At first Izzy had seemed quite happy to go in Phoebe—partly because of Sophie's "therapy" but especially because Sophie had bought a booster car seat for each child and a cat-shaped sunscreen for each girl's window despite the now total absence of sun—but as soon as they reached the end of the road and turned left instead of right and she realized that taking their usual route around the block would not get them to the zoo Izzy started crying and quickly became hysterical. "No *no* NO NO NO NO NO!" she screamed. "GET OUT GET OUT GET OUT."

"My God," Louis said, alarmed, twisting around in his seat. "Shhh, Izzy, it's okay, it's okay. Stop the car," he ordered Sophie. "She needs to get out."

"Hang on," Sophie said. "Just wait a minute. Bella, let's sing."

Louis stared at her. "Sing? Look, she's really upset, so just stop the car—"

But Sophie and Bella had already begun to sing their new and constantly revised version of "Motorcycle Emptiness." Louis watched as Izzy's screams gradually subsided into sobs, and as he recognized the song he sat back in his seat, staring straight ahead at the road. Sophie glanced at him. It was hard to tell what he was thinking, but he suddenly looked like he was miles away. By the time she had turned the car back in to her road, Izzy was calm again.

"It's all right now, Izzy," Bella said, helping her sister clamber out of the car onto the pavement before engulfing her in a hug.

"I hadn't realized how traumatized she is by the accident," Louis quietly said to Sophie.

"But, of course, she would be. She was right there in the middle of it." Sophie quickly filled him in on the details of the accident as the girls hugged each other.

"It's really frightened her, hasn't it?"

Sophie nodded but clapped her hands as Izzy and Bella came over. "But we're making progress aren't we, Izzy? We went quite far then and nothing bad happened, did it?" Izzy shook her head and wiped her new mittens across her nose, leaving a trail of mucus shimmering on her cheeks. Sophie took one of the tissues that she had begun to keep always somewhere on her person and mopped up Izzy's face.

"We go a little bit farther every day. I think that today was just a bit too far all at once," Sophie explained to Louis.

"That's a really good idea," he told her.

She smiled at him. "Thanks," she said. "I read about it in a dog training book."

Louis blinked at her. "Right," he said, raising his eyebrows.

"Well, I'll say one thing for you, you're full of surprises. Excellent. So what's the new plan?"

"Well," Sophie said. "As Bella is dead set against the bus, there is only one plan left. We take the Tube."

It was an interesting journey to say the least. Izzy became convinced that the Tube trains were fire-breathing dragons. Bella took a seat as far away as possible from Louis, and Sophie, who was concerned that a six-year-old girl should not appear to be alone on the London Underground, sat next to her. At this point, Izzy insisted on sitting on Sophie's lap. So they made the whole trip without exchanging a single word with Louis, although Izzy did occasionally throw him a cheery mittened wave.

And when they emerged at Camden Town Tube station because Regent's Park was closed, it was raining. Louis had thought about hats, but neither he nor Sophie had considered the eventuality of rain, probably rather foolishly, as February was making up for the year's early brightness by becoming the second wettest month in recorded history.

"Let's run!" Louis shouted, grabbing Izzy's hand and heading in the direction indicated by the tourist signpost.

"Um, hang on—" Sophie called out to him in vain. She had wanted to point out that it was actually rather far from Camden Town Tube station to the zoo, but it was too late. She looked at Bella, and joining hands, they ran after him. It took them twenty minutes to get to the zoo's entrance, by which time it had stopped raining, but they were all wet through and out of breath.

"That was pretty far," Louis said to Sophie. "You should have told me."

She bit her tongue and said nothing as he paid the entrance fee.

"Two adults and two kids, please," he told the girl in the booth.

"You save eight pounds with a family ticket, sir," she said, fluttering her lashes at him and dimpling prettily. Louis's brow furrowed, and Sophie worried for a moment that he might be about to point out that they weren't *exactly* a family. But then the girl asked him for forty-two pounds for a family ticket and he went a shade paler under his Peruvian tan.

"Right, okay," he said. "Um, do you take traveler's checks?"

Sophie knew that she could and possibly should have stepped in with her credit card, but she decided if Louis was serious about being a dad, he needed to know about things like how much it cost to go to the zoo.

"I only wanted to visit the zoo," he muttered to Sophie as they filed through the turnstiles. "Not to buy it."

She smiled at him. "A bit different from Peru, hey?" she said.

Louis gazed down at her. "I'll say," he replied.

Sophie looked at the bedraggled girls. "Let's get a warm drink, and then we can stand under a hand dryer for a few minutes, warm up and dry out a bit before we look at the animals. What do you think?" Sophie looked at the sky. "There's some blue up there now, look."

Izzy nodded. "Mummy made it," she said.

Sophie thought it was only fair that she should pay the 9 million pounds (okay, eight eighty-six) for the three hot chocolates and a coffee, so Louis and Izzy picked which of the many empty tables they wanted to sit at in the Pelican Café and Bella came to the cashier with Sophie.

"See," Sophie said. "It's not so bad, is it?"

Bella said nothing but looked over to where Izzy was screaming and giggling as Louis tickled her with her discarded mittens.

"It's good to see Izzy laughing, isn't it?" Sophie tried again as she carefully guided Bella and the tray of hot drinks across the café. This time Bella shrugged and mumbled, "*She's* always laughing." Sophie set the tray down on the table and hung the girls' coats over the backs of their chairs.

"Come on, girls," she said. "Let's see if we can dry off a bit."

Izzy was chattering happily about penguins as she sat on the toilet, and Sophie ruffled Bella's hair under the hand dryer until it was mainly dry once more. As Izzy hopped off the toilet and made a big production of pulling up her tights, she giggled at Bella and said, "It's good to have a daddy, isn't it, Bella? 'Cos now Mummy's gone, Daddy can look after us instead!"

Sophie was completely unprepared for what happened next.

Emitting what Sophie could only describe as a growl, Bella flew at Izzy and pushed her violently. The smaller girl fell hard against the stall partition, banging her head with an audible crack.

"Don't you dare say that!" Bella shouted. "I hate him! *I hate him!* I HATE HIM!" Izzy was screaming, tears streaming down her frightened-looking face. Sophie grabbed Bella and had to pull her off her sister, putting her arms around Bella to encircle the child's flailing arms.

"*Bella!*" she found herself shouting. "Calm down *now.*" But Bella did not calm down. Izzy sat screaming on the floor, her arms outstretched to Sophie, desperate to be comforted, and Bella struggled furiously, attempting to break free. For what seemed like the longest time, Sophie thought she would be stuck in the ladies' room at London Zoo forever, caught between the two of them, unable to reach out and comfort Izzy, unable to calm Bella down. Then the door opened and Louis stuck his head in.

"Everything all right in here?" he said. "I thought I heard—" Seeing immediately that it wasn't, Louis came in. "What happened?" he asked.

Sophie shook her head, indicating that now was no time to go into details. "Just take Izzy outside. She banged the back of her head, quite hard I think. You'd better make sure it's not cut," Sophie said over Bella, who was now bright red and sobbing.

Louis reached Izzy in two long strides and scooped her up, but instead of taking her out, as Sophie had requested, he paused by Bella. "Bella, darling . . . , please—" he began.

"I hate you!" she screamed at him. "Go away, go away, go away!"

Louis froze for a moment and looked at Sophie.

"I think you'd better go," she said, desperately nodding at the door.

At last Louis relented and carried Izzy, sobbing into his chest, back to the café.

Hours seemed to pass in the few minutes that Sophie stood there, her arms securing Bella to her body as she waited for her to calm down. Finally she felt Bella's rigid muscles soften, her racing heart slow, and her ragged breaths begin to even out. At last Sophie was able to let her go and turned Bella around to face her, her hands on her shoulders.

"Why did you do that to Izzy?" Sophie asked evenly. She had never seen the girls have a fight any more serious than squabbles over who got the baby doll and who got the felt-tips. And even those they usually resolved between themselves. To see placid, self-contained Bella so out of control was more than a shock to Sophie. It frightened her.

"I don't know," Bella said. "And anyway, she doesn't know anything. They can't make me live with him if I don't want to, can they?"

"No, they can't make you, Bella," Sophie said. "But it's really important that you give him a chance."

"Because you don't want us?" Bella asked accusingly.

"No! It's not that I don't want you—" Sophie stopped herself before she said too much.

"But you said I didn't have to like him—" Bella insisted.

"I know what I said," Sophie said. "But don't stop yourself liking him either. You told me Mummy didn't want you to hate Louis, didn't you?"

"Yes," Bella said reluctantly.

"So why can't you give him a chance and get to know him again?" Sophie asked. "He might be all right." In fact, Sophie thought, so far he had seemed very much all right.

Bella shook her head. "*She* doesn't know anything," she said, referring to Izzy again. "She's just a baby who wants a nice new daddy. She doesn't even understand what's happened!"

Sophie dropped her head. "That's not true, Bella. Izzy misses your mum. Just as much as you do." She was at a loss for what to say next. "I thought you understood that."

Bella screwed her fists into her eyes, rubbing them vigorously. For once she was looking and acting exactly as young as she was. Sophie crouched down and hugged her.

"Izzy doesn't know him," Bella said. "She doesn't remember him going. *I* do. And it's not right, it's not right for her to be all happy about him coming back when Mummy can't."

Sophie's mind seemed to go blank; all the words of wisdom she had been plucking out of nowhere recently had deserted her. For what seemed like an eon, she did not know what to say. And then, in the back of her dark, blank mind, she saw a tiny flame of a memory, which she thought she had smothered long ago, begin to flicker and burn brightly.

"My dad died when I was quite young," Sophie told Bella. "I was older than you. I was thirteen, but it was almost the same as it was for you. It wasn't expected. I said good-bye to him one morning as he left for work. By the time I got home from school, he had gone." Bella watched her, with her dry, dark eyes. "I missed him so much, Bella, I didn't want to feel that pain. The only person who

made me able to bear it was Carrie, your mum. I couldn't go to my
mum because she was as upset as I was. And I didn't have any
brothers and sisters. Your mummy was always there for me, to help
me through it. Always, forever, whatever—remember?"

Bella nodded, and Sophie felt her thighs cramping, so she sat
down on the floor, grateful that the bad weather had kept the
ladies' room empty so far. Bella sat down with her. "Your mum
helped me, not to forget but to control it." Sophie hesitated. She
wasn't sure that this was a memory she wanted to revive. But, she
reasoned, look at where burying her pain and memories had got
her, a lone cold fish. Bella was only six—you shouldn't have to do
that when you were only six.

"Christmas came," Sophie went on. "It was about three
months after Dad had died. We went to stay with some cousins
of Mum's in Suffolk. She thought it would be for the best, she
thought it would be better than her and me looking at each other
across the Christmas table on our own. I hated it. I didn't want
to go and stay with loads of people I hardly knew. I didn't want
to do anything. If I couldn't be with my dad, I wanted to be at
home on my own and forget Christmas."

"That's what I wanted too, but we weren't allowed to stay at
home either," Bella said.

Sophie nodded. "I know," she said. "But it turned out when we
got there that Mum was right. It was good to have some cousins to
hang about with, some other things to look at and listen to. I
didn't stop missing Dad or hurting, but it helped me to turn it
down. Like when you turn the volume down on the telly—do you
understand what I mean?" Bella nodded. "And then on Christmas
Day we were all sitting around eating lunch, and someone told a
joke—I can't even remember what the joke was now, but it made
her laugh." Sophie paused as she remembered the moment. "I
hadn't seen her smile in three months, but there she was laughing

and laughing, for what seemed like forever. I was *so* angry. I got up and I shouted at her. I said, 'How could you?' I ran out of the room and into the garden so fast that I kicked my chair over and my drink too. I was so angry with her, Bella, because I thought her laughing meant that she had already forgotten Dad."

Sophie bit her lip and, reaching out, brushed a strand of Bella's hair behind her ear. "Mum came out and found me. She knew why I was so cross, and she told me that sometimes you have to practice being happy, even when you're not, because otherwise you might forget how altogether. She said that Dad would want me to be happy whenever I could, that he'd never want me to miss a single chance to laugh because of him." Sophie found herself smiling as she thought of her mum. She had taught her something after all, perhaps even more than she realized, even if it was only now that Sophie finally understood.

"It's easier than you think to let being happy go forever, and once its gone, it's hard to get it back again," Sophie said. "I don't want that to happen to you. Mummy wouldn't want it, and believe me, neither would your daddy. Is that why you pushed Izzy? Were you angry with her for being happy?"

Bella regarded Sophie for a long moment and then, clambering up, put her arms around Sophie's neck and kissed her softly on the cheek. "Yes," she said. She took a breath. "But I know really that Izzy misses Mummy as much as me. I just hate him. He makes me so angry, and I took it out on Izzy. I'm sorry."

Sophie scrambled to her feet. It was pointless to press the girl any further, especially when she felt Bella had just begun to really trust her. And Sophie found that having Bella's trust was an achievement that gave her more satisfaction than everything she had done at the office. Because getting Bella to trust her was far, far more difficult than jumping through hoops to impress Gillian every day.

"I think you'd better tell Izzy that, don't you?" Sophie said, holding a hand out to help Bella up.

They emerged at last from the ladies' room, and Sophie gratefully took a breath of air that was not tinged with disinfectant. Bella and Izzy saw each other across the café, and as Bella crossed over to the table, Izzy climbed off Louis's lap and made her way toward her sister. They met halfway and hugged each other tightly.

Sophie stayed a few feet away and looked at Louis over their heads, but he wasn't looking at her. He was looking at his daughters, his face wrought with sorrow.

"We could still go and see the spiders," Sophie said as the girls broke their embrace.

"I want to go home," Izzy said, looking at Bella. "I don't like the zoo anymore. It's stupid, like you said."

"Maybe that would be best," Louis agreed, looking suddenly tired and careworn as he joined the small group with the girls' coats over his arm. "Maybe it was too much too soon. Come on, let's go."

Back at the flat, a little over two hours after they had left it that morning, Bella helped Sophie empty three tins of tomato soup into three bowls and put them in the microwave one by one.

"Right then." Louis appeared in the doorway. "I'll be off."

"Hang on a minute," Sophie said, gesturing that she wanted a word. "Bella, don't touch the microwave when it beeps, okay?" Bella nodded and looked closely at the spoons as her father left.

"So," Louis said as Sophie followed him to the flat door. "Same time tomorrow then?"

Sophie felt every exhausted muscle in her body ache at the very thought of another morning like the one she had just had and longed for simpler times, when the girls would watch TV and she would hover around trying to avert calamity at every turn.

"You're sure you're up to it then?" she asked.

Louis shrugged and opened the door. "I have to be, don't I?" he said. "If I want to make it work. And I really want to make it work." He looked at Sophie closely. "Look, I really appreciate that way you've handled this. A lot of people wouldn't have got involved at all. But you took the girls on, you kept them from going into foster care, and you made sure I found out what had happened. When we first met, I was worried that you hated me." He smiled again, and Sophie felt all of her careful, methodical plans fly away as she was drawn into the depths of his dark eyes, the same dark eyes that had charmed Carrie into giving everything up for him, Sophie reminded herself.

"You might not care either way," Louis told her "but what you've done means an awful lot to me."

Sophie felt suddenly panicked—honesty seemed like the best policy. "I'm not doing it for you," she said. "And I did hate you a bit." She nipped her lip with her teeth. "Look, Louis, there's something I don't understand. And it's worrying me—" He waited for her to continue. "I don't understand why you did what you did. Why you ran out on Carrie and Bella. Why did you just go and never come back or keep in touch?"

Louis's head jerked up, and he took a step back. "That's none of your business," he said, the contours of his jaw hardening as he spoke.

"Isn't it?" Sophie asked him. "While I have guardianship over your children, I think it is, whether you like it or not."

His face darkened further. "Look," he said. "You were Carrie's 'closest' friend, but she didn't tell you what happened." That point did rather hoist her by her own petard. "If she didn't want you to know, then why should I tell you? Anyway, that was the past; things were done and said that caused a lot of hurt and pain. But none of that matters *now*," he insisted. "Now my children are all that matters."

"It matters to Bella," Sophie said, with simple emphasis. "She's furious with you, Louis. Can't you see that?"

His gaze dropped. "I know," he said quietly. "She has a right to be. But what happened between me and Carrie has nothing to do with her, it's in the past."

"Oh, don't be so naïve," Sophie snapped. "It has everything to do with her—and Izzy. If you want either of them to really trust you, you will *have* to face it sooner or later."

Louis's face was very still. "I know I have a lot of bridges to build," he said quietly. "A future to build, but this is my chance to do the right thing by my daughters. I want you to know that."

Sophie's next words sprang out of her mouth before she had a moment to consider them. "It's a shame you had to wait for their mother to die before you made the effort."

The moment she had completed the sentence she regretted it, but she lifted her chin and held his gaze. Louis looked at her as if reassessing his opinion of her and said nothing for a moment. Then he opened the latch and pulled the flat door open an inch. "I'll be back at the same time tomorrow," he said, his tone perfectly even. "I'll see you then."

Louis pulled the door shut behind him, and Sophie stood for a second or two, looking at its smooth surface.

"Should have stuck to Plan Nice," she told herself. She knew that Plan Nice would have worked eventually, but for some reason at that moment when she had looked into his eyes, she'd felt like she could ask him anything and he'd tell her the truth. But whatever she had felt then must have been wrong.

Nineteen

Sophie had taken the girls to see Tess at her office for a change because she had to get out of the flat and Louis had said he would come in the afternoon because he had some business to attend to.

The last eight days of constant heavy rain and no sunlight during the day had finally filled her head with cotton wool that was scarcely improved by the frantic visits she had managed to make to the office. She knew she should be gearing up for the next big event, but where work was concerned she couldn't seem to get out of neutral. It was just as well that the success of the ship party was still carrying her high.

She'd had eight days of Louis filling the flat with his presence to such an extent that Sophie thought it must be shrinking, or else he was growing even taller, Alice in Wonderland style. Eight days of Bella often secluded in the bedroom, alone except for Artemis and her felt-tips, producing drawing after drawing of a sea filled with mermaids. And eight mornings of Louis's perfect politeness, his initial attempt at a warmer friendliness seemingly abandoned.

There had been one occasion when Sophie had thought that perhaps there could be a thaw in relations between them. On the sixth day, a beam of sunlight had fought its way through the clouds, and there had been a break in the relentless wet weather. Louis and Sophie had simultaneously come to the decision that they should take an immediate trip to the park without even having to confer. Sophie had gone and grabbed the girls' wellies from under the bed just as Louis was finding coats and hats. They had bumped into each other in the hallway.

"I thought we could—" Sophie had begun.

"Take them to the park," Louis had concluded. They had laughed awkwardly and set about rousing the girls from their fifth viewing of *The Little Mermaid* that week.

They'd taken the short trip to the park in a truncated column of two by two. Louis and Izzy had led the party, with Izzy skipping, hopping, and swinging on her father's hand, and Bella and Sophie had brought up the rear in almost complete silence.

"You must have seen it a hundred times," Sophie had said, trying to placate Bella's annoyance at having her favorite movie cut short.

"I wanted to see the end," Bella had replied petulantly.

"Look, Bella, you can see it when we get back. Why don't you try doing something radical—like enjoying yourself?"

Bella had looked up at her and sighed deeply. "I'm trying," she'd said. "It's all these days inside that are making me cross. I'm sorry."

Sophie had smiled at her and picked up her hand. "I know how you feel. Come on," she had said as they entered the park. "Let's see how high we can swing on the swings!"

Sophie had been pushing Bella as high as she could when Izzy fell off the slide. She didn't fall very far or very hard, but as she had put out her hands to break her landing, she had grazed her palms quite badly. Sophie had had to resist the urge to run to her in a way that had become an everyday reaction in the last few weeks, especially as Izzy was an expert in getting into the kinds of scrapes that usually resulted in minor injury. She had watched Louis pick the girl up and hold her tightly, but still Izzy had cried.

"So-So-Sophie," Izzy had wailed and stretched out her arms. Louis had brought her over to the swings right away, and as Sophie had sat down on one, he'd lifted Izzy onto Sophie's lap.

"Let me see," Sophie had said, examining the grazed palms very carefully. "Ohhh, that must sting ever so," she'd said and kissed each palm gently. "Is that a bit better?"

"A bit," Izzy had confirmed bravely with a noisy sniff. Sophie had reached into her pocket and pulled out a tissue to blot Izzy's face and a tube of antiseptic cream that had usurped her lip gloss's usual home. In the meantime, Louis had crouched down, his hands on either side of Sophie, holding the swing chains steady. It had felt strange to have this virtual stranger in such close proximity. It had given Sophie a curious tilted feeling, almost like being drunk in the daytime.

Bella had peered over Sophie's shoulder at Izzy's wounds. "Hardly anything there!" she'd scoffed as Sophie smoothed the antiseptic cream on.

Sophie had turned around and shot Bella a warning look. "Don't worry, this magic cream will make it all better, okay?" she'd said.

" 'Kay." Izzy had sniffed again. "But you carry me though." And the small group had returned to the confines of the flat just as they had left it, except this time Louis had walked on his own a few paces behind the slow and lumbering girls, and Sophie had been sure she had developed a hernia.

When Louis had left a little while later, Sophie had followed him downstairs, hoping there'd be some mail for her to collect that wasn't a credit card bill.

"She wanted you, didn't she?" Louis had said as he opened the door. "Wanted you to comfort her, I mean. Kiss it better." He had dropped his chin. "I suppose I shouldn't be surprised. I mean, she's known you longer than she's known me, but well, it made me realize that, even with Izzy, getting her to trust me isn't as easy as just turning up and making her laugh. She still wanted you." It had been the first time in days that Louis had said anything to Sophie that wasn't strictly necessary, and for a moment she hadn't known how to respond.

She had taken a step closer to him. "It will take time," she'd said eventually and inadequately. "But you have to be prepared for it to take as long as the girls think it should take." Sophie had decided to share with him one of the many things she had learned about children recently. "You can't rush the way people are feeling, even little people. They feel emotions too. Properly and really, I mean," she had said, nodding with emphasis.

Louis's mouth had twitched in a smile.

"What now?" Sophie had demanded, fighting her impulse to return the smile. "Look, you might think I'm funny, but I've only been doing this for a month, I've only just realized that children are humans!"

Louis had laughed, and Sophie hadn't been able to help but join in. "I don't know what Carrie was thinking when she made me the girls' guardian," she had said wryly.

"You're doing really well, Sophie. You were so good with Izzy today. It must be amazing to be three and really believe in magic, really believe that someone's kisses can take away all the pain." Louis's smile had dimmed fractionally. "I wish they had wanted me."

Without thinking Sophie had stretched out a hand and rested it on his arm. "One day they will, I'm sure," she had said, knowing that it was probably true and feeling a little jealous of the time when she wouldn't mean so much to the children. When she would just be distant "Aunty Sophie" again.

"You should go now," she'd said, a little abruptly.

"Same time tomorrow?"

Sophie had considered the prospect with resignation. "No chance of a break, is there?" she'd asked him on impulse.

Louis's face had darkened. "A break?" he'd asked. "I thought you understood how much I've got to make up. A break for who? For you? Because this isn't about you."

"I know that," Sophie had snapped angrily. "I sort of guessed that when my normal life went totally to pot just so I could babysit your children!" She'd caught the rise in her voice and forcefully subdued it. "I thought for the girls," she'd lied shamelessly. "A break for them to clear their heads, a chance to relax a bit without you . . . being . . . everywhere they look."

Louis's face had been perfectly still for a moment, and then he'd shaken his head. "Sophie, I'm sorry you don't like me, but like I said, this isn't about you. Same time tomorrow."

The thaw was definitely over.

Tess was trying to explain Louis's position to Sophie, who was only half-listening as she watched the girls run up and down the corridor outside of Tess's office like a pair of Muppets. Occasionally a flash of pink and purple sped by, having been preceded by demented giggles. "He was married to Carrie, you see, which means he is automatically granted parental responsibility—"

"Yes, but every dad has that. It doesn't mean every dad deserves it," Sophie said tartly.

"Well, no, actually, if they hadn't been married he would have no automatic rights at all, not according to the law. But anyway, by leaving the family home, by not contacting the girls or making formal arrangements to support them financially or emotionally, he has contravened the terms of parental responsibility, so if the court considers it proper, they could forfeit his rights. Ultimately it's up to a judge to decide whether or not he should have parental responsibility reinstated and whether or not he should be granted a residency order and with it full custody of the children."

Sophie blinked at her. "And?" she said. "What are they going to decide?"

Tess shrugged and took a sip of her coffee. "I'd say it was almost clear-cut. Louis has come out of his background checks extremely well. Not a blemish on his record in this country, and did you know that when he was in Peru he helped a charity that took homeless and abandoned disabled kids off the streets of Lima? These kids were given a chance at education and a life other than fending for themselves instead of trying to scrape an existence picking over rubbish bins. He was quite literally giving them a chance to grow up."

Tess was going all misty-eyed, so Sophie tutted loudly. "Yes, well," she said. "You see, that whole St. Francis of Assisi thing would play a lot better with me if he hadn't actually abandoned his own children."

"Yes, it is a dilemma," Tess admitted, "but the court makes a point of accepting that good people make bad mistakes. It does not like to split up a family unless it absolutely has to." She was more or less quoting from the book on family law she had been reading the night before just to make sure she was clear on all the proceedings that were even now under way. Louis had not come back from Peru with much money, but what little he did have he had invested in a respectable boarding house and a good solicitor.

And although the legal side was, strictly speaking, down to the authorities' legal team, Tess prided herself on knowing what she was talking about. "And, of course, what the girls want has an awful lot to do with it. That and my recommendations. I have to file my report by the end of this week."

Another flash of color whizzed by the open door. Tess leaned forward on her desk. "What interests me most at the moment, Sophie," she said, "is what you think. What do you want to happen?"

Sophie jerked her head around to look at Tess. "How do you mean?" she asked.

"Well, I more or less pressed you into taking the girls, didn't I?"

Sophie nodded, pursed her lips, and crossed her arms just to show that she still hadn't entirely forgiven Tess for that.

"Well, then it meant either you took them or they went into foster care. I had to rush through the temporary residency order because I was so scared you'd change your mind. That was twenty-odd years of collecting favors gone in two days."

Sophie raised her eyebrows. She hadn't realized.

"When you were looking for Louis, you were doing so in order to provide an alternative to you," Tess went on. "So that it would be between Louis and going into to foster care. So you could get back to your life and not feel guilty."

Sophie looked a bit sheepish. "Ah well. See, that's not *exactly* true . . ."

But Tess waved away her feeble protest. "It is," she said. "But that's not my point. My point is, if I understand what's happening here, you're not just prepared to keep the girls indefinitely until they go somewhere else to live. I think if it came down to it, you would actually have the girls for keeps."

Sophie expected herself to scoff, but the scoff did not arrive. Instead she examined the very last remnants of her nail polish and let a nagging and terrifying thought that had been lingering in the back of her mind since her conversation on the stairs with Bella finally form itself.

"I don't know," she said carefully. "But if it really wasn't going to work out with Louis, then, well— Do you think that I could do it? Give them a good home?"

Tess looked at her. "Actually, I think you could," she said seriously. "But Louis is here now. Something would have to go badly wrong for that situation to arise. You understand that, don't you?"

"I know," Sophie said. "It's stupid to even think about it really. It would never work. I have my career and . . ." She could not think of anything else to say.

Tess shifted in her seat. "Well, the girls have a natural parent alive, present and correct and prepared to take them. And he is doing his best to make himself viable. He's lined up an interview with the National Society for the Prevention of Cruelty to Children and soon he'll probably have a job and a permanent place to stay. He's been asking about when Bella will be found a temporary school. He's worried she's missed too much already, and she has."

"It's the Christmas holidays," Sophie said, as if she knew what she was talking about.

"Sophie, it's February! Anyway, Louis's been in touch with their old school. They are holding a place for Bella. Apparently she was their star pupil. And Izzy's nursery would be delighted to have her back."

Sophie cursed herself. The reason she didn't know about any of this was that she had rashly abandoned Plan Nice. She'd pushed Louis too far, and now he didn't seem to like her much, a consequence she found curiously disturbing because if—as Tess said—it was inevitable that they be returned to him, she didn't want to lose the children completely from her life.

Then she thought about exactly what Tess had just said. "Their old school, in St. Ives?"

Tess leaned back in her chair. "Yes," she said. "They won't be going anywhere until this is all settled and the supervision order is lifted, but I ought to tell you it will be settled soon, Sophie. It could even be in the next couple of weeks. All being well, I think the girls will go back home to Cornwall with their father. And I think that will be the best thing for them."

Sophie tried to imagine what it would be like to have her whole old, peaceful, ordered life back again. "But Bella hates him," she said, deciding not to imagine such a restoration to civilization just then. "She really hates him, and you said it matters what the children want."

Tess nodded. "It does," she said carefully. "It does matter what the children want, but I don't think Bella hates him, not really. She is hurt and angry and worried and confused. But she doesn't hate him." Tess smiled and, reaching over the desk, placed her warm, heavy hand over Sophie's light, cold one, squeezing it for a moment. "I think that what you've done for the girls so far is wonderful, much, much more than I ever expected. You've brought Bella out of her shell, and I know that Izzy's taking short trips in the car now. All that means so much to them. But there's one thing you have to do, the only thing you can do really—you have to help Bella come to terms with what has happened. You have to help her make friends with her dad, and then Izzy won't have to worry about who to be loyal to all the time. And perhaps while you're at it, you could make friends with Louis yourself. It would be so much easier for the girls," Tess added cautiously.

The shouts outside grew louder, and suddenly Tess's office was filled with noise as the girls crash-landed into Sophie, giggling and laughing.

She grinned at them. "Ready, steady—go!" she shouted, and they were off again.

She turned back to Tess, her smile vanishing instantly. "But I mean, what about the reasons why Louis and Carrie split up? What about why he didn't stay in touch with the girls? Doesn't that matter at all?"

"It matters to you, I can see that. But families drift apart for all the wrong reasons every day. It's a tragic fact. It's up to people like me to try to make sure it doesn't happen in the first place, or to try to repair it when it does. We have a really good chance to repair a family here, Sophie—to repair lives. And I have to admit that it is largely thanks to you. Louis is not a criminal, or an abuser. The kind of man he is now is what is important. The past doesn't really matter anymore," Tess said, echoing Louis's words. "If I could just see that Bella and Louis were making progress together, I'd feel so much better," she went on. "Then I think this terrible time of their lives would be over at last. I think they'd be able to start again. Will you help them? Because, I'll be honest, I think that you're the only person who really can."

Sophie paused, feeling as if the pit of her stomach was filling gradually with heavy black stones. There was really only one thing she could say. "Of course I'll help her," she said. "I'll help them both. I just want them to be happy."

It was curious, Sophie thought, as she hurried the girls back to the flat for that day's meeting with Louis, that *she* didn't feel happier. Elated even. She had managed somehow through all the chaos to pull off quite a coup. She'd rescued the girls from foster care and kept a promise to Carrie, made her boss love her, and possibly even secured a promotion in the process. She had located the apparently perfect father more or less single-handedly and was now helping to restore the girls to family life, a family life in the place that they loved and called home. She should feel triumphant. In less than a month she'd have back her bed, she might well have a new job and much more shoe money than she could ever need—well, perhaps not that much—and she would have peace and quiet and all the time in the world to pluck her eyebrows and wax her legs and watch films featuring scenes of sex and violence. She could even start smoking properly again. She should feel ecstatic.

But she didn't, she didn't feel that way at all.

Maybe, Sophie thought reluctantly as she let the girls into the flat, it's because I'm afraid of what I will feel when my "perfect" life is fully reinstated. Perhaps I'm afraid of being something I have always been but never allowed myself to think about before the girls came. Perhaps it's because I'm afraid of being alone—again.

This was probably why she called Jake, even though she had hardly thought of him since the last time they had spoken. He had told her to call him when she figured out what she wanted. Well, she knew one thing, she didn't want her life to go back to the empty, impersonal routine it had been. She was loath to admit that her mother could be right about anything, but maybe she was right about this—Sophie did need someone in her life.

"I thought I wasn't going to hear from you again," Jake said, his voice neutrally pleasant. "I thought I'd blown it. I'm glad you called, Sophie, unless it's to tell me it's over!" He chuckled nervously.

"We haven't even begun yet, Jake," she said tentatively.

"Are we going to?"

"You know," Sophie said with a smile, "you really should ask me what I think about the weather first and then something else general and meaningless before you plunge into all this important stuff."

Jake laughed. "I just want to see you," he said.

Sophie pushed the threatening echoes of loneliness firmly out of her mind and thought about the handsome, kind, thoughtful man who really seemed to care about her. She was sure he would fill the gap that would be left when the girls were gone. She was sure, if she put her mind to it, she could really care about him too. "I want to see you too," she said.

"When?" Jake asked, all trace of neutrality gone.

"This evening?" Sophie said, wanting to see him suddenly quite badly.

"I'll be there."

"Three tickets to see . . ." Louis drew out the suspense to such an extent the Sophie thought Izzy might actually pop. "*The Little Mermaid on Ice*—this afternoon!" Izzy screamed and danced around the coffee table. Louis grinned at Sophie, so pleased with himself that he forgot to be frosty. "Although I've got to say that somehow sounds like animal cruelty to me, but still. . . ."

Sophie found herself laughing and then stopped when she caught Bella's expression. The six-year-old glared at her and then looked down at the three tickets Louis had fanned out on the coffee table. "No, thank you," she said.

Sophie bent down a little and put an arm around her shoulders. "But it's *The Little Mermaid*. You love *The Little Mermaid*!"

"There's only three tickets," Bella said.

Louis caught Izzy as she danced by and hoisted her onto his hip in one fluid movement.

"Ah, yes," he said. "Look, Bella, I'm sorry. I didn't want to leave Sophie out, it's just, well, there were only three tickets left . . ."

Bella stared at him. "I'm not going unless Sophie can come."

Sophie sighed and remembered what Tess had told her. "Well,

perhaps I could buy another ticket at the door?" she suggested. Louis's face fell, and she realized that he had just hoped if he suggested something he knew Bella would love, she might actually want to go with him and Izzy. But mainly him—without Sophie. He had been trying to move out of what he must have seen as an implacable stalemate.

"You won't. It's sold out now. I got those three from a scalper. Can you believe there are *scalpers* selling tickets to see *Mermaids on Ice*? What kind of world are we living in?" he said glumly. He sat down heavily on the sofa, and Izzy landed on his lap with a giggle. "Look," he said. "You three take them and go, I'll see you all tomorrow."

Before Bella could react, Izzy launched her protest. "Nooooooooo," she wailed. "I want to go with Daddy, not Sophie! Bella, *please* come with us! *Please!*"

Bella looked at the tickets again, and at her sister in Louis's arms. "I'm sorry," she said quietly. "I can't." She turned on her heel and walked steadily out of the room.

Sophie sat down next to Louis. "She really wants to go, you know," she said. "*The Little Mermaid* is her favorite."

"I know," he said, clearly uncertain where Sophie was coming from. "Just not with me."

"I don't know. I think she wants to go with you. I think there's something stopping her. It's like she just said. She just can't."

Izzy climbed off Louis's lap and fluffed her fairy skirt. "I need a poo," she told them matter-of-factly and skipped out of the room.

Sophie thought for a moment and then looked at Louis. "I saw Tess today," she said. "She told me you're more or less up for father of the year."

Louis look surprised, delighted, and then wary. "You mean—?"

Sophie nodded. "She says she thinks things will go your way

as long as her report supports you. And I'm fairly sure she's in love with you, so I don't think you're going to have to worry on that score." Sophie thought of Tess's advice. "Look, Louis—we have to clear the air between us. Carrie was my best friend. Even though I didn't see her that much, I never thought there'd be a day when I'd never be able to see her again. I loved her, and I suppose I've been trying to defend her still, which means sometimes I've been a bit out of order with you. I wanted to know what went wrong and why she didn't tell me." Louis began to talk, but Sophie stopped him. "I wanted to know for Carrie's sake, and Bella's, but mainly—for me. I thought I was her best friend. But when it came to the crunch, she didn't talk to me, she didn't tell me anything. Maybe just because I didn't ask her and because I didn't care enough to notice. I want to be a friend to the girls and . . . and you. I'm sorry I was so prickly to begin with. I've been feeling bad myself, but I'm trying to look at the big picture now. So." Sophie offered him a tentative smile. "Can we start again?"

Louis's face relaxed and opened into a smile. "Of course," he said, with a rush of warmth. "God, I'd love that." There was a moment's silence as each of them tried to work out how to adjust their tenuous relationship to a more friendly one.

"I miss her too, you know," Louis said after a while, and it took Sophie a second to realize he was talking about Carrie. "I can't believe that she's dead. She was so . . ." He paused, struggling to find the right words. "She was such a force of nature, she seemed invincible. And I still cared about her, you know, I still hoped that she finally got what she wanted, that everything worked out as she'd planned." He looked down. "I really wish she was here now."

For the first time Sophie got an inkling that perhaps it wasn't Louis who had walked out on Carrie. Perhaps, just perhaps,

Carrie had sent him away. But why, when she had told Sophie often enough that he was the love of her life? There were so many
questions Sophie wanted to ask him, but she had no intention of
making the same mistake twice. Instead she would let her truce
with Louis hold and strengthen. There were other, more important things to think about now.

"You go to *The Little Mermaid*," she told Louis. "Go and take
Izzy with you. I'll stay with Bella. Perhaps I can try to talk her
round."

"Don't you think I might kidnap Izzy or something? What
about having to stay with us?" Louis asked, looking up at her with
that effortlessly intense gaze that he managed so well.

It took Sophie a moment to find her voice. "No," she said, finally managing to speak. "If you'd been taking both of them, I
might have worried, but I know you wouldn't go without Bella."

"You're right," he said. "I wouldn't leave my Bellarina—not
again anyway." He gave a mirthless laugh and glanced out the
window at the afternoon sky glowering darkly over the rooftops.
"I used to take her for a walk every day after work. I worked the
early shift at the printer's so I'd be home by five. Every day we'd
go for a walk except if it was snowing or really cold. When she
was a tiny baby, it was to give Carrie a break, and then as she got
bigger, just because we wanted to.

"In the summer I'd wheel her in her pram along the cliff walk
and we'd look at the birds and the sun on the sea. In the winter
I'd take her past the beach up the hill opposite the town and we'd
watch the light glittering against the sky and try to count the
stars. When we got back, she'd draw what we'd seen for Carrie
while I made her tea. She never got to bed till well past seven, but
it didn't matter. Carrie said it didn't matter, because it was more
important that we had our special time together, that we had a
chance to be friends."

Louis paused and swallowed. "Bella was my best friend. We learned something new together every day." He slumped back in the chair. "I blew it, didn't I? I didn't really stop to think about anyone but myself, I know that now. I've known it for a long time. I just wish I could make her understand how much I've missed her. How sorry I am."

Sophie nodded. "I know."

"Really?" Louis asked.

"I think I'm beginning to," she said.

They watched each other for a moment in the half-light, and Sophie wondered if Louis was seeing her in the same way she was seeing him. As someone she had really only met about four or five minutes ago.

"Right." Izzy reappeared with her raincoat on over her fairy dress. "I've finished my poo, and I did *most* of it in the toilet!"

Twenty

After they had gone, Sophie sat in the shadows and listened to the silence of her home. It was a sound she had grown used to in her years in the flat, the sound of her private life, her very own bubble—a contented background hum. But somewhere lost in the silence was Bella, and suddenly Sophie wished with all her heart for noise and plenty of it.

She thought about Louis describing his daily walks with Bella, their exploration of the coast of St. Ives, the ideas and the stories they'd created as they walked. Either he was an excellent actor and a consummate con man *or* Tess was right—he was basically a good man who'd done some very stupid things. But how do you explain all that to a girl who once idolized her father and had found out that he was only human?

It seemed as if Bella was holding too tightly to herself and her sister to be able to consider letting anyone else, even her father, in. She was trying, with all her might, to hold on to Carrie and to love her in exactly the same way that she had when she had been dropped off for school on the day Carrie had died. No one knew better than Sophie how hard that was and how such an effort could wear you out.

Poking out from under the corner of Artemis's chair was one of Bella's many drawings. Sophie bent over and scooped it up. As usual it was a picture of the sea, drawn with bold swirls of gray, green, and blue felt-tips, leaving intentional gaps of white paper that did make it look as if it were a body of water rising and falling with the tide. In the midst of the sea were the mermaids, ten or so little curly, brown-haired girls garlanded with flowers, laughing and playing. They reminded Sophie of someone—Carrie, of course. In the background Bella had drawn the shore, always the same in each picture, a hill rising out of the sea with little box-shaped houses on its crest, carefully colored around so that they remained white.

Sophie looked at the drawing for a long time, and then she realized. The houses weren't a fantasy, another construct of Bella's fertile imagination—they were the houses in St. Ives. Bella had been drawing home.

Sophie placed the drawing on the coffee table and looked at her watch as she made her way to the bedroom. It was just after two—they had plenty of time before Izzy and Louis would be back from the show. Time to show Bella something that, for some reason, Sophie thought might be really important.

Sophie walked into the room and switched on the light. "We're going out," she said, throwing Bella's coat at her.

Offended by the sudden glare, Artemis scampered out the window with an angry yowl, and Bella sat up, rubbing her eyes as her vision adjusted to the brightness. "I don't want to go out," she said bluntly.

"Yes you do," Sophie said, "Come on, no arguments, just you and me. I'm taking you to see something really special." Sophie did her best to sound enticing and keep her apprehension out of her voice.

"I'm not going to *The Little Mermaid,* am I?" Bella asked with a heartbreaking mixture of belligerence and hope.

Sophie shook her head. "No," she said. "This trip is just for you and me. Come on."

Bella's second trip on the Tube was much less eventful than the first and much quieter. She sat next to Sophie, her hand, still in its glove, slotted into Sophie's. As Sophie counted the stops, Bella stared at everyone else on the train with open curiosity until they coughed and raised their books or magazines a little higher. The train rattled down the Victoria line, through Pimlico to Vauxhall, where finally they got off at Blackfriars.

"Where are we going?" Bella asked again as Sophie marched her briskly through the wet streets, the pavements streaked with reflections of colored light.

"We're going to see a painting," Sophie told her, taking a corner at such a high speed that Bella's feet almost didn't touch the ground as she struggled to keep up.

"A painting?" Bella said, clearly disappointed that it wasn't a musical extravaganza on ice. "Where?"

Sophie stopped at the slope that led down to the entrance of the Tate Modern. "Here," she said.

Bella looked up at the huge bulk of the converted power station standing stalwart against the silvered sky. "Wow."

"Exactly. Come on."

They were lucky. The rain, the season, the day of the week, and the hour had all conspired to keep the gallery relatively unclogged, so for once a visitor could enjoy the functional majesty of the building as well as the exhibits it contained.

"Ooooh," Bella exclaimed, gawking at the huge sculpture that filled the foyer. "It's gigantic!"

Sophie paused and looked up at Antony Gormley's work.

"It is," she agreed, flicking open the folded map. "According to this, I think the painting I want to show you is quite far up the escalators. Let's go and look at it first, and then afterward we can have a look at anything else you want, okay?"

Bella nodded and hopped readily onto the escalator next to Sophie. Sophie felt a knot in the pit of her stomach. She had no idea if what she was about to show the child would mean anything to her. But also she worried that it might mean too much, and if it did, Sophie realized she didn't know what she would do next. But she knew, whatever happened, she had to go forward because there was nowhere else to go. And anyway she had a feeling it would turn out all right, a feeling her mother would call intuition.

With another quick look at her map, Sophie led Bella, whose head was generally pointed in the opposite direction from which they were walking, to the modern British painters' wing and then to a small room at the back of a network of galleries that overlooked the river. She pointed at a sign on the left of the entrance to the room. "What does that say?" Sophie asked.

Bella looked at the sign for a moment and smiled. "The St. Ives School of Art!" she exclaimed. "Are Mrs. Benson's sunflower paintings in there?" she said, hopping toward the door in anticipation.

"No," Sophie said. "At least I don't think so. I think these paintings are a bit older." As they entered, Sophie scanned the room, hoping and praying that the canvas she was looking for was here, that it hadn't been placed in storage when the collection was moved from Tate Britain some years ago. And then she saw it, smaller than a painting should be, she had thought the first time she saw it, almost inconsequential. In fact, when Carrie had brought her to see it in its old home across the river, her first words had been, "A child could do better than that. *I* could do better than *that*!" But then Sophie's appreciation of art had always been much less sophisticated than Carrie's.

Sophie took Bella over and showed her the painting.

"*St. Ives, Version Two, 1940,*" Sophie read out the label for Bella, who studied the painting closely. "It's by a man called Ben—"

"Nicholson," Bella finished. "I know. Mum used to take us to the Tate St. Ives all the time. Some of his pictures are there too." She looked at the painting. "Home," she said, pointing to the top right-hand corner, where Nicholson had painted the beach and part of the town of St. Ives.

Sophie stood behind Bella and rested her hands lightly on her shoulders. She took a deep breath and began to say what she had brought Bella all this way to hear. "They had this big exhibition of St. Ives artists years and years ago, when your mum still lived near me in London. We were doing our A levels at the time. We were supposed to be revising—practicing—for our test. But your mum didn't really like practicing. She said we needed to get out, get some sunshine and fresh air before we went bonkers." Bella smiled. "She brought me to see this painting. Well, not just this painting, she made me see the whole exhibition. But it was this painting especially that really got to her. I don't know why this one, but the minute she saw it she loved it." Sophie paused and moistened her dry lips, realizing she was nervous. Bella stood perfectly still, looking at the picture, but Sophie sensed she was listening very closely.

"To be honest with you," Sophie said, "I never really got it. I think your pictures are better than this one. But your mum said it was called . . . um, abstract constructivism, or something *ism* anyway," Sophie said hurriedly, glossing over the parts she didn't understand. "She said—now let me think—she said that it was so powerful and emotional that the painter had caught a moment in time and trapped it with light on the canvas forever." Sophie smiled as the conversation came back to her sentence by sentence. "I said, 'It looks like a painting of a mug to me,' and she said there was no point in her practicing for her art exam anymore because she'd never be that good. Well, I thought she had gone bonkers, but anyway, she sat and looked at this painting for a long long time. I moped around waiting for her, until eventually I had to drag her away. I think I wanted to go to the café and have cake. Carrie looked at me and she said, 'I'm going there, one day.' 'What? Where?' I asked her, or something like that. 'There, St. Ives,' she said. 'I want to sit exactly where he was when he made that. I want to see that view and feel that light on my face. It's like someone's finally shown me where my home is. And I'm going there as soon as I can. To live and fall in love and have my children and paint. Then I'll be free of this dirty old city and free of my—'" Sophie stopped herself from saying "my mother" and instead inserted, "'free of school and I'll be happy. I just know I will,' she said," Sophie told the top of Bella's head, in Carrie's own words. "I don't know why, I just know that when I'm there I'll be so happy. This painting told me so."

Sophie knelt down beside Bella so their heads were level. "And she *was* happy, wasn't she? Because she had the sea, and the light, and Izzy and you. And she loved you both so much, Bella."

On the last word, Bella crumpled suddenly to the floor and buried her face in her hands. For a split second Sophie watched her shoulders shudder and shake and realized that for the first time since her mother had died, Bella was crying.

"It's okay," Sophie said. "It's okay, darling, it's okay." She put her arms around Bella, who turned in to her embrace.

"Mummy," she said, through her sobs. "I just want my mummy back."

Sophie was glad that the people who happened into the small gallery took one look at the distraught child on the floor and walked right out again. She and Bella sat there for a long time, until Sophie felt the damp of Bella's tears pervade her jacket, until Bella's shoulders stilled except for the occasional long and deep, shuddering breath and at last she was quiet. It was then that Sophie realized she had been rocking the girl. She stopped and brushed the damp hair from Bella's face.

"I'm sorry," Sophie said. "I didn't want to make you sad."

"But I'm sad anyway," Bella said softly. "All the time."

Sophie nodded. "I know."

"Because it was just like a normal day," Bella said, and Sophie held perfectly still, as if any sudden movement might frighten Bella back to silence. "We'd stopped on the corner so that I could walk into school with Lucy like always, and she rolled down the window for a kiss. It always stuck halfway, so I had to stand on my toes to kiss her. And then I ran off and never thought about her again until— I never looked back or waved good-bye or anything."

Sophie didn't know what to say, so she stayed silent.

"One of our gerbils died, before," Bella said. "He was the only person I'd ever known who died, and Mummy got us another one that looked just the same, and after a while Izzy forgot it was a different gerbil. I don't want her to forget Mummy and just remember *him*. *I* don't want to forget Mummy. I keep expecting her to come and collect us. I keep wishing she would just *come*. But she won't."

"No," Sophie agreed gently. "She won't. But listen, Bella, you and Izzy, you're not alone in the world. You have me, and Grandma and Tess, and you have Louis. You have your dad."

"I don't want him," Bella said but without anger.

Sophie kissed the top of her head. "Don't you?" she asked gently. "Are you sure? You must remember how much you loved him once, otherwise you wouldn't hate him so much now."

"He just went too," Bella said. "He didn't say good-bye to me like I didn't say good-bye to Mum. He can't just come back and be all happy when Mum can't. He just *can't,* it's not fair."

Sophie understood Bella's logic perfectly, and she knew that, in some ways, she was right. It wasn't fair.

"I don't think he thinks that he can," she said. "I think he just wants to make friends with you again. He said he wishes you'd never fallen out, and I believe him." Sophie thought about everything Tess had said to her that morning. "Look, when he first came, I was angry with him too, but I don't think he did what he did to hurt you. I think he sort of did it to hurt himself." Bella looked up at Sophie with a furrowed brow. "What I mean is, I think he's a good person and that you should give him a chance."

Bella did not look convinced.

"Okay," Sophie tried again. "I loved your mum and your mum loved me, I think. What do you think?"

Bella smiled. "Yes, she used to tell us about you," she said. "You made her laugh a lot."

"Well, before all this happened, I hadn't seen your mum for ages, for years actually. But I still loved her. I still knew that when we saw each other the next time, things would be like they always were between us, because I still loved her. And when—when I realized that I'd missed my chance to see her again, I was very angry with myself. I still am. But I still let you and Izzy come and stay with me even though you are noisy, messy *brats*." Bella smiled and nodded in agreement. "I didn't do it because I loved you, you pair of hooligans. I did it because I still loved your mum. Even after all those years and even though she was dead, I still wanted to be a friend to her. It is possible to still care about a person even when you are miles away. Even when you don't see them all the time."

Bella studied Sophie's face as she thought about what she said. "Do you like us now?" she asked after a beat. "Me and Izzy, I mean."

Sophie laughed. "Of course I do, I *love* you now!" She realized it was true as she said it.

"Good." Bella clambered to her feet. "Because I suppose I love you too."

She held out a hand, and Sophie let the six-year-old think she was hauling her to her feet.

"Thank you, Aunty Sophie," Bella said, as Sophie stamped her numb foot a few times.

"For what?" Sophie said.

"For bringing me here to see the painting. I don't know why. But I feel better now I've seen it. I feel sort of—lighter."

"I'm glad," Sophie said, with palpable relief. "I truly am. Come on, let's go to the gift shop."

"Oooh," Bella said. "Are we going to buy an eraser?"

There were no posters of Ben Nicholson's painting *St. Ives Version Two* (1940) and no postcards either. The only reproduction that Sophie could find was in a huge yellow book about him published by Phaidon with a price that she assumed was calculated in direct proportion to the tome's enormous weight and bulk.

"That's a lot of money for one picture, especially considering that I'm planning to rip it out," she told the young man behind the counter, who propped his chin on his shoulder as he watched her consider the purchase, the book open at the painting.

"Not a huge Nicholson fan then, no?" he said, giving Sophie

his best cute smile as she glanced up at him. She bit her lip and shook her head, so that a strand of her yellow hair fell over one eye.

"I am," Bella said, standing on tiptoes so that she could peer over the counter. "But I've only got fifty-seven pence."

The man nodded at her. "Cool," he said to Sophie. "Cool kid—yours?" He looked back up at Sophie, who was slightly flushed, her long hair tousled and a little wild.

"Er no," she said, considering the question a little personal.

"Ah, so you're sort of a mentor. Cool," the young man, probably a student, said again. He glanced around the near-empty shop. "Look, hang on a minute." And he took the book and vanished.

In his absence two tourists joined the line, and after a minute or two one began tapping her foot.

"He'll be back soon," Bella told the tourist quite sternly. She stopped tapping. At last the cashier returned and handed Sophie a tube.

"Color photocopies of your painting," he told her, leaning over the counter so that his cheek was close to hers. "Pretty good quality too, and I enlarged them. They're on me." He straightened up again and looked down at Bella. "You can start saving for the book. I reckon you'll be able to afford it by 2010." He winked at Sophie. "Don't tell anyone, okay? I'll get shot, and then I'll never finish college."

Sophie smiled warmly at him and noticed that he was a kindred spirit in the skin department at least, as both of his cheeks flushed a deep red in an instant.

"Thank you so much," she said. "That's really kind."

"Not that kind," the man said. "I made you two copies. My phone number's on the back of one. Maybe you'll call me sometime?"

"Er, thank you," Sophie said one last time.

That was very nice of him, she thought. But quite honestly, she just couldn't think of a reason why she would ever call him.

"He liked you," Bella told her as they emerged into the chill of the dark afternoon.

Sophie laughed. "Don't be silly," she said.

"Oh, Aunty Sophie," Bella said pityingly. "No wonder you haven't got a boyfriend. Lots of men like you, and you don't seem to notice!"

Sophie stopped and looked down at Bella. "What are you talking about?" she asked.

"That Jake, anyone could tell he was in love with you, following you around, helping us home when we'd been shopping that time."

Sophie smiled and felt a gush of warmth toward Jake. "Yes," she said. "That was nice, wasn't it."

"And most men look at you when we're out. Even *he* thinks you're pretty."

"Who?"

Bella looked up at her and shrugged. "Even Louis thinks you're pretty—it's obvious."

Sophie laughed and shook her head. "And why do you think that?" she asked her, only because if Bella was so delusional about Louis, there was a chance she could be wrong about Jake.

"Because," Bella said, "whenever you're not looking at him, he looks at you, and when you do look at him, he has to try really hard not to look away."

"Oh," Sophie said. "Really? I mean, nonsense!"

It was foolish, but for some reason that piece of information started a flutter in the pit of her stomach.

"I'm not saying he loves you or anything, like Jake does," Bella said bluntly. "In fact, he probably thinks you're quite bossy and rude. But he definitely must think you're really pretty, or else he wouldn't look at you and not look at you."

"We're going to be late," Sophie said, hurriedly picking up Bella's hand and starting to walk again. She didn't want to think the thoughts that the girl's offhand comment had stirred up. She wanted to think about Jake carrying all their bags home on the bus instead.

When they got home, Sophie unrolled the two copies of the painting, separated one, and smoothed it out on the table.

"When things have settled a bit," she said, "I'll put this in a frame for you. But for now—" Bella followed Sophie into the bedroom, where she tacked the picture onto the wardrobe opposite the end of the bed. "Now you'll be able to look at the painting whenever you like," Sophie said. "And you'll be able to think about your mum whenever you like. And you can be sad when you think about her and you can be happy. Both are allowed."

Bella nodded and sat on the edge of the bed for a moment. "I think I'll do a drawing," she said, and Sophie breathed a sigh of relief. It seemed as if she had done the right thing after all.

Sophie was engaging the new-to-her art of preparing fresh vegetables when Louis and Izzy came in. She had expected to hear Izzy's hollering long before the three-year-old arrived, but instead Louis just appeared behind her in the kitchen doorway so that when Sophie turned to put the handful of peelings she was holding in the bin, he made her jump. Izzy was fast asleep in his arms.

"The downstairs door wasn't shut properly, and your flat door was on the latch," he said by way of explanation, looking wary of making her cross again. "Shall I put her in the bedroom?"

"No, just put her on the sofa for now," she whispered.

He deposited the child carefully and came back into the

kitchen, where Sophie was peering at the never previously used cookery book. She was attempting lamb stew. It was difficult already, but Louis's presence in the tiny room was making it near impossible. She shut the book with a snap and turned around to look at him. "How did it go?" she asked quickly, feeling the need to breathe in to maintain the foot or so distance between them.

"Great," Louis said, a slow smile spreading across his face as he reflected on the day. "Really great, but my God, she's a real live wire isn't she?" He chuckled. "I thought we were going to get thrown out at one point."

Sophie smiled at him. "Yeah, been there," she told him. "Frequently."

"But she loved it," he said. "She thought it was magic, I mean real magic. It must be great to still truly believe in magical things. It's a shame really that one day she has to find out it's not true."

Sophie shrugged. "I don't know," she said. "Carrie always believed in the magical, she even saw it in all the mundane things around her. I think Izzy will probably be just the same."

They smiled at each other for a moment, and Sophie realized belatedly that she was still holding her cutting knife rather aggressively.

"I'll be off," Louis said, looking rather uncomfortable as Sophie gazed at the potential weapon in her hand with some surprise.

"Oh, okay—right. Well, bye then," she said.

"If you like, you could have tea here." It was Bella.

She stood in the doorway and looked up at Louis.

"Really?" he said cautiously. "With you, you mean."

"And Izzy and Sophie too," Bella said. "Obviously. Although I don't think we'll all fit on the kitchen floor."

"Er—thank you," Louis said, looking at Sophie.

"That's okay," Bella said. And she went back into the living room and turned on the TV. Her slumbering sister didn't even stir.

"You might not want to stay for tea actually," Sophie said, feeling foolish and suddenly nervous.

Louis's face fell. "Oh, right, well, if you think it's a terrible idea—too soon and all that—I suppose—" he began.

"Oh no," Sophie said, smiling at him. "I think it's a great idea. It's just that— Well, I really can't cook."

"Well, that's lucky then, because I can. Move over."

For the first time ever, Louis got Izzy ready for bed, and although she still didn't allow him to do anything for her, Bella let him read Izzy a bedtime story in the bedroom as she sat on the sofa and finally finished her fairy pony story for Sophie.

"The end," Bella said, looking very satisfied.

"That was wonderful," Sophie said sincerely.

"I know," Bella said. As Louis came into the living room, Bella went out, pausing to say a formal good night on the way. Louis sat down on the sofa next to Sophie, uninvited and much more relaxed than he had been in the morning.

She edged away from him, suddenly feeling self-conscious for some reason.

"I don't know how to thank you," Louis told Sophie. "I owe you so much, and I hardly even know you." Sophie just shrugged. "Except I feel as if I've always known you—through Carrie I mean," he added hurriedly.

"Oh well, you know . . . ," she said awkwardly.

Sophie remembered Tess telling her how important it was to stay friends with Louis, but somehow, the more she liked him the harder that seemed to be. And Bella telling her that Louis must think she was pretty had made things worse, shifted whatever kind of fledgling relationship she might have with him, so that she felt nervous and unsettled.

As if sensing that discomfort, Louis stood up and went to look out at the traffic rushing by.

"There's two weeks until Tess files her report and the court makes a decision. It seems like too long and not long enough at the same time. Do you know what I mean?"

Sophie nodded. She knew exactly what he meant.

"I don't know what to do next," Louis confessed. "I thought it would be easy, like it was with the kids in Lima, but although I cared about those kids, a lot, I didn't love them, they weren't part of me. I'm so frightened of messing up this chance with Bella that I keep thinking I'll do or say something stupid every time I see her." He looked at Sophie and smiled. "It's a bit like falling in love."

"Well," she said, taking a deep breath. "I did have an idea today. One that would have to involve all of us to work. But I think there is a way we can finally get Bella to completely relax and open up. And a way of settling Izzy too."

Louis turned and studied Sophie's face carefully. "Really?" he asked. "Tell me."

"Well." She paused. "I think we should use these two weeks to take the girls back to St. Ives for a visit," she said, scarcely believing her own ears. "I mean, you have to go down there anyway, don't you, to find a place to live and a job, so I think we should all go, a sort of a halfway visit. I think you and I should take them home."

They were still discussing how and when, when Jake arrived.

"Jake!" Sophie beamed her best hostess smile at him as she led him up the stairs.

"You haven't forgotten I was coming, have you?" he joked.

"Don't be silly," Sophie said guiltily enough to make him look at her sharply.

She led him into the front room, where Louis was already standing with his jacket in his hand. If Louis seemed to fill up the small room, two men in it made Sophie feel like she could only hover in the doorway. Jake and Louis looked at each other.

"You're the father," Jake said pleasantly, leaning forward and offering a hand accompanied by his all-American smile.

"Louis Gregory," Louis said. He raised an eyebrow at Sophie, who had been somewhat distracted by the sight of two very good-looking men standing next to her sofa.

"Oh, er, sorry, Louis, this is Jake, my . . . friend," Sophie said with an apologetic shrug. The men shook hands quickly and then withdrew, each taking a step back. A bit like pistols at dawn, Sophie thought.

Louis stood up straighter, so that he edged above Jake by a couple of inches. Jake seemed to broaden his shoulders and puffed himself out like Artemis when she was cross.

There was a long moment of silence when nobody moved. Somehow a casual meeting that should have been brief and meaningless seemed charged with tension.

Jake was the first to move. He held out a bag to Sophie. "I picked us up a couple of bottles of Pinot Grigio," he said, with slight emphasis on the word *us*.

"I love Italian wine," Louis said.

Sophie looked at him. "Oh? Well. Do you want to stay and have a glass?" she asked him, compulsively well-mannered.

Louis seemed to consider the offer seriously as he looked from her to Jake and then at his feet.

"I'd better go," he said at last, and the tension, real or imagined, seemed to drain instantly out of the room.

"I'll let you out," Sophie said, deciding she needed the minute or so it would take to get back up the stairs to her flat to figure out what had just happened.

"I didn't know you had a boyfriend," Louis said as they reached the main door. "I don't know why. I mean, it's obvious *you* would have."

"Is it?" Sophie said.

"Well, yeah," Louis said. "I mean you're, you know—great-looking and generally . . . great. Of course you would."

Sophie felt a rush of pleasure at his words. She didn't think she'd ever felt so flattered in her life. Certainly other men, including Jake, had said things that were far prettier and much more romantic, but for some reason none of those words had sounded as completely honest as Louis's did.

"Gosh," she said and then, "did I say *gosh*?"

Louis laughed. "You did," he said. "I like it. Look, it must have made things difficult for you with Jake, having the girls. I hope that your relationship hasn't suffered because of it?"

"Oh no," Sophie said. "Jake's been great, but actually he's not quite my boyfriend. He's more of a sort of date thing. Except we haven't been on any dates yet." She wondered why she was sharing this information so inexpertly with a man whose business it certainly was not.

Because she wanted him to know she was single? She wanted her dead best friend's husband to know that she was single? She refused to think about what that meant on the grounds of taste and decency. But the more she got to know him, the more she was warming toward Louis, which wasn't what she wanted at all. Now was not the time to develop an inappropriate crush.

"Right," Louis said. "So I'll see you in the morning and we'll plan the big trip."

"We will," Sophie said. They smiled at each other as she held the door open, letting the chill of the night air numb her cheeks.

"Good night, Sophie," Louis said. And for a long moment after she closed the door she stood and thought about what it had felt like to be standing next to him. It had to be wrong to feel like she had in that moment. It had to be. There was only one thing for it. She'd have to go upstairs and kiss Jake.

"I was starting to think you'd gone with him," Jake said, holding out a glass of wine.

"Don't be silly." Sophie sat down on the sofa next to him. She looked at his lovely mouth and gorgeous blue eyes and took a large gulp of wine.

"He's younger than I thought he would be," Jake said. "He's younger than me, I think. Don't you?"

"Um, he's my age I suppose," Sophie said, diligently admiring Jake's chiseled nose. "So a bit, I guess."

"And really tall," Jake said.

Sophie laughed. "Anyone would think it was *you* who fancied him," she joked before she realized exactly what she'd said.

"Me as opposed to who?" Jake said carefully.

"No one!" Sophie said hurriedly. "That's not what I meant, I just meant . . ." She looked into her wineglass for inspiration. "I meant you sounded very interested in him."

"I'm always interested in my competition," Jake said, his tone cooling.

"Jake!" Sophie exclaimed. "Louis is my dead best friend's husband! He's not competition!"

"Are you sure about that?" Jake asked her.

"I'm sure." And as if to prove it, she did something she had never done in her entire life. She lunged at Jake and kissed him.

For a moment he was immobile with shock, for a second or two longer he kissed her back, and then slowly and reluctantly he pushed her away.

"You're really screwing with my head," he said.

"I'm not," Sophie said. "That's why I asked you to come over tonight. So we could move things on. You and me—a couple if you want."

Jake sat up and looked hard at her. "Something in you has changed since the party," he said. "You look less reserved, less detached. Actually, that's wrong, you don't look at *all* reserved or detached. You look like someone turned you loose in the world and you're enjoying living and breathing in the middle of it, instead of just looking on from the edges."

"Yes," Sophie agreed, even though she didn't quite get what he meant. "I am. I mean, I am doing those things that you said because of you. *You've* set me free!"

"Nope," Jake said. "It's not me."

"It is!" Sophie insisted, sounding, she realized, a little too desperate for it to be true.

"Sophie." Jake looked sad as he said her name. "It might be that the new challenges life has thrown you have woken you up. Or maybe it's realizing when you found out Carrie had died that life is too short to sleepwalk through it. Maybe it's even those two girls and their father." He looked grim. "Maybe it's him."

"Him!"

Jake cut off Sophie's protest with a wave of his hand. "Whatever it is, it isn't me," he told her firmly. "And I'm not the kind of man to take second best. I thought you'd wake up one day and see what a charming, good-looking catch I am and that you'd want me as much as I want you. But as sorry as I am, I don't think that's going to happen."

"I have," Sophie said. "It is." But even she wasn't convinced.

"I think I'd better go," Jake said.

"I don't want you to go," Sophie said, her voice small.

"I know you don't," he said. "But I think you want me to stay as a safety net to catch you if all this high-wire balancing you're doing doesn't pay off. I can't be that to you, Sophie, as tempting as it is. I can't be your safe option. Whatever you need to make you happy right now—it isn't me."

Jake set his wine down on the table and leaned over and kissed Sophie's cheek. "I'll call you when you're back in the office. We'll schedule a meeting."

"Jake, I . . ." Sophie didn't know what she wanted to say.

"It's okay, honey, I know," he said as he headed for the door. "You've got a lot of other things to think about right now."

Twenty-one

There had been longer journeys in terms of distance and even importance, Sophie knew that. Like Edmund Hillary reaching the summit of Everest or Neil Armstrong playing golf on the moon. Those were, she knew, difficult, almost impossible, and world-changing, humanity-inspiring journeys. However, she was also entirely convinced that never in the history of mankind had anyone taken a journey so tiring, depressing, and remorselessly irritating as the journey she was taking to Cornwall on that cold and rainy day.

A real test of human endurance, Sophie thought, was a daylong car drive with a car-phobic three-year-old, a know-it-all, often-annoyingly-correct six-year-old, and their long-lost, emotionally confused, irritatingly attractive father. And she had come to that conclusion only forty-five minutes into the trip.

It was dusk when they drove into St. Ives. The optimistically anticipated six-hour trip had stretched into an excruciating eight, and at last, the car was quiet. Izzy had finally fallen asleep about twenty minutes earlier, and Louis and Bella had fallen silent for an entirely different reason, Sophie guessed. As they descended into the heart of the town, past hotel after hotel, and a brace of B & Bs, all garnished with a procession of forlorn-looking palms bending in the wind, she glanced at Louis's profile, occasionally highlighted by the beams of passing cars, and in the rearview mirror at Bella, who stared fixedly out the window. Both of them wore exactly the same expression, that of people watching the life they had once known and loved slip silently past their windows like a lost dream. Sophie knew all too well what Bella had lost, and as she watched Louis's face, she realized his sense of loss was almost identical. He must have loved Carrie very much, she realized sharply. He probably still did.

"Louis," Sophie asked, feeling awkward for breaking into his thoughts. "Have you got the directions to the B & B?" She had to repeat the question before he heard her voice and blinked at her.

"The directions? Oh, right. Yes, of course. Sorry, miles away." He fished about in the plastic bag that he had between his feet and pulled them out. "Right, it's on Porthminster Terrace, so left up Albert Road, that's the next left, and then left again."

Sophie nodded and, glancing to her right, saw the sea moving darkly in the gloom. "Oooh, look!" she exclaimed, by force of childhood habit. "There's the sea!"

Izzy did not stir, and both Louis and Bella blinked blankly at the view. "Mmm," they both said with identical laconic cadence. And then the car was silent once more.

Sophie looked around at the family room she was sharing with the girls. It wasn't a bad room, it was clean, and once you got past the pinkness, the rose-patterned wallpaper with contrasting border and the lurid magenta candlewick bedspreads, it was quite pleasant.

"We're less of a B and B and more of a boutique hotel," Mrs. Alexander, the proprietor, had assured them as she showed them this room and Louis's single next door.

"Oh?" Louis had said, looking around him with genuine interest. "What's the difference then?"

Mrs. Alexander had seemed to purse her entire body from the lips down. "Well, I would have thought *that* was obvious," she'd said.

Miraculously, Izzy had not woken as she was transferred from the car to the double bed. She didn't even stir as Sophie gingerly undressed her and exchanged her pants for a pull-up nappy, deciding it was better to be safe than sorry with other people's bed linen.

She carefully tucked Izzy into one side of the bed and looked up at Bella as she returned from the en suite bathroom already in her pajamas.

"You haven't even eaten yet," Sophie reminded her, glancing at her watch. It was only just six.

"But I had all those Pringles in the car," Bella said. "Anyway, I'm tired. You don't mind, do you?"

Sophie now considered herself experienced enough in child care to know that a tube of salt and vinegar Pringles did not constitute what Tess would have called a balanced meal. But she also knew that there was no point in forcing a tired child to stay up and eat broccoli.

"Of course not," she said, pulling back the covers so that Bella could hop into bed, leaving the single free for her. She didn't mind Bella's early night exactly, but while having an actual bed to sleep in was a definite improvement, she had not foreseen the disadvantage of the enforced early bedtime brought about by sharing a room with two children under seven.

"Do you want a story?" she asked hopefully.

Bella shook her head and yawned. "Night," she said, and she was instantly gone, as if she could not wait to escape to the refuge of sleep.

Sophie listened to Bella's rhythmic breathing, complemented by Izzy's squeaky snore, as she sat on her single bed in the dark and looked at the thin sliver of light that ran along the bottom of the door. She glanced at the luminous dial on her watch; she could either stay here and stare at what she supposed to be the ceiling for hours on end until she fell asleep or she could go and see Louis next door. It wasn't as if there was anything wrong with going to see Louis, or as if her going would have any special meaning or anything. It was just that the idea of going to visit him in his bedroom in a B & B in St. Ives felt rather strange. Mainly because, until very recently, he had been the archvillain in everybody's life, including his own, but also because, once she was in his room, Sophie had no idea what on earth they would do for an entire evening, if it wasn't to talk intensely and earnestly about the girls or Carrie. And Sophie knew that she, for one, didn't have the energy to do that. But there was nothing else to do. With her hand on the doorknob, she paused, and then she turned around and crept into the small bathroom, where she brushed her teeth and hair in the twilight and risked the haphazard application of some clear lip gloss.

Louis seemed to have been expecting her; he smiled as he opened the door and stepped aside to let her into the narrow room. Sophie glanced around. His single bed was positioned against the wall that divided their bedrooms. Her bed, she realized, was in exactly the same position but on the other side of the wall, which for some reason that she didn't want to dwell on, disconcerted her.

"Just in time." Louis gestured at a tray of sandwiches and a pot of tea that balanced on a narrow dressing table. "I ordered us food. Apparently providing food in the evening is what makes the difference between a B & B and a boutique hotel."

"Obviously," Sophie said, smiling, partly to cover her surprise that Louis had not only been expecting her but also ordered her sandwiches. She found the plate of white triangular shapes with the crusts cut off curiously touching.

"I thought both the girls would be exhausted," he said, repositioning the tray on his bed and pouring out two cups of tea. "But I got them extra sandwiches just in case. Bella asleep too?"

"Out like a light." Sophie nodded. "Filled up with junk food."

"I felt a bit guilty not being in there helping you, but well, I don't expect Bella would have wanted me barging in, would she?"

He couldn't help but let a hopeful note creep in, so Sophie just said, "She was really tired. Couldn't get two words out of her. I know how she feels." She laughed weakly, hoping he'd take the hint.

Louis nodded and sat down on the bed on one side of the tray, which Sophie took as an invitation to sit on the other side. He held out a cup of tea, which she took with both hands and sipped. Louis nodded at the TV that was positioned on a shelf on a wall opposite the bed.

"There's quite a good film on," he said and helped himself to a tuna sandwich.

It turned out that Sophie didn't have to worry about what they would talk about because they didn't talk at all really, except to make the odd comment about the film, the sandwiches, or the rather pungent plug-in air freshener that Louis finally had to banish to the hallway when the tuna started to taste of petunias. Instead of the intense and earnest discussion that Sophie had feared, time slipped by and their conversation rose and fell as easily and naturally as the tide against the shore.

The music to the ten o'clock news woke her, and she realized that she must have nodded off propped up against the wall on Louis's bed and had probably snored and possibly dribbled.

"Fuck," she said, sitting bolt upright and surreptitiously wiping her apparently dry chin just to be on the safe side. "Sorry."

Louis smiled but did not take his eyes off the TV. "It's cool," he said. "Although I was wondering how we'd both fit into the bed if you didn't wake up." It was a casual remark, but it was still enough to make Sophie feel the heat prickle on her skin as she got a fleeting impression of what it *would* be like for both her and Louis to be closely entwined in that bed . . . Sophie wondered if he'd made the comment deliberately to rattle her and then dismissed the thought immediately. Of course he didn't, she told herself. He had no clue that she was finding it increasingly difficult to be around him, he was just making conversation. She was the one blowing it all out of proportion.

It was classic behavior, Cal would have said. *Cal* would have said she was fixating again on a man she could never have, precisely because she could never have him. Because she preferred to torture herself with hopeless fantasies rather than risk anything messy and physical and real. Well, Cal might have been right, but if he knew how frightening it felt to be this close to the object of her attraction, then he would understand. It was simply better not to let it get out of hand.

"Utterly inappropriate," Sophie accidentally said out loud.

Louis looked at her with a furrowed brow. "Pardon?" he said.

"Oh, nothing." Sophie stood up, smoothing her tousled hair behind her shoulders and pulling her shirt down over her jeans. "Just that I should go to bed. I'll see you in the morning then. We're sticking to plan A, aren't we?"

Louis nodded, but he looked hesitant, unsurprisingly, considering what constituted plan A.

"Louis, are you okay?" Sophie suddenly felt compelled to ask him, despite his obvious reluctance to talk about any of the reasons they were here. He shrugged and stood up, switching off the TV. Suddenly the small room was filled with him.

"I'm all right," he said, looking down at Sophie. "Like you said, I've got to be, haven't I? After all, I am the grown-up here and—" In the silent seconds of his pause, it seemed as if they simultaneously closed the gap between their bodies, just by the tiniest fraction. "And, well, I'm glad you're here," Louis finished. "Listen, are you bored of me thanking you yet?"

Her mouth formed half a smile. "Bored? Never," Sophie said with fragile lightness. "I love gratitude. Bring it on." Louis's smile widened, and Sophie was sure that the oxygen levels in the room depleted.

"Well then. Thank you again," he said, and without warning he bridged the remaining space between them in one swift move and left the remnants of a soft, warm kiss on her cheek almost before she knew what had happened.

"Right then," Sophie said, her voice a decibel higher than usual. "Bedtime for me. See you in the morning. Night then!" And she closed Louis's door behind her before she had finished the last word.

She stood for a moment in the hallway and studied the endlessly swirling pattern of the carpeted floor as she considered the phenomena she had just experienced. Taking a brief audit of her sexual history, Sophie worked out that she had had three lovers in her lifetime, one a boyfriend with whom she'd had the most sex to date. She was fairly certain she had been in love with him, which automatically made sex better according to popular belief. She and Alex had had all kinds of sex, all over her flat *and* his, which meant it must have been good sex, because everybody knows that sex that's not in a bed is good sex. They had done at least three positions, and there had been orgasms. Alex had not always been there, but nevertheless, orgasms had been had while she had been seeing him. Whenever Eve had joked about her near-virginal frigidity, Sophie had confidently scoffed, remembering those orgasms. And as for Carrie's schoolgirl-crude exclamations of what it meant to be truly turned on, Sophie had just laughingly agreed and secretly decided that that degree of sexual pleasure was merely fictional, the sort of thing that women's magazines and slushy novels go on about all the time but that nobody really ever experiences. And nothing, not even Alex, had ever led her to change her opinion on that subject.

Until about two minutes ago, when her dead best friend's husband had kissed her innocently on the cheek, and for the first time in her life, Sophie had felt something that she really could describe only as her knickers. Fizzing.

"Bollocks," Sophie said.

She crept into the room she was sharing with Louis the irresponsible cheek kisser's daughters and, undressing quickly, climbed into her single bed without even bothering to clean her teeth. "Damn," Sophie cursed once more under her breath and yanked the bedspread over her head. She had been really looking forward to a good night's sleep in an actual bed, and now when she finally had the prospect of one, she wouldn't have time to do any sleeping. But it looked like the way Louis made her feel was more than just her usual safe, unrequited crushes. It was hot, intense, and very real.

No, she wouldn't have any sleep tonight. She'd have to spend all night lying awake and worrying.

Twenty-two

We have all been on a long journey," Izzy said with a fair amount of mysticism considering her age. "Haven't we?"

"Yes, we have," Sophie said in her I'm-not-really-listening-to-you-but-I'll-agree-with-everything-you-say voice. She smiled and nodded as Izzy chattered and fiddled anxiously with her napkin. The three of them had been in the breakfast room since seven, the earliest hour permitted, and would have been there a good hour earlier if only they could have got away with it. Izzy had reveled in the cereal selection, and Bella had picked at the edges of fried egg on toast for almost forty minutes. Louis had still not come down, a fact about which Sophie did not know whether she should be relieved or annoyed. On the one hand, she hadn't yet had to endure any embarrassing flashback incidents. But on the other, it struck her as highly ironic that *she* was the one up at five o'clock with the children while their natural father slumbered blissfully unaware, just a few inches of brick and some insulating material away. To be fair, Sophie conceded, she could have sent Izzy into *his* bedroom to practice circus trampolining on *his* bed while *he* was in it, but that would have resulted in her coming face-to-face with him and having to endure even sooner the inevitable embarrassing flashbacks.

Sophie swore at herself. She had to be the only woman since the demise of the great Victorian novel to get so flustered over a totally lame, not remotely special and sexy kiss on the cheek. Maybe if he had grabbed her in his arms and cried "Damn convention, damn propriety—I simply must have you or die!" then flung her on the bed and ravaged her, maybe *then* her total flakiness would have been fair enough. But he hadn't—the thought had never crossed his mind. Furthermore, she would never have allowed herself to get turned on by Carrie's husband—ex or not—while Carrie had been alive, and to do so now when she was dead? Well, put it this way, if Sophie's Catholicism had not lapsed and she'd happened to mention some of last night's wilder thoughts in confession, she was fairly sure that no amount of Hail Marys would have saved her from a specially reserved spot in Hell. But instead of hightailing it to church in search of redemption, she told herself it was all nonsense and silliness and probably just a figment of her wrung-out imagination. When she'd finally got a decent night's sleep and all this emotional wrangling was over and she had her normal life back, she'd realize that she hadn't had fizzy knickers at all. It was probably cystitis.

"Daddy's fab-li-us, isn't he?" Izzy said.

"Yes, he is," Sophie agreed absently just as Louis appeared in the doorway, still damp from the shower and clean-shaven.

"Thanks," he said to Sophie with a broad grin. "You're pretty wonderful yourself. I'm sorry I took so long coming down. I thought I'd better shower and shave before people start mistaking me for a stinky old tramp again." He winked at Bella, who looked studiously unimpressed. "I thought that later on you could have a couple of hours to yourself while I did a solo shift?"

Sophie looked at him. "Lovely," she said, wondering if Mrs. Alexander had any cranberry juice—wasn't that supposed to be good for cystitis?

"What are we doing here?" Bella demanded, pushing her plate away from her. She fixed her gaze on Sophie. "Are you going to leave us here with him?"

Sophie looked at her pale, pinched face. She and Louis had told the girls the day before yesterday that they were bringing them down to St. Ives for a visit. She had expected them to be thrilled to be going home, but instead Izzy had questioned her relentlessly about the mode of transportation and how long it would take to get there, and Bella, seeing yet another upheaval in her already tumultuous life, had said nothing at all.

The night she'd tucked the girls in before they left, Sophie had knelt beside the bed, brushed Bella's bangs out of her eyes, and whispered, "Aren't you glad to be going back home? I thought you missed it?"

Bella had turned onto her side, so that most of her face fell into shadow. "It won't be going home, though, will it? Because Mummy's not there. And going back now means the end of living here with you and the beginning of living with him, doesn't it?"

Sophie had searched the shadows of Bella's face for her eyes and fixed on the two tiny points of reflected light. "Yes, it does," she'd said simply, knowing that any lie, even a white one, would not help Bella. "But I thought you were starting feeling better about that? Better about your dad?"

She had expected more questions from Bella, but instead the two points of light had blinked out for a moment, and then Bella had whispered, "I'm going to sleep now."

She hadn't questioned the trip further until this moment. Sophie looked at Louis, who nodded, reached into his pocket, and pulled out a set of keys, which he laid on the table. Bella and Izzy looked at the keys which were tied together on a faded bit of what was once multicolored ribbon to which was also attached a faded pink troll, its hair matted and sticky.

Bella looked up at Sophie. "Mummy's keys," she said quietly. "He's got Mummy's keys."

"Trollee!" Izzy cried, picking up the key ring and kissing the creature attached to it. "But I mustn't lose you, must I? 'Cos Mummy will be very cross." She said the words like an automatic mantra, before furrowing her brow and placing the keys back down on the table. "But Mummy's not here, so— Well, I'd better not play with you."

All four of them stared at the keys as if they were some kind of talisman, or the way to unlock a secret door to the past. Quickly, before the moment could be filled with any more meaning, Sophie picked up the keys and jangled them as if she could shake all of the significance out of them.

"We're going back to look at the house," she said briskly, as Louis seemed unable to. "Things happened very quickly when you first went to stay with your gran, so we're going back there to get any of your things you might want. And to check that the house is okay before . . ."

Bella frowned. "Before what?" she said.

"Well—" Sophie began out of recently acquired habit, but Louis interrupted her.

"When Mummy died she gave us the house. It belongs to us now, all three of us."

"Mummy gave the house to you?" Bella sounded incredulous, and Louis realized his mistake. Bella was not the sort of child to fall for adult half-truths.

"Well, half of the house belonged to me to begin with, from when I lived there with you, Bella, and then when Mummy died, the other half became mine because Mummy and I were still married."

"You weren't married," Bella said. "Married people live together."

Louis reached out for her hand, which she withdrew and held under the table.

"Yes, I know," he said, resting his hand on the flowery tablecloth instead. "But in the eyes of the law we were still married, and . . . anyway, the house belongs to all of us now, you, me, and Izzy. We're going back there to look at it and decide what we want to do with it."

Bella released one hand and snaked it through Sophie's arm. "What do you mean, do with it?" she said uncertainly.

"Well, we could sell it," Louis said carefully. "Or we could live it in it. You, me, and Izzy."

Carrie's house was in the middle of Virgin Street, a steep terrace that marched down the hillside toward the town's harbor. It was a narrow, whitewashed house, its two front window frames painted bright blue along with the door. As they had walked down the steep road to its front door, Sophie had been able to pick it out without needing to look at the numbers. It was the only one of the row of houses to have a roof glittering with frost in the bright cold morning. A cold, empty house at the heart of a row of warm, busy lives, slotted side by side around the place that had once been Carrie's pride and joy. It hadn't been completely neglected, Louis had told Sophie, who had to admit she hadn't even thought about the house, as if it and all of the physical remnants of Carrie's life would have somehow vanished the moment she died. A neighbor, Louis explained, checked in on it regularly. Turned lights on and off, picked up the junk mail that continued to arrive long after any meaningful correspondence had dried up, and made sure it didn't get so cold that the water pipes burst. In fact, when Louis had spoken to the solicitor who posted him the house keys, he'd discovered that there was something else the neighbor had been doing too, but he wanted to keep that a secret for now.

The four of them stood opposite the house and looked at it.

"Is Mummy in there too?" Izzy said, and it was hard to shake the sensation that she might be. That Carrie might be about to open the front door and ask them where they had all been. "Shall I ring the bell?" Izzy asked, pulling at Sophie's sleeve. "For Mummy to let us in?"

"Mummy's not in there, stupid," Bella said rather harshly. It was the first thing she had said since Louis's announcement at the breakfast table.

Izzy's bottom lip began to wobble. "I'm not stupid," she protested softly. "Mummy's in the sky and the stars and the sea and the trees, isn't she, Aunty Sophie?" Sophie nodded, wincing internally as she realized exactly where Izzy's train of thought was going. "So she could be in the house too, couldn't she?"

It was her fault for agreeing with Izzy every time she asked her, Is Mummy in the lamppost, or the rain?

"Um, the thing is—" Sophie began, before Louis interrupted her, kneeling beside Izzy and hooking an arm around her shoulders.

"Mummy is sort of in the house," he said, trying to hide the strain in his own voice. "Memories of Mummy will be there, things that remind us of her and make us think about her. But Mummy won't be there. She's gone, Izzy."

Izzy buried her face for a moment in Louis's jacket, and Sophie saw Bella watching them intently, emotions racing across her heart-shaped face like clouds across the sun. After a moment Bella put a hand on Izzy's shoulder. "It's all right, baby," she said, using the word as an endearment instead of her usual insult, with Carrie's warmth and intonation in every syllable. "Don't be upset."

Izzy emerged from Louis's embrace and took Bella's gloved hand.

"Right," Louis said, straightening up, one hand still on Izzy's shoulder. "Let's get out of this cold."

For a minute or so, nobody said anything as they looked around the small front room. After a while Louis turned on the light and, going to the foot of the stairs, turned up the thermostat. There was an audible click, and the radiator under the windowsill began to creak.

"Everything's still working," he said, glancing around the room. "Nothing's really changed."

For a second Sophie had to ask him what on earth *could* have changed in a vacant house over six months, but then she realized; this was the first time Louis had set foot in the house in over three years, and who knew—except for him and possibly Bella—under what circumstances he had left it. He continued to look around the room without moving his feet, and then, in one quick stride, he crossed the living room and picked up a framed photo from the mantelpiece. It was a picture of him and Carrie on their wedding day.

Then, as Louis studied the photo, his profile hidden by his hair, Sophie felt herself take a deep, sharp, reflexive breath, and in that moment she knew. Carrie was really gone.

It was being here, so nearly close to her, almost engulfed in the space her absence made that brought the truth home to her.

She really was dead, because if she wasn't here in this house, in this life that Sophie had subconsciously imagined for her even when she didn't give a second thought from day to day, if she wasn't here, then she wasn't anywhere.

Sophie felt her chest tighten and her eyes sting. "I'll just . . . ,"
she said as she hurried through the kitchen to the bathroom, hoping everyone else was so lost in their own thoughts that they
hadn't really heard or noticed her. She pulled open the sliding
door that concealed the apricot bathroom suite. It had always
made Carrie laugh because it came complete with a bidet.

Sophie closed the toilet lid and sat on it. She took deep and
steady breaths, and tried to focus her mind, but still the tears
came, slow and hot. Her shoulders shook and her breath juddered, and she felt Carrie's death keenly in the center of her chest,
like a small but vital part of herself had been ripped out.

"Don't you dare cry," she whispered to herself. "Not now."
Furiously, Sophie brushed the tears from her eyes with the heel of
her hand, repeating the process after every blink, but still they did
not stop. Somehow, as if crying had improved her vision, she saw
everything in the bathroom with startling clarity. A pair of gold
hoop earrings gleaming in the soap dish, an opened box of
Tampax half-concealed by the side of the lavatory. A bra, once
hand-washed and long ago hung across the shower curtain rail to
drip dry, now stiff and dusty. Sophie wept even harder.

She hadn't anticipated this. She had expected to be the strong
one, the emotional prop for the others, who had all suffered far
more deeply than she. She had expected to be there to support the
children, and even Louis if he needed it. But here she was weeping, crying like she never had for Carrie since the moment she
had known that she was dead. It had been so long that Sophie
had begun to believe she would never grieve like this for her
friend. But instead she'd picked the worst time of all to crumble,
crying for Carrie but also crying for herself.

Sophie cried because she missed her friend. But she also cried
for all the things she had lost before Carrie's death. Her father, her
childhood. Her friendship with her mother. Her sense of self. Her

courage and adventurous spirit. The things that losing Carrie had somehow seemed to give back to her, one by one.

She had fallen in love with two children who should never have been hers to love. Somehow this complicated whirlpool of events had woken her up, and now she wanted what Carrie had had and would never have again. And that made Sophie cry all the harder, because if that was true, wasn't she trying to steal Carrie's life? And if she was, she knew she would be hopeless at living it. She could never have a tenth of the energy, audacity, and verve that Carrie had brought to every day. That was the woman whom Louis and his daughters loved and missed so much. Just as Sophie feared she might never pull herself together, there was a knock on the door.

"Aunty Sophie?" It was Izzy. "I need a wee." Sophie took a deep breath, dried her face with her palms, and arranged her mouth into a smile before pulling open the door and ushering Izzy in. Izzy pulled down her trousers and underpants and, lifting the toilet lid, edged her way onto the seat. She examined Sophie's face as she passed water.

"Your eyes have gone all black," she observed. She cocked her head to one side, stretched out both her arms, and said, "Don't worry, baby. Don't be upset."

If just over a month ago anyone had told Sophie that very soon she would be openly weeping in the embrace of a three-year-old girl, who comforted her as she sat on the loo, Sophie would have laughed in her face. But now Izzy's arms around her neck, her hot breath on her cheek were exactly the sensations Sophie needed to feel calm again. Izzy patted her on the back several times as Sophie knelt before her, and after a while Sophie broke the embrace, cupped Izzy's face in one hand, and kissed her forehead. "You're a lovely little girl, aren't you?" she said, realizing she wasn't going to cry anymore. At last she felt connected to the world again, for the first time since that freezing day at the crematorium she stood up, knowing that the first tears she had shed for Carrie wouldn't be her last, but for now at least, she felt lighter and stronger. Strong enough to give the support she had intended. As Izzy concentrated on her business, Sophie looked in the cabinet mirror and washed her face in cold water until all traces of tears and makeup were gone. Her skin remained burnished, but her eyes looked fairly clear, as long as no one looked into them too deeply.

The toilet flushed behind her, and Izzy pulled up her trousers, a trail of toilet paper poking from the back of them like a tail. Sophie plucked it out and put it down the loo. She was about to lift Izzy up to the sink to wash her hands when the little girl picked up a three-legged stool that had been left by the bath and carried it to the sink.

"Do you like coming back here?" Sophie asked her as she washed her hands with the kind of enthusiasm that was bad for the environment.

"I do like it," Izzy said thoughtfully, "and partly I don't like it because, well, it's funny and a bit sad."

Sophie watched her hop off the stool, pull open the door, and head back toward the living room. Sometimes she couldn't tell if Izzy was being curiously insightful or just mimicking the conversations of grown-ups. But on that occasion she felt certain the three-year-old had said exactly what she meant.

When they returned to the front room, Louis was sitting on the sofa with what looked a photo album open on his lap. His expression was unreadable, hidden by the forward seep of his long hair, but Sophie thought she could see the tension and sadness in every line of his body.

"Whassat?" Izzy asked, climbing up and kneeling beside him.

"It's you," Louis said brightly for her's sake. It was strange,

Sophie thought ruefully, how all four of them were pretending to be stronger than they were for the sake of the other three. "It's your baby book. I found it with Bella's. I took all the photos of Bella. I think your mum must have taken most of these. She's only in one of them. I've missed so much." He sighed.

Izzy traced the outline of her own baby footprint in the book and giggled.

"Is Bella upstairs?" Sophie asked, looking up the narrow staircase.

"Yes," Louis said. "She wanted to go and find some things. I offered to go with her, but she said no thank you very politely."

Sophie nodded. The atmosphere was so full, so ripe with Carrie that it seemed easier to be apart from him. To somehow disperse the intensity of emotions.

"That's my girl," she said, before calling up the stairs, "Bella? Are you all right up there?"

"Come up!" Bella called in response. Sophie glanced at Louis, but he didn't look up from the baby book.

Sophie felt foolishly apprehensive as she climbed the stairs. She had never imagined herself to have an overactive imagination, but in this house it was easy to let thoughts run wild. And anyway, after the last few weeks, especially since Louis had arrived in her life, she wasn't at all sure of the sort of person she *was* anymore. She wouldn't have been surprised to find Carrie at the top of the stairs waiting to ask just what she thought she was playing at, falling for her husband.

"Hello?" Sophie called out once on the tiny landing, annoying herself with the note of tension in her voice.

"In here!" Sophie followed Bella's voice to the small second bedroom, expecting it to a child's room. But as she entered she realized immediately it was Carrie's room. Her grandmother's Art Deco wardrobe that she had loved so much dominated the small space, and there was just enough room remaining for a single bed and a former dining chair on which a pile of folded laundry still waited to be put away. Bella was sitting on the bed, her head peeking out of a huge red mohair sweater. She rolled the sleeves up until her hands appeared. "This was Mum's favorite sweater," she said to Sophie, smiling. "It still smells like her a bit. Smell!" She thrust out a sleeve toward Sophie, who sat down on the bed and sniffed the garment, which did have a faint aroma of Carrie's favorite rose oil, and wondered how—out of all of them—Bella seemed to be so relaxed here, and happy. Sophie had expected exactly the opposite, but for possibly the first time since she had met Bella again at her grandmother's house, all of the lines of tension that had characterized the girl's small body seemed to have melted away. Sophie looked at Bella and realized she was six and a half years old again, not some small, noble adult carrying the weight of the world around on her shoulders.

Bella rose on her knees and picked up a black leatherette jewelry box off a shelf that had been put over the bed. Taking it down carefully, she tipped it up and turned the handle to wind the clockwork mechanism before gently lifting the lid, holding the box at eye level.

As the red felt interior was revealed and the tiny plastic ballerina within began to twirl and pirouette, Sophie smiled in recognition. "Carrie got that for her fourteenth birthday," she told Bella, who was watching the tiny dancer. "She said she *hated* it, said she wished she could burn it—that all she wanted was money for clothes and records and that your gran had got her this just to pi—— to annoy her. But she never did throw it away. She always kept her jewelry in it, even when she was grown up." Sophie listened as the tinny rendition of the "Blue Danube Waltz" began to slow. "Maybe your gran knew her better than she thought she did after all," Sophie said. "You'll have to tell her about the box. She'd really like to know."

Bella set the box down on the bed and pulled out a couple of strings of glass beads, dropping them over her head. She took out some earrings and looked at them in the palm of her hand for moment before dropping them back into the box and taking out a butterfly brooch. Sophie pinned it on the sweater for her.

"Can I take this?" she asked Sophie, shutting the lid of the box before tugging at the sweater. "And this?"

Sophie nodded. "Of course you can," she said, and she impulsively hooked her arm around Bella's neck and planted a kiss on her forehead. Unwittingly, Bella was making this visit to Carrie's house easier for her, when it should have been the other way around. "You seem happy to be here, Bella. Do you think you'd be happy living back here with your dad?"

Bella stared at the faded and rubbed gold border that decorated the box's lid for a moment. "This is my home, mine and Izzy's," she said. "Not his."

Sophie was prepared for that response. "But, darling, you know you will have to live with your dad eventually and—"

"I know I have to live with Dad," Bella said with less venom than Sophie had expected, and using the word Dad instead of *him*. "But I want to live *here*, Aunty Sophie. I want to come back home to St. Ives and school and my friends. Here, where I can nearly touch Mummy. It's like I left one morning and I didn't even know that I wasn't coming back. But I didn't. I didn't ever come back until now. And now it seems right to come back even if—even if not all us *can* come back."

Sophie nodded and kissed Bella again.

"I don't know if Izzy feels the same way," Sophie said, releasing Bella from her hug. "And as far as your dad is concerned— well, it's hard to know what he's thinking. But I think you're right about coming back here." Sophie looked around the room. Despite the cold outside, the back of the house seemed to trap the morning sun, and it was bathed in glowing warmth.

"Do you feel happy about living with Louis now?" Sophie asked Bella.

"Well . . . I'm prepared to discuss it with him," she said. "If it means I can come home."

Sophie nodded, trying not to smile at the small girl's formality and trying not feel a sense of rejection.

Suddenly Izzy's scream reverberated through the small house.

Sophie, who was getting used to Izzy screaming the place down over nothing in particular, wondered what they would find as she and Bella went downstairs. But any residual apprehension she might have had dissipated the moment she saw the three-year-old.

Izzy was standing in the middle of the livingroom, her face rapturous as she almost strangled the life out of a huge ginger tomcat.

"It's Tango!" she cried joyously. "Tango! Tango!"

"Tango!" Bella leaped the last two stairs and joined the group hug of which Tango was the remarkably compliant center.

"Okay, guys," Louis said, laughing. "You'll scare him."

"Nothing scares Tango," Bella said, hefting the giant cat out of Izzy's grasp and lumbering with him to the sofa. "He's the toughest cat in St. Ives!"

Louis took Tango from Bella as she climbed up and sat beside him, then plonked the animal back in her outstretched arms.

Sophie, who was not used to seeing cats handled so roughly without the kind of protest that resulted in at least the loss of an eye, looked on in awe. Tango appeared to be twice the size of Artemis, had half of one ear missing and a little bare patch over one eye that meant he must have survived a few fights. He looked like a real bruiser, but there he was purring like a, well, like a pussycat in Bella's arms as she scratched him behind one ear.

"How can he be here?" Bella asked. "He went to a cats' home!"

Louis nodded. "I know, I was going to tell you. Leslie from next door, the lady that was coming in every day," he added for Sophie's benefit, "said she found him here one morning about four months ago. She called the cats' home and they told her he had been relocated in Mousehole, ironic or what? Anyway, he can't have liked it, because he left his new home the first chance he got and came back here. She didn't know how he'd made it so far in one piece or how long he'd been living off scraps and that before she found him. The cats' home phoned his new family and they took him back, but the next chance he got he was here again. So everyone agreed it was best to just let him live here. Leslie's been feeding him. I think he divides his time between here and next door now. They've become quite good friends."

"Tango," Izzy said softly as she knelt at Bella's feet. "Can we take him home too?" she asked Sophie. In a moment of confusion, Sophie tried to work out the logistics of fitting two children and two cats (one psychotic, one freakishly huge) into her small flat before realizing that her flat was no longer home for Bella and Izzy.

"It's not up to me," Sophie said, nodding at Louis as she tried to suppress an unexpected pang of loss. She sat down on a chair.

Louis reached out and scratched Tango under the chin. "All right, old mate," he said, with fond familiarity before saying to the girls, "Well, it's not up to me either." He looked at Bella. "Izzy told me she'd like to live in a new house, when we come back."

"With my own bedroom," Izzy said firmly.

"Well, maybe," Louis said cautiously. "But anyway, Bella— what about you?"

"I want to live here," Bella said into Tango's neck. She glanced up at Louis and pressed her lips together, stubborn and resolute.

Louis looked around the small front room, with good and bad memories stuffed into every corner and crevice. Sophie could see that this was the last place he wanted to come back to. But she could also see that he desperately didn't want to let Bella down.

"It's just, I thought a fresh start maybe . . . ," he said tentatively, "for us all."

"*This* is home!" Bella insisted, her voice heavy with the threat of tears. She pointed at Louis. "You can't just take us away from here and make us forget Mummy. You can't just pretend that we've always been happy and that *nothing* happened. *You* left us here! Here at *home*!"

As Tango twisted anxiously out of Bella's arms and scooted behind the sofa, Izzy stuck her thumb in her mouth and climbed into Sophie's lap.

"I'm not pretending," Louis said carefully, since the wrong intonation could have blown everything. "I know I was wrong to leave you the way I did, Bella. I'm so sorry—"

"But why did you, why?" Bella shouted, standing up, running at Louis, and bringing her fists down on his legs. Izzy buried her face in Sophie's hair and tightened her arms around her neck. Sophie squeezed her back.

Louis leaned forward and put his arms around Bella's stiff shoulders. "I don't know," he said softly. "I was stupid and selfish and wrong. And I've regretted it and missed you all every minute since. And most of all I wish I'd spoken to your mum again and told her how sorry I was. Because I am so sorry, Bella. I am so sorry, Izzy. I am so sorry."

Izzy slid wordlessly out of Sophie's lap and crossed to Louis's, flinging her arms around both father and sister and drawing them together in a hug.

"Don't make us live somewhere we don't know again," Bella said.

"I won't make you do anything," Louis said, but Sophie could see the stricken look on his face. She knew that coming back to this house would be unbearable for him. A permanent reminder of what he had lost, of what it seemed he'd thrown away.

"Why don't you think about it?" Sophie suggested quietly, afraid to intrude on this moment, noticing how Bella had relaxed into the embrace of her family and buried her head in Louis's shoulder. "It's been a very difficult day for you all. Coming back here is a very big step, and perhaps you need to talk and think a bit more before you decide anything. What do you think, Bella?"

Bella's face emerged from Louis's hair, and she roughly wiped the back of her hands across her face. "I need to ask you more things," she told Louis. "And to ask you more things before I know what to do."

Louis tense's and stricken face visibly lightened at words that anybody else might have found intimidating. It was clear he wasn't afraid of might happen between him and Bella. He was just glad that some kind of relationship had started at last.

"And we need to ask Tango where he wants to live too," Izzy added solemnly, fishing the cat out from his refuge and squeezing him hard, and as Sophie looked at Tango, she felt certain he'd want to live wherever Bella and Izzy lived.

"We've got a lot to talk about," Louis said to both of the girls. "But I think we'll work it out." He said it so hopefully it made Sophie's heart hurt.

"Yes," Bella said. "I think we will."

Twenty-three

Sophie waited on the far side of the narrow street as she watched Louis, Izzy, and Bella chatting with their next-door neighbor, who occasionally interrupted the conversation with rapid-fire kisses and bear hugs for the children. The three were gradually becoming a family again, Sophie could see, the bonds between them slowly tightening. Bonds that did not include her. She wished she could at least take some credit, but she felt it would have happened sooner or later anyway, even if the girls had never crash-landed in her life. Even if she'd gone on blissfully unaware, organizing corporate parties on the fourteenth floor of her very own ivory tower, ironing her hair weekday mornings, wearing her pajamas all weekend. *Even without me,* she thought, *they would have found one another.*

As for her, soon she'd be going back to that life, and everything would be exactly the same as it had before. Well, not exactly the same, Sophie decided. *She* wouldn't be the same.

She thought about her job, her flat, and her tiny, insular social life, which she barely managed to maintain, and the same question people were always asking her came into her head: Why? What was all that hard work and near solitude for?

Sophie didn't know the answer, but that wasn't the revelation. What she realized—standing across the street watching Louis, Bella, and Izzy talking to their old neighbor—was that she had *never* known.

The three said their good-byes and crossed over to join Sophie.

"She seems nice," Sophie said automatically, holding out a hand, which Izzy took as she hopped up on the curb.

"She is," Louis said. "She was really pleased to see me." He sounded so surprised that he must have had his own reservations about coming back to a town small enough for everyone to know everyone else's business. He must have wondered if he would be thought of as a returning hero or an unwelcome villain. The fact that at least one old friend had been glad to see him must have come as a relief.

"I've got an appointment with a solicitor after lunch." He glanced at Sophie. "Would you come with me? I could do with a bit of moral support."

She was touched that Louis had asked her. "And the girls?" she asked.

"If you were just outside or in the foyer, it would really help," he told her levelly.

"Oh," Sophie said. "Well, okay then."

She felt a little glow of pleasure that Louis wanted her to just be there. A glow she quickly put out. She had to curtail this crush, she had to, because, unlike her previous imaginary dalliances, she sensed that this one could really hurt her badly.

"And then," Louis continued, entirely oblivious to her inner turmoil, "I suppose we should visit estate agents, and employ-ment agencies." He sighed. "It'll be weird being a wage slave again," he said. "Still, got to be done. Anyway, let's go for a walk on Porthmeor Beach while the weather's good, shall we?"

"Yes!" the girls chorused, and Izzy swung Sophie's hand as they headed down to the beach.

Izzy raced off as soon as they reached the beach, instantly tumbling over and rolling around in the damp sand.

"She'll be wet through!" Sophie worried, but Louis only smiled.

"She's three and she's having fun. Getting wet won't hurt her," he said, chuckling indulgently at his daughter's high spirits.

"I'm going swimming!" Izzy called out to them, her voice al-most carried away by the wind as she raced toward the choppy sea, still dotted with surfers. Unable to employ the kind of lais-sez-faire that Louis displayed, Sophie instinctively raced after Izzy, a fact that thrilled the three-year-old more as she squealed and dodged Sophie's attempts to catch her. Woman and child chased each other recklessly a few feet from the edge of the surf for some minutes, until finally, all her fears forgotten, Sophie grabbed Izzy around the waist and fell backward onto the sand. Izzy turned in Sophie's arms to face her, the rising wind whipping Sophie's hair between their faces, tickling Izzy's nose and making her laugh even more.

"We'll have fun, won't we?" she said, her eyes bright with laughter. "When we all live here in our new house. You and me can chase each other every day!" Sophie extracted a hand from underneath Izzy's body and held her rebellious hair back from her face, fighting that pang of loss again.

"Well . . . ," she began, but just at that moment the tide rushed in a little higher and bathed the left side of Sophie's body with an icy caress.

"Bananas!" Sophie said, remembering for once not to swear. Izzy squealed with delight as Sophie picked her up and they ran out of the reach of the encroaching tide. Once they were at a safe distance, Sophie set Izzy down and looked at the soaking band that ran the length of her jeans.

"We'll have to go back and get changed," she told Izzy, who was running around her in a circle and probably not as bothered about being wet and cold as she was. Sophie looked at the clouds that had grown and darkened. "It's going to rain anyway," she said. "Come on, Izzy, let's catch Daddy and Bella up."

"No!" Izzy said, disagreeing reflexively. "I'm going paddling!"

"Don't be mad," Sophie said, absently scanning the beach for Bella and Louis. "In this weather?" Eventually she spotted a pair of figures, surprisingly small in the distance. It looked as if Bella was walking a step or two ahead of her father, and Louis was talking, Sophie could tell, because he used his hands just as much as language to express himself.

For a moment the wind dropped and a beam of sunlight broke through the clouds as Sophie watched the two distant figures, wishing she could work out what they were saying to each other just by looking at them. And then Bella stopped suddenly, and in one stride Louis caught up with her. There was another beat, perhaps a few more words exchanged, and then, without looking, Bella began to walk on again, except this time she held out her hand, and Louis took it.

And then the wind rose again, this time bringing with it something else.

Izzy was screaming. Sighing, Sophie looked around the beach, expecting to see her in proud possession of a not-so-dead crab or a bunch of seaweed.

But Izzy was not on the beach.

"Izzy!" This time Sophie screamed; a cold drench of fear

flooded her chest. Dimly aware of Bella and Louis stopping in their tracks and turning around, Sophie shouted again, *"IZZY!"* and then she saw her, or rather her red anorak, billowing and blooming as it was buffeted by waves, and her heart clenched in dread.

Izzy was in the water.

Sophie did not know what she was going to do or how she was going to do it, but she knew, she absolutely *knew,* that she had to be there in the water with Izzy. She knew that she must not lose sight of her, that she must not let Izzy's head disappear beneath the waves again before she was at her side. Sophie ran into the surf without feeling the shock of cold as the water rose to her thighs and then to just above her waist, only the resistance of the water slowing her run to a frustrating wade. Somehow Izzy was still afloat and managing to hold her face out of the water. As she got closer, Sophie could see the terror in the little girl's face, and then suddenly the sea was on her side and the tide washed Izzy right into her arms.

Sophie held on to the child, who was still screaming and struggling, as tightly as she was able against the pull of the retreating tide. She didn't know how fast the tide might come in, but she knew she had to get out of the water as quickly as possible before she was forced to try to swim instead of walk ashore. It struck her in a moment of clarity that there was a chance, a real chance that if the tide was strong enough and the wind cruel enough, everything might go horribly, wrong for both of them. She felt a fear sharper than anything she had ever felt before, a fear that made her weak, her legs buckling beneath her. And then she remembered Izzy in her arms, and she tightened her grip on the girl and steadied her legs.

"I've got you," she said as she tried to turn back toward the beach.

Then Louis was in the water with her, lifting Izzy out of her arms and propelling them back onto land. Bella ran into their legs as they emerged and flung her arms around the sodden group, and two or three surfers and some passing dog walkers gathered around them.

"You all right?" she heard a woman ask kindly.

"Do you want an ambulance?" another asked.

Sophie shook her head.

"Bella, careful," she heard herself say to the girl clinging to her legs, her voice remarkably calm. "You'll get all wet!"

"I don't care!" Bella said, and the four stood grouped together, arms around one another for a moment, Izzy still crying hysterically, unable to believe that she was safe.

"Dude, take this," a young surfer, his suit still wet from the sea, offered them a huge beach towel.

"Thanks, mate," Louis said gratefully, taking it and the other towels that were offered. "Come on," he said, his voice shaking. "We've got to dry off."

Louis came into Sophie's room carrying a tray of steaming hot drinks. "Four hot chocolates courtesy of Mrs. Alexander," he said, setting the tray down on the dressing table before looking up at Sophie and the children. She, Izzy, and Bella were huddled under the covers on the double bed, all of them in their pajamas and Sophie with one arm around each child's shoulders. Fortunately, she had found a children's program on the TV, and Izzy watched it intently, sucking the thumb of one hand, a finger of the other twirling her hair round and round. Bella was watching Izzy, her dark eyes fixed on her sister as if even in the safety of the double bed she had to keep an eye on her, just in case.

Louis smiled for the benefit of the group, but his face was still flushed from the cold, and Sophie could see he was still shaken.

"What kind people on the beach," she said. "Helping us to get dry, and that lady that brought us tea from the café."

"Yeah," Louis said, smiling. "That's what I love about humanity. Just when you start thinking the whole world's full of selfish, cruel individuals, you realize that actually, given the chance, all we want to do is be nice to one another and help each other."

"Way deep, dude," Sophie said wryly, but she knew what he meant. She'd learned so much in the last few weeks.

"Anyway, how are you girls feeling?" he asked the threesome, sitting on the edge of the bed. Two of them ignored him, and Sophie just shrugged. She wasn't sure how to answer.

"I'm fine," she said, with a small smile. "I think I'm getting the feeling back in my toes. It might not be frostbite after all."

He nodded, clasping his hands together as if he didn't know what to do with them. "Mrs. Alexander's called a doctor just to be on the safe side. She'll be here in about twenty minutes. It's amazing that Izzy didn't swallow more water," he said, looking at the transfixed girl. "It's incredible that she stayed afloat. I think her anorak must have acted like a sort of temporary water wing, trapping air underneath it."

"Maybe," Sophie said. "I mean, really, it was all over so quickly, wasn't it? I suppose it wasn't that serious at all."

Louis looked at her. "It was serious enough for a three-year-old," he said with feeling.

"I'm sorry, Louis," Sophie said, with unexpected emotion. "I'm really sorry. I just took my eyes off her for a moment . . ."

Seeing she was distressed, Louis reached out and touched her shoulder. "Don't be sorry. I was the one who said getting a little bit wet wouldn't hurt her. Kids get into scrapes, especially Izzy. But you were there to help her. That's what counts. So thank you."

"I didn't do anything much," Sophie said, feeling her skin

flare under his intense scrutiny. She sat up a little so that Izzy's head rested on her stomach. Bella shifted out of the embrace and turned onto her side. She appeared to have fallen asleep. "I just waded in—"

"You were really brave," Louis insisted.

"Not that brave," Sophie said, feeling abashed. "A bit stupid really. I can't really swim."

Louis blinked at her, and the color drained from his cheeks. "Right," he said.

Izzy finally broke eye contact with Barney the dinosaur and reached out a hand to Louis. "Daddy," she said. "Cuddle too."

Louis took her hand and, moving to the head of the bed, put his arms around Izzy, stretching one leg out on the bed, leaving the other planted firmly on the floor.

"She said she wanted to go paddling!" Sophie whispered as Izzy settled back into her program. "I didn't think she meant it! I should have remembered—when a three-year-old says she is going to do something, she really means it. I only took my eyes off of her for a second. I'm so sorry, Louis. I mean, what if—" The now familiar wave of panic surged through her again.

Louis shifted slightly and, using his arm that was around Izzy's shoulders, picked up Sophie's hand. "I said don't be sorry," he said, tightening his finger around hers. "Not you."

Sophie was sure the only thing that saved her from spontaneous combustion was Izzy, rejoining the conversation once again.

"Mummy *is* in the sea, Sophie," she said conversationally.

Sophie looked down at the little girl with surprise. Instead of the nervous wreck that Sophie had expected, with a newly acquired phobia of water to add to her long list of terrors, the child seemed amazingly serene.

"Is she?" Sophie asked.

"Yes." Izzy lifted her head and looked from Louis to Sophie. "It was Mummy that pushed me back to you, wasn't it?

Sophie thought about the swell of the tide that had carried Izzy almost directly into her arms. She rested her palm against Izzy's cheek and smiled down at her. "You know what," she said, feeling suddenly comforted by childish logic. "I think you're right."

Louis tried halfheartedly to persuade Sophie that she didn't have to come with him to the solicitor's.

She pointed out as she clambered out of bed that the doctor had said they were all fine and that in fact a trip would take their minds off of it all.

It was interesting to watch Louis's face then as he struggled with not wanting to go alone but wanting to do the right thing.

"Honestly, it's fine," Sophie said, finding a clean, dry top. She had undone the first two top buttons on her pajamas before she realized what she was doing, dropped the T-shirt like a hot brick, and nodded in the direction of the door. "We'll meet you downstairs."

Louis seemed just as embarrassed as she was by her sudden carefree impulse to undress in front him and needed no further prompting to leave, but just before he shut the door behind him, he turned around again. "You're sure you want to come?"

"We're sure," Bella said. "Because if you're going to look at houses and shops, then so are me and Izzy. You said we'd decide everything together, remember?"

Both Louis and Sophie sensed that Bella was testing him.

"Of course," Louis said. "Of course the three of us will decide together."

Once the door was shut, Sophie dressed herself and the girls quickly in three pairs of jeans purchased especially for the trip and three brand-new pairs of sneakers.

"I look like you!" Izzy said, pointing at Sophie, clearly delighted. "Only I don't have a wobbly tummy."

"Oh, Izzy," Sophie said as she picked up her bag. "You really know how to pay a compliment."

As Izzy and Sophie bustled out of the room, Sophie noticed that Bella was hanging back, picking at the fringe of her mum's red mohair sweater.

"Bella? Come on," Sophie prompted her.

"He really likes you," Bella said. "Doesn't he?"

"A bit, I think," Sophie said. "And I like him too—a bit."

"Does he like you the way he liked Mummy?" Bella questioned her closely. Worried that somehow the six-year-old had seen through her exterior to spot her feeling for Louis, Sophie reacted strongly. "God no!" she exclaimed. "I mean no. Not at all."

Bella bit her lip and looked long and hard before she picked up her coat and walked out of the room. "Good," she said as she passed Sophie.

Twenty-four

"Are you sure?" Sophie asked Mrs. Alexander again as they stood in the foyer of the B & B.

Mrs. Alexander nodded vigorously. "Yes, dear," she repeated. "Those two little mites are out like lights, the pub's only down the road, and if they wake up I'll phone you at this number, okay?" She brandished the Post-it note on which Sophie had written her cell phone number. "I don't usually do babysitting, but we're quiet, and these are extenuating circumstances. Go on, the pair of you, you look like you need a drink."

Louis smiled warmly at their hostess—if she had been a bird, he would have charmed her from the nearest tree.

"Exactly the kind of service you get from a boutique hotel," he said, flirting shamelessly with the middle-aged woman, which was something of an uncomfortable revelation for Sophie, who had yet to see him flirt overtly. He was exceptionally good at it.

"Exactly," Mrs. Alexander agreed, fluttering her lashes coquettishly.

A cold gust of wind enveloped them as they stepped out onto the street, and Sophie pulled her jacket tightly around her. Without comment, Louis dropped the weight of his arm around her shoulders and pulled her into the shelter of his body. Silently they crossed the road and walked into the pub.

"What do you want?" he said, leaning against the bar.

"I don't know. I just don't know!" Sophie found herself wanting to cry out in despair, but instead she asked for a brandy. "Make it a large one," she told him. "For the shock." Only she didn't tell him that it was the shock of having his arm around her that she needed it for, not the whole near-drowning thing.

As Louis ordered, Sophie looked around the pub; it was pretty quiet. Two old men sitting in one corner and group of quite rowdy locals another. Sophie made her way to a third corner and found a table. As she waited for Louis to deliver the brandy, she considered the way he had put his arm around her so easily.

It could have meant one of three things: he now considered them to be such close friends that he felt as comfortable with casual embraces as Cal often was. This proved that he was gay because Sophie had never yet known a straight man who did hugging just to be friendly. Or, it could mean that he knew she secretly fancied him, which she did not anyway because that would be in extremely bad taste, but for some reason he *thought* she did and figured he might have some luck. This made him an amoral philanderer—a description that until recently Sophie had thought would had fitted him perfectly but that Louis had inconsiderately messed up with his irritating bouts of sensitivity and heroism. Or, most likely, being a man, he probably didn't anxiously overanalyze every single gesture he made and worry about its repercussions. Probably, Sophie concluded with regret, it meant nothing at all except that her crush, which she was determined to will into nothing, was getting out of hand.

"Good God," she mumbled to herself as Louis approached the table. "I seriously need to get back to work. I'm starting to turn into Lisa." And for a moment she missed the emotionally flat and tranquil landscape that her life had been a just over a month ago.

Louis set the drinks down on the table, and out of the four seats around it chose the chair opposite her, proving conclusively the arm thing meant nothing.

"So," Sophie asked him, determined not to let her overtired and overly emotional brain do any more unauthorized thinking. "How did it go at the solicitor's?"

She had to ask him because even though she, Bella, and Izzy had waited in the reception area, giving him rather loud and boisterous moral support, when he had come out from his appointment he hadn't said a word. He'd just looked at the children with the expression of a man who had had a serious reality check.

"Let's go" had been all he'd said, and fearing that he'd just been landed with debt, repossession, or worse, Sophie had decided not to question him further in front of the girls.

Louis looked at the top of his pint for a moment. "Weird," he said. "It turns out that the girls and I have got quite a lot of money."

Sophie had not been expecting that. "Really?" she said.

"Yeah, I know," Louis said, looking equally amazed. "When we first got the mortgage, we took out an insurance policy, you know, to cover the cost of the loan and a bit more besides if one of us died. The financial adviser talked us into it. Funny really, Carrie and I weren't exactly known for forward planning—but I think it was the baby coming. We suddenly realized we were grown-ups. But I've got to admit, I didn't really know what the policy meant. I just kept paying into it, even though sometimes when money was tight we were tempted to cancel it. . . . It's not like we ever thought . . . but for some reason, we never got round to doing it."

Sophie listened to him talking about his life with Carrie, as a couple, a unit, and a "we" as if from a distance. Because she had not really known them as a couple, it was hard to think of them that way, even when Louis talked about their domestic arrangements. It was like there were three sets of alternate realities that had nothing to do with one another: Carrie and Louis living life quietly with their two children on the coast, Sophie's absent vision of her friend's life; Carrie on her own, struggling to bring up her kids after Louis abandoned her for the other side of the world; and Louis now, this half-known version of the man Sophie was becoming more attracted to at exactly the moment when she should have been holding back. Three parallel universes that Sophie somehow had to make sense of and draw together without driving herself completely mad.

"Anyway," Louis continued, oblivious. "While I was away, I'd kept paying any money I earned from a few part-time jobs I had into our joint account. I knew Carrie didn't want my help, but I couldn't not do anything, so I kept paying what I had in and the payment didn't get returned, so it made me feel better about things, I suppose."

Sophie watched him carefully, talking about his abandonment of Carrie so casually. And yet she knew he was not a callous, careless person; she was sure of it. So she said nothing and just kept on listening.

"The joint account doesn't amount to much," he went on. "Just a few grand. The solicitor told me Carrie never touched it at all after I left. But the direct debit for the insurance policy went out of that account. The mortgage on the house will be cleared, and there's nearly a hundred-thousand-pound lump sum too."

Sophie blinked. "Fuck," she said simply.

"I know," Louis said. "And that's why I feel weird. When I found out about Carrie, I was ready to come back here and fight for my girls. I was ready to buckle down and get a job, and I knew I'd have to struggle to pay the mortgage on my own but I was determined to do it because this was my chance to makes things right, do the grown-up thing." He paused. "A big part of this was selfishness, you know. A big part of this was to make me feel better about myself. And then, almost as soon as I got back, I realized that the way I felt wasn't important. It was all about my children, my two children. When I saw Bella's face, I realized how I'd damaged her through my own weakness. I couldn't stand to let her down again. But I expected it to be a struggle. I wanted it to be. Somehow having all that cash handed to me on a plate like this seems wrong, it seems really wrong to profit from Carrie's death." Louis struggled to say the last word of the sentence and his shifted in his seat. "So perhaps I should just give it to charity and start again. What do you think?"

Sophie blinked at him again.

"I wish you'd stop the blinking and start talking," Louis exclaimed. "It's freaking me out."

"Sorry." Sophie took a breath. "I just couldn't believe what I was hearing. Louis, don't be mad! You can't give away the money. You and Carrie took out an insurance policy on each other's lives. That's all. And now Carrie's gone, you're entitled, more important, the *children* are entitled to the payout. It still would have paid out if you'd fallen down a volcano in Lima—"

"There aren't any volcanoes in Lima," Louis interrupted.

"Whatever." Sophie held up her palm to prevent further interruptions. "My point is, *you* kept up the payments, and you and the children are benefiting because of that. Those are just the facts. But more important this is exactly what Carrie would want for her children. She'd *want* them to have some security. She'd *want* you to have some breathing space. I mean, think about it. Now you won't have to rush into a job you'd hate, like the one at the printer's. You can spend more time with the girls, getting to know them. Maybe you can even buy a decent camera and start taking photos again."

Louis looked up from the table suddenly and stared at her.

"What?" she asked him, feeling disconcerted.

"How did you know I wanted to get back into photography?"

"Well, you used to run your own business, didn't you, before Bella came and you needed a more regular income? Obvious really. No one would do a crappy job they hated if they had the chance to do something they loved." Sophie watched Louis's expression darken as he broke eye contact with her once again.

"Is that why you went, Louis?" she found the question rushing out of her mouth before she could censor it. "Because you felt trapped into something you didn't want? Because you got married and had a baby before you knew it. Is that why?"

"No!" His voice rose in protest so that the other customers all looked over. "No," he said again more quietly. He picked up his empty glass and stood. "I suppose it's about time we talked about this. I know it still bothers you, and I want you to know the truth." He swallowed. "You've been a really good . . . friend to me. So I'll tell you if you really want to know."

Sophie looked at him. Did she want to know? she asked herself. Because she felt that knowing would bring an end at last to this bubble that she had been living in, kidding herself that she was somehow vital to this fragile family. But she knew that could not be true. In reality, she needed to know exactly what Louis had done to make him leave Carrie so that she could put an end to her crush on him and move on, alone.

"I want to know," she said.

"Okay," Louis said, "but I need another drink first."

Twenty-five

Actually, I was happy," Louis told her, after taking a long draft of his pint. "I was really happy before it all fell apart. I didn't see it coming, and when it did go wrong, it just knocked me completely sideways. I couldn't handle it.

"Everyone said we were doomed to failure, Carrie's mum—obviously—but all of our friends too, even if they were only joking. I don't think from what Carrie said you were that impressed either, were you?"

Sophie considered denying it, but instead she just shrugged. "It did happen very fast," she said.

"I know, but I thought then—and I still feel, even after everything that happened—that just because something happens very fast, it doesn't automatically mean that it's wrong. Sometimes spontaneity is good." Louis waited for a moment, as if he expected her to offer an opinion. When she remained silent, he began talking again.

"We did get together quickly, and Carrie was a bit of a force of nature that was hard to resist—but I didn't want to resist her! When a beautiful, funny, talented woman says she wants you, you don't stop to think about how fast it's going and where it might lead, not when it all feels so good."

Sophie shrugged again. It seemed an appropriately comprehensive reaction to give when she was so unsure of how she really felt.

"And it did feel good. As far as I was concerned, it *was* love. And when Carrie became pregnant, it wasn't a trap—it couldn't have been because I was incredibly pleased. I never knew my dad, and Mum—well, she wasn't exactly the perfect mother. My nan brought me up. And she was wonderful, really wonderful, but I missed all that other family stuff that my mates had. Anyway, Nan died when I was seventeen, and from then on, although I had a lot of good friends, I had no family. Until I met Carrie, and then she and the baby she was carrying became my family. Carrie didn't trap me, there was this one night on the beach when . . ." Louis trailed off, a faint smile on his face, lost in his memories.

Sophie sat quietly, feeling sick with jealousy and guilt.

"I loved Carrie," he continued, "she was my first love. I would have married her with or without the baby. I was going to ask her anyway when we'd been together for a year. I'd more or less decided that I would the day after I first met her. But when she told me about Bella, it just came out. I proposed and she said yes and that was it. When I think about that now, I do wonder if Bella hadn't happened, another six or seven months down the line if we would have still been so in love. But Bella did happen, and I'm glad she did. I don't regret anything. It was a truly happy time."

Sophie thought of the photo of Carrie on the beach with Louis in the background, his arms about another woman, probably flirting with her the way he had with Mrs. Alexander earlier.

"Louis, can I ask you something?" she said.

He nodded, lifting his chin a little as if he expected she might want to punch it. "Were you seeing other women after you were married?" Sophie delivered her blow with swift efficiency.

Louis did not flinch. He held her gaze and shook his head. "No," he said, and he smiled to himself. "Carrie used to say that I was a terrible flirt, but honestly I couldn't see it. I'm just nice to people, and if that's flirting then I flirt with everyone, men included."

Sophie thought about this for a moment. No one could say she was a world expert on the matter, but she was more or less certain he had never flirted with her.

"Except for a person I'm really attracted to," Louis said, "then I sort of clam up." He stopped himself, and an uncomfortable silence hung between them for a beat.

Again Sophie sensed he was expecting her to say something. Again she discovered not only could she not think of any response apart from shrieking hysterically "You've never flirted with me!" but also she was sure that even if she had tried to speak, her mouth would not have opened. She was scared rigid. Too scared to think about what he might or might not be about to tell her. What he might be trying to say.

"I never cheated on Carrie," Louis continued. "Why would I? Carrie was radiant, the most beautiful thing I'd ever seen. Even more when she was pregnant and after Bella was born. She was like a sunrise that got more spectacular every morning. I loved her, Sophie, probably too much. When I look back on it, I think it was almost adolescent. I'd never had a proper girlfriend before Carrie."

"You must have!" Sophie blurted out incredulous, her rebellious tongue probably loosened by an uncomfortable tide of jealousy that rose in her chest as Louis talked about Carrie.

He arched an eyebrow, and a hint of a smile hovered around his lips. "Why?" he asked her inevitably.

"Well, you were twenty-three or twenty-four when you met Carrie," she said, conveniently forgetting that she herself had only ever had one proper boyfriend, and that hadn't been until she was pushing twenty-seven.

"There were girls," Louis said, "but no one I connected with emotionally. That's why when it happened I think I poured so much into it. Maybe too much. You know, I actually think it was my commitment that scared Carrie. All I could see in my future was her and Bella—our family. All she could see was the same thing, and I think seeing that blotted out all of the hopes and possibilities she'd cherished for so long. I think in the end she felt she'd rushed into it."

Sophie let that piece of information sink in. "Are you saying Carrie ended the marriage?" she asked in disbelief. "But she always said you were so happy, even after you'd split up, she told me you were happy!"

Louis shrugged. "Well, Carrie really hated to be wrong," he said.

Sophie wondered if her friend's stubborn streak and phobia of people crowing "I told you so!" was really a good enough reason for her not to have mentioned the split to her best friend. And then another thought occurred to her. Perhaps their friendship hadn't just drifted after the christening. Perhaps Carrie had deliberately begun to cut the ties. It would have been easy to do, as Sophie hardly bothered to maintain them herself. Perhaps she hadn't ever been a really good friend to Carrie. And what use was it, she wondered, being loyal and steadfast to a friend who had gone forever? Sophie had just started to allow herself to feel proud of her rescue job on this family, but in fact, if she had still been the kind of friend who exchanged vows and promises before

Carrie had been killed, then Louis wouldn't have been sitting here telling her everything now. She would already have known.

Sophie dropped her head in shame. She had let her down in life, and now she was secretly lusting after her husband, who clearly still loved Carrie despite all that had passed.

That's it, Sophie told herself silently. The stupidity ends here.

"So," she said stiffly to Louis. "What went wrong?"

He scrutinized her for a moment, probably taking her change in attitude as disapproval, which Sophie didn't mind at all.

"We didn't have much money," he continued. "And both of us working meant that Bella was in the nursery full-time. Neither of us got to spend as much time with her as we wanted. Carrie had stopped painting. I hadn't been near my camera in months. I could see she was finding it all a bit of a grind, the daily routine was wearing her down. So I decided to take more shifts at the printer's. Carrie gave up her shop job. She started painting again, and we cut Bella's hours down at the nursery so she and Carrie could be together more. Don't get me wrong, it didn't seem like a sacrifice. I thought I was doing the right thing for my family, and that made me feel pretty good.

"But Carrie and I hardly saw each other, and when we did I was almost always exhausted. Day by day we lost little pieces of the intimacy that had bonded us together."

Louis paused and took a deep draft of his beer. Sophie followed suit with her brandy, feeling it burn the back of her throat. She wanted to know everything, but the thought of knowing terrified her. She took another sip.

"Then I got in one night, after about two months of me working late, and she was waiting up for me. She said she had some great news that might mean she'd be earning again. This new artist's studio and gallery was opening in town, for local artists only. He was Welsh, but he was looking for two or three other artists to work there too. She'd met him at a friend's house. This bloke called Tony Something. He really liked her work, wanted her to paint in the gallery. She was thrilled, really thrilled, she was so happy, and it was only when I saw her standing there glowing that I realized she hadn't been happy for months. And then she got pregnant again." A shadow of pain passed across Louis's face, and Sophie's chest tightened.

"At first I couldn't understand when she told me why she was so . . . reserved. She couldn't look at me. I thought maybe she was worried that we couldn't afford a new baby, so I tried to re-assure her, told her we'd manage somehow, and she burst into tears."

"I'm so sorry, Louis," she said. "I'm so sorry." And then she said, "I don't think I love you anymore." Louis was no longer looking at Sophie; instead he seemed to be scrutinizing the pub's stone floor as he recounted the memory.

"She said she'd fallen in love with this other man, this Tony, the gallery owner. She said they had been sleeping together for a couple of months. That it was really special. She said she didn't think the baby could be mine because there'd only been this one time in weeks."

"She didn't tell me any of this," Sophie said, shocked. "I used to think that we were so close. That's why I took the girls, because of how close we'd been—always, forever, whatever. That was what we always said. But I must have been wrong. Carrie must have felt that our friendship was over."

Louis shook his head. "I don't think so. Carrie used to talk about you all this time. She was always wishing we had the time or money to see you. If things had worked out with Tony, she'd have told you, I'm sure she would have. But they didn't. And Carrie's dreams were so important to her, and living them for real even more so. It was a matter of pride. I don't think she could bear to see them go wrong, but she would especially hate for other people to see them fall apart."

Sophie's eyes met Louis's, and part of her wished fervently that he was lying, that he was making all of this up to look good, so she could hate him and that would be that. But she could see that he wasn't. Not even the most accomplished con artist could lie with his entire body. Every muscle, every angle of Louis's body, each successive expression on his face told her that he was telling her the truth, a truth that was clearly painful for him as well as for her.

"So she kicked you out?" Sophie asked. "But then how do you know about what happened with Tony?"

Louis took a deep breath and finished the last of his pint. "No, she didn't kick me out. Like I said, the way I loved her was so fierce. I'd invested all of my longing for a proper, stable family into her. The way I reacted was pathetic, childish. I should have stayed, I should have tried to talk things through, but I just went blind with hurt and rage. I went upstairs, I took my passport, my credit card, shoved some clothes into a bag, and I left with no idea where I was going."

Louis paused, the corners of his mouth pulled taut. He passed the back of his hand roughly across his eyes. "The shouting had woken Bella up. She was crying in her bed, calling out to me, asking me to pick her up. I just walked straight past her. If there was one thing that I still wish I could change, it would be that moment. Over and over again I've woken up wishing that I had gone back to her. That I had picked her up and held her. It's the biggest regret of my life."

Sophie wanted to reach out, to put a hand on his arm, but before she could, he seemed to pull himself together, withdrawing his hands from the table and sitting upright in his chair.

"Carrie didn't want me to go," he continued. "She wanted me

to stay and talk, but I had to get out of there. I felt like my perfect life, everything I'd worked so hard to create was ruined. I was like a child who wants to throw away a broken toy. I couldn't even look at her. I just walked out. I didn't even kiss Bella good-bye. The next twenty-four hours were like a nightmare. I can hardly remember them. But I got a train to London and another train to Heathrow. And I got the first standby flight to the States I could get on. Malibu!" Louis's laugh was empty of any pleasure. "It was ironic, because I'd always wanted to go there, before I met Carrie."

He studied Sophie's face. "What are you thinking?" he asked her. "Do you hate me again?"

Sophie shook her head slowly, wishing desperately that she did, because it would make her life so much easier. "I can understand you walking out, but just leaving behind your whole life? That's pretty hard to get my head around," she told him honestly.

"She *was* my life, my whole life. I felt that if I didn't have her, I didn't have anything. And before you ask, I didn't even think about Bella at that point. I didn't think about much at all except Carrie with the other man and— I think I wanted to show her I could be as selfish as she could. I think I wanted to shock her into wanting me back."

Louis took a deep breath. "I was a fool," he said, and it was his turn to shrug. "I lived off my credit card for a while, got drunk a lot." He grimaced. "Generally acted like an idiot."

Sophie guessed she was only now about to find out the extent of his folly.

"And then about a month after I arrived, I woke up one morning somehow sober, and I realized what I'd done to myself and to Bella. By trying to punish Carrie, I'd punished myself and my little girl. I'd got it all wrong.

"I decided to call Carrie. I wanted to tell her I was coming home and that whatever happened between us, I'd be there for my child. I had just enough left on my card to make the call and for a return flight." Louis's face darkened. "Only Carrie didn't answer the phone. Tony answered. I should have asked to speak to Carrie, but I still loved her then. Hearing his voice was like twisting the knife in my gut, so I just hung up."

He sighed. "Again I reacted like a spoiled child. I should just have got that flight home anyway, worked things out with Carrie for Bella's sake. But the thought of doing that hurt too much. Of being near her but not being with her. I decided it would be better to let Carrie build her life with her new family. I told myself that Bella would forget me soon enough and that would be for the best." He shook his head bitterly. "What bollocks. What a fucking idiot."

Sophie watched his profile as he looked out the window trying to find the words to continue his story. It was as if everything he had told her was about a different man entirely from the one sitting opposite her now. Could anyone have changed that much in the space of three years? From someone as impulsive and rash as the man Louis had been talking about to someone capable of bringing up a family on his own. Someone solid and reliable. Could a person change so completely just by growing up? Something tightened in Sophie's chest as she watched him, and sensing her looking at him, he turned toward her and smiled. "Shall I go on?" he said.

Sophie nodded, not quite able to return his smile, which faded when she did not respond.

He took a deep breath and began again. "So anyway, I got a flight to Brazil instead. I decided I was never going home. I decided I was going to travel around South and Central America. But when I got to Peru, I stayed there. It's such a beautiful place, and so different from, well, here—" Louis gestured around him. "It felt like I was finally far enough away for it to stop hurting. I had been in Lima for about six months volunteering for the kids' charity by the time I realized that Carrie would have had her baby. I'd never had myself down as the worthy charity type, but it was good working there. Like being part of a big family. They helped me get a visa, gave me a place to live and food." Louis smiled. "I worked with street children, incredibly brave and resourceful children. The foundation gave them a place to come where they could feel safe for a night, eat a meal, and learn something if they wanted. *Play* if they wanted."

"And in the evenings and on weekends, I worked in a tourist bar in town, so I was never still. I never had time to think. And then one day it hit me. The baby would have been born.

"It took me a long time to get up the courage to make the phone call, but I did. This time I was prepared for Tony to answer, but I knew I had to talk to Carrie to find out how she was, how Bella was. And the baby."

Sophie realized she was sitting on the edge of her seat.

"But Tony didn't answer the phone. Carrie did, and she seemed really pleased to hear from me. She told me she had had a beautiful little girl and that they were doing fine. I said I was glad things were working out for her, and then she seemed to think for a moment before telling me Tony had left. But the three of them were happy."

Sophie could picture Carrie saying those words exactly. She always believed in living with the consequences of her choices, no matter what they were. Mrs. Stiles had said once that Carrie wore her mistakes like badges of honor, and Carrie had said that was the nicest thing her mother had ever said about her. But that was the difference between Sophie and Carrie. Carrie made choices decisively and rode them out no matter what happened. Sophie never chose what happened in her life—she let fate choose for her and never questioned how different things could be.

"Instantly I offered to come back on the next flight," Louis said. "I told her that she'd hurt me badly but I still loved her. I'd come back and we'd work things out. There was this long silence, and I could almost taste the hope in my mouth."

"'I don't want you back, Louis,' she said. 'What happened with Tony is over, but I still don't love you anymore. I know I should, and I did once—so much. But I don't now. It's just gone. There's no point in you coming back for me, I want you to know that. But if you want to see the girls, I'll never stand in your way.'

"We said good-bye, and then she added one more thing. 'There's something else you should know,' she said. 'Your daughter's name is Izzy.'" Louis stopped talking. He rubbed his thumb over his eyes.

Sophie chewed her lip, tasting her hastily applied lipstick. She didn't know what to think about everything Louis had told her. She felt an urge to defend Carrie, but how could she when she had known nothing about any of this? Sophie closed her eyes for a moment and thought about the last time she had seen Carrie, playing the scene back in her head. There had been a moment after the christening when Sophie had thought that Carrie wanted to talk about something else. But she had hesitated and then changed the subject. Maybe she'd been going to tell Sophie all this then. But if she had and decided not to, it meant that even though Carrie had asked her best friend to be the girls' godmother and guardian she had not felt able to tell the truth about what had happened. She must have felt very lonely, Sophie realized.

"Why didn't you come back for Bella and Izzy? Carrie wouldn't have stopped you seeing them."

Louis was silent for a long moment, before taking a deep breath. "At first it was because I still loved Carrie so much. I couldn't bear the thought of going back there and not being with her. It was selfish and stupid and immature. But the grief sort of swamped me. The only way I could get through it was to not think about it. I had to make myself not feel it. Do you know what I mean?"

"Yes, I do," Sophie said so emphatically that Louis paused and raised an eyebrow.

"And then one morning I was working in the vegetable garden with some of the children, and they were slinging mud around and laughing and I laughed too and it was the first time I had really laughed and *meant* it in nearly two years. It was like I suddenly dropped all of this weight that had been dragging me down. All of that pain and hurt that had been crowding out every other feeling finally dissolved. For the first time I could see things clearly. I could see what I had done." Louis shook his head as if he were still perplexed by his own behavior.

"From then on I planned to come back. I knew I wanted to see my *own* children laughing like that. But it wasn't as simple as hopping on a plane again. I had to get together money for a flight home, which took a long time—almost a year. And during that time I was training new volunteers to replace me. I didn't want to leave the children in the lurch. They were like a second family to me. I wanted to come back to England and I knew I had to come back but it was still hard to leave. People had been really good to me there, and I was waiting until I didn't love Carrie anymore, because I thought it would be easier to be around her if I didn't love her." Louis leveled his gaze at Sophie. "I'd been ready to come back for months, but when you called I hadn't quite got the money for the flight together."

It took a moment for Sophie to let that last piece of information sink in. "Did you still want to get back with Carrie?" she asked him, careful not to let any emotion color her voice.

Louis shook his head. "I wanted to see her, I wanted to apologize to her for behaving the way that I did. I wanted to mend bridges and make things right. I had no idea how I would feel when I saw her. Now I'll never know. I left it too late." He swallowed. "It makes me very sad that I can't do that, and I wish she were still here, I really do. But I didn't love her anymore—not like that. All of those feelings had been gone for a long time."

Sophie nodded and let out a long breath. "Did you have a lover in Lima?"

The look of surprise on his face matched her own surprise at having asked the question, which was, after all, none of her business. But instead of being offended, Louis shrugged. "I had a couple of girlfriends," he said. "Not at the same time!" he added hastily. "But it was never anything . . . special." Amazingly, Louis didn't seem to have a problem with explaining himself to Sophie, so she decided to ask him just one more impertinent question that had been in the back of her mind before shutting up.

"When I called you that night, you thought I was someone else. You called me babe. Who did you think I was? One of you girlfriends?"

Louis furrowed his brow as if genuinely confused. "No, I hadn't been seeing anyone for ages and . . ." Then he laughed. "Maureen!" he said. "It was Maureen."

"Maureen?" Sophie asked.

"She was my U.K. contact at the charity. Lovely woman, but always getting the time difference wrong. She was going to help me find a job and a flat to rent back in St. Ives. When they told me an Englishwoman was calling at that time of the morning, I thought it had to be Maureen. I've never met her. I'll be seeing her next week, but she's got two children older than us, so I don't *think* she'll be my type. She's lined me up with a local charity for inner-city kids who need a break from city life."

Louis leaned back in his chair and regarded Sophie for a long moment, the promise of a smile hiding somewhere around his lips. "So after all that, do you think I'm a bastard?" he asked her quietly.

Sophie considered the question carefully. All of this was too much for her to take in. Cal always said she had intimacy issues, and now she realized she had emotional issues too. She could not feel one more thing without imploding. She was feeling pain, loss, guilt, and something else, something hopeful and yearning, all flowing recklessly over a strong undercurrent of attraction to the last man in the world she should feel that way about—her dead best friend's husband.

She realized Louis was waiting for an answer. She struggled to find some words that would sound normal.

"I think you were hurting, and when people hurt they don't always do everything right," she said.

Louis bit his lip and nodded. "I was hoping for a simple no," he said wryly.

"But it isn't simple, is it?" Sophie replied, not exactly sure what she was talking about anymore. "It's really seriously complicated."

They watched each other across the table in silence for a beat.

"Yes," Louis said, without taking his eyes off her. "It is."

"Anyway," Sophie added hesitantly. "It's just a matter of time before Tess calls and tells you the children are yours. It doesn't matter what I think of you."

Slowly Louis leaned forward, resting his elbows on the table as he closed the distance between them by a few inches. "It does matter," he said, his voice low. "It matters to me."

Sophie found that her mouth was dry and that it was difficult to swallow. She took a sip of her drink and moistened her lips.

"For what it's worth, Louis," she said, still desperately trying to prize another meaning into this conversation, and yet terrified of what it might really mean, "I think you'll be a great father. I think the three of you will be really happy. I've already told Tess that too."

Louis shook his head. "Thanks," he said. "That means a lot—but that's not what I meant."

Sophie felt as if each muscle in her body was rigid. She felt that it was entirely possible that she might fossilize right there in the pub. They'd be able to slice her up and sell her in a local gift shop: "Genuine Petrified Woman."

"I didn't really remember you," Louis said. "Before I came back I mean. Carrie talked about you a lot, and there was a photo in a frame. But I never really looked at it." He paused and bit his lip. "So it came as a total shock to me to find out that you're so beautiful." Sophie did not move. "That first night I came to your flat and we were talking in the hallway and you took off your coat and— Well, does it sound corny to say you took my breath away?" Sophie did not know what to say, but luckily Louis didn't wait for an answer. "It does, doesn't it?" he said. "It sounds like a line. But believe me, at that moment I might have thought you were seriously hot, but I never dreamt I'd start to think about you the way I am now. I was so angry when I left that night, with myself and with you. So I thought, I'll just put the fact that you are so beautiful to one side. It was easy at first. I was there for my children and nothing else. You hated me, and to top it off you were my dead, estranged wife's best friend. Not exactly the perfect girl to fancy." Louis smiled. "Actually, I thought you were one of those women who care more about not chipping her nail polish than anything else. And you were a bit of a bitch."

Sophie had thought she had been genuinely afraid for the first time in her life earlier that day, when she had been up to her waist in seawater. But no, actually that had been a walk in the park compared with the pure fear and adrenaline that were coursing through her veins at this moment. What exactly was Louis saying?

"I'm seriously attracted to you, Sophie," he said. "Every sensible part of my body is screaming at me to shut up. But there's something there, isn't there? Between us. I don't know what I'm thinking or feeling here, and I know it's insane for me to be saying all this to you, but I think I'll go insane if I don't."

He picked up Sophie's hand and held her fingers lightly. "Look, I know, if there was ever a wrong time, a wrong place, or a wrong person to say this to, then it's now, it's here, and you're that person. But I have to say it, Sophie. For a while now, every time I look at you I want to touch you. Every time I touch you, I want to kiss you, and if I could kiss you, I don't think I'd be able to stop." He waited for a moment, and when Sophie did not move he let go of her hand. "In my head that last part sounded much less cheesy. Look, I'm sorry. I just thought that maybe— I just couldn't let us go back to our lives without saying out loud how much I'm drawn to you, that's all. Call me impulsive, but life's too short." Louis tried and failed to gauge Sophie's expression. He smiled weakly. "You can slap me now, if you like."

Sophie stood up so abruptly that her chair scraped along the stone floor. She willed herself outside, dimly aware of people lifting their heads to watch her race past them. At last she was bathed in the cold night air, and she felt her skin begin to cool. She crossed the street to the harbor front, leaned against the railing, and watched the foam-topped waves shining in the moonlight as they raced inland. From the moment they had stepped into Carrie's house that morning, the whole day had seemed like a dream. It seemed as if she had experienced more emotion and turmoil in the space of the last few hours than she had since, well, since the day her father died. She heard the rush of the sea more clearly, smelled the chill in the air more sharply, and saw each tiny reflection of light in the dark water perfectly. And she sensed Louis at her side a second before he reached her.

"I didn't know if you wanted me to follow you or not," he said. "So I thought I'd follow you on the off chance."

She turned to face him. "I'm glad you did." Louis opened his mouth to speak, but Sophie stopped him. "Look, if you want me to talk about other people's feelings, then I can. I can do that all night. I am a very good advice giver. But I am not the sort of person who finds it easy to talk about myself. I don't even know what I'm feeling right now or what it means. I don't even understand it. But all of the things you said in there about me, I could say them back to you," she finished awkwardly.

"You mean you feel it too?" Louis asked uncertainly.

"I do," Sophie said with difficulty. Louis smiled, but before he could say or do anything, Sophie put the flat of her hand on his chest and halted him. "But this isn't right, Louis. For us to do anything about it would be wrong. I think it might be really wrong—"

He nodded, his smile fading slightly. "You're probably right," he said. "But, well, would it matter . . . if we had just one night without thinking about anyone or anything else except for this 'thing' that's going on between us?"

Sophie studied him in the moonlight. That was all he was talking about. A one-night stand, a sort of therapeutic session to clear away the sexual tension. She felt simultaneously relieved, sad, and excited, because if that was all it would be, then it didn't really count and there would be no consequences. It could be like stepping off the planet for a few hours and leaving it all behind. And for once Sophie wanted to do something completely foreign to her nature. Tonight she wanted to know what it felt like to be reckless and not care about tomorrow.

"I want to know," she said. "Which probably makes me an idiot."

"That makes two of us," Louis said.

"Do you think so, because . . ." Sophie began again, earnestly trying to rationalize what she was saying.

"Let's stop talking now," Louis said, laying the tips of his fingers gently over her mouth. He watched her in the moonlight, tracing the curves of her lips, and then at last he kissed her so that all she could feel for a wondrous few moments was the heat of his mouth warming every fiber of her being. Sophie broke off the kiss and found she was giggling.

"Not the response I was expecting," Louis said, smiling as she buried her face in his jacket.

She caught her breath and looked up. "I must be drunk," she said. "This isn't normal."

"Well, don't back out on me now. Remember what I said about thinking I might not be able to stop kissing you once I started? I was right." Louis rested his hand on her shoulders, his fingers entwined in her hair. "Sophie, stay with me tonight? Just tonight, please?" he asked her, touchingly nervous.

Sophie looked into his eyes and felt a heady rush of intoxication that she was sure had nothing to do with brandy. "I guess we're going to find out how we both fit in that single bed after all," she said, and she took a step into thin air and kept on walking.

Twenty-six

*I*t was still dark when Sophie woke.

For a moment she lay there waiting for her eyes to adjust as a thin line that ran around the doorframe cast a sliver of light into the room. For a moment, still warmed and comforted by sleep, she stared at the door, trying to work out how it had moved from its previous position.

And then she remembered she was in Louis's room.

Sophie did not leap out of bed, partly because she did not want to wake Louis but also because she discovered that her limbs were so tangled in his that it seemed impossible to move. She lay still, staring into the dark, listening to her heart thumping in her chest. Piece by piece, everything that had happened came back to her in a series of jolting and shocking tableaux.

The moment they had returned to the B & B. A second's hesitation before they'd crossed the doorstep. Their silent ascent to Louis's room, not looking at each other as they climbed the stairs, their fingers just touching on the handrail. Louis looking over his shoulder at her as he unlocked his door. Sophie standing perfectly still with her ear pressed to her and the children's door, looking at the pointed, scuffed toes of her pink knee-high boots—now water-stained and dirty—as she'd waited, holding her breath, for a small voice to call out her name. Not knowing if she'd wanted to hear that voice or not.

Sophie felt again the knot of anticipation that had clenched her stomach into a fist as Louis had held out his hand and she'd taken it, and then . . .

She remembered his kisses all over her face and her neck, in her hair and across her shoulders. Their clothes somehow disintegrating, the heat his body gave off a moment before his skin met hers. The touch of his hands on her breasts, then his lips and teeth. Her own hands exploring the curve of his waist, the length of his thighs. Feeling him harden against the soft cushion of her belly. Feeling him shudder when she touched him and kissed him. Feeling him moving inside of her, experiencing every tiny sensation, every part of him connected to her until she buried her face in his neck, her teeth catching the skin of his shoulder as she came, and a moment later his voice whispering something softly in her ear, words she couldn't make out and did not want to understand.

They'd been silent then and still, seeming to slot perfectly together in the narrow bed like a pair of puzzle pieces. And they must have fallen asleep soon after, because that was exactly how they still lay, Sophie folded inside Louis, his long arms and legs wrapped around her, holding her back against his chest. She edged herself onto her back and turned her head to look at him. Most of his face was in shadow, just the tiniest slice of light picked out one corner of his eye, the curve of his jaw, and the corner of his mouth. His breathing was regular and deep; he was fast asleep.

Sophie was now wide awake, and she could feel her blood pounding around her body. She felt breathless and anxious as the remnants of sleep slowly receded to reveal a sense of raw, wide-awake panic. It seemed as if the reasons for this not happening, which they had hardly talked about and quickly dismissed last night, were solidifying into cold, hard realities all around her.

Sophie frantically tried to close herself off from the feelings that were surfacing with the early morning. Last night it had seemed so possible to do as Louis had said. To explore their attraction to each other free from the restraint of history or circumstance and then go on with their lives as they had been. Louis had seduced her with his reasoning, his looks, and his touches, and she had let him. But she had been wrong when she'd thought there would be no consequences. If she had had a stupid unrequited crush on him last night, this morning it was much, much worse. Spending the night with him had brought all her dreams crashing into the real world, where they could be trampled on and torn apart.

She had gone and fallen in love with him.

She could not do this. She could not be here with Louis. With Carrie's husband, with Bella and Izzy's father. Being here was a betrayal, it was pointless and weak. She should have realized. He might have slept with her, but he'd talked about Carrie with such warmth last night, how could he not still love her? And the place was so full of Carrie—everywhere she looked she felt her friend's presence—her friend who had always been there for her. How could she have even daydreamed about a life with Louis and the girls?

Reaching down to the side of the bed, she felt for her bag and was relieved when she found it almost right away. She took out her cell phone and checked the time.

It was just after five-thirty. The girls could be up at any minute. She had to get up, get dressed, and get back into her own bed before they noticed that she was not there. Immediately Sophie was gripped by panic as she began to grasp the implications of what she had done, and the reckless joy that she had felt in Louis's arms seemed in another lifetime.

"Oh, Christ," she whispered to herself, feeling the prick of tears behind her eyes. "Stupid, stupid, stupid."

Carefully she began to ease herself out of Louis's embrace, but as soon as he sensed her moving, his arms tightened reflexively. The thumb of his left hand ran lazily over her nipple as he kissed the back of her neck, burying his face in her hair. He shifted a little, moving his other arm out from underneath her, using it to prop himself up above her. Sophie felt him looking at her even though she could not see his face.

"Not a dream then," he said softly, and she felt his fingertips run lightly across the contours of her face and neck, traveling over her breasts. For a heartbeat she allowed herself to remain still, closing her eyes even in the dark. And then she closed her hand over his and stopped its exploration. "I've got to go next door," she whispered. "They'll be awake soon."

Louis flopped back onto the bed with a heartfelt sigh. "It's still dark," he protested, his voice warm with sleep.

"I know, but still . . . ," Sophie whispered.

Louis didn't try to stop her as she swung her legs onto the floor and, sitting on the edge of the bed, bent over searching for discarded items of clothing. Instead, as she found her knickers and pulled them over her ankles, he transferred his caresses to the back of her neck and along her spine.

Abruptly, Sophie pulled her underwear up as she stood. "I can't find anything," she said irritably, feeling claustrophobic in the darkness.

"I'll turn on the lamp," Louis said sleepily.

"No, don't—" she said, too late to stop him.

Soft light filled the corners of the room, and all sense of unreality was gone. He was really lying in his bed watching her. She was really standing before him, almost naked and feeling more exposed than she had ever felt before.

"You are so amazing," Louis said, his eyes running over her body. "Come back here, please, just for a moment . . ." He smiled as he held a hand out to her.

Sophie saw her T-shirt lying inside out on the floor and, picking it up, pulled it hastily over her head. She retrieved her jeans lying in a crumpled heap at the foot of the bed, her fingers fumbling as she tried to pull one leg out the right way.

"I can't," she said, her voice tight and nervous. "If the children wake up and find I'm not there or even come in here . . ." Finally she slipped her legs into the cold denim and buttoned the jeans at the waist. "And anyway, that's not what we said, is it?" she made herself remind him, keeping her voice cool. "It was just a one-time thing, remember?"

Louis sat up in bed. "I didn't mean it literally," he said. "I meant—"

"What did you mean?" Sophie asked him, her anger surfacing protectively.

"I meant we could get the lust out of the way and then take it from there." Louis looked at the expression on Sophie's face. "I'm not very good at this," he said quickly. "At words and stuff. Look, I didn't expect this. I didn't expect to . . ." He faltered to a stop.

"To what?" Sophie whispered, conscious of the thin wall between them and the children. "Get laid while you were sorting out your wife's estate? Must have been a real bonus for you."

Louis sat up sharply and pulled on his trousers. "Sophie, please. Why are you so angry?"

Sophie couldn't tell him, she couldn't tell him she was furious with herself for falling in love with him. It was better that he thought she was angry with him. Better than the terrifying possibility that she might show him the reality of how she was feeling.

"I have to go now," she said, gripping the door handle.

"Sophie, wait . . ."

She closed the door on him.

For a moment Sophie stood outside the room where Louis's two daughters were sleeping. She couldn't go in there, not yet, she realized. She was sure the instant that Bella looked at her, she would know something had happened with Louis, something that shouldn't have. Sophie didn't want Bella to know. The last thing she wanted was to wreck the fragile peace that Bella had found both with her father and within herself with one foolish, thoughtless act. Bella trusted her, loved her even. Sophie was determined to preserve that.

She walked past her bedroom door and crept down the carpeted stairs. She pulled on her boots, opened the front door, and stepped out into the dark morning. The cold immediately raised goose bumps on her skin, but Sophie welcomed the chill that numbed her burning cheeks. Her mother had said to her once that the darkest hour was always before the dawn. She meant it, Sophie knew, as an uplifting metaphor, a way to try to get Sophie through the loss of her dad, when she couldn't see any hope, but as Sophie walked down through the near-empty town, still perfectly dark and quiet, she was certain that when the sun came up, her troubles would really begin.

Sophie found her way back to Porthmeor Beach, where she

had run into the sea after Izzy. She told herself that it was a random destination, that it was inevitable she would end up staring at the sea. But she knew she had come here deliberately. It was here that Louis had brought her and Izzy out of the water and here that the four of them had stood together, embracing one another. It was on this beach that Sophie had experienced the very last thing she had expected to feel.

A sense of belonging to each of them. To Bella, to Izzy—and to Louis.

As she sat on the sand, Sophie watched the magic and movement of the ocean begin to reveal itself. "What am I doing here?" she asked herself, a whispered question that was immediately lost on a gust of wind. "How did this happen?"

It had started as an inconvenience, she admitted to herself. Carrie's children forcing a hiatus in her busy and ordered life. It was only now that she realized that life before Bella and Izzy had arrived had been the hiatus, because nothing about Sophie had changed for years until that moment. She had let year after year of her life slip away without anything to mark them out as special or important besides a new piece of jewelry or fabulous new shoes, as her half-forgotten dreams and ambitions quietly stagnated.

Sophie wasn't sure exactly when it happened, but she knew it was only after Bella and Izzy had come that she had started living inside her own life again instead of passively watching it tick by without her. And now, because of Bella and Izzy, she was in love, maybe for the first time, maybe even forever, because they had kick-started her heart.

The trouble was, it wasn't just Carrie's children she was in love with. It was Louis too. Sophie weighed the heavy, debilitating sense of longing that seemed to be pinning her down, and she found it hard to breathe.

It was odd, she thought, and sad that the very thing that had brought her so close to Carrie again—so close that she could almost feel her sitting beside her on the cold sand—was loving the people Carrie would never be able to hold and love again. Sophie felt but did not hear the sob that formed in her throat. She felt so guilty. She felt like a grave robber.

Of course, it was the thought of actually being with Louis that terrified her. The reality of being with a man she wanted so much made the possibilities of it all going wrong horribly real. Cal joked about her intimacy issues, but secretly Sophie knew she kept her distance from love because she could not bear the thought of another man she loved leaving her.

If there was anyone who might make her want to take that risk, perhaps it was Louis, but Louis didn't come on his own. He came with a past that was full of Carrie and with his children.

Even if the children didn't exist, there were hundreds of reasons not to let anything else happen with Louis. He had passionately loved another woman. One Sophie knew for sure had been more beautiful and vibrant than she could ever be, and whom Louis might still love, despite his protests.

He had talked about other girlfriends since Carrie, that was true. Women he must have been attracted to in the same way he was attracted to her. Sophie couldn't exactly remember the way he had described those flings, but she thought the phrase "never anything special" had been used. The panic tightened in her chest again.

What if Louis felt that way about her? What if everything he had said and whispered last night had been a succession of lines, part of a tried and tested seduction routine? She reminded herself that he was still mostly a stranger to her. That despite the last few weeks and the night they had just spent together, she hardly knew him at all. She couldn't bear to be another nameless encounter he might one day refer to as "nothing special."

Amazingly, Sophie felt herself laughing even as the tears ran down her cheeks. She was hilarious. She was insane. She was just as afraid of him loving her as she was of him not caring for her at all.

She shook her head and tried to focus on a way to untangle this mess she had made for herself. She thought about Bella and Izzy, and how she felt about them. She loved them too, and she felt this fierce, overwhelming urge to protect them from anything that might hurt them. She found she wanted more than anything else in the world to know for sure that neither of them would ever be hurt again.

Sophie drew her arms tighter around her and watched the sea.

It was so simple, really. She knew with a sudden clarity that there was no dilemma. All she had to do was what was best for the children, for Carrie, for Louis, and for herself. She had to do the only thing that would preserve each of them from suffering any more hurt.

She had to leave.

If she left now, the girls would still think about her happily, they would still love and trust her, and she would always be someone they could turn to. Sophie felt that by going she would be keeping her promise to Carrie, always, forever, whatever. She would be able to love her friend's memory instead of spending every day trying to compete with her ghost.

And if she left, Louis's pride might be a little stung, but it was better to make this break now.

Sophie knew if she went back to her old life, eventually the routine of work and home would insulate her once again against the threat of love and loss that was looming over her now. She would have back the life she had treasured so dearly. A calm, cool, peaceful life. She would be able to do whatever she wanted, when she wanted.

Knowing that comforted her, but at the same time it made her cry even harder. She forced herself to stand and start walking slowly and stiffly back to the B & B. Sophie knew then that the darkest hour really was before the dawn.

Twenty-seven

The road ahead was clear, so Sophie put her foot down and floored it, watching the speedometer climb steadily past eighty and toward ninety. It was the first time she had speeded since Izzy had arrived in her life and every torturous car journey had had to be taken at a steady twenty miles per hour in the city and a laborious seventy on the motorways. Sophie had expected to find the freedom of having her car back to herself as just a machine—the child seats removed, the Manic Street Preachers silenced at last, and the cat sunscreens stuffed in the glove compartment—much more exhilarating than she did. But driving as fast as she could get away with, nothing but the sound of Phoebe's—the car's—engine quietly humming, had somehow lost its joy.

A mountain of black cloud was building on the horizon ahead, and Sophie knew that somewhere in her near future it would be raining very hard, but she kept her foot down all the same, heading toward the bad weather with steady determination. She had told herself that once she was back in London, back in Highbury, and back in her flat she would be able to hear herself think again and start to make sense of the way her life had turned itself inside out and upside down without any notice or warning. Better still, she decided not to think about it at all. Not have to think about everything that had happened with Louis last night. Not have to think about the way she'd left the children that morning. Not have to think about everything that had happened leading up to that parting, because she was sure that as soon as she got home, everything would be all right.

But home was a few hundred miles away yet, and still Sophie kept playing the events of the last two days back again and again in her head, like trying to make sense of a foreign-language film without the subtitles.

After returning to her room that morning, she had re-dressed herself in clean clothes and then helped the girls as much as they wanted her to as they chattered and giggled and chose each other a rainbow collection of colors to wear. Sophie had looked on, relieved that Izzy seemed to be over the trauma of her tumble in the ocean and was now just enjoying the excitement of it, building the adventure with every rhythmic retelling.

The hour and a half that Sophie had had to wait between joining Louis for breakfast and nine o'clock had seemed like an eternity. As she'd sat across the table from him, Sophie had felt that she was almost visibly smothered in the vividly persistent memories of the night, as if Louis's mouth and hands had left marks on her skin that revealed where each kiss and each caress had been.

She had poked at her breakfast with a fork and sipped her coffee, smiling dimly at the girls as they chattered and made plans for the day. It was exactly as it had been the previous morning, except that Sophie did not speak directly to Louis and he didn't talk to her. It had been clear to Sophie that Louis was just as certain as she was that this had all been a foolish mistake.

When 9:00 A.M. had finally come and normal office hours resumed, Sophie had excused herself from the table and returned to her room, only to find that her cell phone battery was dead. Self-consciously she had slowly descended the stairs, waving at the girls as she fed the B & B's pay phone with a pound coin and a fifty-pence piece, and dialed Tess's number.

"Gosh, I haven't even got my coffee yet!" Tess had exclaimed breezily. "How's it going down there? Any progress?"

Sophie had watched the family of three at the breakfast table, talking and laughing. "Yes," she'd said with mechanical honesty. "It's going really well. Things sort of came to a head yesterday. Bella and Louis had a talk—they're deciding where to live. Bella wanted to stay in the old house at first. But they haven't made up their minds yet." Sophie had paused, realizing that she still didn't know what the two had said to each other on the beach. So many things had happened right after that; she hadn't had a moment even to draw breath, let alone talk properly to Bella. "They seem much more relaxed together now. Both the children seem to be looking forward to staying down here permanently. I think everything's going to work out how you wanted, Tess."

Louis had looked up at that and caught Sophie's eye. She had immediately turned her back on his gaze, although she'd thought she could still feel it touching her.

" . . . excellent," Tess had been finishing a sentence.

"The thing is . . . ," Sophie had begun. "Something's come up at work. They really need me back at the office, like yesterday. And I know Louis still has a lot to do down here, what with having to finding a house, solicitors, estate agents, sorting out the girls' school and nursery and stuff. So I was wondering how long will it be before everything's finalized?" She'd taken a deep breath.

"What I'm trying to say is, Can I leave the girls with him now? Down here?"

Tess had not answered right away. "Sophie," she'd said after a moment, her voice weighted with concern. "What's wrong?"

"Nothing," Sophie had reassured her far too quickly to be credible. "Everything's really fine!"

Again there'd been a moment's uncertain silence.

"Do you need to bring the girls back with you, take them away from Louis? You can tell me if there is *anything* to be concerned about," Tess had pressed her.

"No! God, no, not at all, Tess. He's been fantastic, really. I truly believe he will be a great dad." She had told Tess the truth, even though every word hurt her. "It's just . . . I don't think they really need me now, and work does. And then there's Artemis; she really hates it when I'm away, even with Mum looking in on her, so I thought that if it was all right, I could leave them here. Is that okay?"

"This seems a bit abrupt," Tess had said, still fishing. "Look, Sophie, if you've had another falling-out with Louis, then I'd really like to know—"

"There's nothing wrong, Tess, I promise you," Sophie had said firmly. "The girls will be fine with him. More than that, they will be happy."

"And there's no way you could stay a little longer?" Tess had urged her. "Listen, Sophie, are *you* sure you just want to go like this? Those children—especially Bella—have come to rely on you. This will still be a difficult enough transition for them, even if things are going well with Louis. I know it must be difficult, but if you could stay just a little longer, I'm sure they would really appreciate it—" The pay phone beeped in Sophie's ear as she considered what Tess had said.

"Sophie?" Tess had questioned her.

"I'm out of money," Sophie had lied. "I have to go. Thanks for everything, Tess."

"But what about the girls?" Tess had said hurriedly. "Think about them, please."

"I *am* thinking about them," Sophie had said. "I have to go back. I have to go back because of them."

But the line had already gone dead.

When Sophie had turned around, Louis was ushering the girls up the stairs.

"What did you say to Tess?" he had asked her tensely.

"I told her I have to go back to London today," Sophie had said, unable to look at him.

"You're leaving today?" Louis had asked her, as if he hadn't quite heard. Sophie had nodded.

"Don't worry," she'd said. "I didn't tell her anything."

Louis had taken a step closer. "Sophie, don't leave just because of what happened last night, it was—"

Sophie had stepped back. She hadn't wanted him to say that it was nothing, it wasn't important. "Look," she had told him before he could complete his sentence, "it's time for me to go. I should go now before . . ." She had glanced up at the ceiling. "Before it all gets out of hand. It's for the best that I go." Somehow she had managed to tell him three times that she was leaving, but he had still looked as if he didn't quite believe it. He had probably thought she was making a huge drama out of nothing.

There had been a long pause, and Sophie had got the sense that Louis had been forming and re-forming sentence after sentence in his head, searching for the appropriate thing to say.

"You don't have to say anything," she had told him.

He had just bowed his head for a second before looking back at her. "Just don't lose touch with the girls," he had said eventually. "They really need you."

Sophie had nodded abruptly. "I know they do," she'd said. And then she'd walked back up the stairs, leaving Louis at the bottom, trying to work out exactly how she was going to say good-bye to Bella and Izzy.

The motorway was busy, but Sophie weaved confidently between lanes, overtaking truck after truck and, at one point, sitting on the tail of a car until it moved over to let her speed by, the driver mouthing probably justifiable obscenities at her in her rearview mirror. But Sophie didn't care, she wanted to be home.

As she had knelt to kiss the girls good-bye, Izzy had wound her arms around Sophie's neck and whispered in her ear. "Don't forget, drive specially careful, okay?" repeating the promise that Sophie had made to her before every road trip they took together, regardless of its length and destination.

"I will," Sophie had promised her. It was a promise she had broken more or less immediately, and now she felt an irrational pang of guilt. Reluctantly, Sophie curtailed her speed and moved over to the slow lane. It would take her longer to get home, but at least it was one less thing to feel bad about.

Bella had accompanied Sophie on her final trip to the local grocery store that morning. Sophie had wanted to buy a few cans of Coke and some chocolate for the trip, as she was determined to make it back to London without stopping once and didn't care if she required junk food to do it.

They had walked, hand in hand, down the steep hill that the B & B sat on, following the bend of the road into St. Ives, cutting through the steps that led deeper into the town.

As they had reached the bottom of the steps, they'd paused and looked out to sea.

"It's a lovely day today," Sophie had said. "You can smell spring in the air, can't you?"

"Let's go and look at the waves," Bella had said, tugging her hand in the opposite direction of the store. Sophie had sensed that Bella wanted to say something, so she did not object. They'd walked toward the sea, and Sophie had followed Bella down the harbor steps onto the beach, relieved to see that the tide was out and the sand was dry.

"I wanted to make sure that you're okay with Louis now," Sophie had said. "I saw you talking, but I never asked you what he said."

The breeze had whipped Bella's hair across her eyes, causing her to clamp her bangs back from her forehead with one palm. Sophie had looked into her brown eyes, which were hardly ever so visible. She was such a beautiful child.

"Will you stay if I say I'm not happy?" Bella had tested her. Sophie had touched Bella's cheek. "You know I would," she had said honestly, despite how much it would have cost her. "But are you?"

Bella had released her hair, crouched down on the sand, and begun to dig up half a shell. Sophie had knelt beside her and watched.

"He told me he was sorry for everything that had happened, that he'd been a rubbish dad, and that things had happened differently from the way he'd planned but he was here now and he loves us and would always do his best. He said he'd never let us down, not ever."

Bella had begun to clean the shell with the hem of her T-shirt. "Sometimes grown-ups let you down, even when they say they won't. But it's still Daddy," Bella had said as she cleaned. "It's still Daddy under there. I remember him more now that I've met him properly. I've missed him. I'm glad we've made up."

She had handed Sophie the shell—half a clam—rough and graying on the outside, but with soft pink and a gently luminous sheen on its smooth inner surface.

"Thank you," Sophie had said, running her thumb over its contours. "So you are happy to stay here with him and Izzy then? What about the house?"

"I am," Bella had said slowly. "And we've decided to look at other houses and see if there are any that feel right for all of us. But I still don't want you to go."

Sophie had bowed her head. "I have to," she'd said into the wind.

"You don't," Bella had said, quickly. "I've been thinking. I know you have a job and everything, but people have parties in St. Ives all the time. I'm sure you could get a job doing parties here. And Artemis could come and boss Tango around, he'd like that." Bella had caught hold of Sophie's wrist and tugged it so that Sophie looked into her face. "Please don't go, Aunty Sophie, please don't."

"It's not just work, Bella," Sophie had said, forcing herself to be hard. "I was only looking after you for a bit and—"

"But you do love us, though, don't you?" Bella had asked her anxiously. "You said you did before."

Sophie had put her arms around Bella and pulled her half onto her lap where she was kneeling in the sand.

"I do love you," she'd said. "Can't think why, but I do. That won't change just because I have to go back. We'll see each other often, and write, and you can send me pictures and phone me and . . ." She had paused, willing her tears not to fall, willing herself to be strong for Bella.

Then Sophie had lifted Bella off her lap and turned her around so that they faced each other, both kneeling on the sand, her hands on Bella's shoulders. "Bella, I have to go back," she'd said as she pushed herself into a standing position. "There are reasons that you can't understand . . ."

"What reasons?" Bella had demanded, and realizing that none of them were things she could tell a child, Sophie had brushed the sand off her jeans and begun walking back toward the steps that led up to the harbor.

Bella had caught up with her quickly and hooked her arm through Sophie's. "What reasons?" she had repeated.

"Adult reasons," Sophie had said, hating herself for talking down to Bella. "I have to pay my bills, feed Artemis, look after my mum. Hundreds of reasons. You and Izzy don't need me now."

"But we do! We do still need you!"

Sophie had stopped in her tracks, hearing the tears in Bella's voice. She'd looked down at the child; Bella's cheeks were wet.

"Please, Aunty Sophie, please, don't go back and leave us. We *do* need you," Bella had pleaded.

Sophie had wound her arms around Bella and pulled her into a hug. "I have to go," she'd said.

"You don't have to," Bella had repeated. "Not if you don't want to."

"I do," Sophie had said, holding back her tears. "I do."

Sophie reached London during the peak of the rush hour, rain teeming down. She sat in the tightly packed lanes of traffic, fidgeting with the radio until eventually she turned it off. Home was less than a mile away, but God knew how long it would take to get there. She resisted the urge to rest her head on the steering wheel, or to just get out of the car and walk the rest of the way.

She bit down on her rising frustration, and suddenly an image of Louis just before she left, silhouetted against a clear blue sky, flashed in front of her.

"Don't want to think about *you*," she grumbled under her breath. "Done that already."

Twenty-eight

The heavy scent of the lilies on Sophie's desk mingled with the fresh spring breeze that drifted through her open office window. Two perks of her new job, fresh flowers twice a week and windows that opened on demand. It was curious that, even after a month, she still didn't really feel like she belonged at this desk. But no matter what she had tried to do to settle herself back into her old and new life, nothing had quite done the trick so far.

She hadn't expected to walk back into a promotion. In fact, it was the last thing she had been thinking about when she'd gone into work that day, just over a month ago. So she had been genuinely surprised when Gillian had called her into her office and broken the good news. "It must feel as if a weight has been lifted," Gillian had said when Sophie told her about the girls going back home.

"It does," Sophie had replied, even though the crushing burden of emotion that had almost overwhelmed her on Porthmeor Beach still seemed to envelop her.

Gillian had sat her down and made a long speech about loyalty, strength of character, and fortitude, which had begun to swim over Sophie's head when she heard the word *promotion*.

"Promotion?" she had said quickly.

"Yes," Gillian had told her. "The time has come for me to take a step back. It's been hard deciding between you and Eve, but I think you've shown how much you can do in difficult circumstances. I think that's what won me over in the end." Gillian had stretched out her hand over the desk. "Congratulations Sophie, you've got the job."

Sophie had imagined this moment for such a long time, dreamed about it, enacted how it would be to hear those words and to know that she had finally reached the pinnacle she had been striving for, and now that it had happened? Well, it wasn't quite as satisfying as she had imagined. It was Louis's fault, of course. It was all his fault, he and his children throwing a wrench in the works and upsetting the beautifully oiled machine that had previously been her life.

"Thank you," she had told Gillian, smiling at her, although she'd felt as if her lips were stiff and numb. "I'm so happy."

The thing to do, Sophie had decided on the way back to her office, was to get as drunk as she possibly could, because that was what people did when they were celebrating. Gillian had asked her to keep the news to herself until she could make a formal announcement to the whole company, so Sophie had told only Cal, which was more or less the same thing as making an informal announcement to the whole company. But she'd had to tell somebody, so that person could tell her how marvelous it was. She'd thought she would believe it then.

"So tonight we have to go out and celebrate," she had told Cal intently after he had congratulated her. "We've got that accounting firm do, so we can start knocking back the fizz there, and then—what do you think—a club? I know, I'll call some friends and we can make a night of it. Excellent."

Cal had looked confused for a second. "It's a Monday, Sophie. I'm fairly sure most of the people you know—and by the way, do you actually know any people?—don't go clubbing on a Monday."

Sophie had thought for a moment. Cal was right, she hadn't seen any of her friends in months, let alone spoken to them on the phone. Now she was back and free again, and she was going to change all that, she was going to change everything. She was going to fill her life up with so many events and nights out and dinners with the girls that she would have no time to think about . . . well, anything else.

"You're right," she had said. "We'll just go to that party, and then you and I can go clubbing. I'll get the several hundred people I know out on Friday night. We can have two parties. Hooray!" Sophie had made two small fists and shaken them with forced enthusiasm.

"Hooray," Cal had said, looking slightly frightened.

It hadn't really worked out the way Sophie had planned.

By nine that evening, she had been too drunk to do anything very much other than sleep.

Fortunately, she was not a noisy drunk, just a dedicated one. So when Cal had found her propped up at the accounting do bar, gazing miserably at the martini she was drinking, he had been able to usher her quietly out the kitchen door and into the back of a cab without any of her clients seeing her condition.

"What happened to our night of crazy fun?" he had asked her, after he'd told the driver her address. "You are such a lightweight, Sophie. I knew you'd never manage to stay up past ten. I'll come back with you," he had sighed. "You need a coffee or thirty."

"No, no!" Sophie had flapped her arms in denial. "You gotta stay and sort out the . . . things . . . 'kay?" She had burped noisily and giggled.

Cal had rolled his eyes at the anxious-looking cabdriver and climbed into the cab with her.

"I'll come right back," he had said. "Once I've got you home."

It had been when they were at home and Sophie was stretched out on the comfortable and clean new sofa that she'd bought that Cal had knelt down beside her and asked, "What's up, Sophie? This isn't like you. Something's happened—what is it?"

"It *is* like me—this is the new me!" Sophie had declared and then, rather morosely, added, "I hate this new sofa."

Cal had sat back on his heels. "Is it because now you've got the job you don't think you can do it?"

"Don't be dericiclous . . . relidiclous . . . mad," Sophie had mumbled, deciding it was safer not to attempt any words longer than one syllable.

"Is it the girls?" Cal had asked, as if he had just experienced a revelation. "You miss the little brats running around trashing the place, don't you? Your biological clock has sounded the alarm, and you're panic drinking! Is that it?"

Sophie had turned her face into the cushion.

"Sophie?" Cal had prompted her. "Sophie? Come on, tell me that I'm right, because you don't need a man to get knocked up now, you know. All you need is a willing donor and a turkey baster. I knew these two women who . . . Sophie? Sophie?"

Gingerly he had leaned forward and looked at her face. She had passed out.

Sophie had sat up with a brain-wrenching start several hours later. Cal had left all the lights on in her living room, her head was thrumming, and her mouth was sticky and dry. It had taken her a second or two to work out how she had got there, but once she had remembered, she had flopped her head into her hands. "Oh, God," she had moaned out loud.

Through her fingers she saw that Cal had left her a note on the repolished coffee table.

"Have gone back to save your career. You were out of it. Think you need to get laid ASAP."

"Ha!" Sophie had laughed mirthlessly. "It was when I got laid that everything went pear-shaped. I should have been a nun. I have a lot in common with nuns. I would have been a natural nun. Plus, I look great in black."

For a second, Sophie had caught a glimpse of herself in the mirror, talking to her empty flat. Once she had preferred her own company to anybody else's, now she had to talk to herself just to be sure she was really there. It was all *his* fault.

"You have a great life," she had told herself as she padded to the bathroom and splashed her face with cold water. "You have your own space, some really good clothes, a great job, lots of friends. You did the right thing, you did the only thing you could do. So just get over it and move on." After drying her face, Sophie had gone into her bedroom and looked at the neatly made bed. With a sigh, she had turned around and gone back to the sofa, switching the lights off as she went.

Once in the semidarkness of her living room, Sophie had slipped off her cocktail dress and draped it carefully over the back of the sofa before lying down and pulling a quilt over herself.

For a long time in the half-light she had listened to the sounds of traffic and watched the pattern of headlights flickering across the ceiling. But she hadn't slept; sleep was impossible with her hungover brain fizzing and humming with a chaotic jumble of incoherent thoughts that she could neither make sense of nor silence.

After a while she had heard Artemis come in.

" 'Night, Artemis," Sophie had said wanly. "Sleep well."

But instead of climbing into her favorite armchair, Artemis had done something she had never done before. She had leaped onto the sofa and sat on Sophie's stomach, looking at her with luminous eyes. Carefully, Sophie had stretched out a hand and stroked her behind her ears. Artemis hadn't purred, but she hadn't tried to claw out Sophie's eyes either. Sophie had sat up a little and squinted at the cat just to make sure it really was Artemis and not some randomly affectionate interloper. Artemis had stared back at her. The cat had never sought out attention from Sophie before; it disconcerted and upset her to think that all the upheaval had affected Artemis as well. "Oh, Artemis," Sophie had said, "you must miss them too."

The cat had drawn back from Sophie's strokes and turned her back on her before settling down to sleep.

"I understand," Sophie had said and leaned her head back against her new faux fur cushions. "I don't want to talk about it either."

Sophie had considered the greatest triumph of her career to date, and she had wondered, What did it all mean?

Now, in her new lily-scented office, Sophie closed her eyes for a moment to rid herself of the memory of that particular escapade and concentrated on the caress of the warm air on her cheek, carrying with it the promise of summer, before going back to work on her doodle: a mermaid whose tail reached down the margin of her notebook and flared out across the few notes that she had made on the meeting she was now in.

Oh shit, she was in a meeting.

Sophie looked up, and sure enough everyone sitting around the table had stopped talking and was looking at her expectantly.

"So what do you think about that idea then?" James Winter, one of her new executives, pressed her. "I mean, everybody's done the London Transport Museum and the aquarium, but you've got to agree that's a one-time venue idea, right?"

Sophie glanced at Cal, who was sitting on her right-hand side and had scrawled in inch-high letters on his notepad "CON-CORDE."

"Well, yes, it's a good idea, James," Sophie said, sitting up in her chair a little. "But I think there are some issues that need clarification. I mean, where is the nearest decommissioned Concorde—in London? Close enough to get a busload of people there? And second, aren't they a bit small inside? It might be like having a party in a really long, narrow living room. Maybe if the venue was the hangar and the plane was like a sort of chill-out room . . . but anyway, have you even found out if it's possible to hire one for parties?" James looked sheepish. Sophie was not surprised—his ideas, though original, were often a bit pie in the sky. "Look into it and get back to me. Anyone else got any ideas? No? So, let's catch up on new business leads—anything anyone?"

She knew Cal had some, but before he could open his mouth, Eve's chair slammed forward and she grinned at Sophie from the other end of the conference table. "That'll be me then," she said.

Eight pairs of eyes swiveled in Eve's direction.

Everyone had been surprised when Eve didn't hand in her notice on the day Gillian had formally announced that Sophie was taking over from her. She had made the announcement in the open-plan part of the office, and the collective sigh of relief had been almost audible. Gillian had talked briefly about logistics, asked Sophie to come and see her in an hour or so, and then turned on her heel and returned to her office with a spring in her step that Sophie had never seen before.

Pretty soon everyone else who was still standing about and offering Sophie congratulations had noticed that Eve had not moved a muscle but was standing with her arms folded across her breasts, staring dangerously hard at Sophie. It was at that point that everybody had suddenly remembered a job they had to do elsewhere and scuttled away.

Eve had stalked purposefully over to where Sophie was waiting rather wearily for her, feeling that she should have her gun hand twitching at her holster, if only she had one. "So you're angry you didn't get the promotion?" Sophie had felt someone had to say it.

"Yeah," Eve had said evenly. "But not surprised. I knew you'd get it. All that dead best friend's kids business really gave you the edge, you bitch."

Sophie had considered the statement. Ironically, it was true; being out of the office for weeks on end, looking after the girls, but keeping her hand in at work, really had boosted her in Gillian's estimation.

"So you're leaving?" Sophie had asked Eve flatly. Curiously, she'd discovered she didn't want Eve to go. Gillian had said it had been a hard choice between the two of them, and Sophie had wanted Eve to stay and be her exit route. She had wanted someone able to take her place just in case she got up the courage to walk out of her job and go around the world or something. She didn't think she ever would. She had had her one moment of reckless courage, and it hadn't ended well. But she liked the thought of it being an option.

"No," Eve had replied, eyeing Sophie. "I'm just going to work out some undetectable way of poisoning you."

Sophie had laughed again, but a little nervously this time. "Believe it or not, I'm glad you're staying," she'd said.

"It's mainly because I don't think you'll be here very long. You've gone even softer since you came back from nannying. I reckon you'll find some poor investment banker to marry you and get knocked up before the year's up, so I'm just biding my time really."

Sophie had snorted in response. "Trust me, *that's* not going to happen," she'd said, knowing that she *really* didn't want to marry an investment banker.

"Anyway," Eve had said, "it's probably just as well you got the job and not me."

"Why?" Sophie had asked her, genuinely intrigued.

"Well, you can't hang around outside smoking when you're the boss, can you?" Eve had replied.

"No," Sophie had said with more regret than she'd expected. "I suppose you can't." But it wasn't losing the chance to smoke that had made Sophie feel a sudden pang of regret. It was something else entirely that she wouldn't tell Eve or anyone else. A quiet truth that had been nagging her from the moment she had returned to the office. Now that she had everything she had been working toward for the best part of her adult life, now that she had the power and the prestige and the money, she had made a very depressing discovery.

She didn't really want it.

The huge Friday night event she had planned to celebrate her promotion had had to be put off for a week due to the lack of availability of willing guests on such short notice, and even then the numbers had dwindled rather rapidly to the two or three people from the office who weren't too scared to have a drink in front of the boss: Lisa, Cal, and Christina, the only one of Sophie's friends not currently in the kind of relationship that monopolized Friday nights.

"Thank Christ you're back in town, Soph," Christina had told her as she set two glasses of wine down at their table. "If it wasn't for you, I'd have no one to go pick up guys with. I can't believe it, *everyone* is hooked up. It's so *dull* when everyone is happy."

"Oh, I know," Sophie had said enthusiastically as she took a large gulp of her wine. "Well, I'm not happy. Any time you want to go on the pull, count me in."

"You're so funny," Christina had said, laughing. "I've quite missed you. So, fill me in then—where *have* you been recently? I thought you'd emigrated or something. Didn't somebody die?"

Perhaps if Christina had known what was coming, she wouldn't have bothered to ask, but when Sophie was only twenty minutes into recounting her trials and tribulations of the last couple of months, she had noticed that Christina wasn't really listening. Instead she was gazing rather obviously at someone just over Sophie's left shoulder.

"Chris!" Sophie had attempted to regain her friend's attention. "I'm telling the story of my life here."

Christina had jumped. "God, *sorry.* I just couldn't take my eyes off that man over there. He's *very* handsome. And he looks rich. Probably married of course or—" Christina had sat back in her seat and dropped her palms onto her knees. "Typical, he's talking to Cal . . . I should have known. The best ones are always married or gay."

"Or widowers," Sophie had added without thinking.

"Or what?" Christina had asked her.

"Nothing," Sophie had said quickly. "Anyway, that will be Mauro. Cal's been going on about him nonstop since I got back."

Sophie had turned around to get a look at the man who had captured Cal's attention for longer than two minutes, and as she saw him, she caught her breath. It wasn't Mauro.

It was Jake Flynn.

"Oh, God," Sophie had said just as the music lulled for a moment.

Jake had looked up and smiled at her. Sophie had turned quickly back to Christina and downed her glass of wine.

"What?" Christina had demanded. "Don't tell me he's yours. Seriously, if you get a boyfriend before I do, I'm going to kill myself, because it officially means there is no hope for me."

Sophie wasn't listening; she had picked up Christina's drink and downed that too.

"Hey!" Christina had protested.

"I'll get you another, but I've got to go over and talk to him. You know all that stuff that happened in Cornwall?" Christina had looked blank. Sophie had shaken her head in irritation. "Well, a lot of stuff happened there, stuff I can't seem to move on from or stop thinking about *night* after *night* after . . . And, anyway, I don't know why I didn't think about it before. Jake is the solution, Jake will take my mind off things, he's totally into me, or at least he was. And if he still is, then I'm going to be totally into him. You said it—he's practically perfect."

Luckily, Sophie hadn't seen the expression on Christina's face as she headed determinedly toward the bar, where Jake was standing. If she had, the look of horror and disbelief might have thrown her off a little.

Sophie had planned to approach Jake with the kind of cool sophistication she knew he was attracted to. Unfortunately, she had tripped a little when she was only a step or two from him and ended up stumbling into his chest.

"Oh," she had said, righting herself. "It's these new shoes. Impossible to walk in." She had glanced down to see which of the ten or so pairs she had bought since she'd been back she had put on. Annoyingly, the ones she had randomly selected that morning didn't go at all with what she was wearing.

"Sophie." Jake had smiled at her, his voice carefully neutral. "Good to see you! I heard your news today, and when I went by the office they said you'd be here. I wanted to buy you a drink so you'd know I'm cool about everything and very happy for you, although I guess I'll be doing most of my business with Cal now—you'll be far too important to deal with me."

"I'll always have time for you, Jake," Sophie had said, tossing her hair as coquettishly as she knew how.

Cal had looked from Sophie to Jake. "Good to see you, Jake. I'm off now," he had told Sophie. "Remember what I said."

"What did you say?" Sophie had asked him.

"That you need to get laid ASAP," Cal had replied, and then he had gone.

Sophie had covered her face with her hands, and Jake had gently removed them and smiled at her, still holding her wrists.

"First rule of management, never let your staff see you're embarrassed."

"Oh, I've blown that one about two hundred times already, and I don't even start my new job until next week." Sophie had laughed and noticed Jake had held her for a moment or two longer before he let go. Perhaps it wasn't too late after all.

"I sort of didn't expect you to come back." Jake had handed her the glass of wine he'd ordered for her.

"Didn't you?" Sophie had asked him with real curiosity. "Why?"

"It looked to me like something was going on there. I didn't think you'd be able to leave them. Any of them."

Sophie had sipped her drink and fought the rising tide of sadness that swelled in her chest.

"I missed you, actually," she had said, looking up at Jake. He had watched her for a moment as if he were trying to read her mind, and in response she had tried to banish any thoughts of Louis that might have been lurking in her eyes. She knew what she was doing was wrong, but maybe Cal was right, maybe she did need to get laid. If she had another man in her bed, a man who cared for her and wanted her, then perhaps she'd be able to get the persistent memory of the last one out of her head for good.

"That's not why you came back," Jake had said with a sad, wry smile.

"I'm sorry about the way I acted the last time I saw you, Jake. Throwing myself at you like that. You were right to say what you did, I was confused. I needed to go to Cornwall. But once I was there, I realized how wrong it all was for me. How complicated."

"Just because something is complicated doesn't make it wrong," Jake had said casually. "It's worth pursuing something that will make you truly happy, even if it's difficult getting there."

Sophie had resisted the urge to scowl. Jake wasn't being nearly as helpful as she had hoped he would be.

She had supposed she'd just have to seduce him, and as she had no idea how to go about it, she had decided to be as direct and as blunt as possible.

"Jake, I want you," she had said, somehow holding his gaze and her nerve at the same time. "Sexually."

Jake had had to raise his hand to his mouth to cover his smile, and Sophie had felt her skin instantly blotch. "I'm sorry," he'd said, and his smile was gone in an instant, replaced by that compelling blue gaze.

Finally, Sophie had thought, he was taking her seriously.

"Why?" Jake had asked her.

"Why!" Sophie had raised her voice, and a few people looked across at her. "What do you mean, why?" She had dropped her voice to a whisper. "Isn't it enough that I do?"

Jake had set his glass down and led her away from the bar to a quiet corner near the fire escape.

"You know I want you," he had told her, his voice low and urgent. "I've wanted you for a long time. I wanted you even after I told you I didn't." He had given a brief, mirthless laugh. "You know what? I don't really care if you are into someone else. If you want me to take you to bed just to help you forget that someone else, then I will. That's how much I want you, Sophie. But answer me honestly, do you really want this? Do *you* really want *this*? Because I don't care if I get hurt—but I couldn't stand to see you hurt yourself any more."

Sohpie had looked into Jake's intense blue eyes and had willed herself to say yes, she wanted him to take her to bed.

But she hadn't been able to. She hadn't been able to use Jake like some kind of medication, because it wouldn't work, and anyway he was right, she would only be hurting them both.

She had dropped her gaze to her feet. "Oh, Jake," she had said softly. "I'm sorry. I'm such a fool."

Jake had swallowed and nodded stiffly. "You probably are," he had said. "But not for the reasons you think."

He had turned on his heel and walked out of the bar, and Sophie had not heard from or seen him since. All she knew was that his people called her people whenever they needed anything done.

So, all the going out, all the cocktails and shopping and smoking, and not even Jake had helped. From the moment she had come back, she had tried, really tried, to fit herself into her new and improved life, but nothing she could do would change the most startling and frightening fact: despite her new, frantic city life, she was desperately lonely. And there were only three people in the whole world who could take that loneliness away.

Three people who it was far too late to go back to now—even if she had the courage to make the trip.

The meeting broke up, and Eve paused by Sophie's end of the desk to drop off some paperwork.

"Okay?" she said generally, but Sophie knew she was referring to her vacant spell in the middle of the meeting that she had been supposed to be running.

"Fine, getting a cold or something," Sophie said, with half a smile.

Eve raised an eyebrow before leaving.

Cal checked his watch. "It's lunchtime," he said. "Come on, let's go out for a walk."

Sophie looked at the pile of paperwork on her desk. "I can't, Cal, I have to catch up on all of this *and* read the minutes from the meeting. Has Lisa typed them up yet?"

"You're joking, aren't you?" Cal said, picking up the offending pile of paperwork, arranging it neatly, and dropping it in its entirety into one of the deep drawers of Sophie's filing cabinet. "There, that's filed. Lisa won't have finished those notes until this afternoon if we're lucky. She's out to lunch, in all senses of the word, with the new love of her life. Anyway, it's a beautiful spring morning out there, and we're going for a walk to clear our heads. Come on! I'll buy you a Mars bar."

A few minutes later they sat side by side on a bench in Finsbury Circus looking at a bed of red tulips bobbing cheerfully in the breeze.

"Why is this called a circus?" Cal asked her. "When it's square?"

Sophie shrugged. "Don't care," she said.

Cal sighed. "Look," he said. "When you first came back and were a bit off your game, I thought it was exhaustion. All those weeks of wiping arses and noses, ugh! And when you went through your thankfully short period as a lush, I thought it was the stress of getting a job you probably couldn't really do. I put up with the constant hangovers, the nights out, spending *my* lunchtime taking *your* impulse buys back for you because you're too embarrassed to do it yourself. I thought, She's had a difficult time. It will take time to adjust. But you've been back over three months now, Soph. You keep getting *more* vague and airy-fairy, not less. And I know for a fact you have no social life, so unless you've developed a very boring addiction to heroin, which you haven't because you hate needles, you're depressed. So why are you depressed—as if it isn't obvious?"

Sophie frowned at him.

"I'm fine," she said. "Honestly!"

Cal sighed again and rolled his eyes. "I used to prefer when you were in love with Jake," he said wistfully. "It was much less complicated."

Sophie managed a small smile. "I was never in love with Jake—I wish I had been—and anyway I'll be fine," she said. "I just need a bit of adjustment time, that's all."

Cal looked at his watch again. "Three months not long enough?" he asked. "Look, I'd prefer you to just tell me, but as you're going to make me guess . . . you fell in love with the kids and then their good-looking, mysterious dad, and he toyed with your affections before cruelly spurning you—is that it? Hey, that's a bit like *Jane Eyre*. You could burn their new house down, after evacuating the children first, of course. That'll get his attention. No, hang on, I think that was the mad first wife in the attic."

Sophie did not crack a smile; her gaze remained fixed on the tulips, but Cal persisted. "You could see the girls, couldn't you?" he asked her. "I bet Mr. Mysterious would let you see them, even if he doesn't fancy you. All you'd have to do is pick up the phone and ask."

Sophie wondered if Cal had guessed how many times she had sat with her phone in her hand and thought of dialing the number that Louis had sent her along with a change of address card the girls had made shortly after she got back. He hadn't written anything in the card except for their details, and underneath that Bella had written, "We love you, Aunty Sophie!"

Of course she couldn't just pick up the phone. Of course she couldn't, because picking up the phone would mean talking to him and hearing his voice, and before she knew it, she'd be right back to square one, which would be difficult because she hadn't actually moved off square one since the day she'd left St. Ives.

"I can't," she simply told Cal. "I just . . . can't."

"He must have really fucking spurned you," Cal said, "for you to be so down about it after all this time. If I didn't have such a pretty face to protect, I'd go and beat him up for you." He put an arm around her shoulders. "Look, Sophie, you've got to give up this unrequited love lark. It hurts now, but I promise you it will get better eventually. Really."

Sophie looked at him. "He didn't spurn me," she said on impulse. "*I* spurned *him*." She paused and looked puzzled. "Have you ever noticed when you say a word you don't use much it sounds weird. 'Spurn . . . spurn . . . spu——' "

"Hold on a minute!" Cal's tone snapped her out of her reverie. "*You* spurned *him*! *Why?* I mean, *why* have you been moping around here for weeks on end depressing us all with your miserable face when you could have been romping around the heather or whatever the fuck they have in Cornwall with Mr. Mysterious the whole time?"

Sophie rubbed her eyes with the heels of her hands. It was more or less that very same question that had kept her awake every night since she'd got back.

On the beach, in the cold, in the hours before dawn, everything had seemed perfectly clear. She had felt she knew exactly what she was doing up until the moment she had pulled up outside her flat in London. From that moment she had been running as fast as she possibly could to get away from the persistent, nagging doubt that she had made the worst mistake of her life. That

Louis really wanted her as much as she wanted him and she had denied them both the chance to find out.

Sophie thought she must be the only person in the world who was actually capable of being almost terminally sensible. God knows, it felt like her decision was killing her very slowly and painfully.

"It's too late now," she insisted, giving Cal the same answer she had given herself. "I had this tiny, slim chance of making something happen, and I ran away from it. I mean, of course I did. I'm me, aren't I? I missed my chance. It's just too complicated now."

"Oh yes, it is," Cal said with heavy sarcasm. "It is deeply complicated. You fancy *him,* he fancies *you.* You both love his kids. That's a really tricky one, that is. Better ruin everyone's life, including mine, while you think about it for all eternity." He glared at Sophie. "How, pray, is it complicated?"

Sophie glared back at him. "Because . . ." She struggled to dredge up all the reasons. "He's Carrie's husband. Being with him would be like cheating on Carrie! And maybe he doesn't really like me, maybe he just wanted me for a fling, and then if I fell for him and it all went wrong, what would it do to the girls? Those children have been through enough and . . . and other reasons I forget just now, but which are very sensible."

Cal nearly choked on his Diet Coke. "You are impossible," he told her. "He is in love with you."

"How do you know?" Sophie wailed.

"Because I know you, and I know the reason you ran away wasn't because of any of that crap you just spouted. It was because you *know* he loves you and you're scared shitless."

"I still can't go back, Cal. He's Carrie's husband."

Cal raised both of his beautifully shaped eyebrows skyward. "That is *not* the real reason," he said with some frustration.

"It *is* the real reason," she insisted. "And it's a bloody good reason too, thanks very much."

"Look, even I know that Carrie and Louis weren't together for years before you met him. You haven't told me the whole story, but I've worked out that whatever broke them up, it wasn't just because he was an evil genius. It was probably because, like the rest of us, they were both human. I mean, think about it, Soph—you were in love with Alex, weren't you?"

"I thought I was," Sophie conceded, although she couldn't see the point of the question.

"Exactly. And that was over two years ago. So tell me, how do you—an alive person—feel about the fact that he's getting married in two weeks?"

"Is he?" Sophie said absently. "That's nice." Then her brow furrowed and she glanced at Cal. "How do you know?"

"I don't," Cal told her. "I was just proving the point. If Carrie was here, she wouldn't care about you and Louis being together. *She* would have moved on."

Sophie nodded. "I know," she said. "But she's not here to say it's okay, and that makes it impossible."

Cal gave her a scathing look. "Tell me the real reason you're doing this to yourself."

"What other reason would there possibly be?" Sophie said halfheartedly.

Cal gestured at the cloudless sky. "If Carrie is up there right now, she's probably shouting at you, 'Go to him, you stupid cow!' Oh no, you're not joining a nunnery instead of marrying the Captain and becoming Mrs. Von Trapp, based on some misguided principle. Not even you are that stupid. You're doing it because you're terrified. Terrified of being in love, terrified of being happy, terrified of waking up and realizing that the life you've lived for years on end was actually a shit one." Sophie's eyes widened, but Cal didn't give her a chance to interrupt him. "Yes, Sophie, your life to date has been boring and small and lonely and repetitive—join the club! But if you have a chance to change that, you don't have to just stick it out anyway, like some kind of self-inflicted punishment for being happy. That's just twisted!"

"That's not it!" Sophie said, her protest weakening. "Well, it's a bit it. But it's more than that, Cal. I mean, it's not just him, is it? It's a whole family, a family that's just starting out. What if it all went really wrong with Louis, what then for the girls? Wouldn't it be terrible if we broke up and they were in the middle of it? I couldn't do that to them."

"No one's saying you should run down there and marry him. Just be together, keep it casual, see how you feel. Keep the girls posted. Let them know you'll still love them however it works out. For once in your life, make a choice for yourself, Sophie Mills!"

Sophie considered the words she hadn't dared to say to herself. "Am I strong enough, though?" she asked. "What if it goes wrong?"

"You're strong enough," Cal told her without reservation. "You've proved how strong you are. And anyway, I've got a feeling that this is a choice you won't regret. I'm practically psychic, you know."

"It's a long way to go for dinner on a Friday night," Sophie said, throwing up the last obstacle for Cal to shoot down.

"Are you happy at work, Sophie?" he asked.

"No," she said honestly. "Not anymore."

"Then leave," Cal instructed her. "Rent out your flat, find a place to stay down there. Oh yes, there will be a bit of scandal here. Gillian will disapprove, and Eve will be triumphant, but what do you care? You'll be milking a cow in the country, all blissed up and fat."

"But this is my job, my dream job," Sophie protested weakly. "I loved my job."

"You said *loved*, past tense. And anyway, it's not wrong for your dreams to change, you know. It's just wrong if you don't pursue them with every ounce of the energy and determination that's got you this far. You've got money in the bank, and, I'm sure they have parties all the time in Cornwall. You could get in on that scene. Organize a pig-throwing festival or whatever it is they do down there."

Sophie smiled. "Someone else said that to me once," she said. "But, it's a big risk, it's scary."

"Taking risks is what life is all about, Sophie," Cal said in exasperation. "I thought you would have known that, wearing that shirt with that lipstick. Right out on a fashion limb."

Sophie laughed and felt a sudden surge of adrenaline. "I might do it," she said a little shakily.

"Not might," Cal said. "Just do it."

Sophie looked into Cal's steady blue eyes and picked up his hand. "I'm going to do it," she said, her eyes wide with excitement and terror. "Damn!"

"It will be wonderful," Cal said, kissing her cheek.

"Oh, but hang on." Sophie gripped Cal's hand hard enough to make him wince. "What if . . . what if Louis is no longer interested in me?"

"Oh, shut the fuck up," Cal said. "As if!"

Twenty-nine

*I*t had taken a while to find the cottage Louis and the girls were renting. It was set against the steep rise of the hill about a mile out of town. A small whitewashed building, it looked as if it had weathered a hundred storms, and still stood strong.

As Sophie pulled up at the bottom of the drive, she wondered again if this had been a really bad idea. If she should have at least called first, checked out how Louis was feeling, or even if he had anything planned for the weekend. He might be out; he might be in with some Cornish beauty in his arms. The girls might not care that she was there . . .

Sophie suddenly wished that her mum had broken down when she had told her right after work yesterday what she was planning and begged her not to go. But instead she'd just hugged Sophie and said, "You go, darling, you do what you have to do. And if it all works out for you, you never know, maybe I'll get my dog sanctuary down there after all." And then she'd offered her a packet of biscuits for the journey.

As Sophie sat in the car, she wondered for the last time about the chance she was taking and how it might all go dreadfully wrong or might even go wonderfully right. Knowing that, however her decision turned out, she had to make it anyway. She stopped her compulsive speculation and took a deep breath. It was a beautiful evening, the sun lighting up the foliage around the house with a fiery halo, gilding everything with its glow.

She got out of the car and, opening the rear door, lifted a plastic carrying case carefully off the backseat, where it had been secured with a seat belt. Biting her lips, she went to the front door, but before she could ring the bell she heard voices echo in the air. Peering though the front window, she saw that Louis, Bella, and Izzy were all in the back garden. It looked as if the girls were helping Louis with some planting, although, from what Sophie could see, the gardening had recently deteriorated into an all-out mud fight and Bella and Izzy shrieked with laughter as Louis chased them around in circles, a sod of soil in each fist. For a moment, Sophie looked on at the perfect picture that made her happier and more afraid than she had ever been in her entire life.

"Well, it's now or never," she said.

Sophie did not know how to greet them, so for a long moment she just stood there, case in hand, watching them, her heart in her mouth. And then Izzy saw her.

"Aunty Sophieeeeeeeeeee!" she screamed and hurled her dirt-covered self at Sophie.

Setting down the case, Sophie knelt and wound her arms tightly around Izzy. "You've grown so much," she said, kissing the girl's cheeks several times.

"I know," said Izzy proudly. "I'm nearly as tall as a giraffe."

Then Bella was there, her arms around Sophie's neck, kissing both her cheeks, one after the other. "You're here again!" she said, delighted. "I knew you'd come back! It *is* a long visit, isn't it?"

Sophie untangled the girls from around her and looked over their heads at Louis, who was watching her with astonishment, his hands on his hips.

"Well, maybe," she said, gazing at him steadily. "If you want it to be."

"We do, we do, we do!" both girls sang in unison, dancing around her.

At last Louis spoke. "Girls!" he said lightly. "Come on, you're getting Sophie all muddy! Go and get changed into something clean and dry, okay? It's nearly teatime anyway."

"No!" Izzy protested. "Don't want to!"

Bella looked from Sophie to her dad. "Yes, you do," she said, grabbing Izzy by the arm and dragging her toward the house while tickling her so that her protest gradually morphed into a giggling fit.

"Oh, before you go." Sophie remembered the carrying case. She picked it up and held it out to Bella. "They don't accept cats at the B & B I'm booked into. Will you look after Artemis for me?"

The children squealed with delight, and Bella returned to retrieve the case, carrying it carefully into the house. Amazingly, it began to purr.

Sophie stood up and smoothed her skirt. "I'm a bit of a mess," she said, laughing nervously, not quite brave enough to look at Louis.

"A bit," he said, taking a step closer. "Why are you here, Sophie?" he asked her gently, looking deep into her eyes. "I need to know, because I can't— Why are you here?"

Sophie thought about the hundred or so reasons and excuses she had invented on the journey down to be near Louis without actually having to tell him why: from pretending that she'd been fired from her job to a sudden allergy to cities. But when it came to it, she realized she'd already wasted too much time.

"To be near you," she said simply. "To be close enough to where you are to be able to go to dinner with you on a Friday night, or go for a walk on the beach with you and the girls every Sunday. To be able to be with you when there's nothing else to think about or feel except what it's like to be with you. To get to know you and see if I'm right about the way that you make me feel. To find out if I'm really as in love with you as I think I am." Finally, Sophie looked up at him. "If that's okay with you."

Louis closed the last two steps between them in one movement and held her tightly for a long time. He kissed the top of her head and then released her a little so that he could look at her face.

"It's definitely okay by me," he said. "It's more than okay." He kissed her and kept on kissing her.

Acknowledgments

Thank you so much to the amazingly creative and always supportive Kate Elton and Georgina Hawtrey-Woore, both of whom make the editorial process such a pleasure. And to all the team at Arrow and Random House for the hard work and dedication they put in every day with unfailing enthusiasm.

Thank you to Lizzy Kremer, the world's most dedicated agent, always on the end of the phone, even during maternity leave!

To Maggie Crawford and the fantastic team at Simon & Schuster and Pocket Books, thank you for believing in me and my book.

And to my dear friends who keep me going, Jenny Matthews, Rosie Wooley, Sarah Boswell (and her mum, Mrs. Darby), Clare Winter (and her mum, Mrs. Smith), and Cathy Carter (and her mum, Mrs. Bell). You all give me so much encouragement.

Finally, thank you to my wonderful husband, Erol, whose love and faith never waver, and to my daughter, Lily, who is so clever, beautiful, funny, and kind that I can scarcely believe I'm her mother!

Readers Club Guide

INTRODUCTION

Sophie Mills has worked her Manolo Blahniks off to reach the top of her profession. She seems to have it all: a glamorous job as a corporate events planner, a designer apartment, and her cat Artemis for company. After all, relationships only get in the way of work, and as for starting a family—Sophie hasn't even begun to think about that yet. Until one day, an unexpected visitor brings the news that her best friend Carrie is dead, Carrie's husband Louis has disappeared, and Sophie is now in sole charge of two children under the age of seven. But child care can't be all that hard, can it? Sophie soon finds she is woefully under-equipped to be suddenly thrown into motherhood. But through the eyes of two little girls she learns more about loss, commitment, and true love than she had ever realized existed.

Discussion Questions

1. *The Accidental Mother* opens with Sophie in her office, obsessing over Jake Flynn's lunch invitation. What is your first impression of Sophie Mills, based on this beginning? How does she handle her career? What is her approach to romance?

2. Discuss Sophie's relationship with her coworker Eve. Are the two women friends or enemies? Eve tells Sophie, "You didn't choose this career . . . it chose you." (See page 109.) What does Eve mean? Is she right about Sophie?

3. "There were a lot of things that Sophie was very good at. . . . She was extremely good at pie charts. But she'd always said that when she discovered her limitations, she'd be happy to admit them. That time had come." (See page 26.) Which of Sophie's personal "limitations" come to light, when Bella and Izzy arrive in her life?

4. When Sophie receives a copy of *Dr. Robert's Complete Dog Training and Care Manual* from her mother, she "tossed the book to the floor in disgust." (See page 66.) What unexpectedly handy lessons does Sophie learn from the dog manual? What do you think of this funny statement from Sophie's mother: "That's the trouble with you cat people. No imagination." (See page 66.)

5. The promise "Always, forever, whatever" comes up several times in the novel. What did this promise mean to Sophie and Carrie when they were teenagers? What did it mean for Carrie and her children? What does it mean to Sophie now?

6. Cal tells Sophie, "Taking risks is what life is all about, Sophie . . . I thought you would have known that, wearing that shirt with that lipstick. Right out on a fashion limb." (See page 388.) How does Cal's bold sense of humor inspire Sophie?

7. Sophie's cat Artemis hasn't purred in years, until Bella pets her. Sophie thanks Bella "For making Artemis feel safe and happy." (See page 127.) What does Artemis teach Sophie about taking care of Bella and Izzy?

8. Sophie is fully aware that Jake is "practically perfect." (See page 378.) He's handsome, successful, and very interested in Sophie. So why isn't Sophie interested in Jake?

9. After her father died, Sophie learned from her mother, "you have to practice being happy, even when you're not, because otherwise you might forget how altogether." (See page 248.) How does Sophie help Bella and Izzy practice happiness? How do the girls help Sophie? Do you think Sophie has forgotten how to be happy, since her father's death?

10. What is Sophie's first impression of Louis? How does her opinion of Louis change over the course of the novel? Were you as surprised as Sophie at the real reason why Louis left Carrie? Why or why not?

11. "Carrie made choices decisively and rode them out no matter what happened. Sophie never chose what happened in her life—she let fate choose for her and never questioned how different things could be." (See page 339.)

Discuss Sophie and Carrie's different approaches to making choices. What are the advantages to Carrie's approach? What are the disadvantages? What does Sophie learn from her friend's example?

12. Sophie feels guilty about her attraction to Louis, as if she were trying to steal Carrie's life. But Cal believes, "If Carrie is up there right now, she's probably shouting at you, 'Go to him, you stupid cow!'" (See page 386.) Do you agree with Cal, that Carrie would be happy for Sophie and Louis? Why or why not?

13. When Bella and Izzy first come home with Sophie, she thinks, "A passion for chocolate and an eye for shoes. Maybe she did have something in common with the girls after all." (See page 47.) Besides a sweet tooth and good fashion sense, what else does Sophie have in common with Bella and Izzy by the end of the novel?

14. The ending of *The Accidental Mother* is romantic, but also open to interpretation. What do you think the future holds for Sophie, Louis, Bella, and Izzy? What new challenges could they face?

ENHANCE YOUR BOOK CLUB

1. According to Sophie, "shoes were like fashion magnets. The right clothes would simply be drawn to them." (See page 82.) Find a picture of your ideal pair of shoes in a magazine or catalog and bring a copy to your book club meeting to show off your fantasy "fashion magnets!"

2. Sophie, Bella, and Izzy bond over Carrie's favorite song, "Motorcycle Emptiness" by the Manic Street Preachers. Play the song at your book club meeting to set the mood for *The Accidental Mother.* You can find "Motorcycle Emptiness" on www.itunes.com or pick up Manic Street Preachers' greatest hits album, *Forever Delayed,* at your local music store.

3. In the book, Louis worked at a charity for homeless children in Peru. Do some online research to find an organization that helps homeless children in a community you care about—it can be in your town, or halfway around the world. Bring information to your book club meeting and discuss how your club can volunteer or contribute to a children's charity.

Questions for the Author

1. ***The Accidental Mother* is largely about coping with loss, and yet there's so much humor. How did you manage to balance tragedy and comedy in this novel?**

It's a fine balance. If you are asking readers to trust you as you lead them from a scene that might make them feel sad to another that you hope will make them laugh then you have to be careful to maintain the integrity of the plot and the characters. I don't have a clever way of doing this, however! I trust my instincts and I have a sort of invisible reader sitting on my shoulder who soon tells me if I've got the balance wrong.

2. **One hilarious moment is when Sophie's mother pulls out *Dr. Robert's Complete Dog Training and Care Manual,* which turns out to be very useful to Sophie! Does this manual actually exist? Do you think we can learn something about children from studying animals, and vice versa? Are you a cat person, like Sophie, or a dog person, like her mother?**

I am a pet person and would have cats if it weren't for my asthma. I have a Standard Poodle called Polly (named by my daughter when she was two, although I wanted to call her Holly Golightly) and until a hypo-allergenic breed of cat is discovered, Polly will be my only pet. When Polly arrived, she and my two-year-old daughter seemed to have a very similar mental age and attitude toward life, which was very carefree, happy, and mildly destructive. (Fortunately, only one of them ate shoes.) Not long after we brought Polly home both dog and daughter suffered a terrible fear of cars due to a minor, but very loud, traffic accident that we were all in. I got the idea from my dog-care manual to use the same technique that Sophie uses on Izzy to help them both get over the fear (tiny hand clutching trembling paw). That's where the idea of using a dog-care manual for tips on child care came from.

3. **On the subject of communication with children, Cal says, "It's sort of like learning another language . . . Once you let yourself go enough to get hold of the accent, you'll be fine." (See page 140.) Bella and Izzy's dialogue is incredibly realistic. How did you prepare to write in "child language"?**

I just listen to people and how they talk, the nuances and rhythms in their voices. As for Izzy and Bella, well, my daughter was the same age as Izzy when I wrote the book so I was fluent in three-year-old, and Bella was a mixture of me as a child and my niece. I have very strong memories of my childhood, so referencing that version of me is quite easy.

4. **The Manic Street Preachers' song "Motorcycle Emptiness" is featured prominently in the novel. What significance does this song have for you?**

I love this song—listen to it if you can. It reminds me of a road trip to Wales I went on in my twenties (a good few years after the song was released!) with my best friend Jenny. We went with the intention of finding ourselves, preferably somewhere up a Welsh mountain, and decided Welsh rock would be the perfect soundtrack. We didn't have the epiphany we were hoping for, but we played this song over and over again as we drove in our banged-up old car singing along at the top of our voices. It was in the spirit of that kind of wonderful, close, and lifelong friendship that I decided to use it in this book.

5. **Sophie struggles to balance her career with taking care of the children—and she isn't even a mother. Do you think women must choose between motherhood and career, even in the twenty-first century? Is it possible to find a balance between the two?**

It's so hard to have a career and be a mother. The truth is that many women don't have a choice; they have to do both and they do it amazingly well. The work/life balance for all of us, men and women, in this day and age is difficult to achieve. But I think we should make it a priority to stop and take a breath and appreciate our families—the people we love and the people we are working so hard for. I count my lucky stars that my work as a writer has allowed me to spend more time at home with my little girl as she grows up. I admire both women who choose to be homemakers and those who follow careers; neither choice is an easy one to make. I believe that the trick is to follow your heart and then you'll be a happy and fulfilled person.

6. **Cal is a great source of comic relief in the novel; he always tells Sophie exactly what he thinks, with hilarious results! Who was the inspiration for this character?**

Cal is loosely based on a very dear, very witty, very honest, and sometimes slightly over-the-top friend of mine.

7. **Ben Nicholson's painting *St. Ives Version Two* (1940) helps Bella cope with the death of her mother. When did you first see this painting? Are you a fan of the St. Ives school of art, like Carrie?**

I first found out about the St. Ives School of Art when reading a book called *The Fatal Englishman* by Sebastian Faulks. His description of one ill-fated St. Ives artist led me to find out more and I first saw the painting *Version Two* where it actually hangs in the Tate Gallery in St. Ives. I fell in love with it and the work of Ben Nicholson, Barbara Hepworth, and other St. Ives artists on the spot. I love the idea that they were trying to do something new, create a new world of hope and beauty. St. Ives is a still a wonderful place with a magical kind of light that to this day is chock-full of artists and craftspeople inspired by its unique properties.

8. *The Accidental Mother* **was a big hit in the U.K. Are you excited to bring this book to the U.S.? Do you think Americans can relate to Sophie Mills as strongly as British readers have?**

I am *hugely* excited that my book is being published in the U.S. and I truly hope that the American audience will relate to Sophie Mills as strongly as U.K. readers have! I'm fairly certain they will, though, because Sophie's story is a universal one and her dilemmas are ones that women all around the world experience.

9. **Although the novel ends on a romantic note, we don't know exactly what lies ahead for Sophie, Louis, Bella, and Izzy. Do you envision their living happily ever after in Cornwall? Have you considered continuing the story of this "accidental" family?**

Curiously I hadn't thought about writing a sequel until you asked. Now I'm wondering why I haven't had that idea! I'd love to write a sequel and if circumstances and my existing writing commitments will allow, then I certainly will. For now I see them happy and together, facing the future united.